W9-CDK-941

The shining splendor of our Zebra Lovegram logo on the cover of this book reflects the glittering excellence of the story inside. Look for the Zebra Lovegram whenever you buy a historical romance. It's a trademark that guarantees the very best in quality and reading entertainment.

SWEET YEARNINGS

It was happening again, just like last night. Fiona could only wonder at this as she felt his lips against hers. His mouth followed the curve of her jaw, the line of her neck.

Her moan vibrated throughout her body, and Fiona saw him pause, a spark of satisfaction lighting his eyes.

"I love the way you kiss," he whispered in her ear before nipping at the lobe with his teeth. "I haven't been able to think of anything else since last night."

She felt his warm breath along the side of her neck and Fiona clutched his shoulders. "Zeke, I —" she couldn't seem to control her breathing or her voice. But it didn't matter, for he didn't let her finish. His mouth covered hers again, making her forget what she'd planned to say.

Besides, she didn't want to talk. She only wanted to go on kissing him, feeling the full, hard weight of him against her . . .

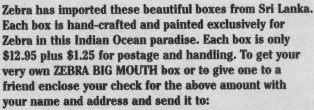

GET YOUR VERY OWN
ZEBRA
BIG MOUTH BOX
...PERFECT FOR THE LITTLE THINGS YOU LOVE!

The Zebra Big Mouth Box is the perfect little place you need to keep all the things that always seem to disappear. Loose buttons, needle and thread, pins and snaps, jewelry, odds and ends...all need a place for you to get them when you want them.

Just put them in the Big Mouth!

Zebra has imported these beautiful boxes from Sri Lanka. Each box is hand-crafted and painted exclusively for Zebra in this Indian Ocean paradise. Each box is only $12.95 plus $1.25 for postage and handling. To get your very own ZEBRA BIG MOUTH box or to give one to a friend enclose your check for the above amount with your name and address and send it to:

ZEBRA BIG MOUTH BOX
Dept. 101
475 Park Avenue South
New York, New York 10016

New York residents add applicable sales tax.
Allow 4-6 weeks for delivery!

Bold Rebel Love

CHRISTINE DORSEY

ZEBRA BOOKS
KENSINGTON PUBLISHING CORP.

To my parents — my mother and the memory of my father —
Thank you for instilling in me an appreciation of the past.
And as always to Chip.

ZEBRA BOOKS

are published by

Kensington Publishing Corp.
475 Park Avenue South
New York, NY 10016

Copyright © 1991 by Christine Dorsey

All rights reserved. No part of this book may be repro-
duced in any form or by any means without the prior written consent of the Publisher, excepting brief quotes used
in reviews.

First printing: March, 1991

Printed in the United States of America

Chapter One

This life has joys for you and I;
And joys that riches ne'er could buy;
   And joys the very best.
There's a' the Pleasures o' the Heart.[sic]
            — Robert Burns
            "Epistle to Davie, a Brother Poet"

Cross Creek, North Carolina
August, 1775

"What in the hell is going on here, Sergeant?"

Fear chilled Fiona MacClure as she gaped up at the man who'd exploded through the bedroom door, demanding an explanation. She thought she'd been in trouble before, but now . . .

One look at the tall, dark, powerfully built man and Fiona knew she'd made a mistake — a terrible mistake. But her sister, Elspeth, had assured her the colonel was in Hillsboro.

"I was coming up from the tavern below stairs and caught this woman sneaking into your room, Colonel Kincaid," answered the burly, blond sergeant who'd surprised Fiona moments earlier as she was, indeed, sneaking into the colonel's room.

"I weren't sneakin'!" The lie escaped Fiona so quickly she had a flash of hope. Maybe she'd be able to wriggle out of this predicament. Maybe the blood of Scottish heroines did flow through her veins. Why, she'd even remembered to affect the dialect of a tavern wench—the dialect that matched her hastily contrived disguise.

The sergeant, who now had a secure grip on Fiona's wrist, snorted. "Claims you sent for her."

"He did send for me," Fiona screeched, throwing herself into the charade. She didn't like her captor's tone. After all, it wasn't inconceivable that someone would send for her. But as soon as she said it, Fiona wished she hadn't. Her outburst riveted the colonel's attention to her. Until this moment, he'd focused primarily on the sergeant.

Now the colonel turned his gaze on her and his scowl deepened. Heroism be damned, Fiona retreated, at least as far as she could before the sergeant's grasp stopped her. "I . . . I could be mistaken." Fiona caught herself slipping into her soft Scottish brogue and paused. "I mean, some bloke did send for me, but I ain't sure it was you. Now that I think on it, it probably weren't. I'll just be takin' my leave now, guv'nor. Sorry for the mistake."

Fiona gave her arm a tug, surprised when the sergeant released it, and reached for the door latch. Relief swelled within her.

"There was no mistake. I did send for you."

"You did?"

"You did?" Fiona wasn't sure who sounded more surprised, the sergeant or her.

"Yes." The colonel strode farther into the room and

6

leaned a hip against the desk—the desk Fiona had wanted to search. He folded muscular arms across his bare chest. "I just hadn't expected you so soon."

Just her luck, the colonel not only was in Cross Creek when he was supposed to be in Hillsboro, but he had sent for a woman. Well, Fiona could take care of that. "That's because I'm not the right one." The colonel's dark brow arched quizzically and Fiona hastened to add, "I'm supposed to go to some other room, I'm sure of it now. And later someone else will come here." Fiona cringed. She sounded like a lackwit.

"It makes no difference." The colonel straightened to his full towering height. With deliberate care his gaze raked her body, from the hem of her too-long gown to the top of her borrowed cap. "You'll do."

Do! Do for what? Fiona was afraid she knew. The colonel had obviously been asleep when she was caught in his sitting room. Asleep in bed. Fiona glanced into the room he'd burst from and saw the high tester bed. It looked nearly as rumpled as the colonel. He stood there, his dark hair tousled, square jaw shadowed by whiskers, and his body covered only by a wrinkled pair of buff-colored breeches. They rode low on his lean hips, were only partially buttoned, and Fiona imagined she was lucky he'd bothered to pull them on at all.

Well, it didn't matter what he had in mind for her, Fiona wasn't about to go along with it. She'd . . . What would she do? If she told him that she really wasn't one of the women who plied their wares from the tavern downstairs, he'd want to know her real name and what she was doing in his room.

Fiona refused to explain that before she had left her home at Armadale, her cousin, Duncan, had mentioned that he'd love to know if the American militia

7

planned to march against the loyalist clansmen in North Carolina. Fiona had agreed with him, not giving it much thought until last evening when her sister had casually mentioned that the militia colonel had been summoned to the Provincial Congress in Hillsboro.

"Are you certain?" Fiona had asked, an idea forming in her mind.

"Told me so himself day before yesterday when he summoned me to look at a knife wound on one of the men he was training," her brother-in-law had answered.

That was when Fiona had decided to sneak into the colonel's room and look through his desk. Surely that was where he kept his orders. She'd been very excited, just imagining the look of surprise on Duncan's face when she told him the American plans. It would be just like the games they'd played as children.

But of course she hadn't expected to be caught. What was the damn colonel doing here, anyway?

Well, she didn't care if he tortured her—Fiona cringed at the thought—she wouldn't tell him the truth. She was braver than that. Besides, if she told him, her grandfather would find out. It didn't matter that he was back home at Armadale, the family's plantation; he'd find out.

Oh, Lord, what was she to do?

"You may go."

Jerked from her musings by the sound of the colonel's deep voice, Fiona thought her prayers answered. But her relief was short-lived. He wasn't speaking to her, but to the sergeant, who obeyed without comment, though he glanced at Fiona suspiciously.

Ezekiel Kincaid rubbed eyes that felt gritty from lack of sleep, and studied the girl standing, poised for flight, by the door. He hadn't a clue as to why she had come to his rooms at the tavern, but it sure as hell hadn't been to satisfy his sexual needs. He'd had his share of paid-for women, and not a one ever clutched a shawl around their shoulders the way this one did. The way she covered herself, Zeke would find it hard to know if there was anything worth paying for.

Not that he wanted to. He hadn't sent for anyone, hadn't even considered it, after the grueling few days he'd had. But here she was. And Zeke would bet his best horse that she hadn't stumbled into his room by mistake. She had a reason, and Zeke meant to find out what it was.

"Come here, woman." Zeke leaned back against the desk.

"Me? Why?" His gruffly spoken command startled Fiona, who had thought the menacing colonel close to falling asleep, he'd stood there with half-closed eyes for so long.

Zeke fought an urge to smile. This woman definitely was not a whore. So what was she—and more importantly, why was she in his room? Zeke might have thought finding out amusing if he weren't so damn tired. "I want a better look at you."

"Oh." Fiona glanced at the door to the hallway, mentally judging how long it would take her to get through it, and came to a disheartening conclusion— too long. Though the colonel appeared relaxed, Fiona sensed his stance deceiving. His body exuded power— latent power at this moment . . . Fiona had a feeling that if she tried to escape, he'd be on her instantly. Deciding her best option was to play along, for the time being, Fiona stepped forward slowly.

"Closer."

Fiona swallowed and moved toward the colonel.

The light from the sputtering candle on the desk behind him outlined his broad shoulders, played across the hills and valleys of his hair-roughened chest.

That candle had been her first clue that something was amiss. It had signaled the turning point in her perfect plan. Getting information from her sister without causing suspicion had been ridiculously easy. Even borrowing the dress and hat from the room of the indentured servant, Hester, and sneaking out of the house just before dawn hadn't caused a problem. And at the tavern, there were so few people, no one gave her a second glance as she entered and marched up the steps. But when she'd opened the colonel's door—he hadn't even locked it—and seen the lighted candle, Fiona had known her luck had turned. Still, if she'd managed to leave without the meddlesome sergeant seeing her, she might not be in this predicament.

The sergeant had grabbed her, demanding to know what she was doing. It was then she'd conceived her ridiculous lie.

Zeke had to hand it to the woman; she had spirit. Even though he could tell she was scared, she walked toward him. After she left the shadows by the door, he could see her better. And he liked what he saw—what he could see. A white cap completely hid her hair, its ruffle partially obscuring her face, but he could make out a short, straight nose and full, gently curved mouth. And skin so pale and translucent it appeared too fragile to touch.

She stood within arm's length now, and Zeke reached out, lifting her chin with his finger. His breath caught when she looked up at him, and Zeke chided himself for his foolish reaction. So her eyes were beautiful, thick-lashed and large—and the exact shade of rain-washed violets. None of that had a thing to do with what she was doing in his room.

Zeke reminded himself that was his only interest in the woman. He examined her more carefully. The defiant gleam in her eyes, the stubborn tilt of her chin as she lifted it away from his touch, told him she wouldn't tell him what he wanted to know—not right away anyway. But if he forced her hand . . . "Well."

"Well, what?" Fiona's mind raced trying to latch onto some plan that would save her. She should have tried to run earlier, before she got so close to him. He was near enough to touch her now—had touched her. Fiona still reeled from the jolt that had caused. If only she could . . .

"Undress."

"What?" Fiona gasped, clutching her shawl tighter.

"Disrobe. Take off your clothes. Surely you don't expect me to take you fully dressed?"

"No. I mean . . ." She didn't expect him to take her at all. Suddenly, flight seemed her only option. Turning on her heel, Fiona lunged for the door.

She had such an expressive little face, Zeke thought. He knew she planned to bolt before she moved. It took very little effort to straighten and grab her back into his arms. She squirmed, trying to twist away, but Zeke turned her around, lacing his fingers at the small of her back, pulling her firmly against him. "Oh, so you like to play a little, first," Zeke said. "Why didn't you say so?"

"I don't. I—" Muffled by the warm skin of his shoulder, Fiona knew he couldn't hear her denial. Tears welled in her eyes, but she refused to shed them. She wriggled, vexed when that motion only nestled her more intimately against her captor. She'd never felt so powerless. The colonel surrounded her. His arms felt like iron bands binding hers to her side; his hard body pressed against her; even the air she breathed smelled of him, musky and male.

He liked the feel of her, a lot. Soft and slight, she fit him well. Wishing he *had* sent for her, Zeke considered playing this game out to its natural conclusion. After all, she was the one who'd broken into his room and lied. Why shouldn't she pay the consequences? Zeke shook his head. Forcing women wasn't his style, and this one would have to be forced. Besides, she'd break down and tell him the truth about why she was here, long before it came to that.

If her trembling was any indication, Zeke guessed she was close to telling him now. A little nudge and she'd confess why she'd come and who'd sent her. Then he could go back to bed and get some sleep. She squirmed and Zeke felt himself growing hard. He decided to procure female companionship, *willing* female companionship, after he'd rested.

The big oaf loosened his grip and Fiona took a welcome deep breath. She also tried to twist away, but couldn't. The movement did make her aware of the rock-hard bulge in the colonel's breeches and the smug smile on his face. "You're making a big mistake." Panic made her words loud and forceful.

"Really?" What a lot of brass she had. As far as he could tell, the mistake was all hers. "What is it?"

What indeed. She had no idea—unless . . . Fragments of a conversation she'd overheard years ago between her cousins, Duncan and William, came rushing back to her. They'd been in the first blush of manhood, thinking themselves quite the thing, and obviously hadn't known she was listening. Whores had been their topic—how to find a good one, how to stay away from those that were—

"I have the pox!"

"The . . ." Zeke didn't know what he'd expected her to say, but it certainly hadn't been that! His reaction was quick and complete. He laughed.

Was he mad? How could he think something like that funny? If she recalled Duncan's description correctly, it was a terrible affliction—one no man wanted.

"Did you hear what I said?" Fiona stomped her foot in aggravation. His laughter, deep and vibrating from his body through hers, grated on her already frayed nerves.

"I heard you." Zeke shook his head, trying to control his amusement.

"Well?" Fiona glared up at him, annoyed with herself for noticing the dimples that slashed his cheeks when he smiled.

"I'll take my chances." He'd never seen anyone less likely to be diseased.

"Ohh . . ." Frustration gripped Fiona. Without thinking of the consequences, she kicked.

Zeke jerked his leg out of the way, missing what would have been a painful blow to his shin. He hauled her up against him, deciding to keep himself more alert, and to get on with finding some answers.

"You're a fighter, aren't you . . . What's your name?"

"Mary," Fiona spit out. The half lie was the best she could do under the circumstances. Though she had been christened Mary Fiona, her grandfather was the only one to call her Mary, and then only when she'd earned his ire.

"Ah, Mary. Sweet name." He didn't believe for a second it belonged to her. "Are you as sweet as your name, Mary?"

Now, what did he mean by that? Fiona looked up in time to see the twinkle in his eyes—blue eyes, she noted—as he bent closer. He was going to kiss her! Fiona panicked. She twisted and turned, trying to keep her face away from his. The colonel's hand left the small of her back, traveling up her spine to clamp on her cap. He yanked it off, burying his fingers in her hair, angling her mouth up toward his.

Her hair was red—not just red, but fiery red. Zeke had never seen so many wild red curls before. They seemed to braid around his hand. Pushing aside that thought, he kissed her, kissed her as he would a woman he'd bought. She hardly responded with the enthusiasm he usually received.

Fiona gasped, but could do nothing to stop his onslaught. She tried to keep her mouth closed, tried to resist the tongue that slipped boldly between her lips—tried to pretend she didn't find his touch exciting.

His tongue skimmed across her teeth, his thumb caressed the sensitive skin behind her ear, and she sighed—she simply couldn't help herself. Her mouth opened; the kiss deepened.

A jolt shot through Fiona's body. Her breasts, crushed against the colonel's chest, tingled, seemed to swell. What was happening to her? She tried to push him away—he'd loosened his hold on her arms—but when her hands touched the warm, smooth skin at his waist they stilled, clung.

His mouth moved over hers, molding it, making her breathless. His tongue plunged, beckoned hers to join the sensual play. His body begged hers to arch into him, promised dizzying delights beyond her imagining. The combination shattered her senses, fragmented her common sense. And then it stopped—abruptly.

Trying to focus, Fiona gazed up at the colonel. He

now held her at arm's length, an expression of bewilderment on his face.

"Do . . ." Zeke paused, waiting for his breathing to steady. The kiss hadn't been at all as he'd planned. He'd meant to frighten her, give her a taste of what would happen if she didn't revise her story. He'd succeeded only in driving himself wild. She was inexperienced, but by the time Zeke had pushed her away, he'd felt his control slipping. He now fought to regain it. "Do you still contend that I sent for you?"

"Sent for me . . .? You said you did." Fiona couldn't think straight. His kiss had—She didn't know what it had done to her. But it certainly had never happened before. She'd been kissed, of course. Last week Thomas MacQuaid had accompanied her out to the gardens at Armadale and kissed her. It had felt pleasant enough, but nothing like what she'd just experienced.

Staring down at her, Zeke admitted, to himself at least, that he didn't know what to do. He'd thought to push her into an admission, but she insisted upon stubbornly standing by her story. Maybe he just hadn't pushed hard enough.

"Very well." Zeke let his hands slide off her shoulders, down her arms. "Let's retire to the bedroom."

"The bedroom?" The pleasant fog lifted from Fiona's mind.

Zeke resisted the urge to gloat. Her face paled to a ghostly white. "Yes. I'm too tired to take you standing up, and the floor looks hellish hard."

Fiona glanced down at the wide planks, and then back at the large, threatening man. She started to protest, but he paid no heed. Grabbing her hand, the colonel pulled her toward the door. "Wait," she yelled, clutching the doorjamb with her free hand. "I'm not who you think I am."

The colonel stopped immediately, glancing over his broad shoulder, his brow raised quizzically. Fiona knew a moment of regret for the admission she'd blurted out. Raised on her grandfather's tales of Scottish heroism, long hoping herself cast from the same mold, she felt a coward indeed. But she couldn't, just couldn't, allow him to touch her again.

"Who are you?"

Sweat trickled between Fiona's breasts, and her knees began to shake. What could she tell him? The truth? Would he believe she'd acted on her own, or would he blame Duncan, or her grandfather? Fiona opened her mouth to speak, not certain what she'd say. "I . . ."

"Come now, woman, I grow tired of these games."

The colonel's growl convinced Fiona that he'd never understand. "I came to the wrong room."

Stubborn little wench, Zeke thought, shaking his head. His frustration was tempered by confidence that in a few more minutes she'd tell all. "I already told you, that matters naught."

He had. How could she have forgotten? Desperation sent her voice aquiver. "But I . . ."

"Enough." Zeke gave a yank, pulling her through the doorway, kicking the paneled door shut with a bang.

No candles burned here, but by now dawn pearled the sky outside the window, gilding the room's interior. Fiona's eyes swept the chamber, searching for some means of escape. Clothes draped the furnishings, littered the floor like windswept shrouds. Apparently the captain had undressed in a hurry, tossing his garments, caring not where they fell. A travel-dusted jacket hung from the washstand, a waistcoat from the bureau. A balled-up shirt lay at the foot of the . . . bed.

Fiona tried to ignore that particular furnishing, but her gaze snagged on it and wouldn't let go. It was high and four-postered; a blue-and-white blanket, partially thrown back, covered the mattress.

The colonel strode to the bed, casually leaned against the side, and began unbuttoning his breeches. "Let's get on with it." He looked up at Fiona and grinned.

She took flight. Grabbing the door handle, Fiona yanked it toward her, only to feel the door slam shut. She closed her eyes, aware of the heat and smell of the colonel close behind her, his strong arm beside her head.

"That will be enough of that, Mary." Zeke circled her shoulders, molding her to his side and dragging her with him to the bureau. He rummaged on the polished top, giving a grunt when he found the key. The brass caught the light as he held it up. "If you continue to insist you're a lightskirt, you will act like one." With that, he let go of her—so quickly that Fiona grasped the chest of drawers to keep from falling—and strode to the door.

He was locking her in—with him! She clutched the smooth wood, her hand knocking against a pewter candlestick. In that moment Fiona knew what she must do.

Glancing at her captor, seeing him bent over, twisting the key in the lock, Fiona seized the pewter and rushed toward him. He must have heard her, for he started to look up, but Fiona brought the candlestick down across his head with all her strength.

The colonel crumpled at her feet. In a panic, Fiona dropped her weapon; it clanked on the wooden floor.

She'd done it! The colonel was unconscious—or dead.

"My God," Fiona mumbled, leaning over his prostrate form. What if she'd killed him? She studied his broad back, looking for signs of life. He'd landed face down beside the door, blocking it. She was going to have to move him in order to leave, in order to see if he was still alive.

Tentatively, Fiona reached out her hand to touch him. His shoulder was hard and warm. Grasping his upper arm, she pulled. He didn't budge. She bent over, shoving with both hands, and finally got him rolled over away from the door. Almost afraid to know the truth, fearing the worst, Fiona laid her palm on the hair-roughened skin over his heart.

She could feel it. The strong, steady beat vibrated through her hand. With a sigh of relief, Fiona sat back on her heels and studied Colonel Kincaid. Now that he lay mobile, he didn't seem nearly so fierce. His nose was finely chiseled and his jaw squarish. Thick black lashes formed a crescent under his eyes—blue eyes, she remembered.

Fiona leaned over further, examining his head. Crimson blood matted the dark brown hair around the cut on his scalp caused by the sharp edge of the candlestick. Wringing her hands, Fiona wished she hadn't had to hurt him. If only he'd let her go . . . Glancing over her shoulder, Fiona wondered if she should dampen a scrap of her petticoat in the pitcher and try to stop the bleeding. Maybe if she bandaged his . . .

He moaned, the sound coming from deep in his chest. With a start, Fiona stood. What was she doing? He'd be all right. A man as big as the colonel wasn't going to be seriously hurt by a candlestick-wielding female like her.

Now her own well-being was a different matter. If the colonel awoke and found her here . . . Well, Fiona didn't even want to think about what he might do. Gathering her borrowed skirts, she climbed over his long legs, turned the key, opened the door, and fled the room.

Downstairs the tavern was empty, a fact that gratified Fiona tremendously. She crept out of the establishment into the early morning sunshine. Taking a route through alleys and gardens back to her sister's house on Cool Spring Street took longer, but at least no one saw her.

Fiona slipped into the back door and up the servants' stairs, not stopping until she reached the security of her bedroom. Once inside, Fiona stripped off her borrowed clothes, stuffing them under the bed — Hester would find them after she'd gone — and began pulling her own clothes from her wardrobe. She'd planned to stay in Cross Creek until Elspeth's baby was born, but she couldn't now.

She had to leave today, before Colonel Kincaid had a chance to find her. This morning's adventure had taught her several things. She wasn't cut out to be a heroine. Intrigue and spying were not for her. And she never, ever wanted to see Colonel Ezekiel Kincaid again.

Chapter Two

His head hurt like hell.

Ezekiel Kincaid's eyes slitted open, then slammed shut as the light increased the pounding at his temple. Tentatively he lifted a hand, exploring the right side of his scalp.

"Ouch. Damnit." A string of profanities accompanied his discovery of the gouge in the side of his head. His fingers felt wet and sticky, and he knew before he even looked that they were smeared with blood.

What had happened to him? He'd been locking his bedroom door when—The girl! His body jackknifed to sitting position. Staring around the room, he tried to ignore the spinning floor.

She was gone.

A quick perusal of the bedroom and what he could see of the sitting room convinced him of that. Lord, she must have hit him with a—Zeke spotted the candlestick on the floor. Lifting the bent pewter, he counted himself lucky she'd been only a little slip of a thing.

"Big enough to best you," he moaned, getting slowly and unsteadily to his feet. The movement only increased the drums sounding surrender in his head.

Clutching the washstand with both hands, Zeke fought a spasm of nausea before pouring water into the bowl. Splashing the cool liquid on his face helped clear his head; the pounding at the door made it feel worse.

"What?" he growled, grabbing for a linen towel.

"It's me, Colonel. Sergeant Simpson."

Ah, the man who'd brought him the redheaded witch. No, more precisely, the man who'd saved him from her. According to Simpson, the woman had been in his room when he'd caught her. If the commotion hadn't roused Zeke, she'd probably have bludgeoned him to death while he slept. He owed the sergeant his thanks. "Come in."

"Sorry to bother you, but you did tell me last night when you rode in from Hillsboro that you wanted to be up and away early." Simpson started talking when he entered the sitting room. " 'Course I didn't know if you felt the same after having that girl, but—What happened to you?"

Zeke threw Simpson a wry look over his shoulder. "Who was that woman?"

"The one I caught in your room last night? Never saw her before."

"You've lived here in Cross Creek all your life, haven't you?"

"Yes, sir, and that's what I thought was strange. I know my way around the tavern wenches in this town, if I do say so." He puffed his barrel chest. "But I never saw that one before."

Zeke studied the sergeant. "You're sure?"

Simpson nodded. "I think I'd have remembered that one, if you know what I mean?"

Zeke nodded. He knew exactly what Simpson meant. She would be hard to forget, with that red hair

21

and those violet eyes—even if she hadn't left her mark on him.

Wetting the corner of the towel, Zeke dabbed at his cut, his face wincing in pain. Simpson stepped closer. "She do that to you?"

"Yeah." Zeke rinsed the linen, turning the water in the bowl a rusty brown.

"Why?"

"Good question. I wasn't able to find out what she—Wait." An explanation that had eluded him last night struck Zeke. He caught Simpson's gaze in the mirror over the washstand as he pressed the towel to the tear in his flesh. "Check the chest of drawers. Is there a money pouch on top?"

"Sure is." Simpson tossed the bag, catching it with the same hand. "Feels pretty full, too."

"I guess robbery wasn't her motive."

"You got anything else that woman would want?"

A sudden memory of her mouth, wet and warm, pressed to his, flashed into Zeke's head, but he dismissed it with a groan. "Not that she'd try to smash my skull for." Zeke looked around, found his saddlebags slung across the Windsor chair by the window, and pulled a clean shirt from one of the pouches.

"What you going to do about her?" Simpson cocked his head to the side. "You think you ought to have Dr. MacCloud look at that?"

"I'm in no mood to be leeched." Zeke's words were muffled as he carefully pulled the shirt over his head. "As for the woman; I intend to find her." And when he did, he'd extract payment for what she'd done to him. Earlier this morning he'd pretended he expected sexual favors from her to find out why she'd come to his room. But the game was over. When he found her, and he had no doubts he would, she'd discover he

22

wasn't toying with her anymore.

Zeke had a moment of doubt about his motives. Was his interest in finding the girl entirely revenge? The blow to his head hadn't dimmed the memory of how she felt, soft and warm in his arms. Or how her red hair curled wildly around her face. Or those eyes. He winced as a new shaft of pain shot through his head. What was he thinking? He had no interest in a woman who'd crack someone's skull for no apparent reason.

"I'll find her," Zeke reiterated. "But I can't start looking yet." He tucked the white linen shirt into his breeches.

"The reason you can't have anything to do with what the Provincial Congress wanted with you?"

"It has everything to do with it," Zeke said, rubbing a hand across his whiskered chin.

For the next few weeks, or however long it took to change a group of stubborn Scotsmen's minds, Zeke's time was not his own. The knowledge still galled. Zeke tried to remember when his luck had taken this turn for the worse.

It had started when he'd been summoned to meet with a committee of North Carolina's Third Provincial Congress. Until that time, he'd been organizing and training companies of militia in Cross Creek and other towns in the area.

He'd ridden to Hillsboro, where the congress was meeting, expecting to present a report on the state of the minutemen in his military district. Instead, he'd gotten an account of the Scotch Highlanders.

They'd been arriving in North Carolina by the thousands since the defeat of the Jacobites in 1745. After the battle of Culloden, which had seen the end of Charles Stuart's quest for the British crown, England's treatment of the conquered Scots had been harsh. They'd outlawed the wearing of the plaid, the playing of the pipes. Rather than live under this tyranny, many Highlanders had emigrated—a large number of them to the Cape Fear region of North Carolina.

Zeke knew all of that, and had said as much to the men on the committee. "Are you also aware that Scottish sympathies lie with the British over our disagreements with the Mother Country?" Thomas Rutherford, a representative from Cumberland county, had asked Zeke.

"I am," Zeke had answered. It hadn't taken him long in Cross Creek to realize that the Scots considered him an enemy. "But the militia is fairly strong. We can forestall any trouble, should they start it."

"We had more in mind to stop it before it ever begins."

"Meaning?" Zeke had sat back in his chair, crossing his ankles.

"We have knowledge that the Scots are flocking around their leaders—lairds. Balls are being held almost nightly to whip up support for the British cause. Flora MacDonald, the Scottish girl who reportedly saved Bonnie Prince Charles from being caught in '45, is said to be a staunch loyalist. Spirits are running high." Rutherford had paused. "But we'd like to inject some reason into this arena, perhaps give the Scots a better understanding of our cause."

"That sounds like a good idea."

"We were hoping you'd agree." The men had looked at each other, nodding.

"Why?" Zeke had begun to get an uncomfortable feeling.

"Because we'd like you to be the bearer of that

reason."

"Me?" Zeke had shot to his feet. "Why in the hell would you pick me?"

"Calm yourself, Colonel Kincaid. Believe me, we've considered this very carefully, and have come to the decision that you're the perfect man for the job."

"Well, perhaps you'd better think it over again."

"For one thing, there's your Scottish ancestry," Daniel Smith, another representative from Cumberland county, had explained, as if Zeke hadn't spoken.

"Scotch-Irish," Zeke corrected. "And lowland Scotch at that. Not considered the same at all, at least not by the Highlanders."

Again, the committee persisted as if Zeke hadn't spoken. "You, of course, are familiar with the vicinity and its people."

Zeke hardly thought staying in rented rooms in a tavern, and training the militia, gave him a great knowledge of the Cross Creek area, and said so. He could have saved his breath. Finally, he'd looked at the men, meeting them gaze for gaze. "I'm not a negotiator."

"That's where you're wrong, Colonel. You've done an excellent job of forming and training militia. You've convinced the men that they need to prepare themselves for what might happen. And of course you'd never have made the success you have of your shipping business without an ability to mold people to your way of thinking."

In the end, Zeke had reluctantly agreed to contact the Highlanders. Looking back on his decision, Zeke knew he never stood a chance of resisting once the delegates reminded him of the bloodshed that would occur if the Highlanders took up arms against the people of North Carolina. And he felt better when the committee informed him that two Presbyterian ministers would probably join him in the negotiations.

"So what did they want you for, Colonel?" Sergeant Simpson's question brought Zeke back to the present.

"I'm suppose to stop an uprising," Zeke said sarcastically. Noting the sergeant's puzzled expression, Zeke shook his head — a move he instantly regretted. "My assignment is to move among the Scottish Highlanders, visit their plantations and homes, and try to convince them to remain neutral during our rebellion against England."

Sergeant Simpson scratched his ear. "But I thought they more or less favored the king's side in all of this."

"They do," Zeke agreed. "Any idea who's the most influential clan leader among the Scots living along the Cape Fear River?" Zeke bent over to pull on his boots and fought another wave of nausea.

"Well . . ." Nathan Simpson tugged on his earlobe. "Since they arrived from Scotland, Alan MacDonald and his wife Flora have kind of become the unofficial head of the group. But they live up in Richmond County, about five miles from Ellerbe Springs."

"She the one who saved the Stuart prince from the British?"

"Sure is. You all right, Colonel? You're not looking so good. No color."

"I'm fine." Zeke waved off the sergeant's concern, but he did wait a minute before tugging on his other boot. He also decided to start visiting Scotsmen a little closer to Cross Creek. Ellerbe Springs was a couple days ride by swift horse, and right now, Zeke wasn't certain he could sit a horse that long. "How about around here? Who would you say has the most influence?"

"Gotta be old Malcolm MacClure." He owns a tar

plantation along the Cape Fear. Haven't seen him for a while, but he used to be a real firebrand. Wore his kilt into town, broadsword hanging by his side. I was just a kid, but I remember he used to scare the hell out of me." Nathan shook his head in silent laughter. "He lost an arm at Culloden, but it didn't slow him down. " 'Course, I hear he isn't as brash as he used to be. His son and daughter-in-law died a few years back, and he's been raising his granddaughters. Figure it must have mellowed him some." Nathan paused. "One of his granddaughters is married to Doc Mac-Cloud."

"Elspeth?"

"I think that's her name."

Zeke shrugged, then decided he'd sit on the bed for a minute—just till his eyes refocused. "Do you think this Malcolm MacClure still has clout with the Scots?"

"Yeah. The MacClures are a big clan. Lots of money and land. And Malcolm's the laird. They listen to him. Other clans do, too. Yes, sir, I'd say Malcolm MacClure's the one you need to convince."

"All right." Zeke gave up the battle and lay back against the pillows. "I'm going to rest a minute, and then I'll start for . . . what's the name of the MacClure's plantation?"

"Armadale."

"Armadale," Zeke repeated. "I'll start for Armadale in a little while."

"Colonel, you sure I shouldn't go get Doc MacCloud?"

"No, I'll be fine. Just need a moment to rest. I'll lie here and think about what strategy I'm going to use with Malcolm MacClure." But as Zeke fell asleep it wasn't an old Scot who filled his mind. Instead, his thoughts strayed to a young woman with wild red hair and rose-petal soft lips—that hid a thorn.

"Fiona! Miss Fiona!"

Galloping down the oak-lined lane, Fiona glimpsed Lucy standing on the wide front porch of Armadale, waving her arms frantically. Though Fiona couldn't hear her over the pounding of hooves, she knew the old black nanny called her.

Fiona cursed under her breath—a habit she'd picked up from her cousin Duncan—and slowed her horse to a more sedate trot.

She'd stayed out too long, ridden too far and she knew it—had known it while she was doing it. And now she'd have to pay. Lucy would yell, threaten to tell Grandfather, and then relent when Fiona promised never to do it again. The next half hour would be unpleasant, but—Fiona grinned—it had been worth it. The day was beautiful, clear, and shining—a gem in late summer. And she'd enjoyed herself immensely.

Fiona reined in her horse at the curve of the boxwood lined drive, sliding to the ground before the stableboy could assist her. "I know, I know," she began, not waiting for Lucy to begin her tirade. "I've been riding too long. It won't happen again." Giving Lucy a hug around her ample shoulders, Fiona smiled when she heard the old black woman's hmph.

"Don't you go hugging up to me, Miss Fiona. It ain't gonna help you this time."

"But Lucy, I wasn't gone *that* long." Fiona opened the door into the wide, cool central hall.

"Ain't my problem how long you been gone, or even that you ain't got no hat on and will freckle for sure. Your granddaddy wants to see you."

"Grandfather?" Fiona's smile disappeared. "What

does he want?"

"Ain't sure." Lucy's expression was smug. "But he called for you right after you left, and hasn't stopped since."

Fiona took a deep breath. "Where is he?"

"In his room. But ain't you gonna change 'fore you go up and see him?"

Pausing on the second tread of the carved staircase, Fiona glanced down at her dust-stained riding habit. Impatiently brushing at the skirt, she shrugged. "He knows where I've been. There's no use trying to hide it."

Or prolong the confrontation, Fiona thought, as she hurried up the steps. If Grandfather had been calling for her all afternoon, it must be something important. Most of the time they spent the evenings together. During the day, her grandfather read or took care of clan and plantation business, while Fiona ran the household. Except when she sneaked off to ride alone, a habit Fiona knew her grandfather disapproved of.

Still, he'd never called her to task for it. She couldn't imagine why he seemed impatient to see her, unless . . . No. He couldn't have discovered what she had done in Cross Creek. He'd accepted her excuse for returning so suddenly — at least he'd appeared to. Besides — Fiona brushed stray curls behind her shoulder — there was no way he could find out about her little adventure.

Her knock on the paneled mahogany door was answered by a robust, "Come in, Mary Fiona."

"Good day, Grandfather." Fiona crossed to where he sat between two open windows and brushed a kiss across his bearded cheek. "You wanted to see me?"

"Indeed, Mary Fiona, and have for some time," he answered in Gaelic.

"I've been riding." Fiona slipped easily into the tongue of her ancestors.

"As I can see—and smell."

Fiona noted the twinkle in her grandfather's blue eyes, and grinned. "Well, I'm here now." Though there were times Fiona feared her actions might bring her grandfather's wrath down around her shoulders, they got along well. Fiona thought it was because they were very much alike.

"It's that wild red hair," Lucy was fond of saying. "No way you and the laird can help running off doing things without thinking. You was branded at birth."

Fiona shook her head. She wasn't impetuous. A memory of going to the colonel's rooms flashed through her head, and she squirmed in her seat. "What did you want to be seeing me about?"

Malcolm MacClure leaned forward, tapping his finger on the paper-littered table beside him. "I received a message—actually two messages—from Cross Creek today."

"Oh," Fiona tried, but couldn't make out the writing on the top letter.

"One is from your sister, Elspeth."

"How is she?"

"She is fine, Mary Fiona, as you well ken. Her concern is for you."

"Me? But I'm—"

"She wonders why you left Cross Creek so quickly, as do I."

Fiona's fingers braided in her lap. "I gave you my reason."

"You gave me *a* reason," Malcolm corrected.

"It was too hot, and I became homesick for Armadale—and you," Fiona added for good measure.

Malcolm looked skeptical, but didn't pursue that

line of questioning. Instead, he examined the post, laying it on his kilt. "Elspeth mentions that you seemed very upset the morning you left."

"I wasn't." Fiona jumped up and walked to the window. Staring out at the tall pines swaying on the edge of the clearing, she took a calming breath. Why couldn't she just forget about what had happened in Cross Creek? Fiona clutched the sill and turned back to stare at her grandfather. "I don't know what Elspeth could mean, but I'll send her a message to relieve her mind."

"That would be a good idea. Elspeth always was a worrier, and now with a bairn on the way . . ."

"I'll send a message right away." Damn that militia colonel. If it weren't for him, she could have stayed in Cross Creek with Elspeth till she had the baby—just as she'd planned. "Maybe Elspeth should come here till the child is born. It's cooler, and—"

"She won't hear of leaving her husband, and a physician can't abandon his patients."

Fiona nodded. Elspeth's husband, Robert Mac-Cloud, was a physician newly arrived from Glasgow. He'd been in North Carolina barely a month when he'd met Fiona's younger sister. The two fell in love immediately, and married a short time later. Grandfather was right. Elspeth wouldn't leave Robert's side.

Sighing, Fiona lifted the dimity curtain. She couldn't help feeling a tiny twinge of envy. Why couldn't she meet someone and fall in love? Elspeth's marriage and now her pregnancy were reminders that Fiona, at twenty, should have her own husband. But though several young men had made their intentions toward her known, she'd managed to dissuade them.

". . . to our visitor."

"I'm sorry." Fiona let the sheer fabric slide through

her fingers, embarrassed to be caught daydreaming. She'd missed most of what her grandfather had said. "But I'm afraid I didn't hear."

"I was telling you of my other message. This one is from a representative of the Provincial Congress. He's coming here to—"

"Why on earth would one of them come here?" Fiona spun around, her balled fists planted on her waist.

"If you'll keep your temper a moment, I'll tell you." Malcolm waited while his granddaughter sat back down. She took her time, spreading the skirts of her scarlet riding habit. "The gentleman wishes to discuss with me the colony's grievances against the king."

"But—"

Malcolm held up his hand. "I believe he is aware of my stand on the issue; however, I see no harm in listening to him. And . . ." Malcolm stood. "I would appreciate you keeping your feelings to yourself, and being polite to our guest."

"Yes, sir." Fiona rose and executed a deep curtsey, brushing back the hair that fell into her face. "Now, if you'll excuse me, I shall retire to my room to make myself presentable for our exalted visitor."

"Fiona . . .," Malcolm couldn't help chuckling.

"Oh, all right. I shall be the height of propriety." Fiona stood on tiptoe to kiss her grandfather's cheek. "But I must get ready for dinner."

"Go on with you." Malcolm waved her off with his hand. He stopped her just as she reached for the latch. "And Fiona, I watched you ride away earlier. I thought I told you to go around the north fence, not over it."

"You did. And I'm sorry. It won't be happening again." Fiona escaped out the door before her grandfather could respond to her apology.

"Well, what did the laird want?"

Fiona shut her bedroom door, leaned against it, and cringed when she heard Lucy's question. "Nothing."

"Hmpf. You don't want to tell me, that's just fine by me."

Pushing away from the door, Fiona unbuttoned her riding jacket, dropping it on the chest at the foot of her bed. "He'd received a note from Elspeth, is all," Fiona relented. "And he wanted to tell me one of the rabble causing so much trouble in North Carolina will be visiting."

"He's already here."

Shrugging, Fiona unwound the stock at her neck, then stepped out of her skirt. "I really don't care. Grandfather said I'm to be polite, and I shall. However, I have no intention of being friendly to the man."

"Might change your mind."

Fiona gave Lucy a wry look before pulling her shift over her head and stepping into the copper bathtub. "Ach, this water's cold."

"I didn't expect you to be as long as you was with the laird. But I suppose I could haul up some more hot water."

"Never mind." Goose bumps sprouted on her arms and legs as she slid down in the heather-scented water. "I shall just bathe quickly."

She dressed quickly, too. Fiona sent Lucy away to stop her from suggesting another ribbon or furbelow to add to her gown. Fiona had no intention of dressing up for the misguided Patriot who was joining the family for dinner. She donned her dark blue silk, adding as her only adornment the MacClure plaid draped over her shoulder and pinned below her waist.

"That should show him where I stand," she murmured, smiling at her reflection in the mirror. Lucy had tamed her hair by pulling it back from Fiona's face on the top and sides and allowing curls to hang down her back. With a shake of her head, Fiona started toward the door.

Thanks to the redheaded witch's blow to his head and the accompanying dizziness, it had taken Zeke a few days before he started toward Armadale. He walked along the upstairs hallway now, wondering if he'd be able to accomplish anything. The laird had greeted him warmly when he'd arrived this afternoon, but had postponed any discussion until later tonight. Zeke rehearsed in his mind the arguments he'd pose to the laird—the arguments in favor of the Scots remaining neutral.

A door opened behind him and he stopped, turning on his heel, a smile of greeting on his face.

It froze as he faced the startled girl.

Panting, Fiona swept back into her bedroom and slammed the door. What was *he* doing here? With fingers made clumsy by fear, she fumbled with the lock, jumping back as the door burst open.

Two strong hands grasped her arms, forcing her against the wall, as he kicked the door shut with his boot. Fiona tried to scream, but she could only gasp for breath. The scowling face she'd seen so often in her mind's eye since that fateful morning loomed inches from hers. His blue eyes shone bright with anger, and triumph.

"What . . ." Fiona's voice squeaked. She stopped and tried again. "What do you want?"

"You," came the colonel's succinct reply.

Chapter Three

Fiona gasped at his arrogant demand. His fingers bit into her arms and his large body pressed hers against the plastered wall. Her heart beat frantically in her chest, sent blood pounding to her head. He had the upper hand—at the moment. But some reason filtered through, and Fiona remembered that *he* was in a house full of MacClures.

She raised her chin, returning his stare. "Get out of my room," she demanded in her haughtiest tone.

To Fiona's chagrin, this tack seemed to amuse the brute greatly. He grinned, exposing those damned dimples, and slowly turned his head.

For the first time, Zeke noticed his surroundings. The bedroom was large—larger than the one he'd been given earlier—and it bore the trappings of wealth.

A large tester bed with yellow-and-green crewel bedhangings and filmy wisps of mosquito netting stood close to the windows. Dainty seersucker curtains fluttered in the early evening breeze. Besides the polished mahogany chest of drawers, and a pair of winged chairs near the fireplace, there was a ruffle-trimmed dressing table in one corner. Atop it a large bouquet of late-summer roses perfumed the air.

The room definitely belonged to a lady, but did it belong to this lady? Zeke glanced back at her. "This your room?"

"Aye," Fiona hissed. Her initial shock had vanished, to be replaced by annoyance. How dare he attack her like this. His very nearness disturbed her. She could smell his maleness, feel the overpowering heat that emanated from him.

Zeke grinned again. "Well now, Mary, maybe this is your bedroom, and maybe it isn't. But the way I see it, it matters naught." The little chit raised her chin defiantly at his words, and Zeke leaned closer to her. "You came to my rooms uninvited. Now I'm returning the favor."

"Ach, you brute!" Fiona squirmed in his hands, her knee kicking up, trying to connect with his groin. But her petticoats slowed her reactions, and he seemed to have no trouble evading her attack. It irked her that he found her attempts so easy to foil.

"Now, now, Mary." Zeke pressed her body harder against the wall with his own. She felt as soft as he remembered, a fact he tried to ignore. "Calm yourself."

Calm herself indeed! Fiona squirmed against the added pressure from his body, stopping when she realized the motion rubbed her breasts across his chest. Though he was dressed today in white linen shirt, silk waistcoat and jacket, Fiona couldn't forget what he looked like with no shirt—his broad, muscled chest swirled with tightly curled brown hair. Fiona reined in her thoughts. "What do you want?" she repeated, amending her question quickly when he cocked a dark brow. "From me, what do you want from me?"

"Perhaps I'm interested in finishing what we started

36

in my rooms."

"What we started? I don't know—"

Zeke knew the exact moment she understood what he meant. The color drained from her face, accentuating the smattering of freckles across the bridge of her nose, and her lovely little mouth dropped open.

"No! If you touch me I'll scream!" Even Fiona thought this a rather ridiculous threat, since his entire body already touched hers in a most intimate way. Besides, if she were going to scream, she would have done it at the beginning. But screaming would bring the entire household—including her grandfather. She'd be saved, temporarily. But Grandfather would demand to know why this man had attacked her. Fiona didn't like the idea of explaining, but she'd risk it before letting this ill-mannered brute have his way with her.

It occurred to Zeke that she hadn't screamed earlier. Now that he thought about it, he couldn't imagine why she hadn't. His own reaction to seeing her hadn't included much thought, but now he realized she could have gotten him thrown out on his ear—or worse. He decided to gentle his attack. "What I really want is to know why you broke into my tavern rooms in Cross Creek."

She seemed relieved that he no longer demanded use of her body, but she didn't answer him. Zeke pulled away enough to examine her. Her dress was silk, and though rather plain, was expensively made. And she wore a plaid draped across it. "You one of this nest of Tories?"

"We are not Tories. We are simply loyal to our king."

Ah . . ."

"What does that mean?" Fiona demanded.

"Nothing." Zeke looked down into her upturned

face. "Did the MacClures put you up to sneaking into my rooms? Maybe even the laird himself?"

"No! No. He knows nothing about it."

Again, Zeke saw panic cross her face, but before he could do anything about it, a knock at the door startled them both. What surprised Zeke was that the woman seemed as unsettled by the interruption as he was. She obviously belonged here. She should be relieved that someone had come to her rescue, but instead she stared up at him with wide violet eyes. Zeke nodded his head toward the door.

"Who is it?" Fiona tried to sound calm. How could she ever explain this man in her room?

"Miss Fiona, you in there? The laird said you was to get downstairs this minute. He says he ain't gonna allow no hiding out in your room."

"I'm not hiding out." Fiona didn't like the idea of Grandfather thinking her a coward. "I'll be right down." Fiona listened as Lucy's clogs clumped along the hall floorboards; then she gave the arrogant colonel a shove. To her relief he moved. But not far.

"We're not finished with our talk."

"I have to go." Fiona squeezed around him and reached for the door handle, surprised when he didn't stop her.

"I want to know the reason."

Fiona ignored him and turned the brass knob.

"Must I seek my information from the laird?"

Squeezing the cold metal, Fiona's gaze shot back to his. She couldn't imagine how this awful man had gotten here, but she couldn't have him bullying her grandfather. "Meet me in the gardens after supper."

"Where in the garden?"

"By the grape arbor, below the boxwood."

"I'll be there." Zeke cupped her shoulder, turning

her to him. He cocked his head questioningly.

"I'll be there, too," Fiona spit out when she noticed the skeptical gleam in his blue eyes.

"Good." Zeke dropped his hand. "Remember, now I know where *your* room is."

Jerking open the door, Fiona strode into the hall. How dare he threaten her like that, and in her own home. She had half a notion to march downstairs and tell her grandfather. He'd show the audacious colonel what happened to anyone who threatened a Mac-Clure.

She stopped, catching her reflection in a hall mirror. Her hair had come loose from the wooden pins, and her plaid was askew. Righting her appearance, Fiona decided to handle this problem herself. She'd started it; she'd finish it.

Fiona hurried down the stairs and into the parlor, stopping short when her grandfather advanced toward her, the colonel by his side. She could only guess he'd run down the servants' stairs to get here ahead of her, but what was he doing with Grandfather?

"Granddaughter." The laird held out his arm. "This is the gentleman I told you about this afternoon, the representative from the Provincial Congress."

Fiona's mouth dropped open. Of course that's what he was doing here. He hadn't followed her bent on revenge. It had been a coincidence—a dreadful coincidence—that he'd found her at all. If she hadn't been so shocked herself, she would have figured it out.

"This is Colonel Ezekiel Kincaid. Colonel, my granddaughter, Mary Fiona."

Fiona caught the subtle lift of his brow when the colonel heard the name Mary. "It's Fiona," she stated as he took her hand. "But you may call me Mistress MacClure." Though Fiona could sense her grandfather's displeasure at her rudeness, the colonel didn't seem to take offense at all. He merely smiled, his blue eyes twinkling as he lifted her hand to his lips.

"It's a pleasure, Mistress MacClure." His mouth was warm and firm and brought back vivid memories of it pressed against her own. Her hand tingled as she jerked it from his grasp.

The meal was an uncomfortable affair for Fiona, though the colonel, even though he was the enemy, seemed to get along well with almost everyone. Several of her aunts, uncles and cousins were present, among them Duncan. He, at least, didn't appear susceptible to the colonel's charm.

Katrine, Duncan's sister, confided to Fiona as they entered the dining room that Duncan had been frightfully rude when introduced to the colonel. Fiona had started to make some comment about Duncan's good sense, when Katrine started gushing on about how handsome the colonel was.

Handsome? Fiona looked across the table at him. He was smiling at something Katrine, who sat at his left, said. Did she think him handsome? Fiona took a bite of chicken. He had a pleasing profile, straight nose, firm jaw. And his dimples were interesting. His hair, which she'd thought black at first, was actually a deep, dark brown. It waved back to a queue tied by a simple black ribbon and was—Fiona paused—attractive. But handsome?

He turned at that moment and met her gaze, his straight brow cocked, his deep blue eyes full of mirth. He'd caught her staring at him, and the arrogant rebel knew it. Fiona blushed nearly as red as her hair, but not before admitting to herself that Katrine was right. He was indeed very handsome.

But that changed nothing. She still didn't like him,

and she certainly wasn't going to simper and swoon around him as her cousin was wont to do. Maybe she'd take Katrine aside after supper and remind her that the colonies were in a state of rebellion against the king, and this man was part of it. No, Fiona reminded herself. After dinner, she had to meet *him*. But what would she say?

Colonel Kincaid wanted to know why she'd come to his room. But she couldn't tell him the real reason. He probably wouldn't take too kindly to someone, especially a Scot, trying to look through his private papers. But she hardly thought he'd again believe her tale of being sent by the tavern—if he ever had.

Sighing, Fiona leaned back in her chair. The lustre overhead was lit, splashing candlelight on the table and guests. Dessert, a variety of late-summer fruit tarts, filled the dishes. Supper would be over soon. And then she'd have to meet the colonel in the garden. Fiona thought again of his threat to come to her room if she didn't keep their appointment. That bothered her more than she cared to admit. Not that she feared for her safety. Fiona really didn't think the colonel would hurt her, but she didn't like the idea of being alone with him—not in so intimate a setting as her bedroom.

Maybe she should tell her grandfather everything. He'd be angry—no, he'd be furious—but Fiona wasn't certain she had a choice. Unless she could come up with a feasible reason for her to have gone to the colonel's rooms—something she didn't think she could do—the colonel would tell her grandfather anyway.

Well, if he did, she'd tell what he had done to her. She'd explain how he had accosted her, forcing himself on her till she was forced to knock him over the head to save her virtue.

Fiona winced. The colonel hadn't mentioned what she'd done to his head, but she must have hurt him. She hazarded a quick look across the table, but could see no evidence of injury. He wore no bandage, and his thick hair covered any sign of a scar.

Taking up her silver fork, Fiona flaked the crust of her peach tart. One thing for sure. Once her grandfather knew what had transpired in Cross Creek, she wouldn't have to worry about the colonel's presence anymore. He'd be kicked off Armadale, wouldn't be received at any other Scottish plantation, and his mission would be over.

Yes, the Provincial Congress's attempt to gain Scottish neutrality would be doomed—and all because Colonel Ezekiel Kincaid couldn't keep his mouth shut.

Fiona dropped her fork, ignoring the clatter it made against her plate, the questioning stares from those around her. The train of her thoughts sent tingles down her spine.

Colonel Kincaid couldn't tell the laird what she had done, because it would jeopardize his mission. Fiona looked across the table, catching the colonel's eye . . . not turning away. He would be the type to take his duty seriously. He wouldn't let anything or anyone stand in his way—and she could.

Should she tell her grandfather and bring to a quick death the colonel's mission that was doomed to failure anyway? Fiona thought of how angry her grandfather would be that she'd risked herself needlessly, and of the punishments he would impose on her. No, as long as the colonel stayed away from her, she'd keep quiet.

A smile turned up the corners of Fiona's mouth. The colonel wanted to see her in the garden—well, she wanted to see him too. Just the expression on his face, when she explained that all his threats were useless, would be worth the anxiety she'd been through.

"You're looking mighty pleased with yourself. Don't tell me you have designs on the American colonel, too."

Fiona realized where she stared and tore her gaze away from the colonel, glancing at her cousin Duncan, seated beside her. "Don't be ridiculous. Though I do think you should speak to Katrine."

Duncan glanced across the table at his sister, then shrugged. "Katrine never did show any sense. You, however, are different."

"I told you I'm not interested in the colonel," Fiona snapped. Surprised by her own irritability, knowing Duncan to be the same by the expression on his face, Fiona touched his arm. "I'm sorry. It's just, I don't like him being here. Do you know why he came?" Fiona whispered, though with the clamor of her noisy family there was no need.

Duncan nodded. "The laird told me."

"Doesn't that bother you?" Fiona knew her cousin to be a zealous supporter of the king. He was the one who'd first given her the idea of finding out if the militia planned to use military force against the Scottish Highlanders. In all honesty, Fiona admitted to herself that he'd never intended she should be the one to attempt such a feat. He'd be as angry as Grandfather if he knew she had.

Duncan took a sip of Madeira, his eyes never straying from the rebel colonel, before answering. When he faced Fiona again, Duncan's pale blue eyes shone with intensity and his ruddy cheeks flared brighter. "General MacDonald has already arrived in North Carolina to take charge of our troops. There is no turning back now. Nothing Colonel Kincaid says or does will change that."

Fiona swallowed, clasped her hands in her lap. This was what she'd wanted her cousin to say, what they'd talked about for months. Then why did she suddenly feel a chill pass through her? The room was warm, the only air coming in the open windows a balmy breeze laden with garden scents. Fiona glanced across the table at the colonel. She wished their meeting was over. She wished she'd never seen him before. Her wool plaid itched through her satin bodice, and Fiona chided herself for wearing it. The colonel apparently hadn't noticed her token of defiance.

If anyone other than she and Duncan were uncomfortable with the colonel's presence, Fiona couldn't tell it. After dinner the family and their guest retired to the parlor. With little persuasion, Angus MacClure, Fiona's uncle, picked up his violin, and Katrine sat at the harpsichord.

Fiona noted with annoyance that Colonel Kincaid agreed to page the music for her cousin. Fine, she thought; we won't meet in the garden. It wasn't my idea anyway.

Sitting back in her chair, watching through the window as darkness overtook the last vestiges of sunset, Fiona let the plaintive music permeate her thoughts. Though she'd never been to Scotland, she'd been raised on tales of her ancestral homeland. She could almost see the craggy mountains rising through the mist, the green glens framing shining blue lochs, the whisper of heather dotting the landscape. The ballad rose to a crescendo and stopped.

It was then Fiona realized that her grandfather now leaned over the harpsichord, turning the pages. Fiona looked around the room, but the colonel was gone. As Angus played the opening bars of "Leather Britches" Fiona slipped from the room.

Even with the full moon, the garden was dimly lit, and Fiona wished she'd thought to bring a lantern. She followed the brick path between the boxwoods, heading down toward the river. The grape arbor stood to her left, a long, tunnel-like structure covered by large leaves and sweet-smelling grape clusters. Fiona glanced about, but could not see the colonel. Peeking inside the arbor also proved useless. The vines blocked most of the light afforded by the moon.

She stepped inside. Why had she picked the grape arbor for their clandestine meeting? She moved farther inside, hearing the swish of her satin overskirt against the leaves. It was dark, only dapples of light filtering through the thickly entwined vines. Hating to admit it, yet feeling fear just the same, Fiona turned, deciding that even if the colonel did come to her room, it would be preferable to this.

A hand reached out and grabbed her, flattening Fiona to the side of the arbor. Her gasp of fright turned to outrage when she made out the colonel's handsome face mere inches from hers. "Must you always wedge me against something?" Fiona pushed at his shoulders with the heels of her hands.

"I wasn't sure it was you," Zeke explained, though he didn't move.

"Just whom did you expect?" Had he made an arrangement with Katrine to meet her in the garden? Fiona chastised herself for such a foolish thought. Besides, he wouldn't treat Katrine like this.

"It occurred to me that you might send someone in your stead."

"Like whom?" Fiona gave up the battle to push him away, with one final aggravated thrust.

"Oh, like the man sitting beside you at supper. He looked as if he'd gladly take a knife to my throat."

Duncan. Fiona almost smiled at the colonel's observation. "Well, I don't have a knife."

"That's good to hear. But the question remains, do you have a candlestick?"

Oh, the insufferable man! Fiona squirmed. She wriggled. But his body held hers prisoner. Finally, with a sigh of resignation, she desisted. "I didn't mean to hurt you."

"Well, for not wanting to, you did one hell of a job."

"I'm sorry," Fiona snapped, not sounding the least apologetic. "But if you hadn't tried to force me to . . . to . . ." She just couldn't say what he'd planned to do when he'd pulled her into his bedroom. "Well, it just wouldn't have happened, that's all."

"Protecting your virtue, were you?" Zeke cocked his head.

"Yes." Fiona looked him in the eye. "Yes, I was."

Zeke snorted, forgiving himself for his cynical remark. There had been a moment when he'd kissed her that he'd come close to taking her. "It might interest you to know, Mistress MacClure, that your virtue was never in danger, at least not from me."

What a cur, to so blatantly lie, when she knew the truth of the situation. "You yanked me into your room, told me to undress. You thought I was a girl from the tavern, you . . . What are you laughing about?"

"Nothing." Zeke shook his head, trying to sober his expression. "I knew you were no lightskirt."

"How?" Fiona thought she'd made a fairly convincing trollop.

"Your kiss."

"My . . ." Fiona's mouth dropped open. "What was wrong with it?"

"Untutored. Now don't get me wrong." Zeke held up

46

his hand to stop her protest. "As kisses go it was more than adequate. But I could tell you lacked experience."

Adequate. She'd had dreams about that kiss, and he described it as adequate. Fiona's back stiffened against the scratchy leaves. "I've been kissed before."

Zeke shrugged. "But not like that."

No, not like that. "Better."

"Hmph."

"What does that mean? Why, I'll have you know I've had lots of kisses that put yours to shame. Lots that . . ." The lie about to cross Fiona's lips died as Zeke's mouth came down on hers.

Fiona's mind registered a quick comparison between this feeling of floating through air and the indifference she'd experienced when Thomas MacQuaid kissed her. The colonel was right. She'd never known a feeling like this—except the first time he'd kissed her. She'd never known it was possible to feel this way.

His lips moved over hers, masterfully, first nipping at the corners, then shaping her mouth to fit his. Fiona lifted her hands to push him away, but found herself clutching the silk fabric covering his broad shoulders instead.

She went weak. Her arms and legs seemed to have lost all strength. Her body swayed toward him. Her will seemed nonexistent. All from a simple kiss. And how did the colonel view it—and her? Adequate.

Pride warred with passion. How dare he think of her as lacking when *his* touch affected her so? His tongue teased the seam between her lips, coaxing. To show him just how well she could arouse him, or perhaps because she had no choice, Fiona opened to him. Her lips parted, abandoning the last defense to his invasion.

His moan of desire enveloped her, emboldened her.

She met the fiery thrust of his tongue with her own, delighting in the dizzying thrill that raced through her body. Fiona ached. Her breasts pressed against his chest swelled, the tips hardening. Fiona welcomed the hand that slipped beneath the draped plaid to caress her back. His palm stroked her spine, making her long for unknown pleasures.

Zeke knew only too well what he wanted. He also knew he couldn't have it. His body, hard with need, pulled back, and he took a deep, steadying breath. Looking down into Fiona's violet eyes, glazed with desire, reminded him that he'd initiated the kiss to teach her a lesson—and ended up learning one for himself. Well, not exactly learning. He'd known from the first time he'd kissed her what kind of effect she had on him. Apparently he'd needed a reminder, though. Or perhaps he'd just wanted one. But none of this would help him with his mission among the Scots.

Cocking his head to one side, Zeke gave Fiona a rakish grin. "You, Mistress MacClure, are a quick learner."

"Hmmm?" Fiona leaned back in his strong arms, examining the slivers of moonlight dancing across the planes of his handsome face.

"No one could accuse you of being untutored now."

"What?" The reality of what she had done shattered the sensual aura surrounding Fiona. "No, never mind. You needn't repeat yourself. Just let go of me." Fiona shoved at Colonel Kincaid, stumbling slightly when he moved away. Color flooded her face and Fiona hoped the dim light concealed her embarrassment. "I'm going back to the house."

"Oh no, you don't." Zeke grabbed her arm as she swept past him. "You still haven't told me why you broke into my room."

Fiona raised her chin, meeting his eyes. "Nor do I intend to."

Zeke suppressed a grin at her stubborn attitude. "Perhaps we need to discuss this with the laird." Just the threat she'd expected, the one that had worried her so—before. "I don't think you'll do that."

"Really?" A dark brow cocked questioningly. "And why not?"

"Because I know why you're here. And even though your mission is a waste of time—"

"It's my time."

Fiona's smile was smug. "And even though it's a waste of time, I don't think my grandfather or any other Highlander will listen to you once I've told them how you manhandled me."

The colonel's eyes narrowed dangerously, and again Fiona regretted her decision to meet him here alone. "Just how will they feel about your breaking into my room, knocking me over the head?"

"Admittedly, they won't like it. Which is precisely why I haven't mentioned our . . . encounter to anyone. However, as angry as my grandfather might be with me, I shall be forgiven. You, on the other hand . . ."

Zeke didn't need her to finish her statement. He knew, as apparently she did, that his welcome among the Scots was tenuous at best. "So we appear to be at a draw."

"It would seem so."

"And you have no intention of telling me why you broke into my room?"

Fiona didn't even dignify that question with an answer.

"Then I suppose we have nothing more to discuss." Zeke chided himself for not giving the girl enough

49

credit. She was intelligent as well as beautiful. And deceitful.

"Just one more thing. I want you to stay away from me while you're here."

"It shall be my pleasure." Zeke's bow was mocking, but Fiona didn't notice. She'd already swished by him, out of the overhanging arbor.

Zeke moved out into the garden, watching Fiona as she walked up the path toward the house. It was time for him to stop worrying himself with the chit and start concentrating on the task at hand: how to persuade fifteen thousand Scottish Highlanders to remain neutral during the coming months.

Zeke shook his head, thinking of the enormity of the problem. He had no time at all to think about one redheaded, violet-eyed woman. Then why did he wait until she'd been swallowed up by darkness, till he could no longer see the moon limning her form, before heading for his meeting with the laird?

Chapter Four

"How much longer is *he* going to be here?" Fiona swept into her grandfather's book-lined study. The echo of the laird's invitation to enter still hung in the hot, humid air, and she could tell her entrance shocked him. It shocked her, too. But as her grandfather looked up from the papers neatly stacked on his desk and absently rubbed the stump of his left arm, Fiona knew it was too late to make amends. Besides, she wanted an answer to her question.

For three days Fiona had put up with the arrogant rebel's presence. Three days too many. Their mutual agreement to stay clear of each other had been all well and good, but it wasn't working. At least not to Fiona's satisfaction.

It seemed every time she turned around *he* was there. Yesterday, while carrying a load of clean linens that partially blocked her view, she'd bumped into him in the upstairs hall. He'd reached out to steady her, and Fiona had nearly dropped the pile of neatly folded bedding. He'd merely smiled that wicked grin of his, nodded and walked on, but Fiona could read the silent laughter and triumph in his eyes. He knew she wanted him gone — and yet he remained.

That same smug expression played on his face whenever he looked at her across the dining room table. Oh, he was very careful not to engage her in conversation, but she could feel his eyes on her. Last evening when she'd sensed his blue stare directed her way, she'd turned and glared at him. But this tactic only seemed to amuse him further, and to her annoyance, Fiona had looked away first.

She was tired of putting up with this insolent stranger—and in her own home. Not ten minutes ago, as she sat in the parlor, diligently stitching a seat cover, he'd appeared on the lawn outside the window. Her uncle Angus stood beside him, and they'd been engaged in an animated discussion—political, she'd assumed—as she did her best to ignore them. But that hadn't deterred Katrine, seated beside Fiona, from singing the colonel's praises.

Fiona had listened as long as she could, but when Katrine began sighing over the way the colonel's broad shoulders filled out his waistcoat, Fiona had thrown down her sewing in disgust and stalked from the room.

"Am I to assume we are discussing the Whig colonel?" Malcolm leaned back in his chair and gave his granddaughter a noncommittal stare.

"And who else would I be talking about?" Fiona began, her voice rising in agitation. She clasped her hands and forced herself not to squirm when she noticed her grandfather's eyes narrow.

"Now, Mary Fiona, I thought I'd made myself clear on that point. I told the colonel I'd listen to what he had to say."

"And you have." Fiona dropped to her knees beside the laird's chair. Her chintz skirt billowed on a gentle puff of air. "You've been more than generous with your time. But now he must leave. Surely you don't want him here when Flora MacDonald arrives tomorrow." The Scottish heroine was even more outspoken in her support of the king than the MacClure laird.

"Whether I want him here or not, he shall be. I've given my word."

"Your word! But why?" Honestly perplexed, Fiona rose, pulling away when Malcolm reached out to grab her hand. What had gotten into her grandfather? A sudden thought of the colonel threatening to tell the laird about her visit to his room flashed before her. Fiona blanched and clasped her hands together.

"What did he say to you?"

"He gives the same reasons for this rebellion as we've heard before. He's perhaps more passionate about his ideas; still—"

"About me?" Fiona resisted the urge to stamp her foot. "What did he say about me?" As soon as the words were out of her mouth, Fiona knew she'd made a mistake. Her grandfather stood, towering over her.

"And why would he be saying anything about you, Mary Fiona? What have you been up to?"

"Nothing." Fiona swallowed, sorry that she'd been so stupid as to voice her concerns, sorry she'd come into her grandfather's study, sorrier still that she'd ever met Colonel Kincaid.

"Mary Fiona?"

The laird's tone, the scowl on his bearded face convinced Fiona he expected more of an explanation. She searched her mind for one, settling on a half-truth that she knew her grandfather hadn't missed. "I haven't been overly friendly to him."

Though she hadn't meant her confession to be funny, Malcolm obviously found it so. He leaned back, his age-tarnished red hair shaking with laughter.

"That is hardly a revelation, Fiona. It's been obvious to everyone that you dislike the man. You've stared daggers at him since he arrived."

Fiona felt heated color darken her cheeks. She hadn't meant to be so transparent. Had her actions amused all her family as much as they did her grandfather? "He shouldn't be here," Fiona insisted, knowing she sounded like a spoiled child.

"However, he is, and at my invitation." Malcolm's demeanor sobered and he looked every inch the formidable Scottish laird who'd led his clan into battle. "And in the future you will make more of an effort to obey my wishes, Mary Fiona."

Fiona's chin notched higher, but she answered that she would, before begging permission to leave the study.

Malcolm's expression softened. "Of course, Fiona. I'm certain you have much to do to get ready for Flora's visit. But cheer up, lass. Colonel Kincaid will be away from Armadale before you know it. He only desires a chance to meet Flora, and then he'll be gone."

"It can't be too soon for me," Fiona mumbled as she closed the study door behind her. So he wanted to meet Flora MacDonald, did he? A smile played around the corners of Fiona's lips.

Flora MacDonald was more loyal to the king than anyone Fiona knew. She would set Ezekiel Kincaid straight. Fiona could just imagine the older woman's indignation when the colonel started spouting his rebellious rhetoric. Why, she'd have him packing back to his silly militia before he knew what happened.

"You look awfully pleased with yourself."

Fiona's hand fluttered to her breast. "Don't you know better than to sneak up on people, Katrine? You startled me."

"I didn't sneak up on you. How could you miss me walking across the hall?"

A red curl bounced against Fiona's cheek as she shook her head. "I don't know. I have a lot on my mind."

"Well, I shouldn't wonder, what with Flora Mac-Donald visiting tomorrow, and then the ball."

"It isn't really a ball, Katrine. Just a gathering of some of Flora's admirers."

"But there will be dancing, and I plan to wear my new gown. You remember the one I told you about, the one I had made in Wilmington. It has an embroidered underpetticoat and a polonaise skirt with —"

"I remember." Fiona was in no mood to hear, again, how the red silk gown set off Katrine's blond hair, or how becoming the neckline was.

If Katrine was annoyed that Fiona cut her off, she didn't show it. "Where are you going?"

Fiona paused, her hand clutching the polished mahogany banister. She couldn't relax — not with the colonel in the house. If he wouldn't leave, then she would. At least for this afternoon. Fiona made up her mind quickly. "I'm going riding."

"But what about Flora's visit . . . and tomorrow night. I said I'd help you with the menu."

Katrine's voice faded as Fiona held up her skirts and rushed up the stairs. "We'll talk about it when I get back. Or better yet, you decide. You're so much better at that than I am, anyway."

"Fiona . . ."

"I won't be long. I promise." Fiona threw this last over her shoulder as she disappeared around the corner of the upstairs hall. She'd have felt guilty about leaving Katrine to plan what dishes to have for tomorrow night's supper, except that she knew how much

55

her cousin loved to organize parties.

"A lot more than I do," Fiona mumbled as she scooted into her room. Ever since Elspeth had married and left Armadale, the task of being mistress of the plantation had fallen to Fiona. She handled most of her duties well enough, but there were some she rather disliked — and shirked. "Planning parties," Fiona grumbled as she stepped out of her gown.

"I should have been a man." Fiona voiced the thought that popped into her head, and nodded with satisfaction. If she were a man she could join the army like her cousin Duncan.

And then she'd show that Colonel Kincaid. He wouldn't find her quite so amusing if she were as tall and big as he. Fiona caught a glimpse of herself in the cheval glass as she moved toward the wardrobe, and stopped.

She didn't look much like a man. Fiona turned, cocking her head to one side. On a whim she snatched her lappet hat off her head and shook out her hair. Shiny red curls twined down around her shoulders, tangling in the ruffles of her shift. Fiona followed one with her finger, tracing the lace-edged border skimming the tops of her breasts, made more prominent by her corset.

Color stained Fiona's cheeks as she remembered how Ezekiel Kincaid's chest had felt pressed against her breasts. He hadn't seemed very impressed — he'd called her merely adequate — but Fiona wondered what he'd think if he saw her now.

Fiona moistened her lips and stared into the mirror, her violet eyes wide with wonder. Would he still have that expression of amused indifference? Or would those indigo blue eyes lose their sparkle and turn an even deeper hue? Fiona leaned forward, placed her hands on her hips, and studied the effect the motion had on her breasts. Handling the American colonel as a woman might be easier than trying to do it as a man.

"What is in your mind?" Fiona jerked upright, grabbing her hair and braiding it with swift rough movements. She had no desire to handle Zeke Kincaid. Period.

She wanted him gone—from Armadale, from her life.

Still, as Fiona pulled on her riding skirt, tucking her linen shirt in before fastening it around her slim waist, she couldn't stop thinking about him. "It's all because of that stupid kiss—two kisses," Fiona corrected herself. She simply couldn't stop thinking about them. With startling clarity she could remember how his lips felt against hers, the smell of his body, the hard press of his arms and chest and . . . "Stop it!" Fiona kicked off her leather slippers and stomped into morocco half boots.

This was ridiculous. What she needed was another kiss—from someone she liked. Thomas MacQuaid would be at Armadale tomorrow night. Maybe she should let him take her to the gardens and kiss her. Of course, that would take care of this stupid obsession she had with the colonel—at least until he left Armadale. After that Fiona had no doubt he'd disappear from her thoughts forever.

Reaching for the emerald-green jacket that matched her skirt, Fiona felt a trickle of perspiration roll down her back. The heat was oppressive, enveloping her like a thick, moist blanket. Her hand trailed down the jacket sleeve. She was uncomfortable enough without adding another article of clothing. Besides, she wouldn't see anyone.

Fiona almost made it to the door before a vision of Lucy's admonishing face flashed into her mind. With a scowl, Fiona turned back and grabbed the floppy straw hat from the shelf. Maybe Lucy was right about sunspots. The old nanny kept telling Fiona how lucky she was, with her red hair, not to be covered with freckles.

Hurrying down the servants' stairs, Fiona slipped out the kitchen door without anyone seeing her. The stables were a little cooler, and Fiona leaned against a stall, surrounded by the ripe smells of horses, hay, and leather, while Joe, one of the stableboys, saddled her horse.

After a boost up, Fiona galloped down the lane. As the north gate came into view, Fiona veered off the path, leaning low over her horse's neck. The bay, used to Fiona's movements, quickened its pace, heading right for the fence. A thrill of anticipation ran through Fiona. She could almost feel herself soaring over the fence, the wind whizzing past her face, the mare's muscles tense and straining beneath her.

And then she remembered her promise to Grandfather about jumping the fence. "Blasted!" Fiona sat up and pulled back on the reins. The surprised horse slowed its pace, and then at Fiona's command headed back toward the lane.

Her horse's hooves kicked up dry red clay as Fiona rode toward the welcome shade of the dense pine forest. Once beneath the long-needled trees, the ground softened by pine tags, Fiona slowed her mount to a walk. Picking their way between the cedar and holly, Fiona guided the bay toward the creek. Not that any guiding was necessary. Her horse knew the way.

More times than not, when Fiona rode away from the plantation house, she ended up down by the bend in the creek. Today, the deep, murky waters guarded by stately pines and rough-barked sycamores seemed especially appealing. She'd lie in the cool grass and relish being alone.

Fiona bent low over the bay's neck to avoid an oak branch. She thought she heard a horse whinny, but it wasn't till she straightened and heard it again that she was sure. Looking around the clearing, Fiona saw one of the horses from Armadale's stables, a black gelding.

Before she could fathom what the horse was doing there, Fiona turned in the saddle and caught sight of a figure lounging on the grass near the creek. He had removed his jacket and thrown it across a bayberry bush. Clad in buff breeches and white linen shirt open at the neck, he lay staring at the cloud-puddled sky. His hands were stacked beneath his head and, though he must have heard her arrival, he ignored her completely.

Sliding from the saddle, Fiona stalked toward him. "What are you doing here? Did you follow me?" Even as she asked the last question, Fiona knew how foolish she sounded. It was perfectly obvious that the man before her had been here for some time. If anyone had done the following, it was she. Realizing that made her all the more angry.

"Well?" Fiona's hands tightened into fists and she jammed them onto her waist.

With infuriating slowness, Colonel Kincaid turned toward her. Leaning on his elbow, he removed a stem of grass from his mouth. "Mistress MacClure, how nice to see you."

He grinned, creasing the dimples in his lean cheeks, and Fiona wondered how he had the power to annoy her like none other.

"Don't Mistress MacClure me." Fiona moved forward, the hem of her riding skirt brushing Queen Anne's lace. "I want to know why you're here."

Zeke lay back down, stretching out to his full length before answering. "I'm here for the same reason as you, I imagine. To gain small respite from the heat. Sit down."

Of all the nerve. He acted as if she had come calling. "I came here to be alone."

"So did I."

Fiona watched him close his eyes in dismissal, and she felt anger boil up within her. This was her place. Ever since she could remember she'd loved to come here—first with her father, and then after he'd died, with Grandfather. Now she came alone. But she wasn't alone now. Fiona swatted at a fly buzzing around her head and glared at the colonel. Her effort was lost on him as he continued to lie on the grassy carpet, eyes closed. He could have fallen asleep, for all Fiona knew.

Well, if she was going to find this situation annoying, so was he. "How did you find this place?" Fiona demanded without preamble. Not that this particular bend of the creek was a secret, but it wasn't close to the road, either. And the thicket of trees all but hid the small glade from view.

"I didn't." Other than answering her question, the only concession Zeke made to Fiona's presence was a slight shrug of his shoulders. "The horse brought me here."

Fiona flipped her braid over her shoulder. Squinting her eyes, she looked over to where the colonel had tied the gelding. What he said made sense. The horse had been to this spot often. And watching him now, munching on some succulent grass, it was obvious he liked it. Still . . . "Who gave you permission to ride him? He's my grandfather's horse."

"The laird himself. My horse's left foreleg is a little inflamed."

"Your horse is lame?" For heaven's sake, now Grandfather would have to lend this impertinent rebel a horse just to get rid of him.

"Nothing serious. He'll be fit enough to ride in a few days." Zeke sat up and grinned. "Wouldn't you be more comfortable if you sat down?"

"I'd be more comfortable if you left." She hadn't missed that he knew why she was concerned about his horse.

The infuriating grin broadened. "Oh, but Mistress MacClure, I was here first."

Fiona started to point out to him that this was her land, but thought better of it. He wouldn't care. After all, it didn't bother him to stay in her house when he had to know how much she wanted him gone. But she wasn't going to let his presence force *her* to leave, either.

With a sigh of resignation that a lift of Zeke's brow told her he'd noticed, Fiona sat down on a fallen log. Carefully she spread her skirts, arranging them around her ankles and feet. Zeke lay some six feet away, but even then she felt as if they were too close. Probably because he continued to loll on his side, staring at her. Fiona refused to be intimidated.

"I would think you'd be using this time to spout your treasonous venom." This didn't get the response Fiona had hoped. The colonel's smile never wavered and his blue eyes twinkled with mirth.

"Which one of us holds the treasonous views is subject to debate, though I have no desire to do that now—with you." Zeke picked up a pebble and tossed it toward the creek. "As it happens, your uncle and I were just discussing the war in the north."

Fiona knew that. She'd watched them through the drawing room window. But she'd never admit that to him. "You're wasting your time with Uncle Angus. He will do as my grandfather tells him."

"So he said."

Fiona was slightly taken back that he would admit that to her, but merely shrugged. She'd expected nothing less of Angus. "Well, Grandfather will never agree to your proposal."

"He'd be wise to."

Standing abruptly, Fiona glared down at the American colonel. "Are you questioning my grandfather's judgment?"

"Simply wondering why he would want to involve himself in a fight that doesn't concern him."

"Perhaps he considers a rebellion against his king a personal affront. There are those of us who consider loyalty an outstanding virtue."

"Count me among that number. However, before I give my loyalty to any cause, I first consider the right and wrong of it and the consequences of my deeds."

"Meaning I don't." Fiona stamped her foot on the sandy soil and glared down at the colonel.

Zeke took the time to give Fiona a slow, personal perusal. She was a feisty little thing, but he'd known that from the start. Much of her hair had escaped the loose braid and curled enticingly around her face. Perspiration molded the linen shirt to her body and the sight of the rapid rise and fall of her breasts sent a surge of lust through Zeke's body.

Her foot was mere inches from his hand, and Zeke resisted the urge to grab her ankle and send her sprawling beside him.

Heat crept up Fiona's neck, flushing her cheeks.

The colonel examined her as if he were deciding whether or not to purchase her. Without thinking, she took a step back. "Are you implying I have not considered both sides of the issue?"

Zeke smiled more at her retreat than at her question. "I wasn't aware we were discussing you. Perhaps I've missed my chance to influence you toward the Patriot views. Do you have much influence among the Scots?"

His words stung. He knew very well she didn't. If her grandfather did any more than indulge her, Colonel Kincaid wouldn't be here now. But her grandfather, and uncles—even Duncan, though he should know better—looked upon her as a pretty piece of fluff whose mind couldn't quite comprehend political matters.

But it wasn't that way with all Scottish women. Flora MacDonald had more influence than even her grandfather. The thought of the Scottish heroine putting Colonel Ezekiel Kincaid in his place creased Fiona's lips with a smile and soothed her hurt pride.

"I think for myself." Fiona looked out across the water, showing him her profile. "But there *are* others you need to convince."

"Flora MacDonald?" Zeke leaned back on his elbow, studying the soft line of her neck.

"Aye. She may be a woman, but she'll not act willynilly because of your manly face."

Zeke threw back his head, frightening a cocky bluejay from an overhead branch with his burst of laughter. "I didn't realize you thought I had a manly face. Should I be flattered?"

"Hardly." Fiona shot him an exasperated look. "I wasn't speaking of myself but of Ka—" Fiona bit her bottom lip, cursing herself for her loose tongue.

"Ah, Katrine." Zeke smiled, his dimples deepening as he said her cousin's name, and Fiona wished for a hard, very sturdy candlestick. "So the lovely Mistress Katrine finds my face manly."

"Oh, don't act as if you didn't know." Fiona swiped at the hair the rising wind whipped into her face. "She's done everything but fall at your feet." In truth, Fiona wasn't certain her cousin hadn't done that, too.

"But you would never do that?" Zeke catapulted to his feet and looked down at Fiona.

Fiona swallowed. Why had the colonel stood? She liked it much better when she towered over him. Now, looking up at him, remembering other times when she'd been this close to him, Fiona completely lost her train of thought.

"Well, would you?" His voice seemed to rinse over her like cool, refreshing water.

"Would I what?"

"Act willy-nilly and fall at my feet?"

"No."

Zeke's grin broadened. "Good. Truly bothersome, having to step over all those females."

Fiona laughed. She simply couldn't help herself. The image of him striding forth, zigzagging this way and that to avoid stomping sighing women, was too much.

Something happened to Zeke when he saw Fiona smile, heard her lilting laughter. He couldn't quite understand what caused the warm feeling that burst inside him. But for one clear moment he wondered if he might fall at *her* feet.

It was silly of course. The woman, spirited and wildly beautiful as she might be, was a nuisance, a millstone around his neck. She had lied to him, bloodied his head, and most certainly done all she could to see his mission fail. They may have shared two rather passionate kisses, but that was all. All there would ever be.

Zeke broke the stare they shared, wondering how long he'd been looking at her, and, more importantly, if she had any inkling of his thoughts. Studying the sky that had rather suddenly changed from pale blue to an ominous black, Zeke pointed to the billowing thunderhead.

"I think we should be getting back." Zeke scooped up his jacket and offered Fiona his arm, a gesture she pretended not to notice.

Instead, she led the way up the slight embankment to where she'd left her horse. Just as she neared the bay, a shaft of lightning split the air, striking a pine tree not fifty rods away. The splintering sound startled Fiona so that she didn't protest when Zeke jerked her back, protectively close to his body.

He felt so wonderfully strong that she stood encircled in his arm, listening to the steady beat of his heart, that somehow had a calming effect on hers. She probably would have remained there much longer if she hadn't heard a horse's frightened whinny. Opening her eyes, Fiona saw the bay rear on her hind legs, then bolt.

"Oh, no!" Fiona sprang away from Zeke, gathering up her skirts and chasing after the galloping horse. "I forgot to tether her." Fiona stopped when fat raindrops splattered against her face.

Her breath coming in shallow gasps, Fiona cursed her stupidity and the man who had so surprised her that she'd forgotten to take care of her horse.

"She'll find her way home." Zeke came up behind her leading the gelding. He appeared not the slightest upset by the turn of events, even though the rain had

65

already soaked his shirt. It lay plastered to his skin, and Fiona could see the darkened shadow of his chest hair through the fabric.

"You could have done something," Fiona said, in what she knew was an unreasonable tone.

Zeke merely shrugged. "*I* tethered *my* horse." Wiping moisture from his eyes, he looked down at Fiona, wondering if she realized how transparent the rain made her shirt. Probably not, he concluded, forcing his gaze above her neck. "Do you want front or rear?"

"What are you talking about?" Fiona yelled over another loud clap of thunder.

"On this horse." Zeke motioned toward the gelding. "Do you wish to ride in front of me or behind?"

Fiona wanted to tell him she had no intention of riding either in front or behind him, but the rain was streaming down her neck in earnest now, and it was simply too far to walk home. "In front, I suppose," she said ungraciously.

In one fluid motion Zeke was astride the horse, reaching down for Fiona. She stuck her hand in his, put her foot in the stirrup, and felt herself pulled up. He settled her in front of him and Fiona pulled at her cloying skirts.

"Comfortable?" Zeke asked, reaching around her for the reins.

"Extremely," came Fiona's sarcastic reply.

Zeke's laughter was lost in the roar of thunder, but Fiona could feel his chest trembling and she smiled in spite of herself.

"Just put your head down, so." Zeke flattened Fiona's cheek against his chest, folding her into the cradle of his body and rested his chin on top of her sodden curls. "And I'll have you home and dry in no time."

And even though the rain continued to come down in torrents, whipped by the lashing wind, the ride did seem to pass in next to no time. When they finally came to a halt in front of Armadale's porch, Zeke had to rouse Fiona from her comfortable nest. "We're here," he whispered into her ear. "I'll take care of the horse. You go on inside and get dry."

He lowered her to the ground, and as Fiona hurried up the steps, Zeke rode off to the stables. Fiona brushed ineffectively at her mud-splattered habit before giving it up and hurrying inside. She supposed it was only fitting that the first person she saw was Katrine.

As she rushed from the parlor into the hall, the expression on her cousin's face convinced Fiona that she had seen the colonel and her ride up. Fiona held up a dripping hand when she saw Katrine's mouth gaping open. "Don't ask. Just don't ask."

Chapter Five

Standing in the doorway to the parlor, Fiona let the mingled sounds of violins and laughter sweep over her. Katrine was right. This was a ball. But Fiona guessed she could expect nothing less, not when Flora MacDonald came for a visit.

Fiona smiled when she spotted the diminutive Scottish heroine nearly surrounded by a group of admirers. Clansmen from near and far had descended on Armadale when they'd discovered Flora MacDonald would be here tonight. And who could blame them? Not a Scot alive didn't know the story of the brave lass who'd saved the Bonnie Prince from capture at the hands of the English. Fiona herself never grew tired of hearing how her clever countrywoman had dressed the prince in the clothes of her Irish servant girl and accompanied him to Skye. From there he had escaped to France.

Pride swelled in Fiona as she thought of the deed. Scotsmen were indeed the bravest of the brave. She glanced across the room, admiring the colorful silks of the women, the handsome kilts on the men. On all except one man.

Fiona's smile disappeared, replaced by a frown, when she noticed Colonel Kincaid striding toward her. She looked around, realizing it was too late to escape his attention. Why did he have to seek her out? Hadn't she spent most of the day convincing Katrine that her wet ride with the American had been nothing but the result of unfortunate circumstances?

"Then why did he kiss the top of your head before lowering you to the ground?" Katrine had asked.

"Don't be a goose. He did no such thing," Fiona had insisted as she went to the kitchen to check on the food for the supper tonight.

"Ach, and I saw it with my own two eyes."

"It was raining too hard to see anything," Fiona had pointed out reasonably. "And besides, don't you think I'd know it if he'd kissed me?" Heat had surged through her body when she'd said that. She had certainly known it the times he *had* kissed her.

"Well, I know what I saw," Katrine had stubbornly repeated.

Fiona had only shaken her head at her cousin's foolishness. She would have launched into a lecture about Katrine caring one way or the other about a man who was their enemy, except that Fiona knew the American would be leaving soon. That would put a stop to Katrine's silly infatuation.

"You seem to have suffered no ill effects from our ride in the storm," Zeke said, stopping beside Fiona.

Anger flared in Fiona as the bold colonel allowed himself a slow, thorough perusal of her to substantiate his claim. When his gaze lingered on the rise of her breasts above the snug bodice of her gown, Fiona could barely resist the urge to slap his handsome face. Her reaction was all the more intense because she knew he'd made her blush—and more, she knew he'd noticed.

Deliberately she turned her back on him, offering him only the briefest glance over her shoulder as she assured him that a little rain would cause her no harm. She would have continued to ignore him, too, if she hadn't heard his deep, sensual chuckle.

"Don't you know, Mistress MacClure, that when a woman spurns a man like you've just done, he finds her all the more alluring? He might even consider it a ploy to pique his interest."

Fiona turned on him so quickly it sent tendrils of red hair curling around her face. "I assure you, Colonel Kincaid, nothing could be further from the truth." Facing him, seeing the devilish gleam in his blue eyes, Fiona realized he'd baited her. He knew very well his presence annoyed her. That's probably why he's here, Fiona thought—to pay me back for splitting his scalp with the candlestick.

"Then dance with me."

"No."

"Spurning me again, Fiona?" Zeke's brow rose questioningly.

"Don't be absurd. I'm simply refusing to dance with you."

"Ah, it sounds more like a challenge to me."

Challenge, her foot! Fiona leaned toward him, her voice a low hiss. "I am not trying to entice you. I am not flirting with you. I want you to let me alone. Go dance with someone else—that is, if anyone will have you."

Fiona realized her mistake immediately. Why had

she moved closer to him? And why had she whispered? Her intimate tone only forced him to bend closer to hear her. They were standing close together — much closer than they ever would have had they been dancing.

He was near enough for his masculine scent to surround her. Near enough for her to notice the prisms of blue that made up his eyes, the thick black lashes that surrounded them. Near enough to remember what it felt like to be held in his arms, to be kissed till . . .

Fiona shifted, only to realize the wall at her back prevented any movement. She would have pushed him away if not for the sudden panicked thought that to touch him would be another mistake, especially when she could tell from his expression that the colonel was remembering their shared embraces as vividly as she.

"Are you enjoying yourself, Colonel?"

Fiona's head jerked around at the sound of her grandfather's voice, and she felt another flush surge through her body. Surely he would see how inappropriately close she and the colonel were standing. But when she caught his eye, her grandfather only smiled at her — and at the colonel. And Fiona realized they really weren't standing that close together at all. It only seemed that way.

The colonel appeared totally relaxed as he scanned the room, then looked back at the laird. "Your hospitality is overwhelming. I was just asking your granddaughter to dance with me."

Of all the sneaky things, Fiona thought — bringing her grandfather into this. She almost expected Colonel Kincaid to bring up the fact that she'd refused him. Of course, now he wouldn't have to. Grandfather would expect her to dance with their guest. A change in the tempo of the music caught Fiona's attention.

The laird noticed it too, for he laughed, motioning toward the dancers who where now engaged in a lively reel. "You should perhaps wait until the musicians play something more sedate, Colonel. We Scots are taught to step dance from the time we first toddle about, but it's not a dance for the novice."

"Oh, but I'm certain Colonel Kincaid can handle anything we Scots have to offer, can't you, Colonel?" Fiona smiled sweetly at the tall, dark-haired man. If he wanted to dance, they'd dance. But he'd get more than he bargained for. He'd teased her about challenging him before; now let him know what a real challenge was. As she led the colonel to the dancers, she only wished she were initiating him into the sword dance. She'd love to see just how high he could jump.

She'd bested him, no doubt about it, Zeke thought as he struggled to keep pace with the quick, complicated steps of the dance. He, along with most of the wealthy youth in Wilmington, had dutifully visited the dance instructor when he'd come to town, but he'd never learned anything like this. And more infuriating than the feeling of having two left feet was the utterly guileless expression on his partner's face. He had the strongest desire to grab her hand, pull her outside and kiss her till her mirth-filled eyes turned smoky with desire.

But of course he wouldn't. Zeke watched as Fiona swirled around, the deep violet silk of her gown lifting ever so slightly. The clock design on her stockings accentuated her slim ankles enough to make him lose his concentration. As the tempo of the fiddles accelerated, Zeke felt himself propelled forward with the other men and almost lost his balance.

Zeke looked around quickly to see if Fiona had noticed, and knew she had. Suddenly the whole thing seemed so utterly absurd. He felt like a strutting rooster trying to gain the favor of the choicest hen, and failing miserably. He threw back his head and laughed, missing another step and colliding with his partner. Zeke grabbed Fiona's shoulders to keep her from falling, then laughed harder when he noticed her scowl. Apparently she didn't think his sense of humor appropriate.

"Would you behave?" Fiona jerked free of the colonel's grasp and gave him her most scathing look before resuming the dance. This wasn't turning out at all as she'd planned. She'd hoped to make him appear a bumbling halfwit, but he didn't. Oh, he didn't know the steps. That was obvious to everyone in the room, but he wasn't totally inept on the dance floor. The most infuriating thing, though, was his attitude.

He should have felt disgraced and foolish, and looked at her in defeat, but he didn't. He laughed, for heaven's sake! And he made her so conscious of him that she found her own steps faltering. Ach, the man was a frustration.

A trickle of sweat ran down Zeke's back as the fiddles thankfully ended the tune with a flourish. Barely able to keep a straight face, Zeke bowed low to his partner and thanked her for the privilege of the dance.

"I assure you," Fiona lied, "the pleasure was all mine." She should have known he'd find that amusing, Fiona thought in disgust when he grinned at her.

"Shall we consider this skirmish yours, then?"

"I had no idea we were fighting." Fiona tucked a sweat-dampened curl behind her ear.

Zeke's brow arched. "Oh, I think you did."

"Very well, then." Fiona shrugged. "I shall claim first blood."

"Too late for that," Zeke chuckled. "I'm afraid you already drew first blood back in my room at Cross Creek."

The brute would have to bring up that unfortunate incident with the candlestick. Fiona clutched a handful of silk overskirt, longing for something more substantial to hold—something pewter. The colonel must have noticed her action, because his laugh became lower, more sensual.

"Don't fret, Mistress MacClure. I still concede the victory on the dance floor to you."

Impertinent man. It didn't help Fiona's reaction to know that she had accompanied him to the dance floor to make him look foolish—to gain a victory of sorts. But she certainly didn't have to stand here and listen to him prattle on about it. With a lift of her chin, Fiona turned to leave.

"Fiona."

His voice, low and deeply masculine, stopped her.

"Beware when *I* choose the battlefield."

"What ever did the wretched man mean by that?" Fiona mumbled to herself later that evening as she opened the door and walked into the library. The tangy smell of her grandfather's pipe smoke trapped in the drapes and in the leather of his favorite chair soothed her, as did the relative peace and quiet of the empty room.

Sitting in her grandfather's chair, resting her silk-slippered feet on the stool, Fiona thought again of her dance with the Whig colonel and the sally that followed it. She'd been led around the floor in almost every dance since, had spoken with countless interesting people, but still couldn't get that single incident from her mind.

He'd teased her about challenging him, yet who could call his parting words anything but the most blatant of challenges?

Well, the only other battlefield she'd see him on was one where bold, sturdy clansmen, brandishing broadswords, cut down everything in their paths. A flash of remembrance sprang to Fiona's mind. She saw the colonel lying at her feet, blood oozing from a gash on his head. The scene sent chills down her spine. Closing her eyes, Fiona assured herself she was only recalling the scene in his room when she'd hit him with the candlestick. It was nothing more.

"Here you are."

Fiona slipped her feet to the floor, tucking them under her skirt as Duncan entered the room. She told herself she should be glad to see her cousin, but at this very moment she would have preferred solitude.

"I've been looking for you. Do you know what *he* is doing?"

By the way Duncan emphasized the word "he," she had little doubt to whom he referred. Duncan's ire at having the Patriot emissary under foot was nearly as great as hers. "He isn't giving dancing lessons, is he?" Fiona couldn't stop a smile from curving her lips.

"I don't consider this a laughing matter, Fiona. He's talking with Flora MacDonald."

"Well, I expected as much. That *is* why he stayed."

"I don't like it."

Fiona motioned for Duncan to take the chair across from her when his pacing began to wear on her nerves. "You can't possibly believe he would do anything to sway her from her resolve."

"She appears quite taken with him," Duncan whined.

"She's just being gracious," Fiona countered, though she wasn't at all certain that was the only reason. For all she'd told the colonel that Flora MacDonald wouldn't be influenced by an attractive man, she was, after all, a woman.

"We need her, Fiona."

"Duncan, I think you're making too much of this." She wasn't sure why his words made her uneasy, but they did. "Flora MacDonald is a true Scotswoman, a heroine. She knows more than anyone else the course we must take."

Duncan's response to this was half moan, half grunt. Suddenly deciding that not only would she prefer the company of many to her cousin at this moment, but that her duty was to play the part of hostess, Fiona stood. "I'd better be getting back—"

The whip-like snaking of Duncan's hand around her wrist stopped Fiona. "I don't trust him."

"He'll be gone tomorrow," Fiona soothed, twisting her hand to free it. "He's just one man."

She really had planned to go back to the party, but as Fiona closed the library door behind her, the thought of heading toward the noise held little appeal. Her conversation with Duncan had been upsetting. She wondered briefly if Duncan had consumed too much punch tonight. His mood was certainly depressing enough. Needless to say, Fiona didn't like the colonel being here, but she didn't think he could cause any harm—not since they'd come to the understanding about keeping each other's indiscretions in Wilmington to themselves.

Even the colonel, though he appeared to be giving

it his all, seemed resigned to changing no one's views regarding the coming conflict. Shrugging, Fiona turned away from the sound of fiddles and headed for the dining room.

Sweetmeats and confections of fruits and sugar lined the sideboard, ready to top the late supper. Fiona's hand inched toward an iced cake, her finger trailing through the frosting, before she stuck it into her mouth and left the room.

It looked as if all was in readiness, she thought, sucking the last drop of sweetness from her finger. She really *should* get back to her guests, but it would be so nice to get just a breath of fresh air.

Lifting the latch, Fiona slipped out the back door, nearly expressing an oath—a particularly vile one she'd heard Duncan use—when she saw the Patriot colonel leaning against the porch stairs.

"Must you always be everyplace I want to go?" Fiona asked, her hands on her hips.

"And must you always follow me about?" he replied, his teeth flashing in the moonlight as he smiled.

"No, wait." Zeke's hand folded over her elbow as Fiona turned to leave. "You stay. I'll leave. You deserve a chance to cool off." His thigh brushed Fiona's skirt as he passed her on the steps.

"No. It is I who interrupted you. I shall leave." Fiona stepped forward, only to feel the pressure on her arm increase.

"I assure you I was about to go in anyway."

"Well, so was I." Fiona moved toward the door at the same moment as the colonel, and collided with firm, hard muscle. The absurdity of their conversation, the entire situation, struck her. Despite her best efforts, Fiona laughed. "Are we actually arguing over who will leave the other in peace?"

"It appears we can agree on very little."

"So it would seem." Fiona looked up at him, so close to her in the darkness, and felt slightly giddy, and very foolish. "I shan't quarrel with you over this. We can both go inside."

"Or stay out here."

Fiona wondered if the colonel knew how tempting his voice sounded, all deep and gravelly and fraught with possibilities. Or maybe it was memory and imagination that made Fiona aware of things that weren't really there. She knew she should go inside, but somehow to do so would be like an admission of cowardice. And Fiona didn't want to be a coward. "Perhaps for a moment. It is warm inside."

"Stifling," Zeke allowed, in an obvious attempt to show he could be agreeable.

Fiona hadn't thought it *that* hot inside, but it was more comfortable out here, where a breeze drifted gently through the trees, carrying the scent of fresh pine with it. Slowly she descended the stairs, mindful of keeping a safe distance between herself and the colonel. She stopped and moved to the side when her feet met the brick walkway. It would be cooler down by the river, past the grape arbor, but she would not turn this test of bravery into folly. She would stay out here a moment with him and then retreat — no, not retreat — simply go back to the ball.

Fiona looked over her shoulder. Colonel Kincaid still stood at the top of the stairs, almost as if he questioned the advisability of moving closer to her. But that was silly. He had no reason to fear her. He'd initiated everything that had transpired between them.

She was going to be mad as hell! Zeke nearly

cringed at the thought. He'd been the object of Fiona's temper before, and though he wasn't afraid of her, it was hardly a pleasant experience. And this time she'd have a reason to be angry. Not that it had been his suggestion. But then, that wouldn't matter to this lovely Scottish she-devil.

Why wasn't he coming down the stairs? Not that she wanted him to, of course, but it was disconcerting. The distance between them was even more uncomfortable than the silence, punctuated only by the chirping of cicadas and the occassional hoot of an owl. Suddenly, the thought of standing here, alone but separated from a man she considered her enemy, seemed inadvisable. Lifting her skirts, Fiona marched up the steps and reached for the door latch. "I'm quite cool now," she said to the shadowy form of Colonel Kincaid as she passed him.

"Fiona." The word was low and intimate. "I need to speak with you."

What an odd man, Fiona thought. He'd stood speechless all that time, and then when she'd tried to reenter the house he'd found his tongue. But not in the normal sense. The timbre of his voice, the seriousness with which he spoke, gave her a moment of dread. But what could it possibly be? He was leaving tomorrow.

"I've met Flora MacDonald," Zeke began, laying the groundwork for his news.

"I saw." Fiona cocked her head. "She didn't change her views, did she?" Fiona didn't allow the niggling doubt to enter her voice. Was that what his serious tone implied? Could he have convinced the beloved Scotswoman to throw her support behind the rebel cause?

"No. You were right. Her mind is firmly made up. She and her clan intend to support King George in any way they can."

Fiona tried not to give him an "I told you so" look, but knew she failed.

"I found *her* charming though—every inch a lady." Zeke knew this was not the time to bait Fiona, but her expression demanded something.

Fiona didn't like the way he said *her*, as if Flora MacDonald were the only charming lady around. Perhaps they did often disagree, especially about politics, but she could be charming—if she chose. And notwithstanding her visit to his room in Wilmington, she was a lady. But she decided arguing with him about it would hardly prove her point. So Fiona agreed with him. "Flora is wonderful. Of course, you know the tale of her saving Prince Charles."

"Of course." Though it had been only a vague recollection from a history lesson until a fortnight ago, he'd heard it enough since then to have it permanently entrenched in his mind.

Fiona shifted, feeling awkward. "I admire her beyond words," Fiona mumbled.

The perfect opening for his news, if ever there was one, Zeke thought, but he didn't follow through. He wished the national heroine of Scotland hadn't come up with this idea. And he wished Fiona didn't look so damn beautiful. Her red hair, gilded by the moonlight, framed her face like a shining halo. Inside, when her lovely violet eyes had flashed challenging sparks at him, he'd wanted to drag her outside and kiss her. Now the urge became damn near irresistible. Zeke wondered what she'd do if he tried. She appeared all soft and sweet now, but any movement on his part might turn her into the firebrand he knew her to be.

Zeke shook his head. She was going to be mad as hell in a minute anyway.

Fiona knew the exact moment the colonel stopped thinking of Flora MacDonald and began thinking of her. He moved toward her, and though she knew she shouldn't, Fiona felt herself swaying to meet him. This was lunacy. But did it really matter? She'd let him kiss her before — and he'd be gone tomorrow to visit other Scots along the Cape Fear. She'd never have to see him again.

The colonel's breath, sweet and warm, fanned against Fiona's cheek and her knees felt weak. His other kisses had been forced. His superior size and strength had left her no choice. But he wasn't forcing her this time. His movements were slow and deliberate, offering her plenty of time to resist him — if she'd wanted to. His arms reached behind her. Then his hands spread, rested softly on the boned silk of her back.

Fiona moved more securely against his body, touching the front of his waistcoat. Through the layers of linen and silk, she could feel the beat of his heart. She melted. Her lips parted in anticipation of the press of his warm mouth.

"How could you agree to such a thing?"

The question, so harsh and demanding, pierced the mood of soft sensuality surrounding Fiona. A whisker-roughened chin grazed Fiona's temple as she turned her head to squint into the puddle of light pouring from the open door.

Duncan stood like an avenging angel, arms folded across his chest. He glared at her — maybe she couldn't make out his features in the imbalance of light—but she knew he glared at her.

And in her opinion, he had a lot of nerve. It was none of his business if she shared the evening cool with Colonel Kincaid. She started to tell him so, felt her breasts press against the colonel's chest with her expanded breath, and jerked away.

All right, so maybe she was doing more than partaking of the breeze, but still, no one had appointed Duncan her chaperone. "It was only a kiss." And it hadn't even been that, Fiona thought. Duncan's outburst had seen to that.

"It's a lot more than that, and you know it."

Fiona's face flamed red at his words, but she didn't have time to think of her own embarrassment. The colonel stepped toward Duncan, crowding closer to her on the small stoop. He raised his chin belligerently and demanded that Duncan apologize to her.

She might have been touched by the gesture, except that a quick glance into the hallway behind Duncan showed her that several people were paying keen attention to the discussion on the porch.

"Stop it. Be quiet," she hissed, stepping between the two men and pulling her cousin onto the already crowded porch, slamming the door to end the other guests' gawking.

Now that Duncan stood on the same level with the colonel, he was considerably shorter, but that didn't stop him from puffing out his chest. "I should have guessed this was the way of it. But somehow I expected better of *you*, Fiona."

Again, the colonel moved to defend her honor, but Fiona stopped him. "That's enough. Duncan, I assure you there is nothing between the colonel and myself.

We were simply—"

"Kissing. Yes, I know. No doubt celebrating all the time you will be spending together."

"Spending time together? Don't be ridiculous. I told you the colonel is leaving tomorrow." Something about the utter silence that accompanied her explanation made the hair on the back of Fiona's neck tingle. She looked at Ezekiel Kincaid, but he stared straight ahead—at nothing. Duncan, on the other hand, couldn't seem to take his condemning eyes off her. She had the strong suspicion he wouldn't be this angry over a kiss that had barely happened. But what?

"You are leaving tomorrow, aren't you? Fiona directed this inquiry to the colonel.

"I am," came his terse reply.

Fiona looked back at Duncan, expecting to see a relaxation of his scowl, but instead, noticed it had deepened. She glanced back at the colonel, but didn't meet his eyes.

"You needn't play dumb with me, Fiona. I just spoke with Flora MacDonald, and she told me," Duncan reproached her.

"Told you what?" Fiona demanded, standing arms akimbo.

"That he won't be going alone, Fiona. I know who's going with him."

"Who?"

"You!"

Fiona stared from one man to the other, for they had both answered her at the same time. Had they both lost their minds? She wasn't going anywhere with the colonel. But neither of them seemed ready for Bedlam. Duncan hadn't lost one bit of his anger. And the colonel, who now apparently deemed it acceptable to meet her eyes, appeared sane.

Without another word, Fiona swept past Duncan, leaving the two men standing on the small stoop as she entered the house. She would get to the bottom of this, and she'd do it right now. Knowing she was being rude, but not caring one whit, Fiona interrupted Eleanor MacPherson, a woman of nearly four score, as she yelled a question at Flora MacDonald.

"I must speak with you . . . now," Fiona said, casting her eyes toward the rug as Flora looked up in astonishment. She would apologize later, Fiona decided — after this misunderstanding was corrected.

But though she did apologize — at her grandfather's insistence — it was not because the issue had been resolved. At least not to Fiona's satisfaction.

Fiona sat in the library staring into the cold fireplace. How could they have done this to her? Fiona tried to see the situation from their point of view. Grandfather and Flora had pointed out that the Whig colonel needed a guide to take him to the different farms and plantations.

"But why me?" Fiona had asked, annoyed with herself for the whining quality of her voice.

"You know the area like the back of your hand, and you're an excellent rider," the laird had said.

Before Fiona could point out that those attributes also encompassed half of the guests at the ball tonight, Flora MacDonald had leaned toward Fiona and in a quiet tone had mentioned that it was her patriotic duty.

"Hogwash," Fiona mumbled, plopping her feet on the stool in front of her. They didn't need someone to keep track of Colonel Kincaid's whereabouts. And even if they did, couldn't someone else do it?

They'd tried to tell her she'd be doing a great service for king and country, but Fiona didn't think that at all. She was simply going to have to put up with the arrogant colonel for a longer period of time.

Flora MacDonald was simply taken by his good looks and charm, Fiona thought; then she shook her head, feeling guilty for demeaning her heroine.

Or more likely he asked for a guide, and suggested me. Ah, this theory had more merit, Fiona thought as she gnawed on her bottom lip. Yes, she had not the least reservation about maligning the colonel. Of course, the whole thing was his fault.

Fiona was so engrossed in her disparaging thoughts that she didn't notice the door open or the man enter the room, until he stood over her chair, looking down at her.

"I brought you some supper." On the table beside the winged chair, Zeke set a plate piled high with ham and vegetables.

"I'm not hungry." Fiona slumped farther down in the seat.

Shrugging, Zeke grasped Fiona's ankles, moving her feet to one side to make room for himself on the stool. "Suit yourself."

Fiona couldn't believe it. She just sat gaping at him. She could still feel the heat where his hands had touched her leg—even through her silk stockings. He seemed totally oblivious to the fact that her slippered foot rested against his hip.

"Your being my guide wasn't my suggestion."

Fiona snorted.

A smile tugged at the corner of his mouth. "I take that as an indication you doubt my honesty."

"Your honesty, your integrity, your intellect, and

your stupid cause."

The colonel leaned forward, his elbows resting on his knees, and Fiona felt herself trapped in the chair. His blue eyes swept over her, and she fought the urge to slide down farther in the soft cushions. Not that she feared him, for instead of taking her words as the insult she'd intended, he seemed to find them amusing.

"You don't believe me?" Fiona lifted her chin belligerently.

"Oh, I don't doubt you for one moment."

"Good. Because I also want you to know that though I may be forced to go along with you, I shan't do one thing to help you."

"Hardly a revelation."

Oh, the man was insufferable, looking at her with that smug expression. "To the contrary, I shall do all in my power to see that the Scotsmen take up arms for the king—take up arms against you and the rebels."

If she wanted his expression to change, she had obviously picked the right thing to say, because he no longer appeared smug or amused—he looked angry. No, not just angry—furious.

"Now you listen to me, Mistress MacClure. We are talking about war. People dying, innocent people. And for what? Don't tell me your sentiments stem from purely political motives. If that were the case, I might understand. But you, Fiona, are advocating violence because you feel you've been taken advantage of. Revenge is never a worthy cause."

Fiona raised her hand, the need to strike him almost unbearable. And in her heart she knew the reason was because he'd come uncomfortably close to guessing her motives. But she never knew the satisfaction of stinging his flesh, for his hand caught hers in midair.

"Don't push me too far, Fiona."

With that he dropped her hand, stood, and left the room.

Chapter Six

She couldn't believe it was actually happening. Fiona rode along the sandy path that snaked its way north beside the Cape Fear River and glared at the broad back in front of her.

They'd been traveling since early morning, and it was well past noon. A glance at the sun through the hickory leaves overhead confirmed what Fiona's growling stomach already knew. It was past time to stop.

But though she was tired—another thing she could blame on the colonel, for worrying about this trip had cost her a sleepless night—and hungry and hot, she wasn't about to suggest stopping. How could she, when she wasn't speaking to him?

Fiona had decided on this tack while tossing and turning, before the earliest songbirds stirred in the oak tree outside her bedroom window. If she had to accompany the Whig emissary—and she obviously did—she would simply ignore him.

A trickle of sweat rolled down between her breasts, and Fiona pressed a damp handkerchief to her neck just above her wilted riding shirt. Goodness, it was hot. The air hung thick and moist, blanketing the land.

Fiona wished she'd taken her jacket off when they'd started. The colonel had. Studying his muscular back covered in only a linen shirt, she could tell he was hot. Small patches of dampness made the material stick to his skin. Somehow it helped to know that he suffered, too.

"We'll stop here for a while, unless you have an objection."

His voice, after miles of silence broken only by the lazy sloshing of the river, the muffled plodding of the horses' hooves, and an occasional droning mosquito, startled Fiona. Leather creaked as the colonel turned in the saddle, waiting for Fiona's response.

She gave him her best facsimile of an unconcerned shrug.

"I suppose we can go farther if you insist."

"No." The word was out of her mouth before Fiona remembered she wasn't speaking to him. "Stopping here is fine."

The colonel's slow grin made Fiona grind her teeth. He'd known she wasn't speaking to him, and had baited her on purpose.

With as much dignity as her stiff limbs could muster, Fiona slid from her horse. Riding as she did almost every day, her muscles should be used to this, but to Fiona's chagrin she found her legs quivering as she stood. Locking her knees against the unwanted weakness, she accepted the parcel of food the colonel thrust her way.

He took the horses toward the river, leaving Fiona standing by the road. Spotting a grassy knoll under the shade of a willow, Fiona spread the checkered napkin and divided the food inside.

"Looks good," Zeke remarked, flopping down on his

side near Fiona. When she did not reply—he hadn't expected her to—he bit into one of the crusty meatpies she'd set out. He was so hungry that he finished it without giving his silent companion another thought.

When they both reached for a boiled egg at the same time and she jerked her hand away from his accidental touch, he was forced to admit her presence. "Still angry about coming with me?"

She only glared at him over the other boiled egg she'd picked up.

"If you were so against it, I don't know why you just didn't tell your grandfather."

"I did," Fiona insisted. If she were against it? Did he think she'd wanted to accompany him, or that she was such a lackwit she hadn't thought to protest? She'd gone to the laird's room after the guests had either left or sought one of the pallets set up for them, and had all but fallen to her knees pleading. Her grandfather had finally put up his hand and ordered her to cease, assuring her that she was making too much of this.

Zeke leaned back on his elbow. "I assume, by the fact that you're here, you got no further with him than I."

"What are you talking about? Why did you talk with him?" Probably to make sure he didn't change his mind about making me go, Fiona thought. Reluctantly, Fiona accepted the canteen the colonel offered, wiping the opening with her hand before drinking.

"When I spoke with him last night, assuring him your presence was not needed on my little journey, he—"

"You told my grandfather you didn't want me to come with you?"

"Don't act so surprised. I told you last night none of

90

this was my idea."

"Well, I know that's what you said, but—"

"But you assumed I was so enthralled by your beauty, so captivated by a few shared kisses, that I would welcome the company of a shrew—"

"A shrew!" Fiona's eyes widened in disbelief. "I am *not* a shrew."

The arching of a single dark brow greeted her shrill denial. "As I was saying, when I spoke with your grandfather, he acknowledged the merit of my arguments, but—"

"Did you tell him you thought me a . . . Did you tell him what you thought of me?" Fiona couldn't bring herself to say the word *shrew* again—she couldn't believe he'd called her that.

"Hardly," Zeke's bark of laughter punctuated the word. "I do value my skin, and though the laird may have only one arm, he looks quite capable of dragging that broadsword off the wall and using it."

"You think he'd find your reference to me as a . . . your reference insulting?" Fiona raised her chin and stared at the man sprawled out beside her.

"Oh, I imagine he would." Zeke picked a blade of grass and twirled it between his fingers. "He, as well as most of your relatives, seem to think of you as sweet, somewhat headstrong, perhaps," Zeke amended, "but sweet just the same."

"Well, I am sweet." The words were out of her mouth before Fiona could stop them. She didn't want to sit here debating her personality traits. What the colonel thought of her didn't matter at all—at least it shouldn't matter.

When the colonel didn't respond, only lay there propped on one elbow, twirling the bit of grass and watching it as if it were the most fascinating thing on earth, Fiona found her tongue defending herself again. "I am sweet." Actually she'd never even thought of that word in reference to herself, but now that the colonel seemed to doubt it, she felt obliged to convince him.

He didn't appear convinced.

The colonel did, however, stop studying the twirling motion of the grass and look at her. "Perhaps," he began slowly, thoughtfully, "you've simply kept that aspect of your personality well hidden."

Fiona ignored that remark. "And I find your reference to me as a . . . a shrew insulting, as well as untrue."

He glanced up at her then and gave her one of those devastating, dimpled smiles that she'd come to expect. "But Fiona, honey, you've already given me your best shot." He paused to rub the spot on his head where she'd cracked him with the candlestick. "And I'm still in one piece."

Fiona didn't think she'd ever been so angry with any human being. She bit her tongue to stop the retort that would keep this stupid conversation going, then found the words pouring out in spite of her precaution. "And tell me why I should be anything *but* hateful with you? Some misguided people — yourself included — are at war with the king. We are enemies," Fiona explained in the simplest terms she knew.

"Ah, the war." Zeke dropped the grass and got up, leaning toward Fiona. "There doesn't have to be a war for you or your clansmen."

"You mean if we ignore the oath taken to defend king and country." Fiona didn't back away from his blue-eyed stare.

"An oath unfairly forced upon Scotsmen as they landed in the colonies."

"An oath freely taken by God-fearing Scotsmen, honorable men who ken where their loyalties lie."

Zeke's shoulders drooped and he rested his chin on a bent knee, giving her a sideways glance. "Ah, Fiona, you owe no allegiance to England. Your people have already borne so much at the hands of a Hanover king. I don't want you to suffer more."

"Well, I think you're more afraid for yourself and your fellow rebels than you are for us."

"You're right. I am afraid. I'm afraid the Scots are going to take up arms, and the people of North Carolina are going to have to stop them. There's going to be needless bloodshed on both sides, innocent people killed. And the worst of it will be that we won't be killing our enemies, not really. We'll be killing our friends and neighbors, people we worked with and visited. People we liked."

Damn, why was he wasting his words on her? If there was one person in this Scot-infested area who wasn't about to change her mind, it was Fiona MacClure. Not that it mattered anyway. She wasn't a leader or even someone that anyone listened to. Hell, she wouldn't be here if she were. She'd made that quite clear.

Fiona couldn't help it. She was moved by his impassioned speech. And it was impassioned. She could tell how strongly he felt by the tight, corded strength of his neck muscles, the grip of his large hands laced around his knees, the intensity of his stare.

But simply because he felt fervently about something didn't mean he was right. There were two sides to this issue. "If it's bloodshed you wish to avoid, per-

93

haps you should convince your compatriots in the north to lay down their arms. It seems to me that they are the ones who started this."

"I'm afraid it's too late for that, Fiona. The seeds of discontent have been sown, and they have found fertile soil in which to sprout. Freedom-loving men will finish what they've begun."

"As will Scotsmen."

Zeke leaped to his feet. "So I fear" was all he said as he reached down toward Fiona.

She accepted his hand after folding the leftover food into the napkins. Brushing off her skirt, Fiona nodded when the colonel said he'd get the horses.

She hated to admit it, but though they'd discussed subjects of much greater import, Colonel Kincaid's remark about her personality was what occupied her mind as the afternoon wore on. When they finally reached Douglas MacDougal's mill, where they would spend the night, Fiona's indignation had reached a fever pitch.

Fiona wished she could push the colonel's hands away when they spread around her waist to lift her to the ground. Instead she gave her frostiest thank you, and started toward the front door of the house. Though not nearly so grand as Armadale, the MacDougals' house sprawled along the ridge of a hillock, a comfortable place she'd always enjoyed visiting—in the past. Of course, she wouldn't be able to enjoy anything with the colonel along.

Before Fiona could reach for the brass knocker, Colonel Kincaid stepped in front of her.

"Still fuming about my calling you a shrew?"

"I haven't given it a thought," Fiona lied, wondering how he knew what she'd been thinking.

"You needn't worry, Fiona." Zeke leaned against the weatherboard siding, barely suppressing his amusement. She really did have the most readable face. But even if she hadn't, he'd have known she was angry by the haughty way she tried to ignore him.

"I assure you, I am not worried."

"I just thought you should know that I enjoy a little spirit in a woman. Never had much of a sweet tooth when it came to the fairer sex."

"Sweet tooth?" Fiona's mouth gaped open. The nerve of him, comparing her to sugary confection. No, he was letting her know she wasn't — and he didn't care. Well, she didn't care what he thought, or what he liked in women, and told him so in no uncertain terms.

"Now, Fiona. I'm not overly fond of vinegar, either."

She threw back her hand to slap his face, he caught her wrist, and that was the way Frances MacDougal first saw them when she opened the door.

"Goodness, I thought I heard someone out here. Fiona, child, what a pleasant surprise."

Her hand couldn't have dropped any faster if it were made of lead. Even as she spun around to face the plump, gray-haired woman, Fiona felt her face flame red. The man at her side seemed to cause her no end of embarrassment. "I . . . we've come for a short visit. If it's all right," Fiona sputtered, annoyed with herself. She'd never been uncomfortable with Frances Mac-Dougal before.

"All right? Well, of course it's all right. You and your friend come in the house this instant."

Fiona wanted to point out that the colonel wasn't her friend, but Frances bustled them through the door and called for Cora, her indentured servant, to bring

95

cider. "And ask Hector to see to the horses, Cora." She turned to Fiona. "Now as soon as you've had some refreshment, you can go up to your rooms and rest. Have you come all the way from Armadale today?"

"Yes, but . . . It really isn't that far." Fiona realized she'd failed to introduce her companion, and proceeded to do so. Frances greeted him as warmly as she had Fiona, even though Fiona pointed out that he was a colonel in the Whig militia.

"Donald will be back by supper time. He left early this morning to take a neighbor's ground corn to her. You remember the Widow Ferguson, don't you, Fiona? She's been feeling right poorly. Just hasn't been the same since she lost her Charles. Lord knows, poor excuse for a son though he was, God rest his soul, he was all the woman had."

Fiona sat on a walnut chair in the parlor, sipping her cider. She gave the colonel a sideways glance as Frances rambled on about the Widow Fergusan's son and his untimely demise — gored by an enraged bull. Of course, Fiona had heard the story before — and more, was familiar with Frances's incessant chatter. But the colonel was not.

He seemed to take it in stride, though, smiling at her and nodding — it was impossible to get a word in — when he deemed it appropriate.

So intent was Fiona on watching the colonel respond to the older woman that she completely missed a question tossed her way. The silence signaled her that something was amiss. That and the fact that the colonel turned at that moment and caught her staring at him.

Flustered, her eyes swept back to Frances, who watched her quizzically, her moon-round face tilted to one side. "I'm sorry." Fiona wouldn't have looked back at the colonel if her life depended on it. "Did you ask me something?"

"Well, yes, I did. I wondered how your grandfather was, but my concern now is for you. Are you feeling poorly, Fiona, child? You haven't looked well since you arrived, all flushed, and now you're wool-gathering. Do you think a dose of my tonic would help?"

"No!" Fiona lowered her voice when she noticed Frances's startled expression, but she'd had the tonic before, and the memory of its taste and the effect it had on her inner workings was still vivid. "I mean, please don't go to any trouble. I'm quite fine, really. Perhaps a little tired," Fiona added when Frances appeared dubious.

"Well, of course you are. And who could blame you, traveling all day in this heat? I told Donald this morning . . . or was it yesterday? No matter, it's been hot for a spell. Well, I just said that I don't recall a hotter summer. Certainly too warm to be riding halfway across the countryside. You must take better care of our Fiona, Colonel Kincaid. After all, she is only a little bit of a lass, not a big, brawny man like yourself."

Fiona's sputtering reply that she could certainly take care of herself without any help from the colonel, who, in case Frances hadn't noticed, was an enemy, was drowned out by the colonel's hearty laugh.

"You're absolutely right, Mistress MacDougal. The best I can do to make amends is to see Fiona to her room."

"Oh, you're such a nice young man. Fiona always sleeps in the room at the top of the stairs, and you can have the one across the hall. I'll call Cora to take you."

"That won't be necessary. I'm certain we can find

them, can't we, Mistress MacClure?"

"Y . . . yes." Fiona was on her feet and being propelled into the hallway, toward the stairs, before she knew what had happened. On the second riser she realized the colonel's hand rested at the small of her back, and jerked her body aside to dislodge it.

"Why did you do that?" Fiona hissed, careful to keep her voice low.

"Do what?" Undaunted by her reaction, Zeke nudged her up another step.

"Act solicitous of me."

"Why, Mistress MacClure, you wound me. It was not an act. I am concerned about your well-being."

Fiona gave an unladylike snort and marched up three more stairs. "And I suppose you had my comfort in mind when you insisted upon riding hour upon hour with no rest." Fiona turned and threw him a challenging look. She was nearly on eye level with him, since he was two steps below her. Easy enough for her to notice the devilment in his blue eyes.

"We rode too long for you?" He acted as if the thought surprised him, but Fiona wasn't fooled. "I would have stopped in a moment if I'd known you were tired. But" — he paused — "you never said a word."

He knew very well she wasn't speaking to him, and he'd also known she was tired. Anyone would have been tired — except him. He seemed as fresh as when they'd started, whereas Fiona felt like an old rag. Turning on her heel, walking with as much dignity as if she wore her finest ball gown, Fiona climbed the stairs, trying her best to ignore his chuckle.

Donald MacDougal was as thin as his wife was plump, as taciturn as she was talkative. He was a great friend of her grandfather, had saved his life at

Culloden, and Fiona liked him very much. When, as a child, she'd accompanied her grandfather on visits, Donald had always slipped her a horehound drop from a supply he kept in his desk. It was their secret, he'd tell her, and Fiona almost expected him to deposit a mint in her hand as he entered the parlor that night.

Instead he kissed her cheek, gave her a satisfied nod, then turned his attention to the colonel. Before Fiona could introduce them, Donald spoke.

"Me wife tells me you've come from the Provincial Congress to try to convince the Scots not to take sides in the coming struggle."

Fiona didn't have long to wonder if the colonel would guess the information came from her. As he answered in the affirmative, his gaze swept to her, and she didn't like the message his eyes held. She knew a moment of guilt—a moment of wishing she hadn't gone to Frances's room and told her the reason they were here.

"And why would you be thinking we would go against our king and our own holy oath?"

"I wasn't aware that Scotsmen held the Hanover king in such high esteem," Zeke countered, feeling more than ever uncertain of achieving his objective. And of course it didn't help that his mission had already been explained, he was certain not in the most complimentary way.

" 'Tis true that at one time we thought it prudent to claim the crown for the young prince. But if that experience taught us anything, it is that uprisings against the king can prove futile."

"And in some cases devastating."

"Ah, so Malcolm told you a wee bit about myself, did he?" Donald smiled for the first time and motioned toward a chair. "Sit, and tell me what you've come to say, so we can get it out of the way and enjoy our dinner."

The invitation hadn't extended to Fiona—she was certain of that—but she sat within earshot anyway. Normally she wasn't included in the gentlemen's talk of war. But since she'd helped get this conversation started by telling Frances why they were here, she imagined it was all right to stay. Besides, they barely seemed to notice she was there.

"You know of the trouble in the North?" Zeke asked, leaning forward toward the older man. Donald MacDougal wore britches instead of the kilt that so many of the men at Armadale seemed to favor, but no one could take him for aught but a Scot. His brogue sounded as if he'd never left the Hebrides.

"Trouble-making Yankees." Donald seemed to dismiss the whole of them with a wave of his gnarled hand.

"It's a great deal more than that. Americans have decided to stand up for our rights. And it won't stop in the North. The Carolinas will see their share of fighting. But it doesn't have to affect the Scottish population."

"We are to sit on our thumbs, then, and watch the king's standard go undefended?"

"British soldiers will invade the South. Rest assured there will be enough guns for us to face," Zeke pointed out gloomily. "We simply don't want to add to those the guns of our neighbors. And I think most would agree that the Scots have suffered enough."

"Aye, suffering seems to be our lot, but that doesn't mean we shy away from something we know the right of."

"And are you so sure you know the right of this?" Zeke rubbed his hand across the wrinkle of his brow, wishing for the tongue of an orator. He knew how he felt, knew the burning desire to right the wrongs of the past and see his country defended, but feared he couldn't convey that feeling to other people.

He'd known from the beginning he wouldn't be able to, from the moment the committee approached him about becoming their envoy. He'd known it, and now he was proving it. For a week he'd been among the Scots, and he'd changed exactly zero minds. And from the looks of Donald MacDougal, he'd be accomplishing nothing here.

"The Patriot cause is just." Zeke almost grimaced at how hollow the words sounded. "But I'm not here to persuade you to join us. That was never my intention." He glanced at Fiona, and she realized he'd known she was there all the while. "I simply would like you to see that you have nothing to gain, and so much to lose, by maintaining the authority of the king. I'm authorized to guarantee your safety and peace if you but remain—"

"You've had your say, and I will give it some thought."

But you won't act on it. Zeke all but shook his head in frustration. This old man would go to war. At a time in his life when he should be reaping the harvest of his labors, he'd risk all again, and probably lose. Where in the hell was that Presbyterian minister who was supposed to join him? Maybe a man of the cloth would have more success, for he sure wasn't having any.

There was no lack of conversation at supper— Frances MacDougal saw to that. Fiona spoke very little, but whether it was from lack of trying or inability to get a word in, she wasn't certain. She did know that she didn't feel quite right about what she'd told Frances. Not that it would have made any difference to Donald's way of thinking. He seemed to be firmly in favor of supporting the king. Still, she shouldn't have said anything, even if she had told the colonel that she'd do all in her power to see his mission fail.

Fiona didn't like it. Feeling guilty wasn't something she did often. And she decided she didn't do it well. After supper Donald and the colonel retired to the library, presumably to continue their political discussion. This time Fiona was decidedly not included. She spent the rest of the evening in the parlor with Frances. But while she usually enjoyed catching up on the local gossip with Frances, Fiona found herself restless. Citing fatigue from her long ride — a fatigue she honestly felt — Fiona sought her room. But she didn't slip into the turned-down bed; she didn't even undress. Time crept along, but finally she heard Frances and Donald climb the stairs, then the sound she'd hoped to hear.

The front door opened and closed. Pulling back the dimity curtains, Fiona watched the colonel's tall form head toward the mill. Grabbing up her shawl, she left the bedroom, bent on apologizing. That would get rid of her guilt fast enough — it always worked with grandfather.

Rustling leaves danced about overhead, now obscuring the moon, now washing the night in pale light. Fiona had no trouble making her way to the mill, nor could she miss seeing the colonel leaning against a pine tree. She didn't think he'd heard her, for he didn't turn around, but he didn't seem startled when she spoke.

"Donald and Frances have run this mill since before I was born. Actually, long before that. They left Scotland on the same boat that brought my grandfather and parents here. The people around here depend on them for . . ." Fiona realized she was rambling, and stopped.

"What are you doing here, Fiona?"

He hadn't turned when he spoke, just kept looking toward the stream and occasionally tossing what appeared to be acorns into the water. Fiona found his actions disconcerting. She knew he was angry with her—and worse, knew he had a reason—but he didn't have to be rude.

Fiona took a deep breath. "I was hot and—" She paused when she heard his low growl, and realized he now stared into her face, and that he didn't look very happy.

"Do you enjoy seeing how far you can push me, Fiona?"

"Push you?" Fiona shook her head, not understanding. "No. I simply decided to take a walk, and saw you—" Fiona concentrated on not stumbling as she backed away from his scowling advance.

"Well, I'd appreciate it if you'd walk elsewhere. The kind of company I'm in the mood for, I seriously doubt if you'd be willing to give. Though if you continue to do things like follow me out into the moonlight, I may be forced to reevaluate my opinion."

Realization dawned on Fiona and she blessed the darkness that hid her blush. How dare he say such a thing about her? She had followed him out in all innocence, but he was acting as if she wished to be seduced. Just as he'd acted when he'd caught her in his

103

room in Cross Creek. Well, she'd come out to apologize, and she'd do it, but then he could go to the devil.

Zeke didn't for the life of him think she'd come out to share a few passionate kisses, though damn if he wasn't game. He'd enjoyed holding her in his arms, thought about doing it again more than he cared to admit. But that was him, not her. He couldn't think of any reason for her to be here, except to gloat. And he didn't need that; he already knew what a mess he was making of this. And though he usually enjoyed their verbal sparring, he just didn't think he could hold his own tonight.

But she surprised him when a moment later she dug in her heels and of all things, apologized.

"You're what?" Zeke knew his manners were lacking, but was too shocked to care.

"I'm apologizing." Fiona stuck out her chin, almost daring him to deny her right. Sometimes he could act like such a dullwit.

"What in the hell for?" He could make a list as long as his arm of things she could apologize for, starting with breaking into his rooms, but he certainly never had expected to hear her say it.

"For telling Mistress MacDougal what you were doing here. I should have let you tell them." Fiona tightened her grip on the shawl when she heard his bark of laughter. Of a sudden, apologizing seemed a poor idea. She should have kept the guilt.

"That's what you're apologizing for? I expected that. You warned me you'd do all in your power to foil me. Hell, Fiona, I just took you at your word."

Insolent bastard! Fiona wished she had the nerve to call him that. "I said that when I thought you'd made me come along with you. Now that I know you didn't,

I—"

"—won't try to undermine my mission," Zeke finished for her, then raised his hand. "Forgive me. You *will* try to undermine my mission, but you will later apologize."

"You've been drinking." The faint odor of alcohol wafted toward her as he loomed before her. She'd retreated as far as she could. The rough bark of a loblolly pine brushed against her back.

"Only a little smooth Scotch whiskey. Do you question my ability to hold my liquor as well as a Highlander?"

The last word was very slightly slurred, and Fiona hid a grin. She had a vision of the colonel and Donald MacDougal, a man famous in these parts for his ability to outdrink anyone, sitting in the library sipping whiskey and talking. "You didn't change his mind, did you?" The question was asked softly, and with no thought of malice.

"Change his mind? Hell, he came close to changing mine." Zeke looked down into her upturned face. The expression of concern shining from those moon-washed violet eyes was unexpected. Without realizing what he was doing, Zeke touched her cheek. It was as soft as he remembered. "It was a joke, Fiona. I have no doubts about my stand, but I don't think your friend Donald has, either."

Fiona fought the desire to lean into him. His thumb idly traced the curve of her jaw, his long fingers splayed on the side of her neck, and she felt warm all over. He'd affected her like this before, but then she'd been angry with him. She wasn't now. She felt . . . Fiona wasn't certain what she felt, but she knew it wasn't anger.

She almost wished she could offer him some hope, but decided the best she could do was reality. "You aren't going to change any of their minds, you know."

"Ah, fair Fiona." Zeke's fingers tangled in her hair, his breath fanned her cheek. "I fear you speak the truth."

Chapter Seven

"Are you ready?"

Fiona gave Frances one final hug, and nodded toward her companion, not meeting his eyes. Zeke gave her a leg up, careful to touch only her boot, and together they set off down the oak lined lane. Everly, a small Scottish settlement on Chisholm Creek, lay less than half a day's ride to the northwest.

Try as she might, Fiona couldn't help a furtive glance toward the colonel. Sunlight filtering through the still-wet pines played across his face, throwing the strong profile into shadow and relief. She couldn't tell what he was thinking, but she knew what was on *her* mind—what had been on it most of the sleepless night.

His eyes flashed toward her, and Fiona jerked, pretending great interest in the lazy swoop of a hawk overhead.

"Today is much cooler. The storm seems to have cleared the air."

Fiona's voice sounded louder than necessary as she rushed to agree with him. The storm last night had done more than lower the temperature. It had sent Fiona and Ezekiel Kincaid scurrying for cover—and it had stopped them from . . . Fiona wasn't certain what it had stopped. She'd spent most of the night trying to figure that out. Oh, she'd told herself it was the wind howling down the chimneys, the incessant rain lashing the windowpanes, the booming thunder, that kept her eyes wide open, but she'd known better.

"About last night." Zeke paused, not knowing exactly how to broach the subject. "I should explain." He'd kissed her before with no explanation — flirted and teased too, if the truth be known — but somehow this was different.

"There's no need," Fiona said quickly, meeting his eyes and then looking away hurriedly. The horses had slowed to a sedate walk, and Fiona resisted the urge to dig her heels into her mount's side. It would seem too much like a retreat. But as uncomfortable as thinking about what had happened last night was, knowing his mind held the same bent was worse.

"You were right. I had drunk far too much. Scottish whiskey can be deceiving."

He didn't seem inclined to drop the subject. The only thing for her to do was act as nonchalant as he. "Indeed it can be, for those not used to it. But Scotsmen imbibe almost from the day they're weaned from mother's milk." What had she said? Trying to steer the conversation from last night hadn't worked. Fiona saw the colonel's gaze sweep down to her breasts when she mentioned mother's milk. By the expression on his face she knew nursing bairns was the furthest thing from his mind.

He'd touched her there.

And she'd let him. But worse — far worse, to her way of thinking — she'd wanted him to do it. Her breasts swelled at the memory, and Fiona only hoped he could see no sign of it beneath her riding jacket. He continued to stare until her embarrassed mumble drew his eyes to her face. This was hardly better, since now his gaze seemed fixed on her lips.

With a supreme effort, Zeke pulled himself together. He didn't know what in the hell was wrong with him, but he couldn't seem to keep his mind on anything but the woman beside him. More to the point, he couldn't stop thinking about what he'd almost done last night. "Still, drink is no excuse. I should never . . . What I mean is, I apologize for . . ."

Zeke couldn't come up with exactly what he should be apologizing for. Perhaps it should be for backing her against the tree and kissing her until neither of them could stand, or grabbing her buttocks and pulling her hard against him, or loving the way she felt writhing, her arms wound around his neck and her body molded to his. But he didn't have to explain. The heightened color on her petal soft cheeks told him she remembered every detail.

"Please." Heat flowed through Fiona as surely as it had last night. "Don't apologize. Can't we simply forget it happened?"

Nodding, Zeke urged his horse to a trot, glad to see that Fiona followed suit. The sooner they got to Everly, the sooner he could be done with this. For last night had proved one thing to him. He couldn't continue traveling around the countryside with her — not and keep his sanity. He needed his mind clear to deal with these stubborn Scotsmen, not muddled up thinking of one fiery, redheaded Scotswoman.

After Everly he was taking her home. And he didn't really care what her grandfather, or Flora MacDonald, or even Fiona, said.

Not that Zeke thought the woman riding beside him would complain. She hadn't wanted to come in the first place, and certainly last night would make her even more anxious to see the last of him. Though she hadn't acted like it at the time, certainly not with her fingers laced through his hair and her open mouth inviting the invasion of his tongue.

With a groan he covered as best he could with a cough, Zeke forced his mind away from those thoughts and tried to concentrate on the task at hand. What novel reason to stay out of the impending conflict could he use when speaking with the next group of Highlanders? He reviewed all the discussions he'd had with the Provincial Congress committee, plus his own considerable thinking on the matter, and came up with . . . nothing new.

He couldn't think of one thing that he hadn't said scores of times before. And the truth of it was, they were all sound arguments; they simply fell on deaf ears. He would feel a lot better if he could convince even one person that fighting against their friends and neighbors would be a mistake — just one person.

Zeke glanced toward Fiona. She'd heard all his arguments; maybe she . . . At that moment she turned her head, her hair streaming behind her like a banner. She stared at him a moment, her violet eyes almost daring him to speak, and Zeke shrugged. No, she'd never change her mind. And hadn't he already decided that it made no difference to him whether she did or not?

Letting go a breath she didn't realize she'd been holding, Fiona watched in relief as the colonel looked away, even urging his horse a little in front of hers. For an instant, she'd thought he was going to mention how she'd melted in his arms last night, how she'd arched her neck and invited his hot, open-mouthed kisses, and his touch . . . But thank goodness he hadn't.

And thank goodness he hadn't asked why she'd allowed it — nay, not allowed it — wanted it — because she honestly didn't know. She did know she couldn't continue to stay with him. But what could she do? She could just tell him. Say it wasn't working and she refused to travel any farther with him. Maybe if she added something about their political differences it would sound more convincing. No, she admitted to herself; he'd see through that in a minute.

Sick. The thought came to her in a flash of inspiration. When they reached Everly she'd feign illness, and he'd leave her behind. Then she could go home and forget all —

"Looks like we're here."

Colonel Kincaid's words interrupted Fiona's thoughts. She looked around as they rode into Everly. Fiona had visited the small hamlet snuggled in a curve of the river several times, but she'd never been so happy to see the neatly laid-out streets and white-washed buildings before. She was tired, tired to the depths of her bones, and more — she knew she couldn't entirely blame it on her sleepless night. She'd sapped what energy she'd had this morning in her unsuccessful attempt to ignore the man beside her.

Not that this was a novel approach — she'd been using it with varying degrees of success since his arrival at Armadale — but it had never proven more difficult. Before, she'd striven to pay no heed to an enemy, a handsome-as-sin enemy who ofttimes caused her blood to heat, to be sure, but an enemy all the same.

Last night she had seen him as a man.

Before, she'd wanted him to fail, had known he would, had cursed the arrogance that made him even attempt to dissuade her people from their pledge of loyalty to the king. But last night — nay, earlier when she'd heard him debating with Donald, she'd known it wasn't arrogance, but conviction, that drove him. He honestly believed his proposals were the right ones — not just for him, but for the Highlanders as well.

He was wrong, of course, but it had still changed Fiona's perception of him. It had opened a chasm in her armor against him, a chasm that was deepened by his vulnerability.

Fiona snorted as she reined her horse in front of the town's only tavern. She always found a man's drinking to excess rather offensive. Why did she have to see it as an endearing quality in the colonel?

"Seems rather quiet for a hotbed of insurrection." Zeke stood in the stirrups and surveyed the village. Small, well-tended buildings lined the street, from the church at one end — Presbyterian, no doubt — to the gaol at the other.

He was joking, of course, Fiona realized when she glanced his way and saw his dimpled grin. Her grandfather, when he'd advised the colonel on an itinerary — a courtesy Fiona had thought unnecessary — had mentioned the patriotic fervor of some of the area clansmen. "I'm certain the locals have better things to do than sit around discussing the actions of some misguided rabble."

Zeke chortled, taking in the flash of her violet eyes, the aggressive jut of her chin. Had he been thinking of her as softening toward him? Memories of last night faded as reality set in. "Well, I suppose it's up to me to

112

stir up this hornet's nest."

She should have come up with some snappy retort, but she didn't. She was too busy watching him dismount. He moved well. Fiona chided herself for noticing, but she couldn't seem to help herself. His buckskin breeches stretched taut over muscular thighs, and Fiona's mouth went dry remembering how they felt pressed hard against her. Hoping he couldn't read her thoughts, Fiona twisted from his grasp—another all-too-vivid reminder of the previous night—as soon as he lowered her from her horse.

Heavy oak beams, darkened by the years, gave the interior of the Cross Boar Tavern an Old World feel. The interior was dim, and it took Zeke's eyes a moment to adjust from the bright sunlight. The common room was void of patrons, but filled with enough benches and rough-hewn tables that Zeke imagined the proprietor did a healthy business.

He surveyed the room, noticing a framed coat of arms centered on the wall opposite the huge stone fireplace. Catching Fiona's eye, he motioned toward the print. "Mac . . ?"

"Lellan," she finished for him. "From Dundee."

"Ah, yes." Zeke remembered the laird mentioning this name. "Another refugee from Culloden?"

"Sufferer, aye. But Alexander MacLellan did not leave his homeland in '45. He tried living under the tyranny."

"What happened?"

"They hanged his last son."

"Last?"

"Aye. He'd had five. They all died in the battle. Only the youngest, Robert, remained after the smoke cleared. But he couldn't live with the restrictions. So

113

he refused to surrender, was outlawed and hunted down."

Zeke had read about some of the atrocities inflicted on the defeated Scots, though it was a subject not heavily covered in his English-published history books.

"Then they caught him, and . . . Well, Alexander had nothing left in Scotland. His land had already been confiscated, so he left."

Fiona turned when she heard someone enter the taproom, smiling when she saw Alexander. The expression on the old man's face told Zeke more than words could how glad he was to see the lady at his side. And it was a good thing, because Zeke couldn't understand a word being said.

Realizing they spoke Gaelic, and not wishing the colonel to think she was passing secret information to the grizzled old man, Fiona smoothly switched to English.

Alexander's change was more reluctant, but he finally followed her lead, pressing her hands in his gnarled ones. "Aren't you a sight now for sore eyes. I was told you was coming, but I could not warrant the truth of it. Yet here you be." .

Fiona squeezed his hands, and turned to introduce the colonel, who'd stood quietly by during her greeting. "Alexander, this is—" She cocked her head back toward Alexander. "How did you know I was coming?" His words hadn't registered with her at first.

"Why, your cousin told me."

"My . . ." Fiona sensed movement in the doorway and turned.

"Hello, Fiona."

"Duncan." Surprise tinged her voice. "I thought you

114

were at Armadale."

"I was." Duncan leaned against the doorjamb, his plaid-trimmed bonnet dangling from one finger. "But I decided it best to keep an eye on things."

Duncan's gaze flicked toward the colonel, and Fiona felt him tense. She knew a moment of annoyance herself. "That's very thoughtful of you, Duncan, but rather unnecessary. As you can see, I'm perfectly all right."

"I'm not sure your cousin's concern was focused so much on your well-being as it was my progress with the Highlanders." Zeke found the young Scot's presence more than unwanted. He hadn't liked him at Armadale—had considered his attitude rude and insulting—but had put up with it. He'd sacrificed his anger on the altar of his mission.

A spark of hatred flared across Duncan's face, and he straightened, taking a belligerent step forward. "No one is interested in your opinions, militia man, so why don't you keep your mouth shut?"

"Why don't you let each person decide that for themselves?" Zeke relaxed his stance. The tavern-keeper wrung his hands, his gaze swinging from Duncan back to Zeke. He probably feared for the row of pottery mugs lining the bar if a fight should break out. And Fiona stood, hands on hips, seemingly ready to deliver a scathing reprimand if this show of bravado should go any further.

Well, neither of them had to worry, because if Zeke had anything to do with it, there would be no confrontation. He'd put up with this arrogant fool before; he'd do it again. The last thing he needed was to trade punches with a Scotsman.

But Duncan seemed to be of a different mind. He

strode forward, puffing his chest fuller with every step. He stopped within arm's length of Zeke and, common sense or no, Zeke had the strongest desire to knock him back on his cocky backside. But he resisted the urge, deciding that holding his ground and peering down at the pompous dandy would have to do.

"We *have* decided, *Colonel Kincaid,* and we don't need you wandering around trying to cause dissent among us." Duncan punctuated every word with a sharp jab of his finger toward Zeke's chest. "And as for Fiona, she doesn't like traipsing all over the countryside with you."

"Now wait a minute." Fiona turned on her cousin. She had a strong feeling that the colonel had been right with his observation about Duncan's motives. He seemed more interested in Colonel Kincaid's political gains than in her—and that was fine. But she didn't like being pulled into this, and started to tell him so.

"Keep out of this, Fiona."

Her mouth gaping open, Fiona glared at Colonel Kincaid. She wanted to tell him exactly what she thought of him for speaking to her like that, but he ignored her completely, turning his attention back to Duncan.

"What are you afraid of, MacClure? If you're so damn sure everyone is strongly planted in the king's corner, my talking with them shouldn't hurt. But that's the problem, isn't it? You aren't sure."

"The hell I'm not!" Duncan accompanied this outburst with a two-handed shove that caught Zeke off balance. As he began to fall, grabbing the curved back of a Windsor chair for support, he heard Fiona's startled gasp. It almost forced reason to prevail. But he received another shove—though he was ready for this one—and he caught a glimpse of Duncan's stupid, boastful expression. All thoughts of what he was supposed to be doing fled his mind. Zeke's fist sprang out and connected with the Scotsman's jaw with a satisfying crunch.

Duncan went sprawling, catching himself on the edge of the handhewn bar. The cocky expression was gone, and Zeke's eyes dropped to Duncan's waistband, relieved to see he didn't have a pistol jammed in his pants. Zeke had little doubt Duncan would have used it, had there been one. As it was, he reached out, grabbing a mug off the bar and hurling it toward Zeke.

Ducking, Zeke avoided the pottery, but it exploded against the back wall, shattering. The second throw missed also, but came close to hitting Fiona, who'd jumped between them, presumably to play the part of peacemaker.

Before Duncan could hurl another mug, Zeke grabbed Fiona, setting her in a chair none too gently before hurling himself toward Duncan. The next right he planted on Duncan's already-purpling jaw gave him even more satisfaction than the first.

Sparing only a glance at Fiona—who, not to his surprise, had sprung from the chair—Zeke dragged Duncan past a stunned Alexander and shoved him out the tavern door. He landed with a plop in a mud puddle at the foot of the step.

Fiona pushed past Colonel Kincaid to stare down at her cousin. Something in the set of Duncan's shoulders as he sat up kept Fiona from running to his assistance. He glared at the colonel, ignoring the muck that clung to his riding britches. Unable to help Duncan, Fiona turned on his opponent. "Ach, and look

117

what you've done!"

"I see." Was there just the tiniest hint of male pride in his voice? Zeke's boots thumped on the step as he went to Duncan and offered his hand. Somehow he didn't think brawling was what the men on the committee had in mind for him to do.

Duncan refused it, snarling some comment in Gaelic that Zeke imagined was less than complimentary. A glance at Fiona's crimson face confirmed it.

"You'll not be staying with this man another minute, Fiona. Get on your horse." Duncan took an ineffectual swipe at his pants.

"Duncan." Fiona's plea was drowned by Colonel Kincaid's booming voice.

"Now just one minute, MacClure. I don't think you're in any position to be telling her what to do."

"That's where you're wrong, Kincaid. Your horse, Fiona."

She didn't know what to do. But she did know one thing. Both men seemed to treat her as if she were a pawn to be won. And she wasn't! Duncan seemed to be the most adamant, but maybe it was because of his wounded ego. Clearing her throat, she stared at him. Logic was what was needed. "Duncan, listen." She brushed a curl behind her ear, trying to buy some time to think. "I know you're upset about the beat— I mean, about what happened." Swallowing, Fiona noticed the veins sticking out on Duncan's neck. Bringing up his thrashing was not a good move.

"The horse, Fiona."

"Be reasonable, Duncan." She was getting sick and tired of his orders, but he was her cousin, a clansman. "Grandfather, your laird, told me to accompany him. I can't just leave."

Zeke did his best to suppress a grin. It was hardly a testimonial, but old Fiona was letting this puffed-up plaid peacock know where she stood—with him. Never mind that just hours before, Zeke couldn't wait to get Fiona back to her grandfather.

"You can and you will."

Zeke glanced back at Duncan. The Scotsman was ignoring him, directing all his hostilities toward Fiona. Zeke was just as glad. Even though he obviously didn't know when to give up on an argument, Duncan seemed to have decided his fight with Zeke was over.

"In the stead of anyone else, I am the oldest and ruling male of the clan, and I refuse to let you alone with this man any longer."

Fiona thought his logic a bit faulty—she'd never heard of this eldest male rule, and doubted seriously if it existed—but she couldn't stand to see Duncan defeated again. He appeared near frantic with wanting her to listen to him. A flash of memory, of Duncan sitting with her when her parents died, came to her mind. When Duncan grabbed her hands, she ignored the mud sliming onto her fingers. "You're right. I should go home. Will you please take me?"

"Now just wait a darn minute! How am I supposed to find these people?" By following the map Malcolm MacClure gave you, Zeke thought, as he heard himself whine with all the finesse of a petulant child. He'd thought for sure Fiona was going to stay with him. By all rights, she should have given that puffed-up cousin of hers a scathing setdown. She sure as hell would have given him one if he'd tried to boss her around.

Dropping Duncan's hands, placing her own on her hips, Fiona faced the colonel. Did he have to cause trouble? Hadn't he done enough by flattening her cousin and tossing him in the mud? Besides, he had as much as told her several times that he didn't want her along. Wasn't this the best solution for everyone concerned? But looking at him, you'd think someone had snatched away his very favorite toy.

Men! Between the two of them, Fiona just felt like riding away and letting them fight it out. No, that would never do. The colonel would beat Duncan to a bloody pulp.

"May I speak with you a moment, Colonel?"

"Go ahead and talk."

"I mean in private." Fiona raised her hand to stall the protest she could feel coming from Duncan. "I'll only be a moment."

"Well, see that you are. I want to get started."

Fiona didn't respond. She'd never known her cousin to be such a colossal pain. Leading the way into the tavern, Fiona noticed Alexander MacLellan sweeping shards of pottery into a dustpan. She bent, taking the broom from the old man's hands. "I'll finish this. But do you suppose I could have a moment alone with my . . . my companion?" She'd almost said friend.

After Alexander left the taproom, Fiona looked up at the colonel. "It's better this way. You didn't really want me along—"

"And Lord knows you didn't want to be along."

"Right." Then where were these little twinges of regret coming from? It hadn't been that bad.

"Here, let me." Zeke took the broom.

"Thank you." Fiona gathered up her skirts and bent down as he swept the broken mugs into the pan she held. "You're quite good at this. Did your mother teach you to sweep?"

"Hardly. I doubt my mother has ever touched a

broom."

"Oh." She didn't know how to respond to that. His voice had taken on a sharp edge she'd never heard before.

"Sorry." Zeke didn't want to get into a discussion of his mother. "When I was a kid, I spent a lot of time at our warehouse down by the docks . . . with my father." He shrugged. "Sometimes I swept up the place."

"I see." This was the first time he'd mentioned his family. Fiona would have liked to ask him more, but there wasn't time, and she supposed that was for the best. They were, after all, enemies. And if she knew more about him, she might have a harder time remembering that.

Better by far to stick with the subject at hand. "You really shouldn't have any trouble finding the rest of the places." Fiona realized she was still squatted down, and that the colonel had lowered himself, his weight on his toes, his arms resting on bent knees.

"I won't have any trouble. I don't know why I said that I would."

"Good." Fiona knew she should stand up. Her skirt billowed around her, his leg brushed against it. They were closer than necessary to perform the simple task of cleaning up the broken pottery, but Fiona couldn't move.

"Are you going to be all right?" Zeke could smell the sweet scent of heather that surrounded her.

"Oh, yes." He really had the bluest eyes. Not pale, washed-out blue like Duncan's, but dark and true . . . beautiful. Fiona pulled her thoughts together. "Duncan isn't . . . Well, he usually is wonderful, and kind and—"

"A real saint."

"You humiliated him." It was fine for her to have some doubts about Duncan's actions, but she didn't like the sarcastic tone the colonel used. Duncan was family.

"He humiliated himself." Why was she always defending the little bastard? Zeke had a sudden thought, one he didn't like at all. They were cousins, for heaven's sake. But in some cultures it was perfectly permissible for cousins to marry. Zeke wished he knew more about the Scots.

How could she argue with Zeke's assessment of Duncan? She hadn't liked the way her cousin had fought. She could even admit that he started it. Still . . . "If this is an example of your persuasive techniques, I don't think you'll be too successful."

She had a haughty little way of sticking her freckled nose in the air that drove him crazy. She was right about his chances of converting the Highlanders to his way of thinking. But there was persuading, and then there was persuading. And Zeke knew it wouldn't take much for her.

"What?" Fiona barely got the word from her mouth before it was covered by his. The dustpan fell from her hands, clattering to the puncheon floor and scattering bits of pottery in a shower around her. His arms pulled her forward till they were both on their knees, thigh to thigh, breast to chest, heart to heart.

Oh, his lips felt so warm and firm, then moist and unbelievably sensual as they urged hers open. The thrust of his tongue forced a moan from Fiona. Her hands moved from his shoulders to his neck, freeing the queue at his nape. His hair feeling like coarse silk braided around her fingers.

It was happening again, just like last night. Fiona

could only wonder at this, as her last shreds of reality faded away. His mouth, open and hot, followed the bow of her jaw, the line of her neck, and she arched for him. His hands, no longer content to trace her spine, played along the curve of her ribs, moved to her breast, and he filled his palms.

Her moan vibrated through her body, and Fiona saw him pause, a spark of satisfaction lighting his passion-darkened eyes before his cheek abraded hers.

"I love the way you kiss," he whispered in her ear, before nipping at the lobe with his teeth. "I haven't been able to think of anything else since last night."

His tongue wet the side of her neck and Fiona clutched his shoulders. "Zeke, I—" She couldn't seem to control her breathing or her voice. But it didn't matter, for he didn't let her finish. His mouth covered hers again, nipping, suckling, then settling in for a complete onslaught that made Fiona forget what she'd planned to say.

Besides, she didn't want to talk. She only wanted to go on kissing him, feeling the full, hard weight of him against her, breathing in his smell, and—

"Fiona! I'm getting tired of waiting, Fiona."

Fiona would have believed thinking out of the question, but the moment she heard Duncan's petulant voice, everything came back to her. Her first shove was ineffectual, but the second, using the heels of her hands, got the colonel's attention.

"What?" He seemed genuinely confused by her reaction. And why not? Fiona thought. She'd given him every reason to expect complete surrender. She was on her knees on a dusty floor, surrounded by broken pottery, and she was pressed intimately against him. She could still feel his large, hard heat throbbing against her thigh.

"Fiona! Damnit. You don't owe that Whig anything. Let's get going."

Apparently the colonel heard this, because his confused expression disappeared. Fiona wished he'd tell her what to do, but no words of wisdom seemed to be forthcoming. Using his shoulder as a brace, she stood up, dusting herself off as best she could. "I'll be right out, Duncan."

"Let me help." Zeke reached around to straighten her riding shirt, and received a sharp smack for his trouble.

"Stop it. Haven't you done enough already?" Her hair tumbled down her back, the ribbon gone, and Fiona wondered if her mouth was as red as it felt.

"Me? I didn't think I was by myself on the floor. At least it certainly didn't feel like I was." This was a less than a gallant attitude, but he didn't like the way she made it seem as if he'd forced her. Especially since they both knew it wasn't true. But she seemed to want to believe it was.

Fiona turned on the colonel, all thoughts of making herself presentable forgotten. How dare he imply that she . . . "You are no gentleman, but then I hardly would have expected you to be."

"Maybe you'd prefer I act like old Duncan out there. Maybe instead of fighting fair, I should start throwing things at people."

"He—"

"Be quiet. I don't want to hear you defend him." Zeke backed her against the wall, holding her there with his body. "You want to pretend I forced you, that's fine by me. But know this: It's a good thing you and I are parting company. Because as much as a pain

124

as you've been, I find that I want you." He pressed himself closer, seeing by the expression on her face that she felt the proof of his statement.

"Well, you can't have me," Fiona hissed, trying to wriggle away, only to find the motion put her more tightly against him.

"Oh, I think I could . . . last night—even here on the floor."

"You pig!" Fiona didn't think she'd ever been so angry. And she feared most of the reason might be that he spoke the truth.

Zeke laughed at her description of him, wondering how they'd moved so quickly from blind passion to hateful words.

"I hope no one listens to you. I hope you don't convince a single Highlander to disavow the king."

"Unfortunately for all concerned, you'll probably get your wish, Fiona."

"Good. Now let me go."

"Gladly." Zeke stepped away with a mocking bow. "But know if you ever push me this far again, Fiona, the ending will be different."

She didn't deem to answer that arrogant threat. She had no intention of ever even seeing him again. With a slam of the door, Fiona marched out of the tavern.

Chapter Eight

"Very impressive, Colonel."

Zeke turned at the sound of Dr. MacCloud's voice interrupting his inspection of the militia as they drilled on the green. "Robert, how have you been?"

Shivering against the January chill, Robert MacCloud laughed. "Things have been right enough, I suppose."

"And Elspeth?"

"Growing rounder by the minute. She asks about you."

"Tell her I'll be by to see her. So she hasn't presented you with that heir yet."

"You know women, especially Scotswomen — stubborn to the end. But it won't be long now."

Chuckling at Robert's description of his wife, whom Zeke considered one of the sweetest, most mild-mannered women alive, he almost missed the doctor's next words.

"Her sister's come to stay with us, till the bairn's born."

"Fiona." Zeke hoped he'd been able to speak without conveying the rush of excitement he felt. He hadn't seen her since she'd ridden away with Duncan, more

126

than four months ago. He'd almost convinced himself it had been for the best, and then he'd said her name.

Annoyed with himself, Zeke turned toward his men, cringing when Baxter, a large, rawboned volunteer from downriver, failed to obey the command to halt and marched into the man in front of him.

"Do you think they'll be ready?"

Robert's words mirrored his own fears, but Zeke answered enthusiastically. "They'll be ready. They'll have to be."

"Any more news?"

Zeke shook his head. "Nothing official. Word is that the royal governor is still quartered on a British warship off the coast, and that he meets with the Highlander leaders often."

"Working them up to a fever pitch."

"I'm not certain he even needs to do that. Most of the Scots I met with this fall were worked up enough without him."

Robert stamped his feet against the cold. "Damn, I wish they'd have listened to reason."

"That makes two of us." As he'd predicted, Zeke's journey among the Highlanders living along the Cape Fear River had done little good. He'd talked, he'd cajoled, he'd cursed, but almost to a man, the Scots had remained steadfast. They would support the king; they'd signed an oath.

A wintry wind ruffled Zeke's dark hair, bringing with it the haunting sound of pipes. "The Loyalists must be drilling too."

"Aye, I passed by their field on the way over here. If it makes you feel any better, your men seem to follow orders better."

"It doesn't, but thanks anyway." Zeke watched the

drill for a moment. He hated to think that this town and other towns like it might soon be torn apart by bloodshed. Now the two factions lived side by side, drilled on opposite sides of town, but soon . . . "This must be tough on you, being fresh from Scotland, your friends and neighbors harboring one belief, and you siding with the Whigs."

Robert shrugged. "It's harder on Elspeth. Her husband's a Whig; her grandfather and sister are fervent Loyalists." Pausing, Robert wrapped the plaid muffler around his neck. "Fiona asked about you, too."

Zeke's brow arched.

"She wanted to know if you were in Cross Creek. I had to assure her you'd gone to Wilmington before she'd agree to come stay with Elspeth."

Zeke couldn't help grinning. He could picture Fiona, her red hair escaping its ribbons, her violet eyes flashing, questioning her brother-in-law. "I got back yesterday."

"Fiona will be thrilled."

"I'll bet." Zeke dug his hands deep in his pockets, thinking about that night before she'd left him. He could still close his eyes and smell the scent of heather that surrounded her, feel her warm and—

"So, will you come?"

Zeke realized thoughts had kept him from listening to Robert. "Come?"

"To supper tonight. I know Elspeth would love to see you."

"And Fiona?" Part of him wanted to accept just to see the expression of shock in her violet eyes; part of him wanted to accept just to see her violet eyes.

Robert rubbed his chin. "That I can't say. But you're bound to run into her sometime."

"However, it doesn't have to be in your house. Besides, I'm not certain Elspeth could take all the excitement. You say she's upset by the controversy. She'd be appalled by how your sister-in-law and I act around each other."

"Oh ho, this is getting interesting. What went on between you two?"

"Nothing." Zeke hoped he was a convincing enough liar. "We just get along like any good Whig and Tory. I'm surprised she hasn't taken off *your* head." Zeke motioned to Sergeant Simpson, signaling him to dismiss the men. Not until he'd finished and turned back to his friend did he notice the lengthy silence. "Robert?"

The young doctor's cheeks were red from more than the brisk wind. "I haven't exactly talked politics with her."

"She thinks you support the king?"

"Possibly. Oh, all right, probably. But she's living in my house, for goodness' sakes, and, as you said, Elspeth doesn't need any extra trouble right now."

"Don't worry about it." Zeke slapped Robert on the shoulder. "You no doubt made a wise move. Just get that baby born and Fiona bundled off to Armadale. Probably wouldn't hurt to send Elspeth there for a while, too."

"You expect trouble?" Robert wrapped his arms around his narrow chest.

"I don't know. Maybe it's just rumors. That's what I'm hoping, anyway."

At Robert's quizzical expression, Zeke went on. "Supposedly Clinton set sail with seven corps of Irish Regulars."

"Destination?"

"No one's certain. But there has been speculation it

might be Cape Fear."

Robert let out a puff of frosty air. "There's been no word of the clans massing?"

"Not yet, but if you hear anything—"

"I'll let you know right away."

Zeke nodded. Despite Robert MacCloud's reluctance to discuss his political views with Fiona—a deception Zeke could hardly fault—the Scottish doctor was a dedicated Patriot.

"I'd better be heading on home. Sure you won't come tonight?"

Zeke only laughed, shaking his head. "Say hello to Elspeth for me."

"Within hearing range of Fiona?"

"That depends upon how much excitement you want at your house tonight."

"I don't know why you're so upset."

"I'm not the least upset, Elspeth."

"Then why are you stabbing the poor shirt so forcefully?"

Fiona glanced down at her mending and forced her hands to relax. "Is that better?" Her tone was sarcastic, and by the expression on her sister's face, she'd noticed it. Fiona sighed. None of this was Elspeth's fault. "I'm sorry. Maybe I am a little tense." She took up her sewing again, making slow, deliberate stitches, hoping Elspeth would let the subject drop.

"That's what I mean. You haven't been yourself all evening."

So much for wishes. "I assure you everything is fine." Fiona smiled, wondering if Elspeth's condition made her more inquisitive. She'd never had any trouble concealing her thoughts from her sister before.

"Well, I'm glad!" Elspeth stifled a yawn, then brushed a light brown curl under her cap. "For a while there I thought you were distraught about Ezekiel Kincaid being in Cross Creek."

"I am *not* distraught." Fiona thought her statement might be more believable if she hadn't jumped out of her seat. To try to cover her reaction, Fiona tossed another log on the already roaring fire. "Goodness it's cold tonight." She hazarded a glance at Elspeth under her lashes. "Where did Robert say he was going?"

"To check on the Fraser boy; then he was going to stop by the tavern. I'm glad he'll have a chance to relax. Robert works too hard, don't you think?"

"Aye," Fiona readily agreed. Thank goodness there was one topic — Robert — that always took Elspeth's attention away from all others. Fiona certainly did not wish to discuss her reaction to learning Colonel Kincaid was back in Cross Creek. Was that man always to haunt her life?

For weeks after she'd left him in Everly she'd been able to think of little else. She wondered how he was doing. Was he able to find all the farms and plantations. Had he persuaded anyone to his way of thinking. Not that she wanted him to, of course. Well, maybe just one person, she'd decided. That would make him feel better.

Duncan had badgered her about her inability to hold onto a thought; Katrine had commented on how thin she was becoming. Even her grandfather had looked at her quizzically.

That was when Fiona had decided enough was enough. So what if Colonel Kincaid could kiss her as if there was no tomorrow, and what if his eyes were the bluest she'd ever seen? She wasn't going to continue to act the ninny.

Right then and there, she'd decided to stop thinking of him. It had worked, too. Except at night. She couldn't seem to control her dreams. But even those were getting a little less frequent. She'd begun to think she was well on her way to a cure from whatever affliction she had—until this evening at supper.

Just the knowledge that he was in town had brought it all crashing down on her again.

"Fiona?"

"Hmmm?" Too deep in her own thoughts to recognize the panic in her sister's voice, Fiona continued to stare into the flames. Only the silence made her look around. "What is it? What's wrong?" Elspeth's face was devoid of color.

"I'm wet."

"Wet?" Fiona's gaze dropped to her sister's skirt. "Do you need the chamber pot?"

"No, no I don't think so." Elspeth's voice quavered as Fiona grabbed her hands. "I think it's the baby."

"Oh. Oh, of course." Fiona felt like a halfwit. She should have known that. Trying to suppress her nervousness, she pulled Elspeth to her feet. Her gown was indeed soaking wet and stuck to the back of her legs. "We need to get you changed." Fiona led her sister to the side of the bed, stopping when she saw her wince. "Does it hurt?"

"Just a little." The moan that punctuated these words showed them for the lie they were.

"Here, lie down. No, don't. Wait till I get your night rail. Can you stand?" Fiona rushed to the chest of drawers and yanked it open, searching through the piles of folded clothes. She was flustered and scared—

and she was here to help. Fiona tried desperately to remember what she needed to do. What they needed was a doctor—Robert, of course. Her breathing slowed. She needed to bring Robert home. He'd know what to do.

More calmly, Fiona retraced her steps, helped her sister out of the soaking gown and pulled the clean one over her head. Helping Elspeth into the tall tester bed took a long time; Elspeth had to pause frequently because of the pain. After pulling the love-knot quilt to just below Elspeth's chin, Fiona brushed a lock of perspiration-dampened hair off her sister's forehead.

"I'll be right back." Elspeth gave her a weak smile. Fiona opened the bedroom door and, forgetting ladylike manners, yelled for Hester. Nothing. "Damn," she mumbled under her breath. Where was the indentured servant when you needed her? "Hester!" Certainly she could hear that.

"What?" Fiona thought she heard something from the bedroom and looked back in on Elspeth. "Did you say something?"

"She's not . . . here. I let her visit her gentleman friend this evening."

"You what?" At the stricken look in Elspeth's hazel eyes, Fiona gentled her tone. "That's all right. We'll simply wait for Robert to come home. He won't be long." She hoped.

Fiona sat down beside the bed, even making a halfhearted attempt to finish her mending, to show Elspeth how calm she was. But the first time she heard her sister scream she was on her feet, clutching Elspeth's hand.

"Robert . . . Robert. I want Robert."

"Of course you do." Fiona stroked the damp forehead, cursing men who could sit calmly in a tavern, drinking ale, while their wives endured this agony. "He'll be here directly." Fiona glanced toward the window where the wind lashed tiny pellets of freezing rain against the panes. She revised her earlier assumption. The weather being as it was, Robert was probably drinking hot toddies.

"Robert!" Elspeth wailed, digging her fingernails into Fiona's palm.

She had to do something. Fiona wasn't certain how long she stood by the bed, smoothing Elspeth's brow, but the pains seemed to be coming closer together. Elspeth would no sooner stop calling for Robert, when she'd start anew.

"I'm going to fetch him," Fiona whispered after the current pain seemed to subside. "Did you hear me, Elspeth? I'll run to the tavern and get Robert. He'll know what to do." Fiona squeezed her sister's hand. "You'll feel better." And so will I.

Elspeth's nod and hint of a smile convinced Fiona she was doing the right thing. "I'll only be a moment." Grabbing Elspeth's cape, Fiona wrapped it around herself before rushing out the bedroom door and down the stairs.

Icy shards stung Fiona's face as she raced out the front door, but she barely noticed. Slipping on the brick steps made her momentarily slow her pace, but once her feet hit the packed-dirt road she bundled up her skirts and ran.

Cool Spring Street was deserted, and black as pitch. By the time Fiona reached the end of it her breath caught painfully in her lungs and she considered stopping—for just a moment. But the wind's plaintive cry as it whipped the cloak around her slight frame reminded her of Elspeth's moans. Hunching her shoulders, ignoring the wet cold soaking through her satin slippers, Fiona pushed forward.

Apparently the town crier had failed in his duty to light the lamps, or else the gusting wind and icy rain had doused them, for the only light came from behind an occasional unshuttered window. Fiona found her way more by memory than sight.

But the tavern's windows shone bright and beckoning. Mixed with Fiona's relief at getting there was a twinge of annoyance with her brother-in-law for being there. She'd let him know what she thought of that later, but for now all her energy was needed to stay upright as she negotiated the slick-as-glass wooden steps.

Raucous laughter and warmth rushed at Fiona as she opened the tavern door. Packed, the taproom was proof that the men of Cross Creek enjoyed sharing a mug of grog at the end of the day.

Throwing back her hood, Fiona squinted, searching the smoke-filled room for Elspeth's husband. She recognized several of the patrons, but saw no sign of Robert. Water dripped from her cloak as the heat melted the ice crystals. Hurrying across to the bar, she left a shimmering trail.

The proprietor, Peter Everett, needed three callings before he seemed to notice her presence. "Robert MacCloud, is he here?" Fiona yelled over the din of masculine voices.

With a deliberate pace that made Fiona wish she had the strength to climb over the polished surface and shake his brawny shoulders, he glanced around the room. "He ain't here. But he was earlier."

"Where did he go?" Fiona tried to keep the panic

135

from her voice, and knew she failed.

"Don't know." Apparently Everett noticed her emotional state, for he turned back toward her, his jaws swaying with the motion. "I think someone came in and got him. Aye, I'm sure of it."

"Who?" Fiona demanded.

"Don't know. Hey, Bruce," the proprietor bellowed toward a man leaning against the brick hearth, a steaming mug in his hand. "You seen where Doc went?"

"He's right over—" The man gestured to a table near him, pausing when he noticed the two men hunched over a pair of dice. "Well, he was there."

"Sorry, mistress. Guess he just ain't here no more."

Nodding, trying to hide the embarrassing tears that now blurred her vision, Fiona turned to leave.

She had to get back to Elspeth.

What had seemed like a good idea—to get Robert— now appeared utterly ridiculous. She should never have left her sister.

If anything, the storm had worsened in the brief time she'd been in the tavern. The first blast of cold air when she opened the door shocked her after the heat of the taproom. She yanked up her hood, wrapped the cloak more securely around herself, and bolted off the porch.

The impact took her breath away.

She started to fall, her feet slipping on the ice-coated wooden slats, but it wasn't the porch she hit. Still upright, she was jerked up against something hard and warm—a man's chest. The flaps of his cape wrapped around her as securely as his strong arms, sheltering her momentarily from the storm. Without seeing him, using only her sense of smell and feeling,

136

she knew who it was.

"Are you all right?" Zeke held the girl at arm's length, squinting as stinging shards of ice pelted off his cocked hat. "Fiona?" He couldn't squelch the stir of excitement that shot through him when he recognized her.

"Let go of me." Though she tried to yell at him, the wind whipped the sound away so that only the breathiest of demands remained.

Zeke chuckled. She was just as sassy as ever. No thank you for keeping me from falling on my attractive little bottom from Mistress MacClure. Of course he didn't expect that, any more than she expected her order to be obeyed. "Well, Fiona, what are you doing about on such a night? You weren't breaking into my rooms again, I hope."

"Let go," Fiona repeated. Why did she have to run into Colonel Kincaid now? And why did his touch bring back all those feelings she'd tried so hard to forget?

"Not so fast, Fiona." Zeke draped his arm around her, pulling her up the tavern stairs when she tried to wriggle free. He'd forgotten just how well she fit against him. "Maybe we should check out the condition of my room before I let you go."

"I didn't go to your room, you . . . you Whig." Fiona couldn't think of a word insulting enough to call him, and by his laughter she assumed he didn't find this one terribly offensive. But she didn't have time to play games. "I need to find Robert."

Zeke pushed Fiona under the eaves, using his body to protect her from the wind. Gone was the teasing tone, the lopsided grin. "What's wrong?"

"It's Elspeth."

"The baby?"

"Aye." Fiona didn't stop to wonder how this colonel in the Patriot militia knew of her sister's condition—he didn't give her time. Before she knew what was happening, he'd bundled her down the stairs, rushing her headlong around the tavern toward the stable in the back. "Would you stop? Where are we going?" Fiona did her best to impede their progress, but the colonel paid her no mind until he thrust her unceremoniously into the musty interior of the stable.

Even then he ignored her as she leaned against the wooden door catching her breath while he bellowed for the stablehand. "Walter, saddle my horse."

Sticking his head out of a stall, rubbing a large hand over his curly, grizzled hair, Walter stared at them stupidly. "Colonel Kincaid, what you doing here? I just done took the saddle off your horse."

"I need him again." Without waiting for the stablehand, Zeke slipped the bridle over the stallion's head.

Fiona decided this was the perfect opportunity to back out of the stable and get back to Elspeth. But before she could turn to leave, the colonel's words stopped her.

"Robert's at the Stewart farm, about a mile out of town. I should be able to get him pretty fast. Is Elspeth having problems?"

His change of topics took Fiona by surprise. "No . . . I'm not sure. She may be. I'd feel better if Robert were here."

"Don't worry, I'll get him."

Fiona didn't think she'd ever seen anyone saddle a horse so quickly. In what seemed like no time, the colonel led his horse to the door. "I'll see you back to the tavern and then get Robert."

"No. I have to get back. Elspeth's alone."

Wasting no time in talking, Zeke shoved open the stable door, allowing a gust of frigid air to enter. Giving the stallion a pat, a silent apology for taking him out again in the storm, Zeke mounted.

Fiona let out a startled cry as he reached down and pulled her up in front of him. "Put your head down" was all he said before wrapping his cape around her. Though her legs and feet were pummeled by the icy wind, the rest of her felt warm and secure, cocooned against his big body as they galloped out into the yard.

Her cheek rubbed the wool of his jacket, moved with each motion of the horse, with each breath he took. The strong, steady beat of his heart sounded loud in her ear, chasing away the howling storm. Fiona sighed, burrowing deeper, wondering how she could feel so safe and secure while worries about her sister enveloped her mind.

Zeke reined in the stallion in front of the small house on Cool Spring Street. Lowering his head, he asked, "Should I come in?"

She wanted to say yes—almost did. Just to have him there with her would be comforting. But she couldn't think of herself. Looking up, seeing the barest shadow of his face so close to hers, she shook her head. "Please bring Robert back quickly." Fiona knew she had no right to ask him to brave the storm, but he didn't hesitate in his answer.

"He'll be here before you know it." He could tell she was frightened; her body had quivered against his as they'd ridden, but she made no mention of it as she slid from his grasp onto the frozen ground. "Have a care, Fiona," Zeke yelled into the darkness that swallowed her up before he galloped away.

"Damnit, I should never have gone to the Stewarts'. Not with Elspeth so close to her time."

As they burst through the front door of the doctor's house, Zeke ignored the outburst—he'd heard this or variations of it ever since he'd told Robert about his wife. Zeke could understand his friend's distress. The storm, which now spit a mixture of snow and ice, had slowed their trip home. Each hour they'd fought the driving wind had heightened Robert's agitation.

Little light or warmth brightened the front hall. The branch of candles on the cabriole-legged table sputtered in guttering wax, and a quick glance in the parlor showed Zeke the fire had long since died in the grate.

Robert's breath frosted the air as he bellowed his wife's name. He was halfway up the stairs, Zeke but one step behind, when Fiona appeared in the upstairs hall.

Hands on hips, red hair curling wildly about her face, she glared at them. "Would you keep your voice down? Such carrying on is bound to wake—" She paused, her head tilted toward the closed bedroom door, listening to the soft keening cries from within. "Ach, you see," she said, before disappearing into the room. "What did I tell you?"

Zeke had time only to shrug at Robert's questioning glance before Fiona appeared again. This time she held a tiny blanket-wrapped bundle against her shoulder. Her singsong mutterings and gentle hands did nothing to stop the wailing.

The cries seemed to jolt Robert. He took the remaining stairs two at a time. "Elspeth?" he questioned, giving the baby in Fiona's arms a perfunctory glance.

"She's fine. She *was* sleeping, but—" The rest of her words were lost on Robert as he plunged through the bedroom door. Fiona looked down at Ezekiel Kincaid. He stood leaning against the banister, snow whitening the broad shoulders of his cape. "It's a boy," she said, feeling suddenly embarrassed around him.

"He seems very robust." Zeke hesitated. "Loud." He couldn't stop staring at Fiona. The front of her gown was streaked with blood, her hair flew every which way, almost crackling with energy, and mauve crescents darkened the pale skin beneath her violet eyes. She appeared disheveled, exhausted, and utterly beautiful. Zeke could barely keep from bounding up the stairs and taking her in his arms—screaming child and all.

He might have, if Robert hadn't chosen that moment to yank open the bedroom door. "Bring him in. Elspeth and I want to see him."

Fiona gave Zeke a whisper of a smile and followed her brother-in-law into the room, closing the door behind her.

Zeke stood on the step, wondering what he should do. It had been an incredibly long night, starting with a trip to visit several brothers in the militia. They'd talked about quitting, complained of the drills taking too much of their time, and cited their belief that nothing was going to happen in North Carolina anyway. It had taken Zeke hours of talking to convince them to stick it out a few more months.

When he'd left their cabin, the storm had worsened, and he'd almost stayed the night with them. But he'd decided to get back to his rooms. They were hardly home, but were the closest thing he had at the moment. It was during his trip back to Cross Creek that he'd passed Robert heading for the Stewart farm. And then, of course, reaching the tavern, he'd run into Fiona.

Zeke's gaze inched up to the hallway, where he'd last seen her. He shook his head. He really ought to get back to his rooms. Maybe he could catch a few hours' sleep, and no one needed him here.

Oh hell, Zeke thought, as he passed the parlor, he could build a fire before he left. It probably wasn't good for new babies to get cold. After he had a good fire roaring in the hearth and the room had lost its chill, Zeke remembered the horses. Grumbling to himself, he pulled on his still-wet cape and trudged outside.

When he came back in, Fiona was sitting in the parlor, her feet resting on the fireplace fender. She appeared to be dozing, and Zeke started to back out of the room. It was only her voice that stopped him.

"Come in, Colonel. You must be near frozen." Fiona stood, offering him her place by the blaze.

"I was just leaving." Zeke realized he was shuffling from one foot to the other, and stopped. "Would you tell Robert I left my horse in his barn? He's been through a lot, and, well, I figured I could walk to the tavern. I'll stop by tomorrow and pick him up."

"Why don't you tell him yourself?" What was she doing? By all rights she should let him go.

"He's busy. I'd better leave."

Fiona couldn't stop moving toward him. "Don't. I know he'll want to thank you." She paused. "I want to thank you."

Zeke shrugged off her words. "Elspeth's all right,

142

then?"

"Oh, yes." Fiona wondered briefly how the colonel knew her sister.

"You did a good job." Zeke grinned at her.

"Elspeth did all the work. I was just there."

Fiona stood there smiling back at him and Zeke wondered what she'd do if he moved forward and kissed her. She'd tried to tidy her hair with a ribbon, the process having almost the opposite effect. But he still thought he'd never seen anyone prettier—or anyone who excited him more.

"Zeke!" Robert came into the parlor, looked over at Fiona and lowered his voice. "I'm glad you're still here." His ruddy smile turned on Fiona. "Don't worry, the bairn isn't asleep, nor is Elspeth. She asked if you'd go upstairs, though."

"Oh, of course." Fiona moved toward the door, pausing in front of the colonel. She offered her hand in a polite gesture that contrasted starkly with the times she'd pressed her body against his. "Thank you again, Colonel Kincaid, for your help."

"It was my pleasure, Mistress MacClure." Zeke touched her hand briefly to his lips, forcing himself not to yank her into his arms.

When she'd gone, Zeke ignored the amused expression on Robert's face. "Well, you have your son."

"Aye. Did you see him?"

"No." Zeke strode toward the fireplace. "But I certainly heard him."

Robert laughed as he poured two goblets of Madeira from a glass decanter. Handing one of the glasses to Zeke, his expression sobered. "I've news. And though I hate to taint the joy of my son's birth by bringing it up, it's something you should know."

Zeke took a gulp of the wine before looking up questioningly.

"The clans are starting to mass. They'll be erecting the royal standard any day now. The Stewarts could talk of nothing else tonight."

"Any word on what they plan to do?" Zeke leaned his arm against the mantel.

"You were right about the fleet under Clinton. It's heading toward Wilmington. The clans will march overland to join the British there."

Zeke let loose with a string of oaths before draining the goblet.

"What do you plan to do?" Robert poured more wine into the empty glass.

"The only thing left to do. I'm going to stop them."

Chapter Nine

"You can't be serious about this."

The expression on her grandfather's face convinced Fiona she should never have burst into his room. But she hadn't been able to stop herself—hadn't been able to keep from riding from Cross Creek as soon as she'd received his post.

"I will thank you to knock before entering my room, Mary Fiona." Malcolm paused, confusion shrouding the anger in his eyes. "Why aren't you in Cross Creek with Elspeth?" he demanded.

Why, indeed? Fiona glanced around the room. Everything seemed in order. Her gaze swung higher, cringing when she saw the pale strip on the wall above the fireplace. Years of smoke and soot had darkened the whitewash, leaving the clear outline of the broadsword that usually hung there. She spotted the claymore, long and double-edged, on the bed, and her stomach tightened.

"Well, have you an answer, Mary Fiona?"

"Why is the claymore down?" Fiona turned on him, hands on hips.

"You will answer me first. Why have you left your sister's side?"

"Because I received your letter." Fiona sank down on a stool, suddenly exhausted. Though the weather had turned mild, the ride from Cross Creek had been long and tiring. "You can't really be contemplating joining the forces around the Royal Standard."

"And why shouldn't I? I am the MacClure, and don't you be forgetting it."

Fiona's eyes strayed to the stump of an arm hidden beneath the folds of his blue velvet jacket. It was an unconscious gesture, one she hadn't meant to make, but one she knew he'd noticed. Hastily, she searched her mind for a reason that would damage his pride less. There was his age, of course, but she didn't think her grandfather would appreciate that being mentioned, either. Yet there seemed no other logical reason why he shouldn't lead his clan.

"Grandfather . . ." Fiona reached out to him.

"Fiona, lass, there's naught to worry your pretty head about. We're only going for a wee bit of a march to meet with the British." His large, strong hand rested on her head.

"But what if there's fighting?" Fiona glanced again at the claymore, wondering if he could still lift it, let alone swing it in battle.

Her grandfather's laugh sounded as craggy as the Highland mountains. "And who would we be fighting? The Whig army is in Boston."

"There's the militia."

His laughter this time was full of disdain. "For all our friend Kincaid seems a likable sort and quite sincere, I doubt even he could make soldiers of the local bumpkins. Certainly not soldiers who could go up against Highlanders." The laird stood tall, shoulders back and chest filled with pride. For a moment, he ap-

146

peared so commanding that Fiona forgot he'd lived nearly three-quarters of a century, and had forfeited an arm fighting for a lost cause.

But it took only an instant for reality to crash back around her. She apparently knew more of the Whig militia than he. Wondering if she should share her knowledge with him, Fiona decided she had no choice. "The Whig militia is stronger than you might imagine."

"You've seen it?"

"Aye. 'Tis hard to be in Cross Creek and not know about the militia. They drill 'most every day on the green. And they don't appear all that bungling."

"You worry too much, lass. There will be thousands of us Highlanders, the best fighters in the world, against a few untried farmers. They'll hightail it and run at the first sight of us."

Fiona hoped her grandfather was right. But as she later sat in the parlor, staring into the fireplace flames, she couldn't help harboring doubts. She'd told him the truth about seeing the militia. She'd been taking a stroll with Elspeth before the bairn was born, and they'd passed by the green. Of course, Fiona had known that Colonel Kincaid was not in Cross Creek before she'd even agreed to go.

Sergeant Simpson was in charge of the troops. Fiona recognized him from that night in the colonel's room. He, thank goodness, did not seem to recognize her. For one thing, he'd been too busy putting the men through their drills. And Fiona had to admit they did follow his intricate orders fairly well.

But that wasn't the real reason she doubted her grandfather's contention that the Whig militia would run at sight of the Highlanders.

147

Colonel Kincaid wasn't the kind to run.

She was almost certain of it, and the thought frightened her. If her grandfather refused to stay home, and the colonel refused to run . . .

"When did you get home?"

"Duncan." Fiona turned to look at her cousin, a smile on her face. It faltered when she saw him leaning against the doorjamb. His mild scowl of rebuke was the same she'd seen ever since that morning in Everly. It was almost as if he blamed her for the beating he'd received from Colonel Kincaid. "I got back today."

He shrugged, walking into the room and tossing his bonnet toward a chair. It missed, falling to the floor with a soft thump. Fiona pretended not to notice. "I figured you'd just stay in Cross Creek."

"I probably should go back in a few days," Fiona answered. She was becoming tired of his attitude, though she did feel somewhat responsible. At least she thought she *should* feel responsible. But Duncan *had* started the fight.

"Didn't suppose you'd want to be away from your friend too long."

Fiona sat straighter in her chair as Duncan slouched in the one opposite her. The way he'd slurred out the words "your friend" left little doubt whom he meant. "I've been in Cross Creek to be with Elspeth."

His lack of response made her angry, and sorry that he chose to act this way. They'd always been close. Closer even than Fiona was with Elspeth, and certainly closer than she was with Katrine. Of all the young people at Armadale, she and Duncan had the most in common. Now he acted as if she were an enemy.

Deciding to make another effort to bridge the gap between them, Fiona smiled. "You should see Elspeth's son. He grows brawnier every day, and loud. Why he can—"

"Did you see *him* while you were in Cross Creek?"

It occurred to Fiona to lie, or at least pretend not to understand him, but she didn't. If he insisted upon acting the boor, she refused to pander to him any longer. "Yes, I did. As a matter of fact, he's the one who rode for Robert the night the bairn was born." Fiona realized this sounded worse than it had been. She decided to tell him how she'd run into the colonel by accident, but he didn't give her a chance.

"You and that Whig colonel are pretty friendly. Has he convinced you to become a traitor to the king?"

"Don't be absurd." Fiona stood. She didn't have to stay here and listen to this. "I'm going to my room."

"Wait." Duncan's hand captured her arm before she'd even noticed him move. "I'm sorry, Fiona. I know where your loyalties lie . . . where they've always been. I had no right to speak to you thus."

"You certainly didn't," Fiona responded, only partially mollified. But she did sit back in the chair.

"The clans are gathering, you know."

From the way Duncan said it Fiona guessed he blamed his sour disposition on that fact. "I know. That's why I came back, to try to dissuade Grandfather from marching with them."

Duncan's expression bordered on shock. "Why would you want to do that?"

"He's old, Duncan, and . . . well, his arm. I just don't think he can take too much."

"He's the laird, Fiona. His place is at the head of the clan. I thought you ken."

"I suppose I do." Fiona pleated the folds of her gown. Apparently no one agreed with her about Grandfather.

Duncan relaxed back into the chair, but his eyes remained alert. "What are the Whigs planning to do about us?"

"I don't know." She looked up. The question and his expression struck her as odd. How would she know aught of their plans?

"What does your Colonel Kincaid say about it?" Duncan steepled his fingers, watching her over the tips.

"My Colonel Kincaid," Fiona said emphatically, "doesn't say anything about it, especially not to me. I only saw him once, Duncan, and that was the night the bairn was born. We spoke of nothing but the child." That wasn't exactly true, but Fiona had no desire to continue this discussion with her cousin. Apparently he was of a different mind, for he stopped her again as she started to leave the room.

"You could probably find out, Fiona."

"Find out what?" She jerked her arm from his hand.

"What the militia plans to do." His voice sent chills down her spine.

"I can't do that." She'd never told Duncan of her one and only attempt at heroism, but thought now maybe she should have. That should cure him of any misguided notion that she could help the Highlanders.

"Certainly you could." Fiona had never heard his voice so chillingly sweet. "That colonel likes you. I saw the way he looked at you." Duncan held up his hand when Fiona started to protest. "All you'd have to do is be nice to him, and he'd probably tell you anything you wanted to know."

Breaking into the colonel's room was one thing, but Fiona didn't like the sounds of this, and she didn't much like her cousin for suggesting it. She told him so in no uncertain terms.

"Suit yourself, Fiona."

"I shall." She walked toward the fireplace, clutching her hands to keep them from shaking with anger. She hated to think about what he was asking her to do.

"You needn't get all huffy about it, Fiona. What I'm asking of you isn't unheard of."

Swinging around, fixing him with her stare, Fiona fought to keep her voice calm. "You're asking me to trade my virtue for some information."

"Oh, don't be so melodramatic. No one said anything about giving up your virtue."

Fiona caught her breath. Duncan was right. He hadn't suggested that. Then why was *that* the first thing that had popped into her head? She didn't want to contemplate the answer to that. Instead she concentrated on Duncan. "Then just how am I supposed to be *nice* to him, as you so gallantly put it—especially since I . . . I detest the man."

"Detest, Fiona?" Duncan's eyes were sly. "You forget, I saw you kissing him last summer."

Fiona opened her mouth to speak, then closed it without uttering a sound. It seemed foolish to point out that she hadn't really been kissing the colonel. Duncan had appeared, putting an end to the kiss before it began. But there had been the other kisses—others Duncan thankfully didn't know about.

Fiona glanced at her cousin. He studied her with an expression not unlike that of a cat who knows the mouse is trapped. But she was no mouse, and she certainly wasn't going to be bullied into doing this because of one little kiss. "I won't do it."

"So you said. I'm not going to force you, Fiona."

"I'm glad to hear that." Now she really was going to leave. At this moment she didn't like her cousin very much. Fiona almost made it to the door—he made no move to physically stop her—before his words gave her pause.

"I just hope the clan doesn't suffer for your selfishness."

"What are you talking about?" Fiona clutched the brass doorknob, but found herself unable to turn it.

"Oh, it's just that without knowing what the Whigs plan to do, the clan"—he paused—"your grandfather—could be in danger. There are several routes to Wilmington. Knowing which ones the Patriots plan to block—if any—would help General MacDonald decide which one to take."

"And there'd be no fighting," Fiona whispered to herself, but Duncan obviously heard.

"That's right, Fiona, no fighting. No one would get hurt."

Wasn't that what she wanted? Fiona bit her bottom lip, her mind catching on all the possibilities. Her grandfather, and all the other clansmen and Highlanders she loved, would be safe. And Colonel Kincaid didn't want any fighting, either. Hadn't he told her several times how dreadful war was?

Of course, the colonel wouldn't want her to do this; Fiona knew better than to think that. But might it not be better in the long run? If the Highlanders joined with the British fleet in Wilmington, the Patriots wouldn't stand a chance. They'd know it and, she hoped, give up without a fight. That would be best for everyone.

Fiona almost smiled at that thought. Still, all manner of rationalizing her motives didn't change the one important thing. "Colonel Kincaid isn't likely to tell me anything. He knows where my loyalties lie. He'd have to be a fool." And Fiona knew that wasn't the case.

"A smart woman can make a fool of any man. Just convince him you've had a change of heart."

"Duncan."

"You wouldn't be the first Highlander to sway toward the other side. There's even talk that your own brother-in-law might have Whig leanings."

"Robert? I don't believe you. Why he's—"

"Have it your own way, Fiona."

She leaned back against the door, her skirts spreading at her side. "Elspeth would have told me."

Duncan didn't answer her. He simply stared at her as if she were incredibly stupid. But he was the stupid one, Fiona was certain of it. After all, she'd stayed with Robert and Elspeth—she knew them. Maybe they were friends with Colonel Kincaid, but that didn't mean they were Patriots. Many of the families in Cross Creek lived together congenially, even if they held opposing political views.

"What about Colonel Kincaid?"

"I'll try, Duncan. But I still don't believe I'll be able to learn anything."

"You underestimate yourself, Fiona."

Duncan started toward her, and now Fiona did turn the doorknob. She didn't think she wanted to be close to him right now. Pausing as she left the room, Fiona turned toward her cousin. "What information are you after?"

"Anything you can find out. How many men they

have. Are they planning to send out to other towns and hamlets for reinforcements? What route they think we're taking."

"In other words, everything he knows."

"Precisely." Duncan smiled then, but it wasn't the same spontaneous grin he'd always given her when they were children. "And, Fiona, when are you planning to go back to Cross Creek?"

"I had thought to stay here a few—"

"Tomorrow would be good."

Fiona couldn't believe he was ordering her about, telling her when to leave. But the more she thought about it, the more she decided perhaps he was right. She didn't much like what she was about to do, didn't much like herself for agreeing to do it. The sooner she got it done, the better.

"That's the third time you've looked in that mirror."

Fiona dropped the hand that patted her red curls into some semblance of tidiness, and caught her sister's eye in the glass. Detecting a knowing twinkle in the hazel depths, Fiona moved toward the window, lifting the curtain to stare into the night. Apparently Elspeth thought this amusing also, because she chuckled as she bent over the cradle to tuck the blanket higher under the baby's chin.

"He'll be here, Fiona. He told Robert he'd join us for our evening meal." Elspeth's foot found the edge of the rocker and she eased the cradle into a gentle swaying motion.

"I wasn't watching for *him*," Fiona insisted, though she knew the lie wasted on her sister. Truth was, she had looked out the window to see if the familiar tall form of Colonel Kincaid was approaching. But certainly not for the reason her sister, with her wildly romantic nature, assumed.

"I didn't think you liked the colonel much."

"I don't." Fiona resumed her seat by the fire, taking up her sewing and ignoring her sister's pale raised eyebrows. "I simply thought it would be gracious of you to have him visit, after what he did when James was born." Fiona leaned forward, peering into the cradle, and smiled at her nephew. "He's awake."

Elspeth barely glanced down, but her foot quickened its pace. "Do you ken what I think?"

Fiona decided it didn't matter if she answered or not; Elspeth would tell her. Too bad the ploy to get her mind on the baby hadn't worked.

"I think you like Ezekiel Kincaid more than you care to admit."

"Don't be silly." Fiona concentrated on her sewing. She'd had to put up with her sister's innuendos for two days now, ever since she'd returned to Cross Creek and suggested the colonel be invited to supper. But this was the first time Elspeth had come right out and said what was on her mind.

And it was so far from the truth, Fiona thought. If her sister knew the real reason Fiona wanted Colonel Kincaid here, she wouldn't have such a smug expression on her face. And if Robert knew the real reason Fiona had suggested the colonel's visit . . . Well, even though she didn't believe Duncan's contention about Robert for one minute, Fiona knew he wouldn't like her using his friend.

As Elspeth began making soft, comforting noises to the baby in the cradle, Robert MacCloud walked into the parlor. Without a word he went to Elspeth and brushed his lips along the side of her neck. The expression of unbridled love that his wife threw his way made Fiona look away in embarrassment and envy. Would anyone ever look at her that way?

"How is our boy doing?" Robert leaned over his wife to stick his finger in the cradle. James immediately grabbed it in his tiny fist.

Moments later, Hester announced the arrival of Colonel Kincaid, and Fiona's heart seemed to race—but only because of what she was about to do, she assured herself.

Unlike Robert, who'd come from upstairs, the colonel carried the frosty night air into the room with him. He handed his cocked hat to Hester, and Fiona watched as he swept off his cape and gave it to the indentured servant. Even though it set off the broad expanse of his shoulders, Fiona found the blue and buff uniform he wore annoying, but she fixed a smile on her face, waiting for him to notice her.

He took his time.

Fiona continued to smile as the colonel leaned over the cradle, admiring James. The baby grabbed for his finger as quickly as he had his father's. When the colonel had his fill of making ridiculous baby noises, he turned his attention to Elspeth. His praise of her was only slightly less lavish than he'd given James. While Fiona gritted her teeth, Robert received a hearty handshake and warm greeting.

Only then, when her smile needed readjusting, did the colonel look at her. As he took her hand, anger expanded her chest inside the gown she'd chosen especially for its becoming décolletage. Thank goodness she remembered her mission, or she might have told him then and there what she thought of his rudeness.

With conscious effort, she smiled again, tilting her head to one side and lowering her eyelashes as she'd often seen Katrine do. "I'm so glad you could join us tonight, Colonel."

Zeke almost laughed, and knew it was only the presence of others in the room that kept him from it. What in the world was she doing? He'd been surprised when Robert told him Fiona had suggested having him visit, but seeing her now, smiling up at him, was shocking—and it didn't ring at all true.

Not that he didn't have a moment of wishing it were, but he knew her too well to believe this little charade. She was after something. Zeke decided the best way to find out what, was to play along—or maybe even force her hand.

Lifting the soft hand he still held, Zeke brought it to his lips, turning it at the last moment to place a kiss in her palm. He thought he heard Elspeth gasp, but was too caught up in the glint that flashed into Fiona's violet eyes to care. She jerked her hand away, seemed to think better of it, and invited him to sit next to her.

"We certainly are glad you could come tonight, Colonel."

Zeke glanced at Fiona, wondering if she realized she was repeating herself, but she studied her sewing as if her life depended upon it.

"You must be very busy," Fiona continued.

"Oh, why is that?"

Accidentally stabbing herself with the needle, Fiona bit back a curse and tried to ignore the pain. What did he mean, "why is that"? Everyone in town knew the militia worked harder than ever now that the Highlanders were massing. Why couldn't he simply talk about it? Fiona had a moment of doubting Duncan's assessment of the colonel. He seemed not to have noticed her gown — a confection of silk and lace borrowed from Katrine — or the extra pains she'd taken with her hair.

Indeed, as she peered at him covertly beneath her lashes, she noticed his attention was again on James. Perhaps Duncan should have asked the baby to get information from the colonel, she mused. As she watched, he looked up, his blue eyes meeting hers with such force her pulse quickened. When she tried to speak, her voice sounded so breathy she paused and started again.

"Certainly the large number of Highlanders rallying around the Royal Standard must be a worry for you." There, she'd broached the subject.

"Your concern for me is touching, Mistress MacClure, but, I assure you, unnecessary."

Concern! She wasn't concerned for him. How like the arrogant man to think so. But then, that's what she wanted him to think. Fiona dropped the sewing into her lap and reached for his sleeve. The wool uniform brushed against her skin as she settled her fingers on his arm. "I can't help it. Do you think there will be fighting?" She fluttered her lashes again.

"Perhaps." Zeke fought to keep the amusement from his voice. "I imagine that's up to the Highlanders." He covered the hand on his sleeve with one of his own, caressing the soft skin on her wrist with his thumb. By all rights she should have jerked her hand away. The Fiona he knew would have. But though her expression darkened for an instant, her hand remained still. She even leaned toward him, allowing a better view of her creamy breasts.

"But surely nothing will happen if they simply move

158

about the colony peaceably."

"Ah, but Mistress MacClure, we both know their objective."

"Yes, but—" Robert's exaggerated throat-clearing made Fiona pause. Her brother-in-law stood, without meeting her eyes, and busied himself with the fire, but Elspeth stared, her mouth gaping open.

What? Fiona looked down. Her one hand lay on Colonel Kincaid's arm, covered by his. And her other gripped the colonel's thigh. When had she done that? The hard muscles beneath his breeches shook and when she glanced up at his face, Fiona knew it was from trying to restrain his laughter.

The speed with which she yanked away almost toppled her from the chair—she'd been a hairsbreadth from sitting in his lap—and she tried to control the blush she felt stealing over her.

Thankfully, Hester chose that moment to announce supper. Gathering what little dignity she had left, Fiona swept from the room, not waiting for an escort. Duncan had said all she'd have to do was be nice to the colonel and he'd tell her everything. Well, obviously that hadn't worked. For heaven's sake, throwing herself at him hadn't worked, either.

Even though Hester had taken James upstairs, he was the main topic of conversation during supper. As much as Fiona loved her nephew, she wished someone—other than she—would bring up the war in the North, or the rallying of the clans, or the colonel's work with the militia—anything to get him talking of his plans for the Highlanders.

But no one did.

By the time Fiona finished rendering her slice of raisin rum cake into a pile of mangled crumbs, her nerves were stretched taut. She silently cursed Duncan for suggesting this foolish mission. From the moment he'd mentioned it, she had known it wouldn't work. Flirting and simpering were simply not things she did well. And Duncan had obviously overestimated her appeal to the colonel. Thinking back on it, Fiona couldn't imagine what had made Duncan assume the colonel had any interest in her. He may have kissed her a few times, but Fiona imagined he did that with lots of women.

Other than that, he seemed to find her amusing. The thought riled Fiona, till she could do naught but glare at him across the table with all the frustration she felt. His answering crooked grin did nothing to cool her anger.

Elspeth played the harpsichord after supper, an entertainment Fiona normally enjoyed. However, the tinkly tunes filled the cozy confines of the parlor, allowing no conversation of any kind.

Fiona, sitting in the winged chair by the fireplace, decided the entire evening had been a waste of her time. Actually, it was worse than that. She'd appeared the fool in front of her sister, Robert—and the colonel. And all for naught. She knew not one thing more now than she had before the colonel arrived. And there would be no other time to speak with him.

Then suddenly, they were alone.

Elspeth excused herself to see to James, and to Fiona's dismay, Robert joined her. She felt certain the colonel would take that as his cue to depart, but he didn't. After bidding her sister and brother-in-law a fond good night, he resumed his seat, and stared at her.

"Now Mistress MacClure, where were we?"

"I beg your pardon." She didn't know what to make of his expression.

"Earlier." He leaned back, stretching his long legs in front of him. "Before we were summoned to supper, we were discussing your concern about the Highlanders." Zeke noted a flash of suspicion cross her expressive face; then she settled into a smile—the same smile she'd given him earlier.

"You . . . your welfare is of interest to me, also."

Almost wishing he could believe that, knowing better, Zeke rubbed his palm across his chin. "Very few of us will remain untouched when the war moves this way."

"If the Highlanders were simply allowed to march to Wilmington in peace . . ." Biting her lip, Fiona stood. She moved to the harpsichord, pretending great interest in the ivory keys. What was she doing? Convincing the colonel to let the Scots army pass was not her job. She was supposed to get information from him, and instead she'd given him some.

"Don't be so upset. I knew the Highlanders' destination. I also know why they wish to go there."

He'd given her the perfect opening. Fiona glanced over her shoulder. "What are you going to do about them?"

Zeke gave her the answer he'd given Robert—the only answer he could give. "I'm going to stop them."

The intensity of his response caught her off guard. Fiona tried not to shudder as her fingers skimmed across the cool keys. Now was the time to ask him more, to find out the particulars of his plans. Fiona swallowed and forced a smile, but the expression in his blue eyes made her look away. "You have so few men and there are many ways to reach Wilmington. How

161

will you do that?"

"What are you after, Fiona?"

"After?" She'd heard him leave his chair, but had no idea how close he was until she turned. He towered over her, the growl she'd heard in his question mirrored in his expression. Fiona tried a sweep of her lashes and failed miserably.

"Are we to trade military secrets for sexual favors?"

"I . . . I don't ken what you mean."

"Don't you?"

Fiona gasped when his finger followed the curve of her exposed breast. She tried to back away, but he'd somehow wedged her between his hard body and the harpsichord.

"You appear shocked, Fiona. But we both know this is what you've been leading up to all evening." Zeke ran his hands down the boned silk, warm from her body, to her tiny waist. "I think you should know that it's my policy never to barter away secret information without first sampling what I shall receive in exchange."

"Why, you bast—" Fiona shoved at his chest, only to find her hands pinned between them.

"Oh, you're right, Fiona. You have offered me several samples of your wares. But then you know us simple-minded Whigs. We have such short memories."

His mouth was on hers—hard and aggressive—before she could turn her head.

She hated him. Tears welled inside her, but she refused to shed them. Fighting him was impossible; he was simply too large and strong. But she'd show her disdain by ignoring what he did to her.

God, she tasted good. Even with her luscious mouth clenched shut and her body stiff in his arms, she excited him. Why did it have to be *this* woman who aroused him so?

When he'd returned from visiting the clansmen, he'd felt almost frantic for a woman. But though he'd hired a goodly number, none could compete with the memory of Fiona. None could even fill him with as much desire as this closed-mouth kiss.

Zeke forced himself to pull away, then found he couldn't. His hands left her side, tangled in her red curls, tilted her face toward him. "Open your mouth for me." He grazed the words against her cheek, never dreaming she'd respond, thrusting his tongue inside when she did.

Gone was any desire to spurn him. The first sensual slide of his tongue across hers saw to that. But why had she allowed it? Why had a gentle plea worked, where force had failed? She didn't know and, as his lips moved over hers, didn't care.

She'd dreamed of him—of this. Fiona wriggled her hands. When he shifted to free them, she wound her arms securely about his neck, hanging on to him, keeping him close. Her body softened, molded into his. Brass uniform buttons pressed into the soft skin above her breast, but Fiona welcomed the hard feel of it almost as much as she welcomed the steely strength that thrust against her stomach.

This was madness, her mind screamed. But feeling him, smelling him, tasting him left little room for reason. Her fingers released the bow at his nape, played in the thick, coarse dark hair. Her tongue met his in a dance of carnal delight. And she moaned when he pulled away.

Zeke tried to control his breathing—tried to control himself. The effort it took to stop kissing her had been

163

colossal. But when he'd felt her arch against him, he'd known stopping then was the only thing that would keep him from taking her there on the floor.

Her eyes fluttered open, and innocent pools of violet stared up at him. But he knew she wasn't innocent — at least not in this instance. She'd tried to use the desire he felt for her. That thought did a lot to cool his ardor. Taking a deep breath, he smiled. "You amaze me, Fiona. Maybe you are worth a military secret or two."

It took her a moment to comprehend his words. He expected anger, steeled himself for the slap he was certain would come. Was surprised to see not rage but tears well up in her eyes.

"Oh hell, Fiona." He suddenly felt drained, tired of the games they played. She'd tried to use him, but hadn't he done the same thing? If he hadn't wanted to kiss her, to feel her body against his, he would have left when Robert and Elspeth did. She tried to jerk away. He didn't let her. "Go home. This is not your concern. If you don't stop trying to make it your business, you're going to find yourself in real trouble."

He moved away from her so quickly, Fiona grabbed onto the harpsichord to keep her balance. She wanted to yell all sorts of vile things at him, but didn't. This was her sister's house and, besides, he'd already slammed the front door.

So he thought she'd get into trouble, did he? Well, maybe she couldn't get information from him by flirting with him — she'd never thought she could. But there were other ways — there had to be. And she'd find them.

Chapter Ten

"What are *you* doing here?"

"Damnit, Fiona, I think that should be my line." Zeke strode into his room, kicking the door shut with a resounding bang. A flickering candle threw a pale glow around his desk and the woman leaning over it. Her startled face looked up at him, then down at the incriminating wealth of parchment at her feet. It struck him that Fiona was either a very messy spy, or she'd dropped the papers when he'd entered the room. In either case, he was ill-prepared for her next words.

"You said you were going to Hillsboro. I heard you tell Robert last night. Were you trying to trick me?"

"Trick you?" Zeke could hardly believe his ears. She stood now, hands on hips, her red hair curling wildly about her face, accusing him of a misdeed, when she . . . "Hell, Fiona, if I'd known you planned to break into my room, *again,* I would have been more accommodating."

"You knew I wanted to know your plans for the Highlanders." Fiona felt near tears, wondered why she hadn't broken down already. How could she be so inept, and, as the colonel pointed out—again?

"Ah, yes." Zeke tossed his hat and cape aside. "Your

little performance of the other night. I suppose since you couldn't seduce the information from me, you thought it fair to use more direct means." Kneeling by the desk, Zeke began piling his papers into some semblance of order. Bills of lading, a letter from his assistant telling him of a problem with one of his ships, and requests from some of his men to leave the militia. They were all important papers, but not one contained a military secret.

Zeke unconsciously touched the front of his jacket. His orders were there, but there wasn't anything secret about them. He simply needed to stop the Highlanders from reaching Wilmington. Yet she'd risked herself—and for nothing.

"Stop right there!"

Fiona froze, her hand suspended in space. She'd just slid it from beneath her cloak reaching for the door latch. He'd appeared so preoccupied with his papers, she'd thought to sneak away. Not that he wouldn't know where to come after her, but she didn't think she could handle dealing with him now. He glanced at her over his shoulder, his arm resting on the bend of his knee, and Fiona swallowed nervously. She supposed she'd have to.

"You're not going anyplace." Anger over her foolish act consumed him, rang in his voice. He saw her chin quiver with fear and was glad. He wanted her afraid, so scared she'd never do anything like this again.

"Colonel, I . . ." Fiona's words came out hardly more than a croak, so she cleared her throat and tried again. She wasn't really afraid of him, was she? The colonel might be her enemy, but he wouldn't hurt her. But the man who stood and approached her didn't seem like the colonel she knew. He seemed larger and more powerful and much, much more dangerous. "I have to get back to Elspeth's. She . . . she is probably wondering where I am."

"I told you, Fiona. You're not going anyplace." Zeke stopped just short of touching her. "Did you honestly think you could just break in here and I'd let you leave?"

"You weren't supposed to be here." She'd plainly heard him tell Robert that he was going to Hillsboro to discuss with members of the Congress the worsening situation with the Loyalists.

"Yes, but I am. As it turned out, there was no need for me to make the trip. I received word that I am to handle the Highlanders as I see fit — all the Highlanders." Zeke ran his finger down the side of her cheek, the corner of his mouth twisting up in a wry smile when she turned away. "Perhaps you should remember that bit of information, as it's all you're likely to get for your trouble."

"What trouble?" Fiona's breath caught when his finger traveled down her neck into the lace of her shift. "What are you doing?" She tried to back away, but only forced herself more tightly against the wall.

"I'm simply showing you what to expect when you come unchaperoned to a man's room, Fiona. If I recall, I gave you fair warning about pushing me too far."

"But I didn't—" Fiona's denial was cut short as his mouth closed over hers.

Punishing. Punishing and harsh was the way he tried to kiss her. He'd told her to go home and forget these attempts at heroics, but she hadn't. Now he meant to show her why she should. The next time she tried something like this it might not be with him. It might be with someone who would really hurt her.

"Don't . . . Please don't." Fiona wrenched her mouth free and stared up at him. "Colonel, please."

"What's the matter, Fiona? Certainly you thought your actions through and realised this might be a possibility. Certainly you decided it was worth the risk."

"No, I never—"

"Well, you should have, Fiona. You sure as hell should have."

"Stop—" His tongue thrust into her mouth before she could get the word out.

He overwhelmed her, making it impossible for her to move, difficult to even think. Just as he'd done last night, and every other time he'd kissed her. But this was different from last night, and she knew it. They were utterly alone. Elspeth and Robert were asleep in their bed, thinking her the same. There was no one to help her.

The whitewashed wall bit into her back, his power and strength pressed into her, and Fiona felt helpless . . . and stupid. He was right. She hadn't considered the consequences of coming here. He'd told her before that he wanted her, not to push him too far, and she had. She'd pushed and pushed, always expecting him to do nothing. And he had—till now. Oh, she'd been so stupid.

He'd stop in a minute, Zeke assured himself. He tried to ignore the pliant softness of her body that fit so well with his and to convince himself that this was only a lesson. He was saving her from who-knew-what in the future. With her unpredictability, there was no telling what she might do—what kind of trouble she might get herself into. Just a moment longer and she'd see the error of her ways, regret she'd ever strayed from her mammy's side.

Fiona's sob startled them both. Zeke pulled back, the anger draining from him in that instant. Wide violet eyes stared up at him, glazed by a veil of tears. Though he'd wanted her capitulation, had tried his best to achieve it, Zeke found he missed the fiery anger that should have shone from her beautiful eyes.

"Did I hurt you?" Zeke asked, his voice rough with feeling. Had he gone too far? He'd meant to scare her, but never to cause her pain.

"No." His hands, so large and sure, were framing her face, forcing her to look up at him. His thumb brushed across her cheek, wiping away a tear.

"I didn't mean to—"

"You didn't—"

"Oh God, Fiona—" The rest of his words vanished as his mouth brushed across hers. There was no thought of punishment this time. There was no thought at all. She'd looked up at him, her eyes vulnerable and the tip of her tongue nervously wetting her upper lip, and he was lost. Somewhere to the north men fought and died, as they soon would here, but for now, for this moment when he held her in his arms, it ceased to matter.

His lips traced the sensual curve of hers, tasting the dewy warmth, wanting more. Her hair, fiery red and silken, tangled round his fingers as he thrust his hands deep into the curls. Angling her head, feeling the heat of her open mouth, he thrust his tongue inside. Soft sounds coming from deep in her throat fueled his passion till he felt ready to explode.

When he tore his mouth away to burn kisses down the side of her neck, Fiona knew she should beg him to stop—felt certain that this time he would. But the rasp of his chin, the warmth of his open mouth along her flesh made her legs weak, and she threw back her head, allowing him more access.

He still dominated her, but now she loved it. Her skin seemed aflame everywhere he touched her. Even through the rough linen gown she'd borrowed again from Hester, she could feel the fire. He smelled of a winter night, of smoke and leather, damp wool and him, and she tried to breathe deeply. But all she could manage were shallow gasps of air.

Fiona grabbed his shoulders when his lips again claimed hers — he made her so weak. His hands left her hair, struggled briefly with the front laces of her bodice, and then a whisper of chill night air puckered her nipples.

"God, Fiona." He held her at arm's length, his eyes boring into her like blue flames. "You're so beautiful." He'd dreamed of her so often, of what she looked like beneath the trappings of civilization, but his feeble imagination had never conjured up such perfection. Soft and round, shining pale in the flickering candlelight, she made the blood pound in his head. His finger traced down over the creamy mound and her nipples tightened, seemed almost to reach out to him, to beg for his touch.

The hot, moist heat of his mouth closed over her breast and Fiona's knees buckled. Slowly, sensually, she slipped to the floor. Her arms reached out to him, but not for support. She simply didn't want him to leave her.

"Zeke." His name was no more than a breathy whisper as he lay down beside her, across her. Again his mouth caressed her breast, his tongue laving the sensitive tip, and Fiona's world tilted. She writhed, arching

170

toward him. Her fingers dug into his scalp. His hair was cool and crisp, the waves falling toward her body, brushing the scalding surface of her flesh. When the heat left her breast, Fiona groaned, clutching his head harder in a fervent plea. But she sighed, wetting her suddenly dry lips when his whiskered chin skimmed down the valley between her breasts and he claimed her other nipple.

He had touched her there before, of course, and the memory had spawned erotic dreams that woke her aching, heavy with longing. And not just her breasts. Liquid heat seemed to flow, to flame low in her stomach, just as it did now. She hadn't known what to do about the near pain, but Zeke seemed to know.

His hand, rough with calluses and chapped from the cold, moved beneath her skirts, inching ever closer to her ache. When he touched her, when the smoldering heat burst into flame, her body bucked, filling his hand. His finger moved, gently explored, skimming so sensually across her passion-moistened flesh that Fiona couldn't lie still. Her hands flayed, hitting the hard floor, then frantically grabbing for him. Her body arched, her legs spreading wantonly, only to clamp together, holding his wonderful hand prisoner. He shifted, his weight, even the bite of brass uniform buttons against her breasts, welcome.

"Fiona." Her name seemed to escape from his thoughts. She opened her gold-tipped lashes and stared at him with passion-glazed eyes. Her face was flushed, nostrils flaring, beautiful red hair spread across the floor in disarray, and his breath caught painfully in his chest. He'd never had a woman so wet and ready for him, had never wanted a woman the way he did her.

Teeth clenched, Zeke slid his finger slowly, sensually over the hard nub of her desire. She tightened, quivering on the brink, her breath escaping on a moan straight from his wildest fantasies. Zeke felt as taut as a bowstring. The arm supporting his weight shook, the tendons in his neck stood ridged from the strain as his manhood began to throb. It took a herculean effort not to spill his seed inside his buckskin breeches.

"No." The sound was more sob than word. But he'd left her. Just when she'd sensed relief for this tantalizing torture, he'd left her. "Zeke?" Had she been dreaming again? No, she wasn't even in bed, but on the hard floor, and besides, her body had never sung like this in her dreams. "Zeke." She called his name again as she opened her eyes. She could make him out, a shadowy figure, beside her.

"Sshh." His finger touched her cheek and her lids fluttered shut. "I'm here, Fiona." Zeke fumbled with the buttons under the double placket of his breeches, yanking one off in the process. Without the restraint of his pants, his engorged sex sprang forward as he leaned over her. He wanted to see her naked, but knew he hadn't the willpower to wait. Next time, Zeke promised himself, as he pulled up her skirts, settling between her legs.

Fiona bowed to meet him. He touched her, yet it wasn't the same. Silky-smooth and rock-hard, he slipped across her, then shifted and probed. Oh, the sweetness of it nearly drove her insane as he lay on top her, his mouth tracing the underside of her jaw.

Fionna arched, moving her hips up to meet him, to accept him. There was more, much more. She'd felt his manhood against her before, knew it to be large, and . . .

172

"Don't. Oh, God, Fiona, don't do that. You'll hurt your—" But it was too late. Even as he gripped her leg, pushing her bent knee toward the floor, he felt himself break through her maidenhead, heard her gasp of pain. He'd known he'd have to hurt her, but he'd meant to slide into her slowly, wanted to ease himself through the barrier. And the worst part was, he wasn't certain if she had forced him inside or if he'd done it himself—a reflex action to her movement.

Zeke paused, his muscles quaking, and looked down at her. "Are you all right?" he asked through clenched teeth. When she didn't answer, only stared at him, her violet eyes dark and unfocused, Zeke brushed a curl off her cheek. "Be still," he warned. "The pain will stop."

"I don't wish to be still." Fiona fit action to words, lifting her hips, opening and accepting all of him. Now it was his turn to gasp. His expression of disbelieving wonder made her smile. There had been a brief stab of pain, but it had swiftly disappeared, replaced by the marvelous fullness of having him inside her.

Zeke pulled back, nearly sliding out of her fiery heat, then slowly let her draw him back inside. He moved again, his breath coming in near-painful pants. In slowly, out with infinite care, trying his best to be gentle. Trying to keep his sanity. But he hadn't counted on the erotic sweep of her tongue inside his mouth when he bent to kiss her, or the rhythmic rise and fall of her body.

He thrust, reflex taking over as her body expanded to accept him, then narrowed and squeezed. Faster and faster he drove, till the only sounds he heard were the harmony of their raspy breathing, the only sensation the pounding force of their joining.

She jerked, her body stiffened, convulsing around him, wiping out his last shreds of self-control. He shuddered, plunged, exploded inside her, his hoarse cry a masculine counterpoint to her soft, sensual moans.

Zeke collapsed. He'd never felt so spent, so utterly drained, and yet so full of life. He'd tell her, he'd show her the mountains he could move—in a minute—when he caught his breath.

Fiona opened her eyes slowly, with a sense of awakening from a dream. But she hadn't slept, not really. She'd been fully awake, her senses too smothered by Zeke to be aware of reality. At least not the reality that grabbed her attention now. Her back and shoulders pressed painfully against the hard, cold floor, made all the worse by the heavy weight on top of her. But more miserable than any physical discomfort was the guilt. She'd assailed Duncan for suggesting she lose her virtue to the colonel, and now she'd done this. What had the colonel said last night? *Trading sexual favors for military secrets.* Well, he'd told her all he intended to—and she'd given him everything.

Fiona squinted, making out only the tousled top of Zeke's head, the curve of his cheek, in the sputtering light from the candle. It occurred to her that moments ago she'd welcomed, nay, craved, his weight, but Fiona thrust that thought aside.

"Get off of me," she hissed, her hands shoving at the immovable strength of his shoulder.

"Hmmm? Sorry. I didn't mean to squash you." Zeke shifted, placing his weight on his elbows, and smiled down at her. His dark brows arched questioningly when he noticed her expression.

174

"Well, you did. Now will you please get up?"

"Gladly." Zeke levered himself up, ignoring her batting hands as he pulled her skirt down over her exposed thighs. She didn't act at all like the same woman he'd just made passionate love to. And he didn't think he liked the change.

Zeke offered his hand when she just lay there, but she looked away, struggling to cover her breasts as she sat up. He straightened, fastening his own clothing, then stood watching her. She fumbled with the laces of her bodice, growing noticeably more frustrated as they refused to obey. Her fingers trembled.

Feeling a bit like a cad for not expecting some negative reaction from her, Zeke hunched down on the floor, his knee touching her outstretched leg. "Fiona, I—"

"What have you done?"

By the way she still struggled with the front of her gown, Zeke wasn't certain if she referred to his bumbling attempt to undress her, or the resulting deed. "Fiona, honey, listen—"

"Don't touch me. Don't ever touch me again. I don't want you to." Fiona's voice trailed off to a whisper.

"You're upset." And who could blame her? He hadn't been the most gentle of lovers, and the cold, hard floor was hardly a fitting place to initiate a maiden into lovemaking.

"Of course I'm upset." Fiona glared up at him, her eyes full of anger. "And don't I have a right to be, after what you've done?"

"Damnit, Fiona." Zeke caught her chin when she would have looked away. "I apologize for not carrying you into my bed as I should have." His fingers tightened as she tried to twist away. "But I refuse to take

175

full responsibility for what happened here." His voice and his hand gentled. "We made love, Fiona. And I, for one, thoroughly enjoyed it."

"I hated it!"

His only response was a maddening grin and a subtle shake of his head.

"You're vile."

"Perhaps." Zeke's grin broadened. "But I don't try to lie to myself."

"Meaning I do?"

"Meaning you loved the way I made you feel just as much as I loved making you feel that way."

"Not only vile, but disgusting." Fiona pushed him aside and stood, yanking her cloak around her with a flourish.

"Aw, come on, Fiona. What's done is done. Maybe this didn't happen under ideal circumstances, but you know we've been heading toward this since we met." Zeke saw immediately, by the widening of her eyes, that his attempt to tease her out of this mood wasn't working. "All right." He leaned against the door, keeping her from opening it. "Then just accept that it's done."

"Let me out of here. You got what you wanted— revenge for my breaking into your room." Fiona worked hard to keep her voice from breaking. "There's nothing else you can take from me."

"Damnit, Fiona." Zeke grabbed her shoulders. "That's not what happened, and you know it."

"You made me feel like a . . . a whore." Fiona hated the sob that accompanied that last word. Why couldn't she be brave about this? And why wouldn't he let her go?

Shock narrowed Zeke's eyes. He shook her once,

then, seeming to have a difficult time restraining himself, shook her again. The curse that escaped his lips was as vile as she'd accused him of being. "If you felt like a whore, Fiona, you felt like it on your own. I never, ever thought of you that way."

"I hate you." The words spilled from her mouth as unrestrained as the tears flowing down her cheeks.

He should have expected that; she'd certainly expressed the sentiment before. But somehow, foolishly, he'd thought what had happened might have changed that. He saw her wince, knew his fingers had tightened painfully on her shoulders, and dropped his hands. "I think you'd better go, Fiona. And I hope this will put an end to your attempts at heroics. Leave the war to those better able to handle it." If nothing else came of this, maybe . . . just maybe she'd learned her lesson.

Fiona started to leave, paused. "You won't tell anyone about this, will you? I mean, my grandfather wouldn't understand, nor would Elspeth."

"Don't worry. Your little spy adventure is safe with me." A cynical smile curved his lips. "You see, though you apparently weren't, I was rather moved by what happened. And I have no desire to hurt you."

Fiona's jaw dropped. She'd been awful to him. Lying and accusing when she knew, as well as he, that she wasn't being honest. She couldn't seem to help herself, was having a very difficult time facing what she'd done. But she'd never expected this . . . this admission from him. It made her catch her breath, rekindled vivid sensations of how he'd made her feel, and it frightened her. Without looking back she left the room.

Thankful for the darkness that swallowed her, Fiona

left the tavern. Making her way to Elspeth's house caused no problem—it appeared to be one thing she could do right.

In her room she quickly changed from her borrowed clothes. The rusty brown streak staining the petticoat made her pause. Closing her eyes, Fiona took a deep breath to quell a fresh onslaught of tears.

What had she done? Oh, what had she done?

All of the thoughts she'd tried to keep at bay came flooding over her. And this time she didn't have her anger with the colonel to forestall them. As much as she wanted to blame this whole mess on him, Fiona knew in fairness she couldn't.

Not that he was completely blameless. Fiona sloshed the petticoat in the bowl's cold water and rubbed at the stain. He certainly hadn't done anything to stop what happened. But then he'd never given her any reason to think he would. To the contrary, he'd let her know exactly how he felt.

And she'd gone to his room anyway.

She scrubbed at the linen harder as that reality sunk in. She'd known what might happen, yet she'd gone anyway. True, she'd thought he'd be out of town, but hadn't such information proved faulty before? Could she possibly have wanted him to find her?

Fiona's knuckles burned and she yanked her hands from the frigid water. She'd rubbed them nearly raw trying to remove the stain, and still she could see it. Biting her lip, Fiona wrung out the fabric and tossed it onto the floor. She'd give Hester one of her petticoats in exchange for this one.

A simple solution. If only everything were as easy as tossing away a soiled petticoat.

Turning away from the washstand, Fiona blew out

the candle she'd left burning on her bureau. Her sheets were cold, having long lost the warmth of the bedwarmer Hester had rubbed over them.

Closing her eyes didn't bring sleep — she'd known it wouldn't. Her mind, her memories, where too active for her to even lie still. As the linen sheets and coverlet tangled around her legs, Fiona relived every detail of the night. She tried not to blame herself — it was so much easier on her conscience to lay the blame at the colonel's feet. But she couldn't. Certainly not all of it.

He'd kissed her, crossing that fragile line that separated sanity from passion. For that she could fault him — would fault him. He knew as well as she what occurred when they touched. Experience, after all, was an excellent teacher.

But she'd tempted fate.

She'd gone to his room again — alone. Never mind that she thought him gone. She'd thought that before, only to be proven wrong — and vulnerable. Even then, when she hadn't known him, when he hadn't teased her, or infuriated her . . . or helped her, she'd found his touch could suspend reality. It had been temporary then, just a brief trip to the edge of the abyss. But now it was more, much more.

Now it was too powerful for her to control.

Except to stay away from him. Absence seemed the tool she needed to break his spell. Hadn't she come close to forgetting him before? Hadn't the dreams subsided?

Absence. That's what she needed. He was right. What was done, was done. But she would see it never happened again. And how hard could that be?

They were enemies, after all. Providence — and her own stupid meddling — may have thrown them to-

179

gether before, but never again.

She would go home, to Armadale. The name seemed to flow over her like a soothing balm. She'd be safe from him there—safe from herself. Fiona closed her eyes, peace and acceptance of her decision relaxing her limbs, helping her drift . . .

She should apologize.

Fiona cringed, her eyes flying open, when that thought popped into her head. She'd blamed him solely—wrongly. She'd yelled, calling him all sorts of awful things. Acted as if he'd forced himself on her, when both of them knew the absurdity of that. She should apologize. But how could she ever do that? How could she even face him after what had happened? And how, Fiona swallowed, could she be certain it wouldn't happen again if she saw him alone?

Chapter Eleven

February's mild weather, a sharp contrast to the bitter cold of the previous month, had teased a few unsuspecting blossoms open. Fiona paused on the brick path and shook her head, spilling red curls around the pushed-back hood of her cloak. Winter was far from over. "I can feel it in my bones," Fiona mumbled, then laughed at herself. She was beginning to sound like Lucy.

Squinting against the unexpected brightness of the sun, Fiona spotted her grandfather, wrapped tightly in his plaid, sitting on a bench by the skeletal vines of the grape arbor. Ignoring the tunnel-like structure, and trying to smother the pang of memory it always evoked, she made her way toward the laird.

Damn, she didn't want to think about Ezekiel Kincaid. If only so many things didn't make him spring to mind.

Forcing a bright smile, she called out, "You wished to see me?"

His answering greeting, and the wave of his hand from beneath the plaid, made her feel better.

"Come, lass, sit a spell in the garden with your grandfather. I fear this warmth is bound to be fleeting." As if to prove the truth of his words, a maverick wintry wind whistled through the pines, swirling the red and black tartan off one of his shoulders.

Fiona tugged it back in place, wishing again that the blossoms hadn't been fooled by the warmer temperature. They were bound to suffer. "Better?" She sat on the wooden bench beside him, gathering her skirts close.

"Aye." Malcolm leaned back. "And how are things with you today? How goes the cleaning of the lustres?"

"The lustres?" Fiona's eyes narrowed till only slits of violet shone from between her burnished lashes. "You called me down here to discuss my housekeeping chores?" She'd begun supervising the lowering and cleaning of the brass and pewter chandeliers two days ago, but hardly thought it warranted her grandfather's concern.

"Not entirely." Malcolm's expression sobered. He shrugged, seeming to come to a conclusion of sorts. "I'm leaving in a sennight."

"Leaving?" Fiona felt a heaviness settle on her chest. She didn't have to ask where he was going. She knew. Since the day she'd rushed home to confront him they hadn't spoken of his joining the Loyalist forces massing at Cross Creek. Foolishly, she'd assumed his lack of discussing the topic meant he'd changed his mind. Now she knew better.

"Aye. I've waited till all was near readiness for our march to save these old bones as much hardship as possible." He smiled, but Fiona didn't return the gesture.

"So, you're admitting age to be a factor, then?"

"It was only a jest, Granddaughter."

"If you think that, you're daft."

"Now, Mary Fiona, we'll have none of this temper.

182

If truth be known, I've put off leaving as much to avoid that as the hardships of camp life."

"And let's not be forgetting the flux you suffered, not a fortnight past. Could that not have something to do with your late leave-taking? Is that not good enough reason to forget this foolishness?"

"I'm as sound as the Scottish Highlands, and I will not shirk my duty as laird of this clan. Not as long as there's a breath in this body."

"Much more of this ridiculous behavior and there won't be." Fiona stomped her foot on the brick path.

"I'm leaving, Mary Fiona."

"Then I'm going with you." Fiona sprang to her feet; her swirling cape spread open as she planted her fists on the curve of her hips.

"And you called me daft. Surely you've lost your mind."

"Not in the least." Fiona tried to steady her voice. The thought of accompanying her grandfather on a march didn't really appeal to her, but then the idea of him going alone left her less than happy also. Besides, Scottish women often joined a march, especially at the onset. "I'll bet Flora MacDonald is at the Highlanders' camp right this very minute."

Actually this was a safe bet, for Fiona knew it to be a fact. It was one of the many tidbits of information concerning the increased tension in Cross Creek that Elspeth's last post had contained.

"And when, lass, did you get it in your head that you should be doing something just because Flora MacDonald does it?"

Red curls bounced as Fiona raised her chin. "I'm going." She could be just as stubborn as he. And as for her being no Flora MacDonald, well, that was certainly true enough. She'd proved it time and time again. But it hadn't stopped both Flora and her grandfather from asking her to guide Colonel Kincaid, and it wouldn't stop her from taking care of her grandfather now. She was simply going, and there was nothing anyone could do to stop her.

Her determination held. It held through her grandfather's grumblings that he didn't need a scrawny redheaded lass to watch out for him. It held through Lucy's scoldings and Katrine's dismay.

It even held through Duncan's shrug and dismissal of the controversy. Back at Armadale for a short visit after helping to muster the Loyalist troops, he seemed filled with his own importance. "Well, Fiona, did you find out anything from your militia colonel?" he asked one afternoon after finding her alone in the parlor.

"Only what I told you in the message." After leaving Cross Creek she'd sent him a note telling him only that Colonel Kincaid had orders to stop the Highlanders — which, despite her sacrifice, was all she knew.

"That's hardly noteworthy, Fiona." He steepled his fingers, studying her over the top.

"Be that as it may, that's all I know." Fiona felt heat creep up her neck as he continued to stare at her. She hoped he couldn't read her mind. Not that she knew anything more about the militia's plans, but thoughts of how she'd received that information, of how Zeke had looked — and felt — when he'd told her that, made her skin tingle.

While none of the controversy at Armadale did anything to break her resolve to accompany her grandfather, thoughts of Zeke came close. She was, after all, going to Cross Creek. And that's where he was. She did *not* want to run into him; especially since she hadn't sent her note of apology.

That was the alternative to seeing him in person

she'd come up with. And she'd meant to write it, she really had. She'd even wasted several pieces of parchment in the process. But everything she wrote sounded so stupid, and thinking of what had happened between them only upset her, so she didn't send it. But thoughts of him still played in her mind, annoyingly so, as she prepared to leave Armadale.

Fiona and her grandfather, who'd been given the rank of major in the British army, left the plantation on the tenth of February. Most of the clan MacClure, including her Uncle Angus and cousins William and Duncan, had preceded them.

If Fiona had any misgivings about accompanying her grandfather, the trip dispelled them. It was obvious he needed someone to help him. It was also obvious he shouldn't be going at all; Fiona suspected he'd had a recurrence of the flux. But he held his head so high, and his eyes, even when weariness set in, were so bright, she hadn't the heart to argue with him.

Any thoughts of an embarrassing encounter with Colonel Kincaid disappeared as they neared the Loyalist camp on the outskirts of Cross Creek. Fiona had never seen so many people in one place. Thousands of Highlanders milled about. She recognized the tartans of the Clan MacKenzie, the Clan MacRae, the Clan MacLean, MacKay, MacLachlan, MacLeod, and of course, the Clan MacDonald.

Everywhere there was noise and activity. The shrill of bagpipes formed a backdrop for the animated conversations among men who hadn't seen each other for months or, sometimes, years.

After finding the bright banner marking the MacClure clan's encampment, Fiona helped get the laird settled in. She rejected her grandfather's suggestion that she stay at Elspeth's house, instead packing away the few things she'd brought with her under a cot in the corner.

"Mary Fiona, 'tis not proper for you to be staying in this camp with all these lads."

"And are you saying you can't protect me, then?" Fiona asked, with a cocky lift of her head.

"Mary Fiona!" For all Malcolm tried to sound intimidating, his tone lacked the fire of old.

"I'm staying," was all Fiona said in reply.

The evening of their arrival in camp, Malcolm, with Fiona in tow, took their evening meal with the MacDonalds. As Fiona had predicted, Flora shared the tent with her husband Allen, laird of the clan.

The commander of the Loyalist troops, General MacDonald, was present too. Though no close relative of Flora's husband, who could deny the pull of clan? General MacDonald, a man in his mid-sixties, appeared pleased with the number of Highlanders assembled.

" 'Tis an awe-aspiring sight, to be sure," the general said, raising his pewter goblet in toast. "Just to see all the loyal subjects of King George, all these proud Highlanders, stirs the blood."

His speeches were inspiring and Fiona felt pride well within her. It almost dispelled her misgivings about her grandfather, and the general's next words made her feel even better.

"We shall do our best to avoid any confrontation on the way to Wilmington. That is, if the local militia is so inclined."

His amused chuckle joined those of his audience—except for Fiona. She wondered if she should mention her last interview with Colonel Kincaid, wondered if they'd believe her when she expressed the colonel's determination to stop the Loyalists from reaching the coast. She decided they wouldn't. Besides, if she mentioned the conversation, would she be called upon to relate where and how it had taken place? Fiona didn't think she could talk about it without arousing suspicion.

Also, she'd told Duncan, and he supposedly had the ear of those in command. And General MacDonald said they would steer clear of a fight. Remembering the size of the camp as they'd entered it today, the multitude of kilted Highlanders standing ready to march, Fiona didn't think the militia, paltry by comparison, would dare start any fighting. Ezekiel Kincaid was, after all, only a man. She'd had proof enough of that. He couldn't work miracles.

Feeling much better about everything, Fiona accompanied her grandfather back to the MacClure tents. Darkness had fallen, the air had chilled, and she was thankful for her plaid.

For as far as Fiona could see, campfires dotted the landscape like so many twinkling stars, testimony to the number of Highlanders who'd answered their king's summons. Melodies of fiddles and bagpipes blended in the night air, calling to mind the glories of the past.

Glancing at her grandfather, who seemed lost in those memories, Fiona was almost glad they'd come. He'd be all right. She'd see to what needs she could handle, and when Robert joined them, he'd take care of any medical problems the laird might have.

"When do you suppose Robert will be here? I imagine he wants to stay with Elspeth and the bairn as long as possible, but I thought we might have seen him today. Tomorrow, if you promise to rest while I'm gone, I might ride into town and visit with—" Fiona stopped. She'd rambled away, not noticing until this minute that her grandfather had yet to respond to anything she'd said. Something about his silence made her stare up at him.

Light from a nearby campfire illuminated him, cast bizarre shadows upon his face and beard. Even in this light she could tell he'd gone deathly pale.

"What's wrong?" Fiona didn't know whether to summon help or not.

"Robert won't be joining the Loyalist army, Fiona."

"Oh." She let out a sigh of relief. She could understand her grandfather being upset. In times like these, a man wanted all his kin by his side, but she supposed if anyone had reason not to leave Cross Creek, it was Robert. "I imagine he's needed here, Grandfather. He can't run off and leave the town without a doctor, no matter what his heart might say."

"He's joined the rebel militia."

It took a moment for her grandfather's words to sink in, but when they did, Fiona felt her blood heat. "Nay, Robert would not do such a thing. I don't believe it. Whoever told you, spoke false." She immediately thought of Duncan, and damned him for spreading such vicious lies.

" 'Tis Robert's own word I have on it."

"But it can't be." Fiona grabbed at her grandfather's plaid, studying his face in the flickering light. "Elspeth would . . . She would have said something. I stayed there near a fortnight, and we talked. . . ." But never about the war, she thought — nay, never about the war.

Elspeth and Fiona were too different — like opposite sides of the moon — to be really close. Each woman had known it for years, accepted it. Yet each knew they could count on the other, and they'd always trusted each other. Fiona felt that loss like a sharp pain.

"You could speak to him, remind him where his loyalty lies." Fiona followed her grandfather into the tent and pulled the heavy canvas flap down.

"I have talked to him, lass. 'Tis no good to brood on it. You must let it go, Fiona."

"I can't." As she began to unwind her plaid, Fiona's hands stilled, then dropped to her side. "It's Colonel Kincaid." She stared at her grandfather, repeating the accusation when he seemed not to understand. "This is his fault. I know it." Fiona rushed to where her grandfather sat on the edge of the campaign bed. "They're friends. I didn't think anything about it at the time, but now I know that must be the reason. Zeke Kincaid persuaded Robert to abandon his kin."

"A man can't be swayed unless he wishes it."

Fiona lay abed that night thinking about her grandfather's words. She still couldn't believe that Robert had joined the Whig militia. There must be some mistake. What it was, she couldn't imagine, but she meant to find out. And if it were true—well, she meant to know the how and why of it. And the reason they hadn't told her.

The next morning when the laird went to meet with General MacDonald and his staff, Fiona saddled her horse. Riding the short distance to Cross Creek gave her more time to consider what she would say to Elspeth and Robert. Surely they didn't realize the full import of their decision.

Hester answered the door and showed Fiona to the second floor nursery, where Elspeth sat contentedly rocking her son.

"Fiona, I did not expect to see you."

"I suppose not." Fiona shut the door, leaning on it a moment before crossing the room. After staring into the golden flames of the fireplace for a moment, she

189

turned. "Is it true, Elspeth?"

The rocker's pace quickened, the creaking floorboard beneath groaned in protest. "True?"

"That Robert is a Rebel? That he joined the militia?" Fiona didn't need to hear anything. The answer was written clearly on her sister's face.

Thoughts of changing Robert's and Elspeth's minds gave way to a need to know why they hadn't told her.

"I wanted to," came Elspeth's reply when asked. "But—"

"But what? How could you let me live in this house with you, thinking . . . talking." Fiona threw up her hands. "We're sisters Elspeth. I just don't understand why you didn't tell me."

"Because I told her not to."

Looking around as Robert entered the room, both sisters were surprised. Elspeth's expression quickly changed to a welcoming smile. Fiona's did not.

"I hope you don't mind my joining you." Robert leaned over the back of his wife's chair and gave her a quick kiss before rubbing his son's downy head. "Hester mentioned your sister came for a visit."

"I don't mind at all."

Fiona wasn't the least amazed that Elspeth answered. It was obvious his question had been solely for his wife's benefit. Fiona imagined he didn't give a fig if she minded his interruption.

"So, Fiona." Now Robert addressed her. "I understand you think an explanation is due you."

"An explanation and a possible reconsideration on your part." Fiona folded her hands in front of her, tightening her fingers when she heard Robert's chuckle.

"That's not likely to happen, but I will try to explain why we"—he glanced down at his wife—"didn't tell

190

you earlier."

Fiona tapped the toe of her low riding boot, growing impatient while he seemed to search for the right words. When he finally spoke, Fiona wished he'd waited longer. "You thought I'd create a row because of my temper?" She nearly yelled, then lowered her voice, realizing she was doing just that.

"Fiona, try to understand. . . ."

Fiona turned her gaze from Robert to his wife, then back again, as he finished her thought. "I didn't want anything upsetting Elspeth in her condition. We all knew how you felt, and . . . well . . . it seemed better to let you think we shared your views."

"You thought I would do something to jeopardize Elspeth?" Fiona could hardly fathom that.

"Not intentionally. But even now, I worry about what this scene is costing her and the baby. They aren't as strong as you, Fiona." As if to emphasize Robert's words, James, bundled tightly in Elspeth's arms, began to whimper.

Taking several deep breaths, Fiona tried to calm the temper they accused her of having. It wasn't easy, but she did it. She'd show her brother-in-law that she could have a rational conversation, that his lying, and forcing Elspeth to do the same, wouldn't affect her. Heaven knew, by the expression on Robert's face, there would be no changing his course. But hadn't Grandfather told her as much?

Wishing, not for the first time, that she'd heeded her grandfather's advice, Fiona moved toward the door. The bairn was crying in earnest now, and Fiona resisted the urge to take him from Elspeth's arms and sing him one of the silly ditties she'd made up for his amusement.

"Fiona, you don't have to go. Tell her she doesn't

have to go, Robert." Elspeth grabbed her husband's arm, tugging at his uniform jacket.

"I think Fiona knows she's always welcome here, don't you?"

"Aye." She continued to back toward the door. "But I must get back to Grandfather."

She didn't think either of them were fooled by her hastily said good-byes. But she thought if she didn't get out of this house now, she'd either lose her temper — thus proving Robert right — or break down in tears, proving herself a fool.

This wasn't the way it was supposed to be. They were family — clan. They all fought on the same side. Even in Scotland, when some clans were divided in their loyalties to Prince Charles, the MacClures never were. They stuck together.

Fiona trod down the stairs, growing angrier by the moment. Maybe Robert wasn't a MacClure, but he'd married into the clan. He had no right causing this dissension, no right at all.

And what about the oath he'd signed? Did that mean nothing to Elspeth's husband? "The man has no sense of honor or loyalty," she mumbled, grabbing her cloak from the chair in the hall where Hester had draped it. With a vicious jerk, she swung it around her shoulders, nearly losing her balance when she heard a deep voice.

"What are you grumbling about?"

"You!" Fiona's eyes grew large as saucers, then narrowed suspiciously. "What are you doing here?"

Zeke leaned a shoulder against the doorjamb, smiling. He'd known she was here, had been in the study when Hester mentioned her presence to Robert. And he'd told himself it was best if he kept out of sight. After their last encounter, she wasn't likely to have any desire to see him.

But he couldn't help himself. He'd heard her stomping down the stairs, could guess the cause of her anger, but none of that diminished the fact that he wanted to see her. She continued to glare at him with an expression more suitable for muck dirtying the hem of her dress, and Zeke couldn't help chuckling. "You don't seem in the best of tempers, Fiona."

"My temper's fine." Why did everyone seem to concentrate on that? "You startled me, is all. And I didn't expect to see you here." That certainly was true. Didn't expect nor wish to see him. "Shouldn't you be off somewhere gathering your little army?"

"Perhaps. Did you come to Cross Creek to cheer yours on?"

"Perhaps." She'd never let him know she planned to be part of it. Fiona turned and started for the front door, swirling around before she opened it. He was still standing in the same lazy, nonchalant way, watching her, and Fiona found it infuriating.

"I suppose you think you've won?" When the colonel cocked his head questioningly, Fiona continued. "Robert. You've finally convinced a Scot to change his mind. I wonder if you took joy in the fact that he's married to my sister."

"I have nothing to do with Robert's political views."

Her snort of disbelief made him push off from the wall and move toward her. "Believe what you like, but—"

"I shall." Fiona took an involuntary step backward, locking her knees against the weakness she felt when he looked at her like that. She swallowed. "Why should I believe anything you say?" She wished he'd stop coming toward her. "You're a liar, a blackguard, a scoundrel . . ." Fiona was running out of hateful things to call him, and his nearness, and the blue gaze that seemed to bore through her, made it difficult for her to think.

"You're not angry about Robert."

"I most certainly am. I—"

"At least that's not what has you in such a dither now."

He was so close, backing her against the door, that she could feel the heat from his body, smell the maleness of him. "I am *not* in a dither."

"Keep your voice down, or we'll have Elspeth and Robert down here wondering what the problem is."

"They know what the problem is," Fiona retorted, but she did speak more softly.

"Oh, I don't think they do. I'm not even sure you know."

Fiona's chin shot up. "Then why don't you tell me why I'm angry, if it isn't the fact that you bullied my brother-in-law into forgetting his loyalties."

"You're angry because of what happened in my room."

Fiona knew the color drained from her face, then in the next instant felt the blood rush back to stain her cheeks a vivid red. How could he mention *that!* Of course she'd thought of it. When she'd seen him standing in the doorway, undeniably handsome in his uniform, despicable as she found it, she'd very nearly expired of embarrassment. But she'd been saved by anger, righteous indignation over what he'd done. Now he'd stripped even that from her. "I hate you," she hissed, incapable of a more creative rejoinder.

"I know you do, Fiona." Zeke's breath left him in a rush. He turned away, sparing her the power of his stare, only to pierce her with heightened intensity when he looked back. "That makes it all the more difficult."

"Makes what difficult?" Fiona wanted to run, knew she should. What difference did it make if he thought her a coward? But she couldn't. Though he didn't touch her, he kept her as firmly bound to the spot as if she were chained.

"The fact that I don't hate you. Oh, don't get me wrong. I hardly find you faultless." Zeke shrugged, as if he didn't understand it himself—and he didn't. "I can't even say I particularly like you. But I do find you—" he hesitated—"intriguing, alluring."

"Don't touch me." The words came out of Fiona by rote, but pressing her cheek against his hand showed they lacked conviction. What did he mean he didn't like her?

His kiss was hardly unexpected, but knowing it was coming did not diminish the jolt it sent through her system. Before, his kisses, the touch of his lips warm and firm on hers, had turned her resolve to ashes, her bones to molten liquid. This kiss, mingled with the memory of all they'd shared, rocked the foundation of her being.

Fiona grabbed his shoulders, luxuriating in the sensation of being swept away. She moaned; he deepened the kiss. Her body molded against his—and he pushed her away.

Fiona's eyes shot open. She tried to make sense of the hands that now roughly held her arms, the face that studied her not with passion, but with a tinge of sorrow.

What had gotten into her? Now that he'd stopped kissing her, she could think. And the first thing she decided was that she'd been crazy to stand here and discuss what had happened in his room. She tried to twist away, fumbling with the latch, till he brushed her hand away and opened the door himself.

"You needn't run off," Zeke said, retrieving his hat from the hall table. "I'm leaving."

He started through the door, paused, then looked back to where Fiona stood, trying to steady her breathing. "You know what the damnable thing about this is? I can't stop thinking about you. And I can't seem to stop wanting you."

The door shut before Fiona had a chance to say anything—even if she could have thought of anything to say. He tossed her emotions around like a tempest, and then he left.

"Was that Zeke leaving?" Robert asked from the top of the stairs.

"Yes." Fiona turned, her hand fluttering to her throat. She wondered how long he'd been standing there.

"That's strange. We'd planned to leave together."

Robert's words reminded Fiona of the reason she'd come. She couldn't stand here all day daydreaming about a kiss. All things considered, it had been a colossal mistake to come.

Mumbling her good-byes for the second time, Fiona left her sister's house and rode back to the Loyalist camp.

Chapter Twelve

The Highland army began its march from Cross Creek on the morning of February eighteenth. The shrill of bagpipes, the heartbeat of drums, vibrated through Fiona's body as she sat her horse, waiting to join the long line of men, horses and wagons. Glancing at her grandfather, she wondered how he fared midst all the excitement.

He'd hardly slept at all last night; she knew that. Long past the time when the din of camp life had quieted, she'd heard the creak of the wood-framed camp cot as he tossed and turned. And more than once the wedge of tent opening spread to let in light from the dying campfires as he made his way out back to the privy. She felt certain he was having a relapse of the flux, but just as certain he'd not admit to it.

Yet now he sat tall in the saddle, the feather on his bonnet tilted at a jaunty angle, his gargot shining in the weak winter sunshine that filtered through the low-lying clouds. Even the plaid fell in gentle folds, disguising the stump of his missing arm, making him appear strong and vital. Love for him swelled in Fiona's heart. Pretending to rearrange her own plaid, draped around her head, she impatiently swiped at the moisture blurring the stream of colorful banners passing by.

" 'Tis an awesome sight, lass." Malcolm's horse whinnied and sidestepped, restless at the delay in joining the march. "It reminds me of the Hebrides, and of the times before Culloden."

"Aye," she agreed. If Malcolm noted the slight huskiness of her voice, he made no mention of it. But then, his, too, sounded more emotional than usual. A Scot's heart was still in the Highlands, remembered or imagined.

Fiona's attention shifted back to the columns of marching men. Some wore leather breeches, but most sported the colorful tartan kilt of their clan. Interspersed with the stomping feet of men came the rumble of supply wagons as they rolled along the road, churning up dust.

Her grandfather was right. The sight was awesome — and formidable. "It will be all right." Fiona didn't realize she'd voiced the sentiment till she felt her grandfather's gaze on her.

"You needn't worry, lass."

"I'm not. Not really," she amended. "General MacDonald seems optimistic."

"Aye, and he should know."

"Aye." Fiona leaned forward to pat her mount's neck as the MacClure clan eased into the march. She hadn't even tried to count the stream of men preceding her, nor could she estimate how many came behind. But certainly it was enough to intimidate the colonial militia. Certainly there would be no fighting — at least not until they joined the British troops.

But General MacDonald had been disappointed in the number of Highlanders who'd heeded the call to join the Royal Standard. Fiona hadn't been meant to hear that, she was certain, but she wasn't deaf. She'd been sitting to the back of the tent Flora MacDonald shared with her husband, supposedly talking with the older woman, when the conversation took place.

Several of General MacDonald's officers, including Flora's husband, Allen, and the MacClure laird sat hunched over a roughed-out map of the area. From the gist of the hushed discussion, Fiona gathered that a goodly number of Highlanders had stayed at their homes, ignoring even the British inducements of two hundred acres of land to enlist.

Had Colonel Kincaid influenced any of their decisions, Fiona wondered? She imagined he had. Shaking her head to dislodge the tartan, Fiona blew out a misty fog of air on a sigh.

She'd felt sorry for Colonel Kincaid when he seemed doomed to failure, had even wished him a small measure of success. But she'd never wanted his mission to make a difference. And she most assuredly hadn't wanted him to persuade members of her own clan to turn against their families.

Fiona forced thoughts of Robert and Elspeth from her mind. She hadn't told Grandfather about her visit to their home, and she had no intention of doing so. He hadn't mentioned either of them since their first night at camp, and neither had she. It simply was something she refused to think of now.

But later Fiona heard a cheer swell among the men and, squinting through the dust, she realized the army was marching down Cool Spring Road, the street where Elspeth lived. The soldier's huzzas had nothing to do with Elspeth, of course, but were caused by their sighting of Flora MacDonald sitting astride a huge white horse.

The realization that all she'd need to do would be to

lean forward in the saddle and turn her head to possibly catch a glimpse of her sister and nephew was too great a temptation for Fiona.

Even knowing she might see them didn't prepare her for the sight of them bundled in a MacClure plaid, standing on their front porch. Fiona glanced toward her grandfather, but he stared straight ahead. She might have thought he hadn't seen them; certainly anyone who knew him less well would have believed it. But Fiona recognized the expression, the stubborn tilt of his chin. He'd seen his other granddaughter, and great-grandson, but it would accomplish nothing to mention it.

Not that Fiona had any desire to discuss it. She didn't know what to think, let alone say, about her sister's desertion of the clan. But thoughts of Elspeth and little James alone in Cross Creek made her uncomfortable.

Robert would be gone, of course; he'd be with Colonel Kincaid. Rumor had the local militia with General Moore's men about seven miles from town near the Rockfish Creek bridge, blocking the most direct route to Wilmington.

By the time the Highlanders encamped for the night, they'd traveled a mere four miles, but Fiona felt as if it were four hundred.

Scouts confirmed the earlier speculation: American forces were in front of them. Continuing on one of the two roads leading from Cross Creek to Wilmington, the Brunswick Road, would result in a confrontation with the Whig forces.

Fiona ate a sparse dinner, saw to her grandfather's needs, and fell onto the narrow camp cot too sleepy to worry about what the Highlanders would do.

But the next morning Fiona watched nervously as

the troops were paraded and preparations made for a battle. Flora MacDonald, who'd accompanied her husband and son this far, rode by and, noticing Fiona standing by a rough-barked pine, dismounted.

"I'm leaving in the morning for Cross Creek, and would be glad for your company, Fiona," the Scottish heroine said.

"Though I thank you for the offer, I think I should be staying with my grandfather."

"A battle is no place for a lass such as yourself."

To herself, Fiona could only agree; she wanted to go back. It amazed her to realize how much she longed for the safety, the comfort, of Armadale. Oh, to sit in her room and stare out at the pine forest, to simply bask in the peace and quiet. How often had she taken such simple luxury for granted?

But she couldn't leave. As frightened as she was to stay, she knew fear for her grandfather would not let her return to Armadale. She thanked Flora, but assured her the decision to stay was the right one.

More than once, as she watched Flora MacDonald ride among the troops, calling encouragement to the men, Fiona was tempted to summon her back and accept her offer, but she didn't.

That afternoon, under a flag of truce, General MacDonald sent a message to the Patriot forces under General Moore. When Malcolm told Fiona its contents she nearly laughed aloud. MacDonald had enclosed a copy of Governor Martin's proclamation commanding all loyal subjects to rally to the Royal Standard, and his own belief that the men blocking the bridge were unaware of this, else they'd be with the Loyalist troops. He did allow them until noon the following day to mend the error of their ways.

Fiona could certainly imagine Ezekiel Kincaid's reaction to such a dictate if he were in General Moore's camp. But to her surprise, a messenger returned with General Moore's promise that he would discuss the governor's proclamation and General MacDonald's letter with his officers.

"They're stalling for time, hoping their reinforcements arrive," Malcolm informed his granddaughter as they took their evening meal.

"Certainly General MacDonald won't allow that."

"There's naught he can do about it. But do not worry yourself. Our main objective is to reach the coast and join the British. The general has no desire to clash with the locals."

Yet the thought of doing battle obviously had crossed General MacDonald's mind, for later that evening he called a council of his officers. When her grandfather returned to their camp, she didn't need the flurry of rumors that had flown about to tell her something was wrong. His face appeared even more drawn than usual.

" 'Tis true then, what I've heard?"

"That depends upon what it is you've heard, lass."

Refusing to be put off, Fiona followed him into the tent. "Are men from the Anson County Regiment leaving?"

"Aye!" Malcolm produced a flask from the pocket of his wool jacket and swallowed a healthy draught of whiskey. "Nearly two companies of them." He took another swig. "The filthy cowards."

"What does this mean?" Fiona sank onto the side of a cot.

"It means nothing except the miserable lot are gone, and good riddance."

"But doesn't it . . . it greatly reduce our numbers?"

"We've still enough brave Scotsmen to whip a hand-

202

ful of rabble."

"And are we going to have to—whip them, I mean?"

Malcolm lowered the flask, wiping the back of his hand across his mouth before answering. "Aye, the possibility does exist."

Fiona could not stop thinking of her grandfather's words later as she lay abed, courting a slumber that would not come. More bad news had filtered through the Loyalist camp as night had fallen. Farquard Campbell, a man whose loyalties were questionable, had arrived with word that a force of six hundred men were marching to join General Moore. Patriots seemed to be materializing from nowhere, and rallying to stop the Highlanders.

Zeke was out there too; she could feel it. And he wasn't going to let the Highlanders pass without a fight.

Fiona pulled the rough woolen blanket under her chin and shut her eyes, trying to pretend she didn't long for the smooth linen and cozy quilts of home. Somewhere in the camp a piper, perhaps as homesick and scared as she, played a mournful tune.

What would tomorrow bring? The Highlanders and the Patriots seemed at an impasse, and she could see no way out but to do battle. And there would be people hurt. She wasn't so concerned for herself, but the thought of something happening to those she loved terrified her.

Her grandfather was so vulnerable, and if she knew him at all, he'd be right in the thick of any fighting. And there was Duncan. For all their squabbles of late, she cared for him. And Uncle Angus. And William. And Zeke.

Fiona's eyes shot open, and she stared unseeing at the eerie shadows dancing upon the tent walls. Why had she included Zeke in a list of those she loved? All right, she admitted to herself, she didn't like the idea of his being hurt. But that didn't mean she loved him.

"Yet you made love with him," a little voice in her head whispered, and Fiona groaned aloud. Listening to make certain she hadn't awakened her grandfather, whose even breathing she could hear from across the tent, Fiona tried to banish thoughts of Zeke from her mind. But he wouldn't leave; like the piper's soulful tune, he haunted her. And as dawn pearled the horizon and she fell into a fitful slumber, Fiona had almost convinced herself she hated him for it.

By noon, when General Moore's reply arrived, Fiona knew there would be no battle — at least not this day. Not that the Patriot general had backed down. To the contrary, he reported that his officers unanimously agreed that they could not join the Loyalist forces and assured him that they considered their actions in defense of the liberties of mankind.

However, General MacDonald decided a strategic retreat was in order. Thus, the following morning the Loyalist army retraced their path to Cross Creek, crossed the Cape Fear at Campbell Town, and started for the coast along the Negro Head Point Road.

It sounded simple enough, and Fiona supposed it was, but that did nothing to alleviate the constant discomfort she felt. A damp chill seeped through her clothing and into her bones, and she wondered if she'd ever be truly warm again. She tried to convince herself that she was young and healthy — that it was her grandfather's comfort rather than her own that should concern her. And it did.

Fiona did all she could to keep the laird as dry, warm, and comfortable as possible, but she couldn't help wishing they were both safe at Armadale.

Still, the fact that there'd been no battle greatly cheered her, even when she had to clench her teeth to keep them from chattering. According to the scouts, one of whom was Duncan, the Highlanders' abrupt march had caught General Moore unaware. He'd expected an attack, was prepared for it, and hadn't even realized till the next day that the Loyalists had escaped.

General Moore wasn't likely to follow, either, Fiona thought with a smug smile, as she ladled a watery stew from the kettle onto her grandfather's plate. General MacDonald had ordered the destruction of all the boats the Highlanders had used to cross the Cape Fear.

Pushing aside the tent opening, Fiona carried the food in to her grandfather. She shook her head when she saw him sitting on the side of his cot. "Ach, and didn't you promise me you'd stay in bed today and get some rest?"

"I'm on the damn cot now, aren't I, lass?" Malcolm continued grumbling as Fiona bundled some bedding to form a bolster, then pushed him back.

"Here, eat this." Fiona handed him the unappetizing stew, vowing to listen the next time she was offered cooking instructions.

Her grandfather's narrow-eyed inspection of the runny brown liquid shimmering with grease had her amending her vow. She'd seek out help for her culinary talents.

"How goes progress with the bridge?" Malcolm took a bite.

"Uncle Angus stopped by while you were sleeping. He said that it will be ready for the wagons to cross tomorrow."

"Good. We shall show the local rebels that we can

not only out-fight them, we can outwit them as well."

Fiona's smile mirrored her grandfather's. Uncomfortable as she was, she couldn't help being hopeful. The Highland army was proceeding toward the coast. Perhaps they traveled a bit slowly because of the need to repair bridges and the worry of ambush, but that allowed more time for her grandfather to rest.

Fiona's spirits sank on February twenty-third as they approached Corbet's ferry only to receive word the enemy was encamped there. The army halted, formed battle units, and marched forward—to discover the Patriots were on the far side of the river.

General MacDonald moved his army farther down the river, built a bridge and crossed unimpeded. Again, Fiona gave a sigh of relief, and the Highland army continued their march to the sea.

Now the general seemed to push the men for greater speed. Duncan told Fiona one evening that they were trying to beat Colonel Caswell, a leader of the Patriot forces they'd come close to fighting before crossing the river, to Moore's Creek Bridge. "He's on his way to reinforce your old friend," Duncan said, tossing his just-cleaned knife into the sandy soil around the campfire. He watched the hilt quiver for an instant, then looked back to meet Fiona's eyes. "Don't you want to know who I mean?"

Fiona straightened her back and didn't evade his gaze, though the expression of hatred on his face made her long to turn away. "I assume we're discussing Colonel Kincaid."

"That's right, Fiona. That no-good son of a bitch is there with the militia. And we're going to destroy them."

"General MacDonald doesn't want a fight."

"Ah, but he's not going to be able to avoid this one.

We need to get over that creek, and there's no other way." Duncan rose, walked around the campfire, and leaned toward Fiona. "But you needn't worry, Fiona. We'll beat Caswell to the bridge and then we'll annihilate the militia — and their leaders. After all" — Duncan patted her cheek and Fiona tried not to flinch — "that's what we all want, isn't it?"

That night Fiona dreamed of Zeke. To her annoyance, this was nothing new. But instead of the sensual mist that usually surrounded these nocturnal journeys into her subconscious, Fiona found herself fighting through a thick gray fog. It enveloped her, but not in the pleasurable way it usually did. Though she couldn't see him, couldn't see anything, she knew he was near. His scent surrounded her. But again it wasn't the same. He called to her, his voice as low and exciting as always, but tinged with a sadness, a pain she couldn't understand.

She tripped, stumbled to her knees, then saw him lying on the ground waiting for her. In her dream she forgot guilt, forgot propriety. She wanted to lie with him again. Wanted to feel the weight of his body pressing hers. Wanted to know again the magic his hands and mouth could do. Wanted to tingle with anticipation, soar through the heavens, tumble gently back to his arms.

But when she snuggled down beside him, he didn't rouse her with passion. She pulled on him, wrapping her arms around his shoulders, his head, feeling passion rise within her despite his lack of response. And then she saw it. Blood. Bright crimson, it streamed from his head, from the thick waves of his dark, silky hair. And she screamed. And screamed.

Fiona gulped in air, felt the gentle rocking, and knew that she was in her grandfather's arms. "Shhh now, lass. 'Tis all right it will be. Was only a bit of a nightmare you've been having. And who can blame you?"

She let herself be lulled, let her grandfather treat her just as he'd done when she'd lost her parents. But she felt guilty for, as he droned on about it being perfectly natural for her to have bad dreams, with all that was going on, she knew he thought her afraid. She was. But he thought her afraid for herself, or him, her clan. How could she tell him she feared for Zeke Kincaid — the enemy?

Fiona's last hope that a battle could be averted died when she heard of General MacDonald's illness. His inability to lead made an opening for younger, more aggressive officers to push for an offensive.

At one o'clock in the morning the Highlander army began a six-mile forced march toward the Widow Moore's Bridge — and the Whig army.

Fiona refused to stay behind. The arguments her grandfather put up did no good, nor did his attempts to order obedience.

"Leave me and I shall follow," she said while tying the strings of her cloak under her chin. "At least with you I am safe, but if I must travel on my own . . . who knows what may happen?"

"You are too stubborn for your own good, Mary Fiona. And foolish. Don't I have enough to worry about with the clan, and the Whigs? Must I have an obstinate, rebellious, insubordinate lass to devil me also?"

"Apparently so. Don't forget your plaid. There's a decided chill in the air tonight."

Though the laird refused to speak to her, refused to even acknowledge her presence, Fiona was glad for his sake she'd refused to stay behind with the ill general.

The ride was harder—harder than any she'd endured to this point. At night, unfamiliar with the terrain, the army quickly became bogged down in the swampy ground. Often during the long, drizzly night they had to stop so that the supply wagons could be pulled from the mire.

Near dawn the dying campfires of the Whig army were spotted and, as the Loyalists divided into three columns for the surprise attack, Fiona did agree to stay behind with the supply wagons. Unable to rest, she paced along the line of wagons, stopping here to touch the velvet nose of a horse, there to run her hand along another's flank. But always listening, anticipating the staccato report of gunfire.

So intent was she upon listening for that particular sound, she almost missed the galloping hooves and the voice of the messenger sent back to camp.

" 'Twas a trick," he yelled, and before Fiona realized what she was doing she'd run over to where the man conferred with the sergeant who had been left in charge of the wagons.

"What is it? What's happened?" she asked, ignoring the sergeant's startled expression.

"That snake Caswell wasn't where he was supposed to be. He and Kincaid moved across the creek, leaving their campfires burning so's we'd think they was all sleeping like babes." The messenger seemed to have no qualms about telling his tale to anyone who'd listen.

Secretly Fiona thought this a rather clever trick; it was probably Zeke Kincaid's idea. But the messenger's next words, spoken around a stream of tobacco, pushed that thought from her mind. "They're getting ready to attack the bridge."

"But isn't that dangerous?" Her question sounded so naive that Fiona cringed.

"Sure as hell is. Pardon me, ma'am." The messenger made a crude attempt at a bow, though Fiona hardly noticed his cursing, or his attempt to make amends for it. "What I'm meaning is, those damn Whigs done took the planks off the damn thing. Nothing but the sleepers left."

"Then how —" Fiona began, but the messenger had already remounted and started back toward the impending battle. The sergeant seemed unwilling to enlighten her as he turned back to check a harness, so Fiona continued to wander on her own.

Her grandfather had told her Moore's Creek was about fifty feet wide at the bridge, and that the swampy waters below were nearly five feet deep. How could the Loyalists cross the creek?

The eerie sound of cheers floated through the misty predawn air, and Fiona strained to hear more. Drums began pounding, pipes shrilled, and she clutched her cape tightly to stop her shivering. It didn't seem to help; nothing did, until she heard the rifle shots. She started, feeling almost as if the guns were shooting at her, and let out the breath she'd been holding. For good or ill, it had begun.

Fiona had no idea how long she stood in the middle of the marshy road, surrounded by pine forests, listening, trying not to think of what was happening. But it couldn't have been long.

It was barely light when the first men burst through the trees, ignoring her as they ran for the supply wagons. At first it was just a few; then more, some wounded and straggling behind, yet all intent on their flight, came from the direction of the bridge.

"What happened? What's going on?" She grabbed first one soldier, then another, but no one answered. Yet she didn't really need their words to tell her the

210

battle was going poorly for the Loyalists. The shock on their faces, their general appearance — so different from the confident Highlanders who'd ridden from Cross Creek with regimental banners waving — spoke eloquently.

Moving slowly, against the tide of men now streaming past her, Fiona searched for her grandfather. Artillery sounded and the ground trembled. Fiona fought to keep her footing, fearful she'd be trampled if she fell, but it never occurred to her to stop, not until she felt herself grabbed from behind. "Fiona! What in the hell are you doing?"

"Duncan. Thank God." She sagged against her cousin. He smelled of gunpowder and fear, and she pulled back to stare into his blackened face. "Where's Grandfather?"

He looked away. "I don't know."

"You don't know?" Fiona could feel her voice rising, though she could hardly hear her own words over the din of battle. "You told me you'd watch out for him. You said—"

"Damnit, Fiona. There was no chance. They were waiting for us. The last I saw him he was trying to rally some of our clan. But it was no use. They mowed us down like hay." Duncan shook his head, then grabbed Fiona's shoulders. "We have to get out of here. They've forded the creek and are attacking from the rear. There's no telling when they—Damnit, Fiona, what are you doing?"

"I'm not going." Fiona batted at his hands, struggling to pull away from him.

"Did you not hear a word I've said?" Duncan bent over her, his face close, the abrasive quality of his question impossible to miss.

"I heard." Fiona wrenched free. "I'm going after

Grandfather."

"Are you crazy? You'll never find him. Besides, he's probably already dead."

Fiona didn't bother to reply. She had no more time to waste on Duncan. She thought she heard him call her name as she wriggled through the retreating line of men, but she couldn't be certain, with all the noise around her. She didn't look back.

The terrain sloped downward, the pine trees became more sparse, and more wounded littered the spongy ground. Dashing from one prone figure to another, Fiona began to think Duncan was right, that she'd never find her grandfather. There were simply too many. Then a breeze shifted the haze of gunsmoke, and she saw him leaning against a tree trunk.

"Grandfather." Fiona ran to him, sinking down in the mud beside him. She grabbed his hand, rubbing it frantically between hers, sobbing with relief when he opened his eyes. She dropped his hand, her eyes, then her fingers, searching for his wound. He was covered in dirt and blood, and it took her precious time to find the hole in his side. He groaned when she touched it—a weak, defeated sound that tore at her heart and spurred her to action.

"Can you stand?" Fiona finished tying the strip of petticoat around him, and tried prying his shoulders away from the tree.

"Don't. Leave me here, lass, and go." Malcolm resisted her efforts to get him standing.

"Come on and try, damn you." Fiona wriggled her shoulder beneath his and pulled, sweat dampening the bodice of her gown as she strained against his weight.

"No use. Listen."

Fiona paused more for breath than to follow his order. She cocked her head to one side, hearing the low,

212

sad song of a mourning dove above the moans of the wounded. "There's nothing to hear. Now raise your arm." Again she strained to pull him erect.

"The guns have stopped. They'll be coming." Malcolm tried to push his granddaughter away.

"Then you . . . better get up," Fiona grunted. "Because I'm not leaving without you."

"Stubborn, stubborn Fiona." Mustering a small reserve of strength, and using Fiona and his broadsword as props, Malcom pushed himself up.

She'd never have guessed he could be so heavy. His weight nearly tumbled her forward, but Fiona stiffened her knees and moved toward the throng of men heading back to the supply wagons. She'd get her grandfather to one, and then drive him back to Cross Creek—or better yet—to Armadale. They could take care of him there, and they'd be safe. Everything would be all right. She'd make sure—

Gunshots again pierced the morning air, but these were close—too close. Fiona glanced behind her, almost stumbling over her skirt, to see mounted Whig soldiers riding toward the retreating men. Without thinking, using only an inborn sense of self-preservation, she veered into the thick underbrush to her left. They did fall then, tumbling down a small incline to land in a marshy area covered with tall grasses. But at least they were out of sight of the Patriots.

Fiona rolled her grandfather onto his back, motioned for him to stay quiet, then inched her way up the slope. Most of the retreating Loyalists had thrown down their arms, if they still possessed them, and were surrendering to the Whigs. Resting her forehead against her arm, Fiona breathed in the peaty decaying smell of the swamp and gave a sigh of relief. At least she'd spared her grandfather that.

They stayed in the hiding place till late afternoon, till she could no longer see or hear any activity from the Whigs. Her grandfather's wound had started bleeding again, so Fiona tore off more of her petticoat to make a fresh bandage. Then she pestered the laird till he agreed to rise, and again they stumbled forward, one painful step at a time.

By nightfall, amid a thicket of pines she found a small shed with a meandering stream nearby. She had no idea whose it was or what it was used for, nor did she care. She gave a prayer of thanks for the shelter and helped her grandfather onto a bed of pine needles she'd gathered.

The small fire she started with the flint in her grandfather's knapsack produced more smoke than heat, but she couldn't worry about the lack of a chimney. The cleaning of the encrusted blood and dirt from her grandfather's wound proved too much for him, and he passed out.

After wrapping him in his plaid and her cloak, Fiona slid down on the packed dirt. Deciding she couldn't do anything until morning, Fiona leaned her head against the rough boards. She clutched her grandfather's clayborn and began her lonely vigil.

Chapter Thirteen

"Sorry to be bothering you, Colonel sir, but . . ."

Zeke rubbed a hand across eyes weary from listing the spoils of the battle. Dropping a very dull quill onto the makeshift desk, he looked up. "What is it, Sergeant Simpson?"

"Well, I know you said not to bother you for a while, and I wouldn't, except . . ."

Leaning back on the stool, Zeke rolled his shoulders, trying to loosen the kink that had been steadily growing for the past two hours. He couldn't remember ever being so tired, but then he imagined everyone was. He'd marched his men hard to get them here in time to fortify the bridge. Then they'd spent several days—and nights—digging earthworks. And this morning, before dawn, they'd been awake, alert for the attack that came. Since then there'd been the rounding up of prisoners and supplies, the caring for the wounded, and now this report he was writing for the Provincial Congress.

They'd be happy about the rifles and shot bags, swords and dirks the Whig army had captured. And then there'd been the two medicine chests straight from England that had fallen into their hands—

Robert had been especially pleased by that. He wasn't so sure what Congress would do about the large number of prisoners they'd taken.

General Moore had put him in charge of escorting them to Wilmington—After that, Zeke didn't know what the Patriots planned to do with them.

Standing, Zeke realized the sergeant still hadn't stated his reason for entering the tent. "What's the problem, Sergeant?"

"Well, sir, there's this prisoner who insists upon seeing you. Now, I told him you was busy and all that, but—"

"Does this prisoner have a name?" Searching through his knapsack for a candle, Zeke lit it with the sputtering remains of the one on his desk.

"MacClure. Says he's Angus MacClure. Says he knows you."

"He does." When Sergeant Simpson had first said MacClure, Zeke had felt a surge of emotion. It was irrational to think of Fiona now—he knew that—but that's what his first thought had been. He sat down on the stool, stretching his legs forward in the cramped space. "I'll see him. Oh, Sergeant," Zeke called out before the other man dropped the tent flap, "he's not wounded, is he?" So many of the Scots were wounded and dying, victims of their brave but foolish storm across the bridge.

Zeke rubbed his hand over his jaw, not even noticing the three-days' growth of bristly whiskers. The bridge had been a perfect place to stop the Highlander army. He'd known that even before studying the map, even before his scouts informed him the Loyalists were heading that way. He'd traveled the area often, knew the swampy terrain that would force the enemy to funnel toward that one narrow bridge.

He'd counted on their coming to this point, pushing

his men to the limits of their endurance to fortify the area. When Callis arrived, first camping on the far side of the creek, the unfordable water at their backs, Zeke had sent word for him and his men to cross the bridge and join the militia behind their earthworks. Zeke even had the bridge dismantled, the sleepers stripped of bark and slicked with grease and tallow. His men had made the bridge unpassable; they'd forced the Highlanders' hand. Zeke had expected either retreat or battle, but he hadn't expected what had happened.

This morning the Scots, spurred on by the shrill call of bagpipes, assailed the bridge. By twos, they'd tried to cross what was left of the structure, using their broadswords thrust into the slippery logs to assist their progress. But they'd struggled across the sleepers only to meet their death. The Scots, for all their fierce determination, had been no match for the dead-eyed Patriots waiting for them.

Sergeant Simpson stuck his head back inside the tent. "He's not wounded so's I could tell. But if he didn't stop yowling for you, I was going to see what I could do about it."

Zeke grinned for the first time that day, and set about sharpening a new point on his quill. So Angus had given Sergeant Simpson a hard time. Zeke shook his head. That didn't seem like Angus. He'd been very mild-mannered when Zeke had met him last summer—at least compared to most of the other Scots. He'd certainly been nothing like his son, Duncan. Zeke shook his head again when he heard the commotion outside his tent. Battles—losing battles—appeared to change people.

"Get yourself in there and settle down, or I'm a-going to have to use this on you." Sergeant Simpson waved his beefy fist under the Highlander's nose be-

217

fore giving him a shove. "Now you behave, 'cause I'll be right outside with this." He patted the stock of his Brown Bess.

"I don't think it will be necessary to use that, Sergeant." Zeke glanced down at his pistol, primed and ready, lying next to the parchment on his desk. He could handle Angus if the need arose. Hell, he could take care of him without the gun. But he didn't think he'd have to.

The Angus that barged into his tent bore little resemblance to the quiet man Zeke had discussed politics with this summer. He was dirty, his clothes matted with dried mud, and wild-eyed, his voice rough from a combination of gunsmoke and yelling.

"What have you done with Malcolm?" he demanded without preamble.

Zeke raised a brow questioningly, then motioned toward the stool on the opposite side of the desk. Angus ignored the gesture.

Zeke's initial reaction was surprise—not only that Angus would accuse him of doing something with the laird, but that the older man had come with the army at all. But then, knowing the MacClure, he thought the man probably didn't consider advanced age and a missing arm sufficient reasons to stay home.

Zeke studied Angus for a moment, taking in the dirt-tarnished kilt and torn jacket. Again he indicated the chair, and this time Angus sank into it heavily.

"Now. Would you care to explain what you're talking about?" Zeke began. "Is Malcolm one of the prisoners?"

"No. I've looked through them pretty good, and he's not there."

"Well, then, I assume he escaped." His men had returned just before nightfall with a large group of Highlanders who'd managed to flee the scene, but

Zeke was not so foolish as to think they'd captured all of them.

"I saw him fall," Angus insisted. " 'Twas impossible for me to get to him, but I could tell he was hurt badly."

Zeke tried to ignore the pity he felt for the once-proud warrior who didn't know when to stop fighting. But he couldn't explain what had happened to him any more than Angus could. "I'd be willing to bet he isn't among the wounded, or the dead." Robert had reported to him not over an hour ago. He'd certainly have mentioned it if his wife's grandfather was among the wounded. And Zeke himself had supervised the gruesome task of identifying the dead.

"Then I cannot imagine what has happened to him." Angus leaned forward, his grizzled head resting heavily in his hands. "Unless . . ." Angus raised his head, a spark of hope brightening his eyes. "Unless Fiona—"

"Fiona!" Zeke's body jerked upright, his knee knocking against the table leg. "What does she have to do with any of this?" Zeke didn't realize how loud and aggressive he'd been until he saw the startled expression on Angus's face.

"I was just thinking that perhaps she managed to get the laird away. She—"

"How in the hell could she do that?" Zeke stood, looming over the captured Scot and waiting for an answer—fearing he already knew.

"She came with the army."

"Damn her!" Zeke's palm smashed down on the wobbly table, sending the candle flying to the packed earth-floor.

Retrieving the still-lit candle, Angus set it back in place and studied the Whig colonel as he paced the confines of the tent. "She came along to aid the Mac-Clure. None of us approved, but there didn't seem to be much . . . Well, you know Fiona when her mind is set."

He knew her, all right, though at this moment he fervently wished he didn't. Zeke raked fingers through his disheveled hair and took a deep breath, trying to get himself under control. Though he felt like ramming his fist through something, he doubted that would do much good. He'd save his bottled-up hostility for when he found that redheaded she-devil.

Zeke turned on Angus. "Where would she go? Does she have any family close, any friends?"

Slowly Angus shook his head. "Nay, none that I can recall. But even if she did, I think she'd try to get home, to Armadale."

"Well, Armadale is a hell of a ways from here. And you did say the laird was wounded."

"Aye." Angus hung his head again.

"Sergeant!" Zeke bellowed for the man, who popped his head inside the tent moments later.

"Right here, Colonel."

"Take the prisoner back and pack me some supplies. I'll need a few days' ration and an extra blanket."

"What are you planning to do?" Angus asked, trying to get the colonel's attention.

Zeke straightened from reaching for his musket where it stood in the corner. He'd tried to warn her, to show her where her impetuous actions would lead her. Hell, he'd even made love to her in the process. But he'd never envisioned her doing something like this. Just the thought of her marching with the Loyalist army, or out there somewhere in the dark, made his jaw clench. She was foolish and a damn nuisance. And he could not stop himself from going after her. "I'm going to find her . . . them," he amended quickly.

Four hours later, as the first traces of dawn streaked the sky, Zeke was doing just that. Mounted on a chestnut, he rode out of camp. As anxious as he'd been to start searching for Fiona and her grandfather, Zeke had realized he'd never find any sign of them at night. Besides, he'd needed the time to question his soldiers and the prisoners. He'd moved among them, hating to jostle them awake, but needing answers.

Finally he'd found a man, one of Colonel Crewel's troops, who'd thought he'd seen a woman on the battlefield. "Yeah," he'd mumbled, still groggy from sleep, when Zeke had pressed him. "A woman with curly red hair."

Anger had surged within Zeke, and he'd strode to Colonel Crewel's tent, waking him also. The colonel had agreed to wait until the following day to begin the march to Wilmington. "It will probably take us at least that long to sort through this mess, anyway," he'd said, sitting on the edge of his cot and rubbing large-jointed hands over his face. "But, Colonel Kincaid," he'd said, looking up and blinking at the lantern Zeke held, "shouldn't you take some men with you? We've rounded up quite a few Tories, but I'd be willing to bet there's more out there. They'll be desperate, and they won't take kindly to a militia officer riding about alone."

"I'll be careful," Zeke had assured him, but as he eased his horse off Negro Head Point Road, caution was the last thing on his mind. Mist, eerie in the early gray dawn, billowed around his mount's withers as Zeke leaned forward, trying to find any sign of Fiona.

He'd crossed the creek at the ford Callis's men had found during the battle, and followed the road toward Cross Creek for a few miles. Deciding that if she'd gone that way, the militia would probably have picked her up, he'd turned back toward the battlefield. Since then he'd systematically worked his way back toward the spot where the Loyalists had begun their attack.

But searching the swampy area of hollies and live oaks proved difficult. The underbrush ran thick, and if something had happened to her — if she were lying somewhere hurt — Zeke knew he could ride right past her without even knowing.

He sat up in the saddle, straining his eyes, hoping to see something. So intent was he that he almost missed the change in smell as the wind shifted. Luckily his subconscious mind registered the whispery scent, and in the next instant, Zeke twisted toward the faint odor of burning wood.

Ten minutes later he found the ramshackle wooden structure in the small clearing. By now the sky had become a dull pewter gray, allowing enough light for Zeke to make a quick perusal of the shack. It was small, windowless, and he imagined it was used as a storage shed for hunters or trappers.

A lazy haze hung above the roof. Since he saw no sign of a chimney, Zeke imagined there must be at least one hole in the roof to allow the smoke to escape. Someone was inside. But who? He hoped it was Fiona and her grandfather. But reality forced him to admit it was most likely some Loyalist stragglers from General MacDonald's men. Dismounting, Zeke reached into his saddlebag for his pistol, checked it, and made his way toward the single door.

Fiona's head bobbed forward, the movement waking her with a start. She'd fallen asleep — again. Glancing across the smoky space between them, she saw her grandfather. He lay much as he had the last time she'd looked. Through most of the night she'd alternately tried to force water down him and dampened his burning forehead with another section of petticoat. He was still, and Fiona anxiously watched his chest for movement. She sighed when she saw it, and leaned back against the rough boards.

She should get up and check his bandage, Fiona told herself. She would in just a moment. The wound had stopped bleeding during the night, and there didn't seem to be any sign that it had started again. Still, she should check.

Fiona pulled up her legs, barely suppressing a moan as her cold, stiff muscles protested. Sucking in her breath, she clutched the broadsword hilt tighter and closed her eyes. Would she even be able to move, let alone get her grandfather to safety?

The next moment she had the answer to the first part of that question.

As a scream of fright stuck in her throat, Fiona jumped to her feet, clutching the heavy sword, when the door splintered open.

His pistol leveled, Zeke stepped through the door he'd just kicked in. He squinted, trying to make out shapes in the murky interior. What he saw made him freeze in his tracks.

For long moments they stared at each other, their eyes locked, their weapons ready. All the anger Zeke had felt since learning of Fiona's latest escapade evaporated as he saw an expression of relief flash across her face. He wanted to go to her, to take her in his arms and tell her everything would be all right. But now she looked at him with fear, and as he glanced down her tattered dress he noticed the broadsword, pointed threateningly at his chest.

The realization that she held a weapon made Zeke notice the aggressive aim of his pistol. Slowly he lowered it to his side, arching his brow questioningly when she did not do the same. "Do you intend to run me through, Fiona?"

Fiona shook her head slowly, but seemed unable to make herself move other than that. When she'd first recognized Zeke, she'd known a wild surge of relief.

He hadn't been hurt during the battle! She hadn't even understood the niggling worry that had pulled at her — worry for him — until she saw him standing before her.

But now that she knew him safe, new worries assailed her. Even with the pistol lowered he looked dark and dangerous. The dim light made his hair, unbrushed and windblown, appear almost black. Dark whiskers camouflaged his rugged jaw, hiding the dimples and making his mouth appear hard and unyielding.

He was the enemy. Fiona had to remember that, no matter how glad she was to see him safe. But she let loose her hold on the clayborn and heard it hit the dirt with a dull thud.

She thought he might come to her then — a small moment of truce between the battles — but he didn't. A low moan from her grandfather caught his attention, and he moved toward the laird. Before he knelt beside him, Zeke whipped off his cape and tossed it to Fiona. "Put this on."

The gruffness of his command hurt. Fiona came very close to throwing it back at him, but she was so cold. When she wrapped the dark blue wool around herself, the warmth and smell of him flooded her senses.

Zeke didn't know much about wounds, but he'd bet Malcolm MacClure was in pretty bad shape. For one thing, his forehead felt on fire. "How long has this fever been on him?"

"Since last night." Fiona knelt down beside the colonel at her grandfather's head. Maybe he had no feelings for her, but the colonel respected her grandfather — he'd told her so. And he did seem willing to help him. That, not hurt feelings, had to be Fiona's first concern. "I've been trying to keep him warm."

Zeke had noticed the laird was wrapped in both his plaid and Fiona's cloak. That was one of the reasons he'd given her his. That and the fact that she'd looked so damned small and vulnerable standing there with the huge sword lying at her feet. He'd been afraid if he'd taken her in his arms, warmed her the way he longed to, he'd never have done the things he knew needed to be done.

Peeling away the plaid, Zeke noticed fresh red blood brightening the rusty stain caked on the bandage. Fiona must have noticed it, too, for she brushed her fingertips across the laird's cheek and sighed. "I thought the bleeding had stopped."

"We need something else to use as a bandage." Zeke leaned back and searched through his pockets.

"No, wait. I've . . . I've been using my petticoat."

Zeke could swear he saw a blush creep over her wind-chapped face, was sure of it when she stood and turned her back on him to tear off a strip of relatively clean cotton from under her skirts. He wanted to tell her that her modesty was misplaced—he'd seen, touched, caressed, far more of her than he was likely to glimpse now. But he didn't.

She seemed to want—to need—to pretend they'd never allowed their passions to rule their judgment. He would give her that—for now.

Watching as Zeke wadded up a piece of cotton and pressed it into the hole in her grandfather's flesh, Fiona sank back down on the cold ground. The colonel seemed to know what he was doing. After he'd tied another, longer, strip around her grandfather's side, Fiona could restrain her curiosity no longer. "Why are you here?"

Zeke pulled the MacClure plaid, its red and black checks nearly obscured by blood and dirt, back over the laird and rested his arm across the bend of his knee. Leveling Fiona a look she didn't shy away from returning, he answered, "You didn't think I'd leave you out here, did you?"

"But how did you know?" She wasn't sure if he referred to her or her grandfather, but his words, the power of his stare, made her feel warm inside. Fiona fought the urge to lean into him.

"Angus told me."

"Uncle Angus?" When could the colonel have spoken with him, unless—

"He's one of our prisoners."

"I see." Fiona glanced toward the glowing embers of the small fire. "Is he . . . is he all right?"

Zeke's nod released the breath Fiona didn't realize she held. She wanted to ask him of the others, of Duncan and William—but she didn't think this was the time. Besides, she had to concentrate on her own problems. And right now the main one was getting her grandfather to safety. Her eyes met the colonel's. "Angus told you about grandfather and you—"

"He also told me about you." Zeke found his anger building again.

Fiona sensed it, knew that it was directed at her, but chose to ignore it. "So you came to help us?"

Zeke stood, not bothering to brush the dirt from his already filthy breeches. "I guess that's about it."

Hope bloomed within her. She wasn't going to have to do this alone. "Do you have a horse?" Of course he'd have a horse. No one—except someone as desperate as she—would wander around here without a horse. But Fiona was too overwhelmed with gratitude to think about what she said.

"He's tied up near the edge of the clearing."

"If we can get grandfather up on him, it should only take us a day or two to reach Cross Creek. Then we could get a wagon and head for Armadale. We might even be able to find a farmer's wagon before Cross Creek. That would be so much more comfortable for him, and—" Fiona had rambled away so steadily that she hadn't noticed Zeke's lack of response till he interrupted her.

"We aren't going to Armadale."

"What?" Fiona stood, but he still towered over her.

"You heard me, Fiona. I'm not taking you to Armadale. For one thing, the laird would never make—"

"Where are you taking us?" Panic laced her words.

"Back to camp."

"As prisoners?"

"Fiona, listen." Zeke raked his hands back through his hair in exasperation. "That's the closest place where your grandfather can get medical help, and he needs it badly."

"But we'd be prisoners." Fiona's voice was shrill and she didn't wait for his confirming nod to leap toward the broadsword lying in the dirt at her grandfather's feet. Her hand touched the cold steel of the engraved hilt, but before she could tighten her fingers, the metal flew out of her reach, kicked by the colonel's boot.

A heavy weight crushed onto her, flattened her, pushing her cheek into the gritty dirt and stealing the breath from her body. Fiona felt herself jerked around and forced to look into the colonel's dark, angry face. He straddled her hips and glared at her with such intensity that she couldn't think to fill her lungs.

"What were you doing, Fiona?"

His words, and the angry shake he gave her shoulders, forced her to gasp for air.

"I asked what you were doing? Were you planning to use that sword on me?" Zeke shook her again when she continued to stare at him in mute disbelief. "Well, were you?"

"I don't know," Fiona whispered, the best she could do with his accusing eyes riveting her.

"You don't know," Zeke repeated in disbelief. "Well, the next time you reach for a weapon, you better damn well know what you plan to do with it." Zeke tried to take a calming breath, to gain control of his anger, but he was having a difficult time. When he'd realized what she planned to do—a split second before she dove for the sword—he'd felt anger, and something else—betrayal—greater than he'd never known before.

He'd worried about her all night, had shifted his responsibilities to someone else so that he could search this infernal marsh for her, and how did she show her gratitude? She was going to slice him up with a broadsword rather than let him get her grandfather some help.

All because of some misguided sense of heroism.

"I . . . I didn't want to hurt you." Fiona looked up at Zeke, hoping he'd believe her. She hadn't had any plan in mind when she grabbed for the sword. Threaten him—that's all she would have done—she was certain of that. How could she hurt him, when she'd been so concerned for his safety?

"You didn't want to—" Zeke stared down at her in disbelief. He loosened his hold on her wrists, because he sensed he might be hurting her, then stretched them high above her head, but he didn't let go. "What do you think a sword does but hurt, Fiona? It isn't like a candlestick."

"I didn't mean for that to happen." Fiona's voice was little more than a sob. She felt so vulnerable stretched out beneath him. Her skirts had flown up when he'd tackled her, and she could feel the cold dirt beneath her thighs.

"That's the problem, Fiona. You never mean for things to happen."

"You keep pushing me till—"

"Pushing *you!* You think I push you?" Air hissed from between Zeke's clenched teeth.

"No." How could she have said something so stupid? She was simply so scared.

"You're damned right I haven't. Every mess you've gotten yourself into has been of your own making. And I've been damn patient about all of them. Most men would have—"

"Why?"

"Why what?" She'd all of a sudden started looking at him with the strangest expression in her violet eyes, and Zeke was having a difficult time holding onto his anger.

"Why have you been so patient?"

Her question, asked in the softest of tones, seemed to startle him. He looked almost as if he couldn't comprehend what she'd asked. Fiona decided to elaborate. "I know I've caused you problems, breaking into your room—twice," she added. "And now this, but I only did it to help my grandfather, and I'd do it again; but it caused you trouble, and I really don't know why you—"

She'd thought his lips looked hard surrounded by the growth of beard, but they felt soft and sensual when he pressed them to hers. Even the whiskers, so dark and foreboding, tingled and abraded in the most pleasurable way. He let go of her wrists, and Fiona wrapped her arms around his neck as he stretched out beside her. His tongue sought hers, but Fiona could tell he kept his passion leashed, not allowing the full power of it to take control. She didn't know if she were glad or not. She just knew that he was holding her as she'd longed for him to do since he'd burst into the shed.

Zeke raised his head, then brushed his lips over hers

again. "Does that explain it?"

Stunned by his kiss and her reaction to it, Fiona searched the depths of his blue eyes. "Not entirely," she breathed.

He nodded, tracing her bottom lip with the pad of his thumb. "I don't understand it completely myself. But that doesn't change the fact that I'm taking your grandfather back to the Patriot camp." Zeke shifted, throwing his leg across hers. "Now stop wriggling and listen to me. The laird's in bad shape. You have to know that. He'd never make it farther than camp. Hell, I'm not even sure he'll make it that far. And we have plenty of medical provisions." Zeke didn't add that they had them thanks to the Loyalists.

Fighting his weight was impossible, so Fiona stopped trying, but she continued to glare at him as he explained what they would do. When he'd finished, she asked, "What's going to happen to my grandfather?"

"I don't know," Zeke answered honestly. "But he's an old man, and he's wounded. I can't imagine the Provincial Congress will be too hard on him. They'll probably parole him."

Fiona sighed. "He's not going to like this. He doesn't like to surrender."

"That seems to be something he has in common with his granddaughter." Zeke reached down for Fiona's hand after getting to his feet. "Now I want you to behave yourself, because whether you believe it or not, going back to camp is the best thing for him."

Not liking to admit it, but conceding to herself, at least, that Zeke was right, Fiona gave him her hand. Her grandfather probably couldn't make it far in his condition. But when he'd recovered, she'd see him home to Armadale. "What do you want me to do?"

Picking up the claymore—just to be on the safe

side—Zeke started toward the shattered door. "Just keep him warm, and see if he'll drink some water. I'm going to rig up some sort of litter."

It took Zeke the better part of an hour to fashion two poles from pine saplings, lashing them together with woven vines. Then he draped the extra blanket he'd brought over the poles and attached them to the stirrups.

"Do you think this will work?" Fiona asked, moving around the front of the horse and patting his nose.

"It should." Zeke pulled on the litter, testing its strength. "We don't have far to go." Then he looked up at her.

"What are you grinning at?"

"You." The sun had risen above the tree line, throwing splashes of dappled light across the clearing and illuminating Fiona.

"What about me?" Fiona tugged at a snarled curl, then shoved it behind her ear.

The smile broadened. "You're looking a little . . ." Zeke cocked his head to one side—"the worse for wear."

"Ach. And why shouldn't I be? 'Tis not a picnic I've been to—or one that I'm going to, either, if truth be known. Besides"—Fiona planted her hands on her hips and gave the colonel a slow perusal—"you've looked a sight better yourself." She didn't add that, as dirty and unkempt as he appeared, she still found him appealing. But apparently she didn't have to, because he certainly didn't take her insult seriously.

He laughed. Threw back his head and laughed so hard that Fiona stalked toward the shack. "Let's get going, if we're going to do this."

Zeke caught up with her before she reached her grandfather, and stopped her with an arm around her stiff shoulders. "It's going to be all right, Fiona. And

231

that remark I made about your appearance—"

Fiona turned on him, wrenching herself free from his hold. "Do you think I care a fig what you think of my looks? My grandfather might be dying, we're on our way to an enemy camp, and . . ." Fiona felt a sob building deep in her chest and was afraid to go on. She did care what he thought of her, and she couldn't for the life of her understand why.

"Well, I'm sorry anyway." He'd actually thought she looked charming, the sunlight turning her hair into a riot of flames, even with her dirt-streaked face, but she wouldn't want to hear that right now. She'd knelt down beside the laird, who was still unconscious. "Are you going to help me, or must I carry him by myself?"

In truth, she only walked along beside Zeke as he carried her grandfather to their makeshift litter. But she refused to ride, insisting she needed to stay back with the laird. So she solemnly trudged behind the horse that Zeke led, watching her grandfather for signs that the bumpy ride worsened his condition, and wondering what would happen when they reached the enemy camp.

Chapter Fourteen

"I don't ken how this could have happened."

"Now, Granddaughter." Malcolm paused as a fit of wheezing coughs racked his body. Though he probably didn't notice the way he protectively clutched his wounded side, Fiona did.

"You should have been paroled!" Unable to contain her feelings of anger and betrayal any longer, Fiona bounded off the rough-hewn bench and began pacing the length of the tiny cell.

"The Provincial Congress considered me a leader of the insurrection."

"Ach, the Provincial Congress." Fiona spit the words out with obvious contempt. "If you be asking me, they're the ones fostering an insurrection. And mark my words, it won't be long till King George puts them squarely in their place." Fiona stopped short of kicking at the heavy paneled door — the locked door — and turned, hands on hips, toward her grandfather.

Her further tirade toward the government body that had imprisoned her grandfather in the public gaol died on her lips when she saw him trying to control the shivers trembling through his body.

"You're ill." Fiona dropped to her knees beside him. Pulling the hand-knitted shawl from around her shoulders, Fiona tried to drape it over her grandfather. "Take this. It will help keep you warm."

"You'll not see me wearing a woman's shawl, Mary Fiona, and I'm feeling as well as can be expected."

"Your side . . ." Fiona tossed the knitted shawl on the bench, hoping he'd use it after she left.

"Is healed."

"Hmph. You may be telling the others that, but I don't believe it for one moment. And further, if you'd not insisted that you were fit as a fiddle, 'tis likely you'd have your parole."

"I'll not be shirking my duty as laird, Mary Fiona."

"And where is it written 'tis your duty to be sent to Philadelphia and locked in a gaol?"

"That will be enough, lass. What's done is done, and there's naught can be done to change it."

"I could go to the Congress—appeal to—"

"Nay, I tell you!" Malcolm lowered his voice from the roar that had interrupted her. "I've had my trial, and the decision's been made. I'll not have a Mac-Clure pleading my case before the very ones who judged me guilty. Besides, you are the one that concerns me now. I want you to get word to Armadale. They will send someone to get you."

"I can travel to Armadale without any assistance," Fiona said, with a dismissing wave of her hand.

"Send for someone, Mary Fiona. I'm liking the idea of your traveling by yourself even less than your staying alone in this town."

"I'm not alone," Fiona insisted, but her grandfather paid her no mind. He refused to believe she was comfortable and being well taken care of in the home of a Scotswoman—a widow, Mrs. MacLinn. Robert had found the lodging for her as soon as the Whig army arrived in Wilmington with its prisoners.

Fiona had made it clear to Robert, and anyone else who would listen, that she wasn't leaving her grandfather. And though she wasn't a prisoner, he was.

After promising to get word to Armadale—though she really didn't know who was there to help her— Fiona left the gaol and headed up Water Street toward Mrs. MacLinn's house.

Spring gentled the breeze drifting off the Cape Fear River, and another time, Fiona might have appreciated the new blush of green in the grass surrounding the houses she passed, or the unfurling leaves overhead. But now as she walked along the live-oak-lined street under a canopy of fluttering Spanish moss, she could think only of all her grandfather had been through—and what lay ahead.

At first, after the battle at Moore's Creek, when Colonel Kincaid had taken them back to the Whig camp, Fiona had reluctantly agreed that it was the right thing to do—at least, she would have agreed with him, had she ever seen him. But he'd been busy organizing the prisoners and wounded for the march to Wilmington. And she'd scarcely done anything but nurse her grandfather.

Now—Fiona kicked a stone along the path—if she saw Colonel Kincaid now, she'd tell him what she thought of him for what he'd done. Her grandfather's side might be improving, though Fiona didn't think it as healed as he boasted, but this Rebel government— Zeke's government—was going to kill him. Oh, they hadn't called for his execution. But Fiona felt strongly the trip to Pennsylvania, plus further imprisonment, would accomplish that for them.

Fiona sighed, remembering how Robert had removed the ball from the laird's side. It had taken weeks for Grandfather to calm down after he'd discovered who'd doctored him. But finally common sense had won out over anger and feelings of betrayal.

In the beginning, Fiona had found it difficult to be civil to Robert. But later, as they worked together to help Malcolm through his fever, she found herself thinking less and less of their differences. She'd even been sorry to see him leave when the militia left Wilmington.

That had been a fortnight ago. By that time, Grandfather had seemed much improved, and Fiona had eagerly awaited the Highlanders' trials, sure that her grandfather would be paroled and they could go home.

But he wasn't. General MacDonald and Allen MacDonald, and his son, and most of the other clan leaders, including Malcolm MacClure, were to be turned over to the Rebel government in Philadelphia. And though Malcolm insisted to all that he suffered no more from ill health than any of the other prisoners, Fiona knew differently. What she didn't know was what she could do about it.

Her grandfather had overlooked or shrugged off a fair number of indiscretions by her, but Fiona didn't think he would forgive her going to the Congress to plead his case. If only he hadn't specifically forbidden her to do it.

"There has to be something I can do," Fiona mumbled to herself as she climbed the brick steps of Mrs.

MacLinn's house.

"Is that you, Fiona, dear? I waited tea for you."

Fiona shut the front door of Mrs. MacLinn's small frame house and peeked into the parlor. Despite the mild spring temperature, a fire blazed in the hearth, testimony to Mrs. MacLinn's "thin blood". The little white-haired lady sat in a chair by the tea table. She wore widow's weeds today, as she had every day since her husband had died thirty years ago.

"I'm sorry I'm late, but you should have gone ahead without me."

"Nonsense. You hardly eat enough to keep a bird alive as it is. Now come in here and tell me all about the laird, while you have some rum cake. How is the dear man today?"

Suppressing a smile at Mrs. MacLinn's description of her grandfather as a "dear man," Fiona sat in the chair the older woman indicated. After accepting a cup of tea and a generous slice of cake — Mrs. MacLinn thought most of the world's ills could be cured if everyone had access to her rum cake — Fiona unburdened her troubles. When she'd finished her tale, Fiona leaned back against the carved cherry wood. "I simply don't know what to do."

"I wish I could help you, dear."

"I know, Mrs. MacLinn." Fiona reached over to touch the black-sleeved arm. "And believe me, you have. Why, if you hadn't allowed me to stay with you, I . . . What is it?"

The wrinkles around Mrs. MacLinn's eyes crinkled deeper and she tapped a gnarled finger against her chin. "I just had a thought. Perhaps your brother-in-law could assist you."

Fiona shook her head sadly, brushing the flyaway

curls off her cheek. For an instant she'd thought perhaps there was an answer—Mrs. MacLinn had seemed so animated about her idea. But it wouldn't work. Not that Fiona, in a moment of desperation, hadn't thought of it herself, but after facing the facts, she'd dismissed it. Even if she could reach Robert—the militia was reportedly guarding the lower end of the Cape Fear River—Fiona didn't think he had enough influence to do much. "Robert's with the militia," Fiona stated. Poor Mrs. MacLinn's memory was not the best, but Fiona thought she'd remember that.

"But they're back, dear. At least some of them are. I ran into Colonel Kincaid today, and—Are you all right, dear?"

"Ezekiel Kincaid is in Wilmington?"

"That's what I said. Have some more tea, Fiona. You look pale."

"No." Fiona held up her hand to cover the rim of her cup. "Thank you. I'm fine, really." Fine and angry. She wouldn't be in this mess—her grandfather wouldn't be in this mess—if it weren't for Colonel Ezekiel Kincaid. And even though it would accomplish nothing, she intended to let him know. "I'll take you and your grandfather back to the Whig camp and everything will be all right," he'd said, or at least implied. And she'd trusted him. Oh, maybe she'd had no choice, but she'd trusted him all the same.

The kiss had done it. It had knocked all reason out of her head. He'd made her think he wanted to help her. But she should have known, when he all but ignored her in the Whig camp, when he left Robert to see her settled in Wilmington, that it had all been a ruse. Well, she wouldn't be taken in by him again.

Fiona stood, brushing at her skirts so hard the silk crackled. First thing in the morning, before she visited grandfather, she'd pay a visit to Colonel Kincaid. She'd let him know exactly what she thought of him for making her grandfather a prisoner. It might serve no purpose other than to vent some of the pent-up hostility she felt, but that was something.

Then she'd decide what to do to help her grandfather. Maybe if she sent word to Armadale, someone—anyone there—could help. Uncle Angus was a prisoner, but Fiona thought Duncan had escaped—at least she'd heard no mention of him here. And she had seem him running away. Yes, maybe Duncan could—

"You know, Fiona dear, *he* may be able to help you."

Fiona dragged her attention back to Mrs. MacLinn. She knew the white-haired lady couldn't have followed her thoughts about Duncan—as far as Fiona knew, she didn't even know he existed. "Oh, you mean Robert. I really don't think he has much influence with the Congress, but I could—"

"Not Robert, dear. The colonel."

"No!" Fiona noted the shocked expression on Mrs. MacLinn's face and softened her voice. "That would never work."

"I'm not so sure." Mrs. MacLinn was obviously warming to her idea. "He is a colonel, you know. And, if I remember correctly, he even went on some sort of mission for the Congress, so they must think well of him."

Oh, Fiona knew all about *that*. But though the Congress trusted him, thought him a saint, for all she knew, the truth was, she didn't.

She knew him too well. Fiona tried to force her thoughts away from just how well she had known him. She had to forget that moment of insanity. On second thought, maybe she should remember it — remember exactly what it was that Zeke Kincaid wanted from her. He'd told her, he'd shown her, but still she'd thought there was something more.

Mrs. MacLinn might think him the perfect solution, and by the way her dark eyes glowed she did, but Fiona knew better. The colonel wouldn't be interested in helping her unless . . .

Fiona sucked in her breath. How could she even think such a thing? It was wrong, immoral, an affront to everything she'd been taught — and it would probably work. Eating a huge bite of rum cake didn't dislodge that last thought from her mind. Aye, it probably would work. But was she willing to do it?

"You're very quiet, dear."

"I'm sorry." Fiona replaced her tea cup. "I suppose I'm tired." And worried that I might just decide to try it, Fiona added silently.

"Of course you are. You should take a nap. And try not to fret too much about your grandfather. You'll come up with something to help him. I know you will."

She already had. But she certainly couldn't tell dear Mrs. MacLinn. Though Fiona hadn't made up her mind to do it — yet — just the slightest hint that she might, would send the poor woman into an apoplectic fit. Maybe, Fiona thought, she should take that as a sign. But before she left the parlor to take her nap she paused. "Mrs. MacLinn, where is Colonel Kincaid's house?"

* * *

240

Zeke kicked his boot, knocking mud from around the docks onto the side of the brick porch. He opened the back door to his house and stepped into the hallway lighted by brass wall sconces. It was late; his growling stomach and the dull ache in his head would have told him that even if the grandfather's clock hadn't picked that moment to toll the hour.

Ten o'clock, he mused, heading for the spiral staircase. He'd see if Mrs. Steel, his housekeeper, could get him something from the kitchen. He'd missed supper by hours, but if he knew her, she'd have something warming for him. Not that Zeke cared if the food was cold. He'd eaten enough cold, unappetizing food in the last month that anything would do him. Besides, all he really wanted to do was sleep.

Perkins, the man he'd left in charge of his shipping business, had fired numbers at him all day, interspersing them generously with excuses. After his assistant left, Zeke had stayed, trying to make some sense of the disaster his business was in. Between the war with England and his absence, Kincaid Shipping was running far from smoothly. It had taken hours to muddle through the mess of paperwork and put it in some semblance of order.

Zeke started back toward the hall, trying to decide just how he was going to handle Perkins. It was clear the man was incompetent, but finding someone to replace him wouldn't be easy. And for all he'd cost the shipping company by sending partially laden vessels along the coast, Zeke liked the man, and, he supposed, felt sorry for him.

Shaking his head, Zeke caught sight of the sliver of light shining from beneath the parlor door just as

241

Mrs. Steel came from the back of the house.

"Ah, there you are, sir." Mrs. Steel's gray dress was neat and crisply starched, as was the cap that covered her equally gray hair.

"Yes. Sorry I'm so late, but do you suppose there's something for me to—What's the matter?"

"You have a visitor, sir." Mrs. Steel's eyes flicked toward the parlor door and Zeke could swear her lips thinned.

"A visitor? Who is it?" The last thing Zeke wanted was to entertain members of the congress.

"*She* didn't give her name."

"She?"

"Yes, sir. The young lady arrived some two hours ago, and has refused to leave, though I've repeatedly pointed out the time."

Zeke heard only the beginning of Mrs. Steel's explanation before he threw open the parlor door. "Fiona."

Jumping from her seat when she heard her name, Fiona braided her fingers. "Hello, Colonel Kincaid."

Zeke didn't know how long he stared at her—it was Mrs. Steel who made him realize what he was doing. "Will you be wanting anything else, sir?"

"What? Oh, yes. Something to eat, if you don't mind. I missed supper." Zeke looked back at Fiona, noticing the changes in her appearance since he'd last seen her. She'd lost weight, and now appeared so fragile a stiff wind might blow her away. And her eyes, though still the deep, vibrant violet he remembered, were smudged beneath with lavender crescents that spoke of sleepless nights. "Make that enough for two, please."

"I didn't expect to see you here in Wilmington,"

Zeke said as he entered the room and closed the door. His remark sounded inane; after all, she'd been here when he left. Not that he'd seen her, of course. He'd purposely stayed away from her after that morning he'd found her near Moore's Creek. But he'd kept track of her whereabouts through Robert. As foolish as his words were, Zeke felt they should do something besides stand there staring at each other. And Fiona didn't seem inclined to break the silence.

Something akin to anger flashed in her eyes before she lowered them to study the hands clasped in front of her. When she looked back at him her expression was more composed. "I can't imagine you thought I'd leave Grandfather."

"No. I never thought that. But I heard rumors today that the trials were over, and I assumed—"

"Grandfather wasn't paroled."

"I see." Zeke had known this possibility existed, but he'd expected the Congress to be lenient, considering the laird's age and physical condition.

"Is that all you can say—'I see'?" Fiona tried to keep her voice calm, but knew she failed. None of this was going as she'd imagined. When she'd gone to her room at Mrs. MacLinn's she'd pondered her choices, finally coming to the conclusion that she had none. She had to keep her grandfather from being sent to Philadelphia, and she knew only one way to accomplish that.

But even with her decision made, Fiona realized accomplishing it would not be easy. This fact was emphasized when she'd opened the wardrobe and dragged out the one decent gown that had been rescued from the supply wagons. Though the dress, a yellow silk, had fit her tolerably well before, now it simply hung on her. "I should have eaten more rum cake," she'd mumbled, pinning it in as best she could at the sides of her waist. Her hair had proved another problem. After nearly a month of not caring about her appearance, it was almost impossible to control. Even now she knew curling tendrils escaped the tight braid she'd twisted around her head.

Though not a vain person, Fiona felt she needed to look her best for this encounter, and it hadn't taken the disdain in the housekeeper's voice, or her critical perusal, to know she didn't. The housekeeper had treated her like a cross between a servant and a whore. Fiona twisted her fingers. Could she truly fault the older woman for that? At this moment, Fiona didn't care what the housekeeper thought of her. However, everything depended upon what her employer thought.

And Zeke wasn't likely to be impressed, even if he could overlook her appearance—if she didn't bridle her temper. She could, and she would. Fiona took a calming breath. "I . . . apologize." Fiona tried, but couldn't meet his eyes, afraid he'd see the insincerity there. She wasn't sorry for what she'd said. She'd say a lot more if the circumstances were different.

She was angry—he could tell by the rigid way she held her body, even if she wouldn't meet his eyes— and he supposed she had every right to be. But she was trying to hide it. She hadn't meant a word of that mumbled apology, Zeke was certain of that.

A knock made them both look toward the door. "That will be Mrs. Steel with some food. Are you hungry?"

After the housekeeper had set a silver tray on the tea table, and left the room, Fiona spoke. "I don't think she approves of my visit."

Zeke shrugged. "Mrs. Steel has been with the family for over twenty years. She runs the house, but not me. Don't let her bother you. I, on the other hand, though not disapproving of your visit, am curious to know why you're here."

Fiona swallowed. Now that she'd been given the opportunity to state her purpose, she found her throat too tight to speak. She swallowed again.

"Perhaps we should eat first." Zeke indicated a chair beside the table, and removed the tray's covering. Two blue-edged plates were piled high with ham and fish, potatoes and biscuits.

Fiona wished she could do justice to the food, for the sake of her gown, if nothing else. But she couldn't seem to force a bite past her tight throat.

She wished she'd spoken quickly and gotten this over with as soon as he'd asked her why she'd come. He didn't seem the least interested in talk now, as he ate like a man enjoying his last meal. He appeared to have completely forgotten her presence, so Fiona took the opportunity to study him from beneath her lashes.

He'd lost weight, too. Perhaps that was the reason for his ravenous appetite. He was darker, also, his face bronzed a deeper hue by long hours in the sun. But all in all he looked the same as she remembered—strikingly handsome.

Annoyed with that thought, Fiona stabbed at a piece of meat. He could look like the devil himself, for all she cared. She wasn't here because she wanted to be. None of this had anything to do with the fact that he was handsome, or that he could kiss her senseless, or even that she'd momentarily lost her head and made love to him. She needed someone to help her, and Colonel Kincaid fit the bill. He also professed to want something she had.

Exchange.

Period.

By the time Fiona had stuffed three forkfuls of food into her mouth, she'd almost convinced herself that was all true.

"I'm glad to see you decided to eat." Zeke pointed the tines of his fork at her. "You're a bit on the thin side."

"You . . ." Fiona started to talk, realized her mouth was full, chewed, swallowed, and tried again. "You could use some fattening up, too." She'd meant to insult him, but by the smile he flashed her, she assumed it hadn't worked.

"Rigors of war, Fiona," Zeke said, patting the russet waistcoat covering his flat stomach.

"Was there much fighting?" Fiona asked. Though meant to tease, his words brought visions of Moore's Creek bridge back to her. The blood, the dying, the cries of the wounded were as real to her now as they had been then, as they were in her nightmares.

Zeke's smile disappeared when he noticed the haunted expression in her eyes. "No," he assured her, "only a few skirmishes with some Tories . . . excuse me, Loyalists."

"Scots?"

Shaking his head, Zeke took another bite of fish. "There's been no more trouble with the Scottish population."

That wasn't surprising, Fiona decided, since most of the leaders were either in the gaol or dead.

"What about you?" Fiona heard the colonel ask.

"Me?"

His blue gaze swept over her, stopping below her breasts, then returning to her face. The flush that brightened her cheeks made him toss her a lopsided grin. "It's hard to believe Mrs. MacLinn isn't feeding you."

"She is feeding me," Fiona insisted. "She's taken very good—" Fiona paused, her eyes narrowing. "How do you know about Mrs. MacLinn?"

He knew because he'd suggested the widow's house to Robert as a place for Fiona to stay. But he didn't think Fiona would want to hear that. Knowing her, she might even refuse the good woman's hospitality if she realized how she'd come to receive it. Zeke shrugged. "Someone must have mentioned it."

"Robert?"

"Probably."

"Is he here, in Wilmington?" Fiona was beginning to wonder if Mrs. MacLinn's original idea, to have her brother-in-law intercede in the laird's behalf, might not be the best plan after all. Colonel Kincaid had shown no sign that he still . . . Well, he'd shown no interest in her, except to fill her with food.

"No. He returned to Cross Creek."

"Oh." Fiona bit her lip. She didn't think there was time to get word to him, and then have him come back to Wilmington—if he would—and then appeal to the Congress, and . . . "I'm sorry. I didn't hear you." Fiona realized she'd been so preoccupied she'd missed what the colonel had said. She supposed she should at least feign interest in his conversation, since she was back to considering him Grandfather's only hope.

"I was merely explaining that Robert didn't feel he

247

should leave the colony when we go to—"

"You're leaving North Carolina?" Fiona didn't have to pretend interest now.

"Yes." Zeke leaned forward, feeling an unexpected thrill of elation at her obvious concern. "The militia will join the Continentals when they march to South Carolina. It's thought Clinton plans to attack Charleston. Don't look so shocked. I'm not telling you any military secrets."

"I know. Talk around town has been of little else." Fiona laid the fork down beside her plate, then continued to stare at it. "I just never thought you'd go with them."

Zeke studied the plaited crown of gleaming red hair on top of Fiona's head. He couldn't see her eyes, only the tip of her small nose and the fan of thick, burnished lashes, but he could tell she was upset—by his leaving. And, God help him, the thought excited him.

Fiona excited him. He'd tried to pretend otherwise, tried to stay away from her when he couldn't pretend any longer. But now she sat in his parlor, showing every indication that she felt something for him. He considered reaching for her, honestly didn't know what kept him from doing it. "Fiona, I—"

"When are you leaving?" Fiona glanced up, her heart skipping a beat when she saw the desire in Zeke's eyes.

"A sennight, maybe two."

"Oh." Fiona hoped her relief didn't appear too obvious. But when he'd first mentioned leaving, she'd thought he might be off on the morrow—before he could help her. A week or two should give him time to convince the Congress, if he'd do it. The desire

248

she'd read in his eyes earlier gave her hope, but she'd never know until she asked. Taking a deep breath, Fiona began.

Unfortunately, the colonel started to speak at the same time. He chuckled, his dimples deepening, and swept his hand toward her. "You first."

"No, you," the coward in Fiona said.

"I insist." Zeke reached for her plate. "Are you finished?" he asked. Seeing her nod, he cleared the dishes off the small table, stacking them haphazardly on the silver tray. Then he resumed his seat and stared at her expectantly.

Seeing no course but to plow straight ahead, Fiona began. "You may be wondering why I'm here."

"The question did cross my mind."

"Yes, well . . . I came to ask a favor."

"What sort of favor?" Zeke would warrant it had something to do with her grandfather.

Fiona ignored his question. "And to make you an offer . . . a trade."

"I see," Zeke said, though he didn't at all. The favor he understood, had already anticipated. Actually, he'd decided when she'd first mentioned her grandfather's imprisonment that he'd see what he could do to help the laird. But what did she think to offer in exchange? Whatever it was, she didn't seem inclined to tell him. Now that she'd given him a peek at her reason for coming, she reverted to silence. "Fiona," Zeke urged.

Standing, Fiona started pacing the room, her feet measuring the length of the Caucasian carpet several times before turning toward Zeke. "I want you to get my grandfather freed. He's—"

"I'm not certain I can do that, Fiona." He'd

249

thought to talk to Congress, urging them to spare the old man as much hardship as possible, but to get him freed altogether . . .

"He's ill and wounded. I'm afraid he'll die if he's sent to Philadelphia." Fiona stopped twisting her fingers and turned to him, her eyes as pleading as her voice. "Please, you must help me."

"Hell, Fiona." Jerking out of his chair, Zeke strode to Fiona, cupping her fragile shoulders in his hands. "You don't know what you're asking—"

"Are you afraid what I have to trade won't be acceptable? Is that it?"

"I don't care about—Damnit, Fiona." Zeke's hands tightened when she tried to wrench away. "Would you stop wiggling and listen?"

"No." Fiona's voice caught on a sob as she pushed against his muscular chest. This wasn't happening the way she'd hoped at all. In defeat, she stopped struggling. Taking a calming breath, she stared at the top silver waistcoat button. "You once said you wanted me. . . . Did you mean it?"

Shocked by her abrupt change—and by the question—Zeke could only blink and look down at her.

"Well, did you?"

"Yes, I meant it."

"Do you still?"

Unconsciously Zeke moved his hands over the canary yellow silk covering her shoulders. He could feel her heat seep into his body. "Yes."

Letting out the breath she hadn't known she was holding, Fiona lifted her eyes. "Have my grandfather freed, and that shall be the trade," Fiona said, wondering how she could speak so calmly when her heart pounded painfully in her chest.

"What the hell are you talking about?"

Must she spell it out for him? "I'm talking about a trade . . . a bargain."

"Yeah," Zeke growled, resisting the urge to shake her. "I understand that part. I even understand what you want me to do. What the hell I don't understand is what you're going to give me if I do this little favor for you."

"Me." Fiona swallowed. "Whenever you want me."

Chapter Fifteen

"Let me make sure I have this straight. You're offering yourself to me . . . sexually," Zeke growled the word. "In exchange for my getting your grandfather paroled?"

Thankfully he'd released her shoulders, so that Fiona could retreat from his murderous scowl. She tried not to cower as the echo of his question vibrated through her. Pride, what little she had left, forced her to stop her backward steps and face him, her chin notched high. "Aye. . . ." Fiona's courage faltered when she noticed the muscle in his cheek begin to throb. "Yes, I am. It's what you want."

"What I want," Zeke raked his hands through his hair, fighting to gain control of his temper, "is to know what is in your mind."

"You needn't act so . . . so shocked." Fiona couldn't fathom his reaction. She'd thought he might object to his part of the bargain, but never hers. "It isn't as if we haven't . . . haven't . . ."

"Made love?"

Fiona swallowed. "Aye."

"For God's sake, Fiona," Zeke said, noticing the blush that bloomed across her cheeks. "You can't even say it, yet you'd prostitute yourself for—"

"I would not!"

Zeke's dark brow arched questioningly. "No? Then what in the hell do you call this?"

The end of hope; the beginning of true despair. Fiona suddenly saw herself as Zeke saw her, and the picture filled her with humiliation. She turned, determined to erase the scorn from the depths of his eyes the only way she could. A thrust of his hand against the paneled door kept her from opening it. "Let me out of here."

"Oh, no. Not until you've answered a few questions."

"Like what?" Fiona yanked on the brass doorknob even though she knew opening it was impossible.

"Who else received this proposition from you?"

Fiona sucked in her breath. "No one." She glared at him. "I wouldn't say this to anyone but you."

"And that's supposed to make me feel better?"

"It's not supposed to make you feel any way at all. I don't know why you're so angry."

He didn't either. It wasn't as if he'd never bought a woman before. He'd thought little enough of it those times, wanting only to slake his lust on a willing female — even if that willingness came at the cost of a few coins. But damnit, this was Fiona. "You don't understand, do you?"

"I understand one thing." Fiona's hand dropped from the latch and she turned to face Zeke, drawn by the calmer tone of his voice. "I need this favor . . . desperately, and I thought I was offering you . . . what you wanted."

She looked on the verge of tears, and Zeke, now that the worst of his anger was spent, didn't think he could handle that. Jamming his hands into the pockets of his jacket, he strode to the fireplace, giving the fender a kick with the toe of his boot. "I'll see what I can do about your grandfather."

Fiona could hardly credit what he said. She'd jumped at the sound of leather against brass, had almost decided to escape the room while she had the chance, but now she took a cautious step forward.

As if he sensed her movement, Zeke looked around, pinning her with his blue gaze. "I can't promise to get him a parole, but I'll talk to some members of Congress. Maybe . . ."

"Thank you. I—"

"And I want you to know that I planned to look into this as soon as you told me about your grandfather."

Fiona's gaze dropped, and she studied her fingers as they pleated the yellow silk folds of her overskirt. She offered herself, humbled herself, and for no reason. But she wouldn't retract her offer. What was done was done, and a Scotswoman did not go back on her word. She took another step toward him. "Zeke, I—"

"Don't!"

Fiona's head jerked up at the harshness of his voice.

"Before you say another word, I want you to know I'm not interested in your part of the bargain."

"You're not?" Somehow these words seemed as cruel as those he'd hurled at her earlier.

"No." Zeke turned to face her, his hands clasped behind his back. "I want you to go home . . . and stay there. I don't want to hear from you or see you again. Is that clear?"

Thrusting her chin forward, ignoring the sting of tears behind her eyes, Fiona answered, "Perfectly."

"Good. Now get your cloak and I'll see you back to Mrs. MacLinn's."

"I'll get my own self back, if it's all the same to you." Fiona was in the hallway before he caught up with her. Grabbing her upper arm, Zeke twisted her toward him, lowering his face till it was mere inches from hers.

"Well, it isn't all the same to me," he hissed. "And for

once I'd like you to think about the consequences of your actions *before* you act."

Fiona jerked her arm away, and scooped up her cloak from the walnut chair in the hall. There didn't seem to be any way around enduring his presence for now, but she would do nothing to prolong it. She wanted to be away from the colonel as much as he apparently wanted to be away from her. The fact that she'd never have to see him again after they walked the few blocks to Mrs. MacLinn's house kept her feet moving steadily in that direction.

It was dark, puddles of light from street lamps the only illumination as they walked toward the river. The man beside her was silent, the sound of his booted footfalls the only proof of his existence until they reached the small frame house.

"There are no lights on." Zeke stepped in front of Fiona when she would have rushed through the iron gate.

"Mrs. MacLinn must be in bed." Why did he have to prolong this?

"But surely she would have left a candle lit."

"She doesn't know I'm out." Fiona blurted out the truth as her only means of quick escape. She didn't want the colonel waking up the household to make certain everything was all right.

"I see." Zeke leaned against the fence, still blocking Fiona's way. "And if I'd taken you up on your offer, were you ready to stay the night?"

He *would* bring it up again. Fiona clenched her fists, anger overriding embarrassment. Her head raised at a defiant angle, she doubted he could see in the dim light, Fiona stepped up to him. "As you didn't choose to accept, you'll never know." With that she pushed past him and hurried along the brick path to the front door. Luckily none of the servants had discovered that she'd unlocked it, so she was able to slip inside.

Hidden behind the door, her motive for erecting her facade no longer able to see her, Fiona's composure crumbled. By the time she maneuvered through the darkness, knocking her elbow on the carved newel at the bottom of the stairs, tears streamed down her cheeks. Closing the bedroom door behind her, she fumbled toward the tester bed, great sobs racking her slender body.

Alternately pounding and weeping into the dimity coverlet, Fiona tried to gain control of her emotions, but to no avail. She should be happy, Fiona told herself, during a particularly frantic fit of tears. She'd accomplished what she'd set out to do. The colonel was going to see to her grandfather's release — as much as she hated him at this moment, she didn't doubt he'd do it.

Then why was she so miserable? Fiona asked herself around a hiccup. The colonel had said some awful things to her — accusing her of prostituting herself. Fiona sobbed again. And that had hurt, but mostly it made her angry. He'd acted as if she had a choice, when clearly she hadn't. But she'd been angry with him before, and he with her, and never succumbed to such a mass of weeping misery.

He rejected you, and further, he never wants to see you again. Fiona sat bolt upright when that thought hit her. Rubbing her knuckles across eyes that ached from crying, Fiona tried to reject that as the reason she felt so awful.

But she couldn't.

"I never want to see him again either," she mumbled into her pillow, thinking perhaps hearing it aloud would prove more convincing. And it might have, had not the pillow slip been damp from her renewed tears.

But though she'd decided the cause of her misery, Fiona fell asleep, trying to decide why it was she cared one way or the other.

* * *

"Damn, damn, damn!"

Zeke dismounted, tying his horse's reins to the wrought iron fence, and stood hands on hips, staring at the small white house. He'd already run the gauntlet of damning first Fiona, then her grandfather, the Provincial Congress, and finally, and most emphatically himself. Now he was reduced to mumbling ineffectual curses at things in general.

Currently he was lamenting the fact that he was forced to march into this house and face Fiona again. In the light of day. After the things he'd said to her.

Not that she didn't deserve every last syllable he'd uttered. But if he hadn't been so emotionally involved, he knew he'd have handled their meeting differently. And if he weren't so emotionally involved, he probably wouldn't mind the solution the Congress had thrust on him.

Shaking his head, Zeke opened the gate, and headed for the front door. Fiona wasn't going to like this any better than he, but there was no help for it.

As he lifted the seagull knocker, Zeke wondered if Fiona would even receive him. After all, he'd told her he never wanted to see her again.

A small dark woman led him into the parlor. Apparently Fiona hadn't aired her anger with him to Mrs. MacLinn, for the old woman greeted him as warmly as ever.

"How are you Ezekiel, dear boy?"

Zeke bowed over her hand, then kissed the wrinkled cheek she tilted his way. She smelled of lavender, and Zeke smiled as she squeezed his arm. "I've been very well, Mrs. MacLinn. And you?"

"Just fine now that you've chased the British away."

"I had a little help with that," Zeke chuckled, seating

himself in the chair the old lady indicated.

"Nonsense. Governor Martin on the *Cruizer* was terrorizing the town until you showed up."

"I think you're forgetting Colonel Moore's regulars and the rest of the militia."

"Have it your way." Mrs. MacLinn tapped his arm. "You always were a modest boy."

Zeke didn't think that true, but held his tongue. Besides, Mrs. MacLinn had already launched into another subject — one of her favorites — the high price of foodstuffs since the outbreak of the war.

"Why do you have any idea what Mr. Decker wants for a pound of sugar," she finally asked after reciting the cost of flour, eggs and tea.

"No, actually I don't, Mrs. MacLinn. Is Fiona . . . Mistress MacClure in by chance?"

"Ah." Mrs. MacLinn gave Zeke a knowing look and shook her finger under his nose. "You've come to see Fiona, have you? And why didn't you just say so from the beginning so I wouldn't have gone rambling on."

"As a matter of fact, I did come to see you." Zeke grinned. "But I thought since I was here, I might give my regards to Mistress MacClure."

"Liar," the old woman chuckled. "But then you always could get away with anything when you flashed those dimples."

Laughing, Zeke bent forward and gave Mrs. MacLinn another kiss.

"We'll have none of that, now," she chastised, but her smile belied the words. "Actually, I'm very glad you came to see Fiona," Mrs. MacLinn said after she'd asked her servant to fetch the young woman from upstairs. "She's been so downhearted lately. Perhaps you can cheer her up."

Zeke seriously doubted that, but he listened as Mrs. MacLinn related how she hadn't seen Fiona smile in days. "And you know what a charming smile she has. I know she's upset about her grandfather, but it almost seems as if there's something else troubling her."

About to ask what Mrs. MacLinn thought it might be, Zeke's attention instead focused on the doorway, drawn by the gasp of surprise he heard.

Having been in her room drafting a letter to Armadale begging Duncan for assistance, Fiona hadn't considered the possibility of a visitor, when Mrs. MacLinn summoned her. Even if she had, she'd never have imagined *this* visitor.

Fiona watched as the colonel sat a moment staring at her, before remembering himself and rising. She knew that was her cue to enter the room, but Fiona wasn't certain she could do it. He'd said he never wanted to see her again, yet here he was. Realization that only news of her grandfather could have brought him — though even then she'd have expected a message at best — finally propelled her into the tiny parlor. A room that seemed so much smaller with him in it.

If Mrs. MacLinn thought the silence that hung between Fiona and Zeke unusual, she didn't let it keep her from babbling away. "Colonel Kincaid came to call upon us, Fiona. Isn't that sweet of him?"

"Yes, sweet." Actually, Fiona doubted the colonel had done anything you could call sweet since he'd been removed from leading straps, but she had to say something with Mrs. MacLinn staring at her so expectantly.

"In truth, though the dear boy denies it, I believe he came to see you."

"Me?"

"You're far too perceptive, Mrs. MacLinn." The colonel leaned toward the old woman, and to Fiona's amazement, her landlady reached up and patted his cheek. Then he turned to Fiona, pinning her with the full power of his blue gaze. "Since Mrs. MacLinn has found us out, would you care to walk with me?"

"Walk?"

"Yes. You and I strolling along, out of doors."

Fiona mentally shook herself. She was acting the dimwit, and by the expression on his face, a slightly crooked grin, he noticed it. Well, she didn't want to see him at all, cared even less to be alone with him. Whatever he had to tell her could be said in front of Mrs. MacLinn.

"I really don't think—"

"Nonsense, dear. I know what you're thinking, but don't mind me. It is almost time for my rest anyway. But it was kind of you to worry about me. That's so like our Mistress MacClure." This last the older lady had addressed to the colonel.

"Indeed," was his only response. But the look he shot Fiona convinced her he knew concern for Mrs. MacLinn had little to do with her reluctance.

"Do run along, children, and enjoy this spring weather."

"I really am not dressed to go out." Fiona made a final effort to avoid what she feared was the inevitable.

"Nonsense, dear. You look lovely, doesn't she, colonel?"

"Lovely."

Fiona wished to goodness he'd stop agreeing with everything Mrs. MacLinn said. She, as well as the other two people in the room, knew she looked dreadful. Her dress was faded and worn, and her hair only tied in a ribbon at her nape. She'd planned to change into a better gown before visiting her grandfather, wished she'd done it sooner.

Presentable or not, Fiona felt herself nearly propelled out the door on the colonel's arm by Mrs. MacLinn. She barely had time to grab her wide-brimmed straw hat before her landlady, with a gleam in her eyes

Fiona took for matchmaker fever, closed the door behind them.

Fiona waited till they were out of earshot of the house before turning toward the colonel. "Why did you do that?"

"Do what?" Zeke bent down to catch a glimpse of her face beneath the bonnet, but could see nothing but intriguing shadows.

"Make that poor woman think we are . . . are . . ."

"Lovers?"

Now she looked up at him and glared. "That wasn't what I was going to say." Fiona began walking again — at a faster pace.

"Sorry. My mistake." Zeke stifled a smile. This was hardly the time to tease her. Soon she'd be angry as hell. But sometimes he could barely resist.

"Friends." Fiona bit out the word. "You made it appear that we are friends."

"I wanted to speak with you alone, and you didn't seem very willing to —"

"Never mind." Fiona waved her hand impatiently. "Did you get my grandfather paroled?"

"No," came his succinct reply. "Wait a minute. Where are you going?"

Fiona tried to shake the hand off her arm without drawing too much attention to them as they walked down Water Street toward the river. "Back to Mrs. MacLinn's. I was writing a letter when you arrived, and I might as well get back to it."

"I know."

"You know what?" He'd let go of her upper arm, but now held her elbow in such a way that she couldn't get loose. He steered her off the street and started down a path toward the bank of Cape Fear.

"That you were writing a letter. You have ink smudged on your nose."

Fiona tried to swat away the thumb that rubbed across the tip of her nose. "Would you stop that?"

"Hold still. Now look up here." Zeke cocked his head, examining her critically. The streak of ink was gone, though the skin on her nose had pinkened from the chafing of his thumb. But it wasn't her nose that held his attention. He couldn't seem to stop looking into those violet eyes, continued to do it, until she made a small sound of protest. "There, that has it," Zeke added somewhat lamely.

She'd almost let him do it to her again. He'd come close to kissing her — and she'd come close to letting him — or at least not stopping him. And after he'd just told her that Grandfather — her main concern at the moment — would not be paroled! What was it about this man that caused her to forget reality — or at least to want to forget it? He looked at her — he touched her — and rational thought sailed, like the gulls circling overhead.

Stepping back in the sandy soil, taking a deep steadying breath, Fiona glanced around her. He'd brought them to a small clearing in the trees by the water's edge. The river, wide, dark and lazy, lapped at the shore. It was picturesque and secluded — and at the moment, Fiona wanted neither.

"May I leave now?" Though he didn't touch her, seemed almost relaxed as he turned to gaze out over the water, Fiona sensed the same coiled strength she'd noticed the first time she saw him.

"Don't you wish to know what *is* to happen to your grandfather?" Zeke tossed a twig into the water, watching it bob about before being picked up by the current. Then he turned his head toward Fiona, arching his brow questioningly.

"I assume he's to be sent to Philadelphia."

"He's not."

Fiona stepped forward, batting at a pine bough in her way. "Is he to stay in Wilmington?"

"Yes."

"In the gaol?" Fiona tried to keep her voice hopeful. Even if he had to stay in the damp wooden structure, at least he wouldn't have the trip to contend with. And here, closer to home, perhaps she could get some help from Duncan or other Scots. Perhaps she could even help break him out of—

"Not exactly."

The colonel's words made Fiona pause, her plans of escape stilled. "What do you mean 'not exactly'?"

"I mean . . ." Zeke leaned against an oak tree. "That though he'll remain a prisoner, he won't be in the gaol. He's being made the responsibility of one man."

Fiona's eyes narrowed. "Who?"

"Me."

"You!" The explosion of sound sent a heron to flight. Fiona lowered her voice. "You," she said again. "Why you?"

"Because I'm the one who went pleading for him, I suppose." Picking up a fallen branch, Zeke sailed it out over the water with a flick of his wrist.

"My grandfather is to be your prisoner?" Fiona had a difficult time comprehending this new development. "But that will never work." She wasn't certain why it wouldn't, but she knew it wouldn't.

"Damnit, Fiona. Do you think I like this any better than you?"

She'd never considered how he might feel about it, and truthfully, it wasn't her main concern. For suddenly she realized if her grandfather was not to be held in the gaol, but he was still a prisoner, then he must be held . . . "Where is my grandfather to stay?"

"My house."

"What . . . what about me?"

263

"There also." Zeke watched the color drain from her cheeks. "The Congress agrees with your assessment of his health, and though they refuse to let him go, they do want to see him properly cared for."

"I have to stay at your house . . . with you?" Fiona tried to follow the colonel's explanation, but her mind snagged on that alarming fact. How could she possibly live in the same house after all that had passed between them? Why, she'd even offered herself to him, and been rejected. And by the looks of him now, he'd reject her again if he could. What had he said? He didn't like this any better than she did.

"You won't exactly be . . . with me," Zeke explained. Though damn close enough, he thought. He'd wanted her to leave, to go back to Armadale, so he could somehow forget this . . . this obsession he had with her, but now . . . "My house is large," he reasoned for his benefit as much as hers. "You and your grandfather will have plenty of privacy. And he'll be much more comfortable."

"That's true." Fiona tried to concentrate on that fact as she stripped the leaves off a willow branch. But all she could think of was being around Zeke day and night, of the strange effect he had on her — and the fact that he didn't want her there. Slowly she raised her gaze to meet his. "Perhaps there's some other way."

"There isn't. Believe me, I've thought this through thoroughly."

She was certain of that. With his eyes, blue as the sky forming his backdrop, staring at her as if he'd been condemned to spend the rest of his days in the darkest dungeon, she was sure he'd tried all he could to get out of this. That realization seemed the most discomforting of all. "I suppose there's no help for it then."

"None."

Fiona studied Zeke's spread-legged stance, as he

turned to stare out across the water. His broad shoulders, covered by dark blue superfine, appeared tense, as did the large hands he clasped behind his back. For long moments they stood like that, Zeke looking toward the opposite shore, Fiona, shredding the twig to nothingness, her thoughts in a state of confusion, wondering why she cared so much that he didn't want her.

"I suppose we should be getting back." Zeke turned, surprised by the expression on Fiona's face. She appeared vulnerable, almost as if she were appealing to him for understanding. But she quickly looked away, and when her eyes met his again, there was none of the soft confusion he'd noticed before. She stared at him with the same guarded anger she'd shown before. Zeke decided a trick of sun and shadows beneath her wide-brimmed hat had played havoc with his senses.

"When are we to . . . when is this to happen?"

"As soon as possible. Tomorrow." Zeke raked his fingers through his hair. "I had a physician look in on your grandfather — he'd refused to see one since Robert left — and I think the sooner he leaves that damp cell the better."

Fiona's shoulders stiffened. "What did he say?"

"Nothing we didn't already know. The wound is healing, though it still causes a great deal of discomfort."

"He never says anything to imply it hurts him."

Zeke shrugged. "He also appears to be suffering from dysentery. Probably picked it up in the gaol."

"He had it before joining the Loyalist Army."

The look of shock Zeke sent Fiona made her rush to explain. "He refused to admit it as vehemently as he refused to remain behind at Armadale."

"How is he going to feel about this change in developments?"

"I'm not certain." Zeke had started walking back along the path and Fiona kept pace.

265

"Would you like me to speak with him?"

"No." Fiona brushed a pine branch out of her way. "I think it would be better coming from me."

Nodding, Zeke took Fiona's elbow, to guide her around a rotting log. He dropped his hand as soon as the path was clear again.

Fiona pretended not to notice, then wished she'd have jerked her arm away when she first felt the pressure of his fingers.

Fiona left Zeke the moment they returned to the main street of town, and headed for the gaol. She didn't take time to notice where he went, and if truth be known, didn't care. All her energies were focused on deciding how she'd tell her grandfather of their move to the colonel's house.

He wasn't going to like it—of that she was certain. And more, he'd most likely conclude that she had something to do with it. Maybe, Fiona decided as she trudged along Market Street, her own disfavor with the idea would keep him from jumping to that conclusion—even if it was correct.

"You're right late today, ain't you, Mistress MacClure?"

"I suppose so," Fiona answered the guard sitting with his heels propped on the scarred oak table. He called himself a sergeant, though he hardly looked the part with his grubby buckskin breeches and soiled shirt. But Fiona had discovered that now most everyone seemed to have some sort of rank in either the militia or the Continentals. They all seemed proud of sporting a doe's tail in their hats too. That symbol of resistance to the king was everywhere.

Still, Fiona decided as she followed the lumbering sergeant back to the narrow hall, he'd been cordial to her in his gruff way, allowing her visits whenever she wanted. He'd even managed to look the other way

266

when she smuggled extra food and blankets into the laird's cell.

"I'm right glad you showed up." The sergeant stopped short, blocking Fiona's path. For a second, she thought she may have read the intent of his kindness wrong. Was he about to suggest some lewd way for her to repay his concessions toward her? But his words brought other fears to mind. "I thought about sending for you myself, when I saw the laird this morning."

"Why? What's wrong?" Fiona tried to push by him, but he captured her shoulders, holding her still.

"Now settle yourself, little missy. It ain't as serious as all that. But I do think your grandpappy is feeling right poorly today."

Fiona stepped cautiously inside the cell, cringing when she saw her grandfather lying on the narrow cot. Ever since his fever broke he'd greeted her sitting on the rickety chair in the corner. "Grandfather." Fiona strove to keep her voice calm.

She walked across the straw-covered floor, letting her breath out when the grizzled red head turned her way. "Fiona, lass." Pushing on his shoulders when he tried to sit, Fiona edged onto the side of the cot. She touched the whiskered cheek, then brushed a strand of gray-streaked hair off his forehead.

"I understand you've had a wee bit of trouble today," Fiona said, careful to keep her smile in place.

"That nosey sergeant told you that, didn't he?"

"Perhaps. But even if he'd not said a word, I've got eyes, don't I?" To Fiona's surprise, her grandfather didn't utter a word of protest. He merely shrugged his shoulder.

"I do have a bit of a chill."

For someone who rarely admitted anything was wrong, those words seemed revealing indeed. Besides, Fiona had proof of his condition when she touched his face. He felt hot and dry. No wonder he had a fever, his cell was damp and chilly, even though the day was anything but.

Standing, Fiona took a deep breath and began the speech she'd practiced on her way to the gaol. "The Provincial Congress has decided to move you from these . . ." Fiona lifted her hand, indicating the cell. "Accommodations. To something more comfortable." Before grandfather could argue, Fiona rushed on. "Tomorrow we are both to become guests of Colonel Kincaid."

There, she'd said it. Fiona patiently waited for the barrage of complaints and accusations. Why was he to be treated differently than the other prisoners. He was the laird, and should go to Philadelphia with the rest. What had she done to change the Congress's mind? Fiona had tried to come up with a feasible argument to offset anything he could say.

But he said nothing. He only closed his eyes, and nodded, then suggested she go on to Mrs. MacLinn's so he could rest.

Fiona stepped outside into the late afternoon sunshine, and leaned against the whitewashed building. Because of his illness, telling her grandfather of their move to the colonel's was much easier than she'd anticipated. And with this newest complication of his health, it probably was for the best.

Fiona sighed. If only she could convince herself that being in the same house with Zeke was something she could handle.

Chapter Sixteen

And to think she'd wasted time worrying about staying in the same house with Zeke.

Fiona stood, rubbing the dull ache in the small of her back, and walked absently to the window. Pulling back the heavy drapes, she stared at the steady downpour of rain that streaked the windowpane. With a sigh, she dropped the material and glanced back at the bed where her grandfather lay sleeping.

He had improved. That was enough to be thankful for, Fiona reminded herself. She could imagine how dank and cold his cell at the gaol would be in this damp weather. Why, if he'd had to stay there much longer, let alone travel through these early summer rains to Philadelphia, he'd probably be dead. Instead, he was resting peacefully on a thick feather tick, in a large, comfortable room with a cheery fire that kept the evening chill at bay.

Aye, she should be thankful, Fiona thought, as she trailed her fingers along the brocaded coverlet at the foot of the bed. Grandfather's fever was gone. He'd regain his strength soon, and then . . .

Using the brass poker, Fiona nudged the burning logs, decided against adding another, and sank into the winged chair by the hearth. She imagined they'd stay here even when her grandfather's health improved. They were prisoners, after all — at least the laird was. But, Fiona had to admit, there certainly were worse prisons. Allowing her gaze to drift about the room, Fiona noted the expensive furnishings — the Chippendale bed and bureau, the Turkish rug beneath her feet.

The entire house reflected wealth and taste, and she had the run of it — the run of the entire town — if she wanted. All things considered, she really had no right to complain, Fiona thought, as she again sighed.

Especially since Ezekiel Kincaid was leaving in the morning for South Carolina.

Brushing an imaginary speck of lint from her silk skirt, Fiona bounded to her feet. She covered the distance to the window quickly, then paced back to the chair. She was glad Zeke was leaving. Glad and relieved. Now she wouldn't have to concern herself with being around him. She could forget this annoying pull — nay, attraction — she felt for him. With him away trying to repel the British invasion near Charleston, she'd be able to purge him from her mind.

That's just what she'd do. Fiona plopped down in the chair, deciding she liked the word *purge*. With him gone, she'd finally be able to do it. She would realize dislike and anger were the emotions she should feel toward him, and she'd make sure that's all she felt.

The problem was, she should have been able to do that now, because she'd hardly seen the colonel for a fortnight. Not since she'd walked with him along the riverbank had she spent more than a quarter hour in his presence. She'd been living in the same house with him, eating his food, sleeping in one of his beds, and the only time she'd seen him was the morning she'd risen before dawn.

Not to see him, Fiona assured herself for the hundredth time. She'd simply awakened early. After dressing, she'd wandered downstairs, into the dining room. And there he sat. Since he obviously hadn't noticed her, Fiona stood in the doorway studying him. His hair had been freshly brushed, tied with a simple black ribbon into a queue. She'd wondered at the time if he ever wore a wig. She'd never seen him in one. But then, it would be a shame to cover that thick, dark brown hair.

He'd turned, seeing her, and he'd stood so quickly, she'd been startled. "I . . . I thought to have some breakfast," she'd mumbled, for lack of anything better to say.

Inviting her into the room, he'd waited until she was served to continue with his meal, though Fiona could tell he was eager to finish. They'd eaten in silence for some time, the quiet so uncomfortable that Fiona was barely able to swallow her ham, before he spoke. "I understand your grandfather is much better."

"Aye. His fever is nearly gone, and his appetite returning." Fiona had paused. "Thank you for sending the doctor."

He'd waved off her gratitude. "He isn't Robert, but he's the best I could do."

The smile he'd flashed then had made Fiona realize how foolish she'd been to come downstairs. It made her want to throw herself into his arms. Luckily, he'd left shortly after, pleading urgent business at the docks. But Fiona had wondered if it wasn't simply an overpowering desire to be away from her.

If that was his desire, he'd accomplished it well, Fiona decided as she left her grandfather's room and entered her own. But tonight was his last night at home. Certainly he'd spend the evening at home, Fiona thought, as she let down her hair and began

271

brushing the thick red curls. Tomorrow he'd leave for South Carolina, leave to fight the British. Fiona tried swallowing back the uncomfortable feeling that gave her.

He'd be all right. Twisting her curls into a braid, Fiona wrapped it around her head coronet-style, jabbing in wooden hairpins to secure it. Zeke was big and strong and certainly knew how to take care of himself. Fiona pinched her cheeks, examining the effect in the cheval glass. There was no reason to think he'd meet the same fate as the dead and wounded she'd seen on the battlefield at Moore's Creek. She pinched her cheeks again, wondering why she suddenly looked so pale, and left the room.

Fiona ate supper alone.

Looking down across the Irish linen tablecloth set with Chelsea porcelain, she wished she'd taken the meal in Grandfather's room. That had been her policy since arriving here—and it was a good one.

Fiona sighed, shaking her head when a servant offered to pour her more wine. There was no sense prolonging this. He wasn't coming home. And it wasn't too difficult to figure out what—or rather, who—was the cause.

In the hallway, Fiona met Mrs. Steel—another reason not to come downstairs.

"Good evening, Mrs. Steel."

"Mistress MacClure."

Though Fiona had tried to initiate several conversations with the older woman, she had responded very curtly. Fiona was pretty certain the housekeeper thought she was Zeke's mistress, a notion that amused Fiona, since she rarely saw him. If there was a mistress—and Fiona thought that a strong possibility—it certainly wasn't someone in this house. The man was never home.

Fiona started climbing the stairs, looked over her shoulder to see the housekeeper watching her, then continued. She'd play cards with Grandfather, and go to bed early.

He'd had too much to drink.

Zeke didn't need Mrs. Steel's reproving expression to convince him of that as he came through the front door. But that didn't stop her from giving it. Zeke shook the raindrops off his hat and laid it on the hall table. "I'll be in the library, Mrs. Steel."

"Will you be wanting a meal sent in? It's been hours since supper, but—"

"No." Zeke concentrated on walking down the hall. "I don't think I care to eat." Or could eat, he added to himself.

The library was dark except for the remnants of a fire lit earlier, but allowed to slowly die when he didn't return. Zeke ignored the lack of light as he sank into the leather chair behind his desk.

He fingered the decanter of Scotch, poured himself a liberal portion, then leaned back in the chair, resting the glass on his flat stomach. He'd spent the evening at the Sign of the Gull, a waterfront tavern. Though he'd drunk his share of grog, he'd kept himself from crossing the line into drunkenness, promising himself he'd step across when he returned home. But he didn't want Scotch; he wanted a Scotswoman.

Annoyed with himself, Zeke brought the glass to his lips, hoping the heady smell and strong taste would clear his mind. It didn't. Closing his eyes, too tired to fight it, Zeke gave in and let his mind fill with thoughts of her. She'd become almost an obsession with him. An unwanted obsession.

"One that will end tomorrow," Zeke mumbled, as he

took another drink. One more night of living in the same house with you, he thought, lifting his glass to toast the invisible Fiona that haunted him. After tonight there would be no more lying awake, wanting, knowing her mere rods away.

Absence. That's what he needed to rid himself of this foolish bewitchment. And absence was what he'd get. Not the pseudo nonappearance he'd forced on himself for nearly a fortnight, but true separation. Separation of space, and more.

With Sir Peter Parker's fleet confirmed off the coast of Charleston, he'd be too busy to remember how soft her skin was, or the deep violet her eyes could become when caught in the throes of passion.

Zeke rubbed his hand over his jaw. It wasn't like him to be so maudlin, but then this wasn't an ordinary day. Not only was it the last he'd spend in Wilmington for a while, it was the day he'd received a letter from his mother. The first in nearly ten years.

Letting his eyes stray toward the parchment lying on his desk, Zeke picked it up. It didn't matter that the light was insufficient to read the flowing script, Zeke realized he had the words committed to memory.

She wanted to see him, wanted him to come to Fountainhead, her family's plantation in South Carolina. Just like that. "After twenty-two damn years." Zeke threw the letter onto his desk. "She writes once in twenty-two years." Zeke shook his head. "And now—now—she wants to see me. Why can't she just leave me alone like she always has?"

He'd been seven years old when she'd left—left for good to return to Fountainhead. Not that she'd been available to him much before then, but he had known she was there.

Zeke leaned back in the chair, propping his legs on the desktop.

Judging from the discussion he'd overheard the day before his mother had left, she hadn't been available to his father, either. Though he hadn't understood that part of their argument at the time, he'd known it was important.

His father was begging.

Zeke could still remember how it had felt to sit high in the magnolia tree, camouflaged by the large leaves, and hear the pleading tone in his father's voice. His large, dark, robust father gave orders to employees, answered Zeke's questions firmly and completely, and often laughed—but he did not whine. Yet he was doing it. Begging his wife to let him touch her.

Though Zeke hated to hear his father in such a state, wished they hadn't stopped beneath the tree he was playing in, he couldn't help feeling some empathy toward the older man. But Zeke had long since given up hoping his mother would touch or cuddle him. At seven, he'd decided he didn't need what she'd never offered. But apparently his father did, because he couldn't seem to stop asking, telling his wife she would want to stay if she'd only let him touch her.

At first, when Zeke realized his mother had gone, he blamed his father. If touching her would have made her stay, why hadn't he just done it? He was certainly bigger and stronger then she. But later, when he first experienced the touch of a woman, when he fully understood the argument he'd heard years before, Zeke had known better. Nothing would have kept his mother from returning to the place she loved more than anything else—to Fountainhead. Just as nothing would keep Fiona from returning to Armadale.

"Don't think about it," Zeke mumbled to himself. "You don't really care."

Taking another drink, Zeke decided to go to bed—try to sleep. Dawn would be here before he knew it, and then he'd march his men south.

The rain still hadn't stopped. Fiona could hear it
steadily droning against the window as if mocking her
attempts to sleep. The air was cold, yet she could
barely tolerate the restricting blankets. Even the finely
woven linens, the delicate night rail, seemed too abrasive on her sensitive skin.

She was a fool. "A fool," Fiona repeated, as she
swung her legs over the side of the high mattress.
She'd been in bed for hours, yet sleep escaped her.
Her body was tired, ready to accept the oblivion, but
her mind wouldn't let loose. Fiona raked both hands
through her hair, pushing the heavy red curls away
from her face.

She needed something to take her thoughts off
Zeke. The truth she'd been trying to fight caught her
off guard, but she was willing to concede the point.

That was her problem. She couldn't stop thinking of
Zeke, wishing she'd been able to see him one more
time. Tomorrow she'd stop this foolishness, Fiona assured herself. When he was gone. But that wouldn't
help her sleep tonight.

After lighting the bedside candle, Fiona glanced
around the room, hoping to find a diversion. Her eyes
snagged on the stitching she'd left on the table near
the fireplace. Too mindless. Besides, she'd spent nearly
an hour tatting the edge of pillowcase before she'd
climbed into bed, and it hadn't helped.

A book might work. But she'd replaced the one
she'd finished yesterday, and hadn't chosen a new one.
If she wanted something to read, she'd have to go
downstairs. She hesitated, not wanting to chance upon
anyone, then realized the entire household — even
Zeke — would be asleep. With a sigh, Fiona slipped off

the edge of the bed, almost scurrying back when her bare feet hit the cold floor.

Instead, she hurried to the fireplace, tossing another log onto the fire before wrapping a shawl around her shoulders and leaving the bedroom.

The candle she cupped with her hand splashed light ahead of her as she crept down the stairs. Fiona paused at the library door, hesitant to invade Zeke's private domain. But she'd done it often enough to get books during the weeks she'd spent in his house. He had told her to make free use of his home. There was just something about the night that made it more intimate.

Pushing open the well-oiled door, Fiona stepped inside. The servants had failed to bank the fire, and the last of the glowing ashes filtered silently through the grate. Placing her candle on a cabriole-legged table, Fiona snuggled deeper into the folds of her shawl.

Two walls of the room were lined with bookcases, filled with books. Fiona hurried to the one surrounding the fireplace. If she remembered correctly, she'd noticed a copy of Fielding's *The History of Tom Jones, a Foundling* on the fifth shelf. She'd passed by the book before, but tonight she imagined it offered just the involvement she needed. Standing on tiptoe, Fiona reached toward the book.

"What in the hell are you doing down here?"

Startled as much by the speaker—she recognized the deep baritone immediately—as the fact that someone was in the room with her, Fiona whirled around. She dropped the book she'd managed to retrieve, but didn't even look down to where it thudded onto the cushioning carpet.

Searching the deep shadows, she found him, sitting behind the mahogany desk. As she watched, wide-eyed, he stood, filling the space with his tall, broad-shouldered form. When he started toward her, large, dark and dangerously powerful, Fiona knew a moment of déjà vu. He looked much the same as the first time she'd seen him.

A loose linen shirt, carelessly opened down the front, reflected the glow of the solitary candle which dimly lit the study. The stark white material contrasted with the snug deep-blue breeches, the tangle of brown hair covering his chest. Fiona raised her eyes to his face, dark and wickedly handsome in the grainy shadows. Instinctively she stepped back, only to feel the biting edge of a shelf wedge into the small of her back.

"I asked what you were doing down here."

His voice had softened, but it still held the gritting timbre that sent tingles down Fiona's spine. Ignoring the sensation, Fiona stared back at him. He'd frightened her at first—in truth, still frightened her, though her mind knew he wouldn't really harm her. But he had no right to speak to her so. He had given her run of his house, and the last time she'd noticed, the library was part of it. She supposed she should have knocked before entering, but who would have thought he'd be sitting here in the dark at this hour?

She lifted her chin. "I came for a book."

"This one?" Zeke nudged the fallen volume with his boot.

Fiona swallowed. "Aye."

"Then please get it and leave."

Gasping, Fiona scowled, her arms akimbo. Why, the big oaf wasn't even going to pick it up for her. And as far as his rudely delivered order went . . . "I have as much right to be here as—"

"Damnit, Fiona!" Zeke tightened his already clenched fists. "Don't you know better than to parade in front of me dressed like that?"

The midnight-blue eyes that raked down her body heated Fiona as no roaring fire ever could. It drew her own gaze down for a quick self-inspection. The knitted shawl she'd wrapped around her shoulders now lay in a rose-colored tangle at her feet, but she was still demurely covered. The white linen night rail buttoned primly at her neck and wrists, and covered everything but three small pink toes on each foot. She might be in her night clothes, but compared to him, she was quite properly covered.

"You're hardly the one to be complaining of someone's attire. Yours is hardly that of a gentleman." Satisfied with her retort, Fiona became bolder, and made a frightful mistake. Lifting her hand, she continued, "This is positively indecent."

And then she touched his exposed chest.

Heat from his hair-roughened flesh flared through her. She tried to pull away, but his large, callused hand covered hers. Looking up, she caught the devilish gleam in the depths of his eyes.

"I didn't say I was complaining. And I never claimed to be a gentleman where you're concerned, Fiona."

"Let me go." Fiona's voice was no more than a breathy whisper. She could feel his heart's rapid beat beneath her flattened palm, knew it matched the cadence of her own.

He should release her. Zeke tried to control his breathing, and stared down into her upturned face. If he'd had an ounce of sense he wouldn't have made his presence known. If he'd kept quiet while she got the damn book she'd never have seen him — and she'd be gone, back to her safe little room.

He'd almost managed it, too. Watching through heavy-lidded eyes, he'd ignored the tightening of his stomach muscles as she walked in the room. But when she'd moved toward the hearth, when those glowing coals had illuminated her, turning her night rail nearly transparent, the ache had moved lower. Challenging her, moving close to her, certainly hadn't helped.

She looked even more beautiful, more alluring, since he was near enough to see the violet eyes, the full, inviting mouth. Red curls flirted with the light from the flickering embers, seemed to blaze with a fire of their own. Her hand on his chest drove him crazy. And he was so hard he hurt.

She was making a mockery of her demand. Fiona knew, they both knew, the light pressure of his hold allowed her freedom—if she wanted it. Yet she stood, staring up at him, unable to move. The clock on the mantel ticked away the seconds, proof that time didn't stand still, but Fiona could swear that was happening. She forced herself to breathe deeply, hoping to break his spell, but the scent of leather and whiskey and him only deepened it.

"I . . . I should go back upstairs." She could control her trembling voice no more than the coursing blood through her body.

"You're right," Zeke agreed, though when he released her hand, it was to trail his fingers along her arm, catching her elbow in a sensual squeeze.

Fiona felt herself being tugged closer to his heat, and went willingly, unable to resist the pull. Her breathing slowed when his thumb traced lazy circles on the linen covering her inner arm, caught when his lips lowered toward hers. "Just one good-bye kiss," she heard him murmur before his other hand tangled in her hair, tilting her face to meet him.

Passion flared white-hot.

Zeke's mouth skimmed across hers in a futile attempt to move slowly, then, consumed by the heat, he plunged deeper. His tongue probed, and a groan vibrated from his chest when she opened for him.

Her world tilted, spun, the weakness in her knees forcing her to cling to him. His large hands traveled impatiently down her back, clutched her rounded bottom and pressed her closer. Molding to him, Fiona felt a wild surge of erotic power. He throbbed, hot and hard, against her, proof that he wanted her as much as she wanted him.

Fiona dug her fingers through his hair, tasted the moist heat of his mouth, and longed for more. Her breasts strained against his chest, the nipples unbelievably sensitive to the fine linen separating flesh from flesh.

His mouth ravished hers, taking and giving with the same wild abandon. Sensation flooded her. His heat turned her body to molten fire. She wanted to surround him. Impatiently his lips slid from hers to torch the skin along her cheek, down the side of her neck. His lips were soft, demanding, the tip of his tongue sensual. The whisker-roughened jaw abraded the underside of Fiona's chin and she moaned.

Zeke caught the sensual sound as his lips again claimed hers. Hunger and need raced through him like wildfire. Bending her back in his arms, he ground against her, almost losing control when she shifted, instinctively spreading her legs to accommodate him. He could feel the moist heat of her womanhood through the heavy cotton of his restraining breeches, the filmy fabric of her nightgown. The heady scent of passion enveloped them.

Dragging his open mouth down her flesh, he followed the curve of her breast, found the dark, hard shadows beneath the night rail, and suckled. Her legs opened wider, his need raged with raw power. His hands flexed, balling up fistfuls of fabric, lifting the night rail higher and higher. He'd take her here, on the floor. He'd . . .

Squeezing his eyes shut, Zeke fought the logic that burned at the edges of his mind. He wanted her, she wanted him. And tomorrow he'd leave . . . and she'd be sorry. Sorry she had given herself to him on the cold floor — again. She was caught up in passion, passion he knew how to ignite in her, but if she had time to think, she wouldn't do this. And she'd have plenty of time to think while he was gone — maybe even a lifetime.

Silently cursing himself, Zeke tore his mouth away. Sucking air into his deprived body proved painful. Or maybe it was the look of bewilderment in her smoldering eyes. She slumped forward, would have fallen if not for the strong hands cupping her shoulders.

"You'd better go," Zeke said, when he could trust his voice.

"Go?" She tried to understand him, couldn't.

"Back to your room." Zeke started to turn her, unable to bear seeing the hurt in her eyes.

"But . . ."

"It was a good-bye kiss, Fiona, nothing more." The lie almost choked him.

A good-bye kiss? A good-bye kiss! He'd driven her to the edge of sanity, and to him it had only been a good-bye kiss. Anger steeled Fiona's limbs. She jerked away from him, her hair flying about her face. Her breast felt cold, and looking down,n she noticed her wet night rail plastered against her still-straining nipple. Hastily she grabbed for her shawl, tossing it around her shoulders.

"Do you still want the book?" Zeke bent over, retrieving it from the floor.

"No!" Fiona rushed toward the door. "I don't want anything from you."

If only that were true. Fiona slammed into her bedroom, balling up the shawl and tossing it onto the bed. "I hate you, Ezekial Kincaid," she mumbled, stalking to the window. "I hate you. I hate you." Lifting aside the drapes, pressing her forehead to the chilled glass, Fiona sighed. "But, oh, how I want you." Closing her eyes, letting her warm breath dew the pane, she held on to that truth.

She wanted him. Not just physically, though Lord knew all he had to do was touch her — nay, look at her — and she longed for that. But she wanted his strength, his comfort. She wanted him to tell her he didn't want to leave. That he'd be all right — that he'd come back.

And he, he wanted a good-bye kiss. Nothing more.

Fiona held her breath when she heard footfalls in the hallway. Zeke. Going to his room. She listened, waited, as they reached her door, expecting to hear him continue down the corridor. But the sound of leather heel against wood stopped. Turning, Fiona stared at the paneled door, knowing he was on the other side.

She gasped in air, felt her heart pound, when she heard his knuckles rap against the wood.

Chapter Seventeen

She shouldn't answer it. Then he would continue on his way — out of her life. The knock had been tentative. He wouldn't force himself in, if she simply said nothing.

Fiona's hand pressed against her chest, trying to calm her pounding heart. And she waited. Seconds trudged by, and still no sound of retreating footsteps. It couldn't be much longer till he left — her room, Wilmington . . . her life.

Biting her lip, Fiona blinked back the tears threatening to spill over her lashes. And then, unable to stop herself, began moving.

He appeared startled when she jerked open the door. His arm, draped high over the jamb, dropped. His head, which, in that moment when she'd first seen him, had rested against his powerful forearm, snapped around — to stare at her.

Their eyes met, even when Zeke took a hesitant step forward. "It was more than a good-bye kiss," he allowed, his voice husky and low.

"Aye, it was."

"I want . . . need more."

"So do I."

Her soft-spoken admission filled Zeke with awe. He'd sat downstairs after forcing her away, wondering how he could ever let her go. He had no choice but to leave in the morning, but he'd finally decided he couldn't, without telling her how he felt—at least as much as he knew himself. But he hadn't expected, even dared hope, to hear like sentiments from her.

Zeke shut the door, then slowly took her into his arms. She trembled when he lifted her chin, brushing his lips softly over hers. "This has nothing"—Zeke hesitated, running his hand unhurriedly over her shoulder— "nothing to do with you and your grandfather staying here . . . in my house."

"I know." Fiona smiled and he nibbled at the upturned corner of her mouth.

"I don't want you to think I'm collecting payment, because I'm not."

Fiona touched his cheek. She couldn't remember ever feeling so warm or protected, or safe. "I should never have suggested such a thing."

"You were desperate."

"Aye." And she was beginning to feel desperate now. Zeke's mouth skimmed a heartbeat away from hers. His breath mingled with hers; when he spoke, his lips met hers in fleeting butterfly caresses, but she wanted more.

"Tell me to leave and I will."

"Leave?" Fiona studied the dark blue eyes that stared at her, as her fingers traced his strong jaw. "I've never known you to be so . . . so . . ." Fiona couldn't think of a word to describe him at this moment, so she changed her tack. "You've always boldly taken what you want."

Zeke tried to still his hands, but they seemed bent

on relearning the form and texture of her slender back. "I don't want to take you." Zeke sucked in his breath when Fiona pressed closer to him. "I want to make love with you."

"Ezekiel?"

"Hmmm?" Zeke wondered if he had the strength to leave if she asked. He loved the feel of her, the smell of her, the taste of her. Her hand was behind his neck, playing in the hair at his nape, driving him insane. He felt the pressure, the downward pull, at the same time he heard her sensual siren song.

"Stay, Zeke. Please. . . ."

Fiona's last plea was lost as his mouth swept down on hers. He lifted her up against his body, and Fiona wondered how he'd ever stood talking so long, when he was so obviously aroused. Then his tongue plunged inside her mouth, and she couldn't think at all.

Her arms locked around his neck, urging him ever closer as he held her against him. When he tore his mouth away so they could breathe, Fiona gasped in air while kissing his nose, the tip of his chin, the bold sweep of his brow.

"God, Fiona, you drive me crazy. I want to go slowly, to savor this time." Then he belied his words by kissing her so deeply, Fiona went weak.

Scooping her into his arms, Zeke carried her to the bed. He laid her down, watching the abundance of red curls fan across the pillow. "So beautiful," he murmured, following her onto the high tester bed.

The mattress sank beneath his weight, cradling Fiona in the dreamy soft feathers. She spread her legs, offering him the comfort of her body, gasping when he snuggled down on top of her.

"Am I too heavy?"

"No," Fiona breathed, then, because she couldn't help herself, added, "You feel so good." The touch of arrogance in his grin made Fiona smile. "You really are an insufferable man."

The grin broadened. "And you are the most tempestuous woman."

"Tempestuous?" Fiona's eyes opened wide, and she glared at him as he leaned on his elbows, staring down at her. "I am n—" His deep, drugging kiss cut off the rest of her denial—proved it false.

Fiona couldn't seem to get close enough to him. Her fingers pushed away the linen shirt and dug into his bunched shoulder muscles as he settled more intimately against her. His skin was smooth, velvet over steel.

When Zeke broke off the kiss, there was no trace of his earlier grin. His eyes, smoldering a smoky blue, searched her face, the flushed cheeks, the parted, kiss-swollen lips, then traveled lower, watching his suddenly inept fingers. He'd never known buttons to be so small, so stubborn, so aggravating. He could see the dusky shadows beneath the fabric, longed to taste the torrid tips that flirted with him as her breasts rose with each ragged breath. His thumb skimmed across her nipple, once, twice, answering her erotic moan the only way he could.

The sound of ripping fabric momentarily startled Fiona, but then his moist heat surrounded her breast, and she was lost in the sensation. His teeth grazed, traveled the thin line between pleasure and pain so skillfully, Fiona thought she would surely lose her mind. She moaned, she arched, she writhed, she called out his name on a ragged breath.

"I know." His words were muffled against her chest

287

as he flicked his tongue over the hard bud of her other breast, a promise of things to come, and tore away more fabric.

Fiona's heated flesh flashed cold, then hotter than ever as he leaned back on his knees, admiring her nakedness. His hands skimmed down her ribs, her stomach, then lower, spreading her thighs with no more than a suggestion of need. She arched up to him as his fingers tangled in her nest of moist curls.

"God, Fiona," she heard him say, his breath fanning the flames, the core of her heat. "You look like you're on fire for me."

"I am. I am. I . . . oh . . ." Fiona never knew anything could splinter reality so completely as the touch of his tongue did. Again and again he caressed her. Her legs tightened, pulling him closer, the feel of his whisker-roughened cheeks on her inner thighs an erotic contrast to the scorching liquid heat of his mouth.

She burned. Like a blaze flaring out of control, her body flamed. Wave upon wave of molten fire raged through her, consumed her. Clutching handfuls of Zeke's hair, Fiona began to tremble, couldn't stop trembling, as the inferno reached a fevered peak. Then, like so many glowing embers, she drifted back to earth.

Zeke slid up her body, relishing the taste of her, the feel of her surrender. He still ached with unfulfilled need, but his thoughts were on Fiona, on the pleasure he knew he'd given her, the pleasures yet to come. Brushing away a tangle of hair strewn across her mouth, he touched her lower lip. "Tempestuous," he whispered before claiming her mouth with his, but there was no teasing lilt to the word.

Fiona thought all her energy was spent, but the first taste of his tongue proved her wrong. He ignited her banked passion, sent her arms around his lean waist. His shirt was gone, but as her hands moved lower, the heavy material of his breeches impeded her exploration. Zeke shifted, moaned into her mouth when she followed the firm slope of his muscular buttocks. "Did I hurt you?"

"Oh, God, no." Zeke rolled to his side. "Feel what you do to me." He guided her hand, pressing it hard against his swollen length. She squeezed and ·he groaned, the sound vibrating from deep in his broad chest.

Now it was Fiona fumbling with buttons. His were larger, more easily unfastened; still, she had a fleeting thought of rending the fabric before she managed to unclothe him. Zeke raised his hips, allowing her to pull the breeches down, clenching his teeth when she touched him.

He was magnificent. Fiona had once spied her cousins swimming in a pond near her home. She'd been twelve, devilishly curious, and just as disappointed when she'd had her fill of watching Duncan and William frolic in the water. But either men changed drastically as years passed, or Ezekiel Kincade was a marvel.

Fiona ran her fingers along the thick shaft, watching in awe as he throbbed up toward her hand. Desire pooled, awakening the ache deep inside her as she wrapped her hand around him.

Then so suddenly she gasped, he had her on her back, her legs spread, ready to take him. His first thrust was deep, expanding, overpowering, his second even more so. Fiona arched, draped her legs around his hips, welcoming his power and strength as he drove into her. His arms trembled, the muscles heavy and bunched. His body heaved, the coarse curls on his chest rubbing against her straining nipples as his movements accelerated, pumping wildly out of control.

"Zeke!" His name, his groan of release, echoed in her ears as her body convulsed, fragmented around his, urging the last vestiges of his vibrations free.

When his mind had cleared enough to realize he might be crushing her, Zeke rolled to his side, pulling Fiona along to face him. His leg still rested cozily between her thighs, his hand on the small of her waist. She blinked once, then stared at him, bewilderment shading the deep violet of her eyes.

"Are you all right?"

"Aye." Fiona tried to turn her face away, found his hand guiding her chin back toward him.

"Are you sorry?"

"About this?" Making a small sweep of her hand to indicate their intimate position, Fiona cursed the blush she felt creeping up her neck. Except for the hand that now drew lazy circles over her ribs, he seemed impervious to their nakedness. And while earlier it hadn't bothered her, either, now she found the fact that her breasts brushed against the hair on his chest every time she breathed disconcerting.

He apparently didn't, because a lopsided grin formed slowly. "Yes, I mean this. Do you wish you hadn't let me in?"

"I don't —" Again he forced her to look at him when she would have turned away.

"Please don't regret this, Fiona." His expression turned serious so quickly, the indentations from his dimples remained. "What I said earlier is true. Our lovemaking had nothing to do with Patriots or Loyalists."

Trying to ignore the sensual sweep of his fingers down her side, Fiona sighed, rolling onto her back. "If only it were that simple."

"Damnit, Fiona. It's as simple as we want to make it." Zeke scowled down at her, his weight resting on his bent arm.

"Why? Because you say so?" Her attempt to sit up was foiled by Zeke's hands pushing her shoulders back on the mattress. Taking a steadying breath, Fiona tried to explain certain things to him—things she'd forgotten in the heat of their passion. "You say this has nothing to do with you being a Patriot, my feelings about the war. But that's like saying it has nothing to do with us. Because those things are part of us."

Zeke continued to stare at her, the incessant beating of the rain the only sound. Then abruptly he flopped onto his back, throwing his arm up and across his face. "Are you saying what happened tonight means nothing?"

"I could never say that." Fiona watched him lift his arm just enough to peek at her, and smiled. "It just isn't as uncomplicated as you think." Sitting up, Fiona swiped a tangle of hair from her eyes. "For heaven's sake, Zeke, my grandfather's your prisoner. I can't just forget that and make love to you."

"He isn't my prisoner, damnit. And as far as forgetting about it, you seemed to be doing a pretty good job of it earlier. I have scratches on my back to prove it."

Zeke never saw the hand that cracked against his cheek, but he was able to stop the punch she aimed for

291

his stomach. His demand to stop it had no effect as she rose to her knees, then propelled herself at him. Though it was obvious she meant him physical harm, Zeke found her fascinating at that moment.

Her red hair fanned out around her slender body. And she either didn't care about her nakedness anymore, or in her anger had forgotten it. But Zeke noticed, and he was hard even before he caught her wrists, pushed her onto her back, and rolled on top of her. She tried kicking, bucked several times, but she was no match for his weight. That didn't stop her tirade, though. She shrieked, calling him everything from a bastard to a pig. When she questioned his manhood, Zeke decided it was time to shut her up.

One thing about kissing her when her mouth was open, it saved him from coaxing it that way. Not that it would have taken much effort. He'd barely touched his lips to hers, when he felt the fight flow out of her. He deepened the kiss, considered carrying it out to its destined end. His body was ready, and if the tiny sexy moans she made were any indication, so was hers.

But Zeke wanted more than her body, though now, sprawled on top of her, her softness cradling him, it was difficult to keep that in mind. He lifted his head, pleased to see she was as out of breath as he. "Are you ready to listen to me?"

Listen to him! Why the—"You've said plenty, you—"

"I'm sorry."

"What?" Fiona had started to wriggle again, but stopped at his softly spoken words.

"I apologize. I should never have said that to you. Lord knows I didn't mean it." Zeke combed his fingers through her silky hair, fanning it out on the pillow.

"Everything about being with you was beautiful . . . perfect."

His words lulled her. "You don't wish I were more"—Fiona searched for a word—"subdued?"

His bark of laughter made her tense, but his smile had her arms winding around his neck. "I don't want you any different than you are now." Zeke traced his thumb across her lower lip. It was soft, full, still moist from his kiss. "All I can do is think of you." The admission was out before he could stop it.

Searching his face for signs of teasing, Fiona caught her breath at his earnest expression. "You think of me?" *He* barely left her mind, but she had no idea it could be the same with him.

"All the time."

His teeth nipped her earlobe, the words vibrating against her neck. His revelation, the feel of him long and hard, nestled in her softness, was fast driving everything else from her thoughts. With effort, Fiona held on to reality. "That's only because I cause you so much trouble."

Zeke shifted, interrupting his pleasurable exploration of the area behind her ear. She had the softest, sweetest-smelling skin he'd ever known. "You do that," he conceded, chuckling when her eyes narrowed.

She'd wanted a denial, pure and simple, Fiona thought, realizing how much his good-natured agreement hurt her. Her fingers stopped playing in the black curls at his nape. "And I suppose I haven't been sorely provoked."

"By whom?"

"By you."

"Me?" Zeke grinned, wondering how long it would take him to mellow the flash of temper in her eyes to

293

passion. He set about seeing, while he listened to her summary of his supposed transgressions.

"You came to Armadale, trying to gain support for the Whigs. Don't do that."

"What? This?" Zeke obligingly moved lower when she nodded. "My visit wouldn't have bothered you so much if you hadn't broken into my room and tried to bash my skull in with a candlestick," he pointed out, between nibbles.

"You dragged me into your bedroom."

"I wanted to find out why you were there. Does this feel good?"

"Aye," Fiona conceded, trying to keep her breathing steady. "Is that why you kissed me?" Her body arched toward his tongue. "Colonel Kincaid, are you listening to me?"

"You have my complete attention." Zeke rose up on his elbows. "I kissed you because I wanted to." The deep violet eyes had lost the sting of temper, but they still weren't as smoky purple as he wanted them. "For the same reason I'm going to kiss you now."

When he lifted his head again, Fiona's hold on reality was tenuous, but she felt she had to point out the obvious. "This doesn't change the basic facts."

Zeke's hand drifted down her body. A low moan escaped her when he cupped her moist heat. "Which are?"

"You . . . you're a Patriot, and I'm . . . Oh, Zeke. I'm a Loyalist."

"We're going to have to have a serious philosophical discussion."

"Now?"

Zeke stared at her flushed face. "No, Fiona, not now." The last thing he saw before sliding into her fiery sheath was the agreement in her passion-glazed eyes.

Something soft and fuzzy aggravated him, disturbed his peaceful slumber. In an attempt to hold on to the last threads of his dream—a decidedly sensual dream centering around a redheaded siren—Zeke rubbed the back of his hand across his nose. His fingers tangled in skeins of thick, curly hair.

Opening his eyes, Zeke smiled. There was more to this dream than a phantom lover. Fiona lay warm and softly pliant in sleep, snuggled against him. Her hair curled around his face, fluttering with each breath he took. Reaching up, he brushed it away, realizing a strand was caught in his whiskers. He released it, running the silky ringlet through his fingers.

He'd never given much thought to hair color before, though thinking back over the women he'd known, he guessed he'd preferred dark hair to light. But now, he couldn't imagine ever liking anything but hair the color of fire. He brushed the strand along her arm. Or skin of milky white, he added to himself, touching his lips to her shoulder.

She made a soft, sleepy sound, then snuggled her rounded bottom more firmly against him. He should get up. Though he didn't give a damn for himself what anyone thought, Fiona probably would fare better if he wasn't found in her bed come morning. Besides, he needed to meet his men shortly after dawn, and though he didn't know the time, there couldn't be that much of the night left.

He'd leave in a minute, Zeke promised himself, settling back onto the pillow. The fire in the grate had burned down to ashes, but they were warm and cozy beneath the quilt Zeke had pulled over them before falling asleep. He closed his eyes, savoring the sweet feminine smell of the woman beside him. Damn, he didn't want to leave her.

He liked waking up beside her, liked making love to her, talking to her, looking at her. Hell, he even liked arguing with her. Especially if they could end each disagreement the way they had last night.

Not that Zeke thought they'd really solved anything—not in her mind, anyway. She still saw them on different sides. And maybe they were. But that didn't mean they had to stay that way. He was certain she'd see the right of his way of thinking sooner or later. It might take a while, but he was a patient man—usually. They'd talk. But he couldn't do anything until he returned from South Carolina, and he had no idea when that would be. Thank goodness she'd be here, relatively safe, in his house. Zeke's hand tightened over her breast, noting with pleasure that even in sleep she responded to him.

He must leave. Right now. Just get out of the bed and leave. His eyes strained to catch a glimpse of the sky through the small space between the drapes. It seemed dark, but even though the rain appeared to have stopped, the dawn would be shadowed by gloomy clouds. If he rose now, he could dress, have breakfast, and hope she'd be awake in time to bid him good-bye.

If not, he would leave her a note. That might be best. She needed her rest. Zeke couldn't help grinning as he remembered why she was so tired. It stood to reason that he should be as exhausted as she, but in truth he felt wide awake, rejuvenated. And damn sorry he had to leave.

296

He could stay. The thought crept into his mind, snagged, and wouldn't let loose. He was a colonel in the militia, not the continentals. His main duty was to remain in North Carolina, to protect her from enemy attack. He certainly didn't have to volunteer to go outside his colony's borders to fight. But the truth was, he had. And more, he'd convinced others in the militia to do the same.

"We need to help our allies in arms. Show the British we are united in our stand against tyranny," he'd said. Oh, he'd been inspiring as hell. Most of his men had rallied to the call. And most would be shocked if they could know his mind at this moment. All because of a slip of a redheaded woman.

"Fiona." Zeke whispered her name as he brushed his lips over the curve of her shoulder. He tried to move his hand, but hers reached up to enfold it, pressing his palm against her straining nipple.

Her name came out on a moan this time. "Fiona, honey, I need to leave."

"Stay. Just a little longer," Fiona mumbled, hovering on the filmy edge between sleep and consciousness.

"Fiona, sweet—" A deep groan cut off what would have been a brilliant explanation of why he must go at this moment. All because she'd wriggled her soft bottom closer to a part of him that was anything but soft. "Honey"—Zeke drew in his breath—"you don't know what you're doing."

"Don't I?" In the next moment she proved him wrong by doing it again.

"I'm not going to be responsible if you keep—"

Her low chuckle and the movement of her hips made him pause. His hand glided down her stomach. "I never knew you were so . . . playful first thing in the morning."

"You've never been around me first thing in the morning." Fiona peeked over her shoulder at him. She could barely make out his shadowy form in the near darkness, but she thought she caught a flash of white teeth as he grinned.

"True enough."

"And besides," Fiona continued, rubbing against his hardness, "I think I've seen all you can do."

"Oh, you think so?" Zeke asked, his fingers sifting down through her tight curls. She was warm and sweetly moist.

Now it was Fiona's turn to moan, and her voice wasn't quite as teasing when she responded, "I do."

"Well, I consider that a challenge," Zeke growled against her ear. "And I never . . . well, rarely ever, pass up a challenge."

He thrust deep inside her before Fiona could catch her breath. Fiona's lips fell slack, as the motion of his body quickened, matched that of his finger. It took mere moments for the tension to reach a peak of unbearable beauty. She teetered a heartbeat on the edge, then soared off toward the heavens.

Wild and uninhibited, her convulsive release triggered the savage explosion of his own. Zeke collapsed back on the pillow, totally spent. Nothing short of her breathless admission could make him open his eyes. "You are full of surprises."

Shaking his head, Zeke rolled her onto her back, hovering over her. "You don't know the half of it."

"Goodness." The laughter in her voice didn't completely disguise the anticipation.

"Unfortunately" — Zeke brushed his fingers across her cheek, feeling the lightheartedness she'd inspired

298

drift away—"you'll have to wait until I return to experience the rest of it."

Fiona stared up at the face above and so close to hers, trying to make out his features. She'd awakened, safe and warm, and fully aroused, in his arms, and he'd almost made her forget that he was leaving.

She shouldn't care. Fiona knew that. At least her mind knew that. But her heart couldn't stop feeling as if the world were coming to an end. He kissed her lightly, then rolled over. Fiona started to follow, but his words stilled her. "There's no reason for you to get up. 'Tis chilly for summer. The rain, I suppose. Stay in bed where it's warm."

But you've taken the warmth with you, Fiona thought, wanting to argue with him. But she could hear him hastily pulling on his breeches. He wanted to be gone. And he wanted her to stay.

She didn't know what she'd expected. Not a long, sorrowful good-bye, of course. That wasn't like him. But certainly more than this . . . this dismissal. He began talking again in the same detached voice. Telling her of the coin he'd leave for her in his study. That she was to use it as she saw fit, purchasing what she needed, what she wanted. But Fiona paid no attention. She merely snuggled down under the quilt and wished him gone.

But when the door closed quietly behind him, Fiona remembered her grandfather's adage about being careful what you wish for. The room seemed empty without him. Lying on her back, staring at the ever-lightening tester, Fiona tried to reason through what had happened last night and this morning. Things had changed between them, but she wasn't certain how or why. They had made love, yet there'd been no words of love. Not that she wanted them, Fiona assured herself quickly. But it would have helped to order things in her mind.

He'd wanted her. And, Lord help her, she'd wanted him. So much she'd let the consequences be damned. Last night, even this morning, nestled in his arms, it had seemed the most natural thing in the world. But now she wondered.

He'd been angry when she'd suggested becoming his mistress. Last night he'd denied that his desire had anything to do with her grandfather. But what was she, if not his kept woman?

He said they'd talk, but she'd have to wait till he returned from South Carolina. Fiona shoved away the nagging fear that he might not return. He'd come back. But it could be weeks, months. She didn't know if she could wait that long.

Jumping out of bed, Fiona slipped her feet into the satin shoes she'd discarded last night. Too rushed to dress, she pulled on a shift, then searched through her wardrobe for her dark blue cloak. Chances of anyone else being about this early were slim.

His room was empty, as was the dining room when she burst into it. Deciding she'd missed him, that she would have to wait till he returned, Fiona leaned against the table. It took her a moment to realize the horse she heard could belong to only one man. But when she did, she dashed out of the house and toward the stables.

The rain had stopped, but muggy air surrounded her as she splashed through puddles, bright with reflections of the mauve sunrise.

"For God's sake, Fiona!" Zeke drew back sharply on the stallion's reins, twisting the horse's head and skidding him to the side. His heart pounded fiercely against his ribs when he thought about what might have happened if he hadn't noticed her as he rounded the corner of the stable.

She grabbed his leg before he could dismount, and looked up at him so earnestly he forgot to lecture her on keeping herself safe. "Are you all right?" Zeke reached down, brushing the wildly curling hair from her face.

"I think so." Fiona tried to catch her breath. She'd seen him riding toward her a split second before he'd veered to the side.

"What are you doing out here?" Mist rose around her in soft, silent billows.

"I don't . . ." With him staring down at her, his eyes as blue as the promise of a new day, the heat of his body beneath her hand, she couldn't remember what urgency had driven her.

"I'm glad you're here."

"You are?" Fiona looked up in surprise as he leaned toward her, his hand sifting through her hair.

"I wanted to come back, kiss you good-bye properly."

"Why didn't you?"

The grin he flashed was disarming. "I was afraid seeing you again"—he hesitated—"like I saw you this morning, might make me want to do more than just kiss you."

"I see." Fiona hoped he'd think her red cheeks caused by the rosy wash of dawn.

"And I have to leave. My men are waiting."

Fiona nodded. For the first time she noticed the bedroll attached to his saddle, the knapsack and canteen.

"Probably safe enough kissing you here, though."

Fiona looked down at the soppy ground, agreeing somberly. "I'd say so. I imagine you can resist tumbling me in this."

"I don't know." Zeke rubbed his chin. "Mud might be fun. But I don't think I'd like any of the servants as spectators." He bent over, pulling her up against him and anchoring her there with one arm, before she knew what he was doing. His kiss was deep and lingering. By the time he lowered her enough for her sodden toes to touch the ground, Fiona had forgotten her reason for wanting to talk to him.

"Be good," he said huskily before he gave her a lazy salute and rode out of the yard.

Fiona waited until he turned onto Market Street, till she couldn't see him anymore, before turning back toward the house. Trying to ignore the strange tightness around her heart took so much effort she forgot her worry about being his mistress. Until she stepped into the hallway.

Mrs. Steel stood by the door, her back ramrod straight, her lips pursed. It only took one look at her crisp clothing for Fiona to remember her own disheveled appearance.

"Will you be wanting to break your fast now, Mistress MacClure?"

"No." Fiona tightened the muddy-hemmed cloak around her. "I was just—"

"I think we both know what you were doing . . . what you are."

Although the housekeeper did not elaborate, the possible words flew through Fiona's mind all too easily. She was a kept woman, a mistress . . . a whore.

Turning on her heel, Fiona marched up the stairs.

Once in the privacy of her room, she pulled parchment from the writing table. Without glancing around, making certain to notice nothing that might remind her of her night with Ezekiel Kincaid, Fiona wrote a plea for help.

Dressing quickly, Fiona left the house and headed for Mrs. MacLinn's, knowing full well she'd wake the poor woman at this early hour. But if she waited, if she had time to think, Fiona feared she might not ask Mrs. MacLinn to send her message to Armadale. And deep down, Fiona knew that was what needed to be done.

Chapter Eighteen

Fiona lurched forward, fighting the hand that clamped over her mouth, smothering her startled scream. Struggling, she kicked at the unknown assailant who'd exploded from the stand of oaks behind her. As he jerked her back against him, Mrs. MacLinn's warning rang through her mind. "You shouldn't go walking down by the river all alone, Fiona dear. 'Tis not safe for a lass like yourself," the old woman had said.

But Fiona hadn't listened, and now as she raked her nails across the hand biting into her jaw, she fervently wished she had. No solitary stroll was worth this.

She heard a muffled curse, then jerked her head around as her captor mumbled something in Gaelic. Above the broad-fingered hand her eyes widened in shock.

"Duncan! What are you doing here?" she insisted when he loosened his grip. In answer, he clamped tighter over her mouth.

"For God's sake, Fiona, will you keep your voice down?" He waited another minute before releasing her, then took an involuntary step back as she turned to face him.

Arms akimbo, Fiona spit a strand of hair from her mouth. "What are you doing? You nearly frightened me to death. Why, I thought . . . Never mind what I thought, but—" Fiona held up her hands when she noticed her cousin starting toward her again. "All right, I'll whisper. But you *will* tell me the meaning of this!"

"I've come to rescue you."

"Rescue me?" As far as she knew, the only rescuing she needed had been about two minutes ago.

"The letter, Fiona. I've come in answer to your plea for help." He must have noticed the bewilderment on her face, in her voice, because his held an impatient ring.

"Oh, of course, my letter." The one she'd sent the morning Zeke left for South Carolina. How could she have forgotten? It was just that it had been nearly a month ago, and she'd given up on anyone from Armadale responding to it. She'd also become accustomed to being here. With the major exception of Mrs. Steel, whom Fiona had learned to ignore, her life here was fairly pleasant.

But that didn't mean she wouldn't rather be home.

In the next instant she propelled herself toward her cousin, wrapping her arms around his neck. "Oh, Duncan, I'm so glad to see you. To know you're safe."

"If you don't shut up, I won't be for long."

The chill in his tone had her backing up, studying his face. It looked gaunt, darker than she'd ever seen it, the freckles blending together over the prominent cheekbones, disappearing into the scraggly red beard. And his eyes were hard, a pale, icy blue, and angry. At her? "What is it, Duncan? What's wrong?"

"You're making too much damn noise."

"Well, I'm frightfully sorry." Her tone sounded any-

305

thing but. "It's just that I tend to get a trifle excited when I see my cousin after months of not knowing if he was alive, or when someone jumps out of the bushes at me. Why did you do that, anyway?"

"I'm a wanted man, Fiona."

"Wanted?"

"Aye. You may have sold yourself to the enemy, but I haven't."

"Sold myself!"

Duncan grabbed her hand before she could slap him, and hauled her against his side. "Don't think I don't know whose house it is that you're staying in."

"Colonel Kincaid's," Fiona hissed defiantly. "*He* helped me, helped Grandfather, when we needed it." Fiona hadn't forgotten begging Duncan to help her find the laird on the battlefield, and the expression on his face when he'd jerked away from her, heading in the opposite direction.

"Aye, he helped you. What I'd like to be knowing is what manner of payment he demanded."

"Nothing." Fiona tried to yank her hand away. "He didn't demand anything. You're hurting me." Duncan let her go so quickly she stumbled backward. Rubbing her wrist, Fiona studied her cousin carefully. "Why did you come here, Duncan?"

"I told you. I've come to play the knight in shining armor. To rescue the fair Fiona."

"And . . ." She sensed there was more to this.

"And perhaps to eliminate one pesky Patriot colonel."

"He isn't here." Fiona strove to keep her voice calm.

"So I gathered. I haven't seen him leaving the house."

"You've been spying on us?"

"I wasn't going to walk into any trap."

"Trap?" Fiona was indignant. "You think I would lure you into a trap?" Duncan's shrug infuriated her, but she tried to keep her temper in check. He must have noticed the supreme effort it took, for his expression softened.

"Look, Fiona, I didn't come to argue with you. I guess I'm a little nervous. I see Whigs behind every bush, and I don't want to be hauled off to Philadelphia, or worse, hanged."

"But why would they—"

"Never mind." Duncan waved her question aside with a flick of his wrist. "The important thing is to get you and the laird back to Armadale. Is he able to travel?"

It hadn't escaped Fiona that Duncan hadn't asked about their grandfather's health, even though she had mentioned his wound in her letter. She took a calming breath, watching an osprey sail above the Cape Fear River a moment before answering. "He's weak." She shook her head. "The physician thinks it is his heart. His hands and legs keep swelling. They bleed him, but . . ."

"Is he able to travel?" Duncan repeated his question with a twinge of impatience.

"I suppose so. But not by horse. Carriage, maybe."

"Well, I didn't bring a bloody carriage with me, Fiona."

Sucking in her breath at his sharp tone, Fiona studied him for a moment. "A wagon, then. I'm certain there's one in the carriage house. And it will be easier to use fording the streams and creeks."

"All right. It will slow us down, but we'll take a wagon."

"Good." For a moment she'd feared he would make her grandfather ride, and she felt certain Malcolm couldn't handle that. "I'll go home and get him ready."

"Why don't you simply alert the entire town while you're about it?"

Fiona stopped, turning back to stare at her cousin with something akin to distrust. "What are you talking about?"

"You're going to have to keep quiet about this, about seeing me, until the time is right to leave."

"And when will that be?"

"Tonight, maybe tomorrow night. I'll let you know. I'll come up with some diversionary activity to keep the town busy. A fire, perhaps."

"A fire? Duncan, many of these people are our friends. They've been kind to Grandfather and me. I don't want to see anyone hurt."

"They're the enemy, for God's sake!" In his excitement, Duncan forgot his own rule and his voice rose above a whisper.

"Duncan. I mean it. Besides, there's no need. Grandfather isn't guarded. We can simply leave."

"All right. All right. No one will get hurt. Now you just go back to that rebel colonel's house and keep calm — and quiet. Do you understand?"

"Aye."

Duncan stepped forward, and though he wasn't very tall, Fiona was forced to tilt her head to meet his gaze. "See that you mind your mouth, Fiona." Then he disappeared into the trees beside the river.

Fiona stood staring out across the river for a moment, then forced herself to walk back to Zeke's house slowly. She tried not to let anything about her expression reveal her excitement, but it wasn't easy.

308

She was going home!

After nearly six months of being away from Armadale, she'd soon be there. What had Duncan said? They'd leave either tonight or tomorrow? Travel would of course be slow, but perhaps within a sennight they'd ride up the familiar oak-lined lane.

Fiona's thoughts skittered to Zeke Kincaid. He wasn't going to like it when he returned and found her gone. He wasn't going to like it at all. He might even look on her leaving as a betrayal. Fiona pushed open the gate in front of his town house, and bit her bottom lip. There was no "might" about it. Her grandfather was his prisoner, and she planned to help liberate him.

Colonel Ezekiel Kincaid would be furious when he found out.

But that would be a long time from now. He'd been gone more than a month, with nary a word from him. There was no reason to think he would be home soon. As far as Fiona had heard, the Charlestonians, and their reinforcements from North Carolina and Virginia, were still waiting for Admiral Parker's attack.

Besides, Fiona decided as she climbed the stairs to the wide front porch, Zeke Kincaid's reactions weren't her concern. Her grandfather was. And she was certain his health would improve if he could only get home.

Entering the house, Fiona went straight to her grandfather's room. She smiled when she saw him sitting by the window, staring out at the garden. Brushing aside the light summer curtains, Fiona followed his gaze. "It's a lovely view."

"Aye. Near as nice as that from my window at home."

The dimity curtains fluttered from Fiona's fingers.

309

Smiling at the subtle scent of roses that drifted through the open window, she sat on the stool at her grandfather's feet. "You miss Armadale, don't you?" She'd decided not to tell him about Duncan's visit, but now, as she saw the sheen in her grandfather's eyes, her resolve wavered. Certainly she could trust him to say nothing.

In the end, though they talked longingly of the pine forests and cool, sheltering house, Fiona kept the secret to herself. There was no sense in risking his disappointment if Duncan didn't return.

She did organize the laird's belongings, deciding she'd slip back tonight after he'd gone to sleep and pack what he'd need for the trip.

That night she packed his things, as well as her own. But though she lay awake listening till near dawn, there was no sign of Duncan. Nor did he come the next night.

By the morning of her second sleepless night, Fiona began to think she'd imagined the scene by the river — or that Duncan had been captured. He'd said he was a wanted man, who saw Whigs behind every bush. Maybe one of those Rebels was more than an illusion. And maybe he'd caught her cousin.

Vowing to find out, Fiona first went to help her grandfather with his breakfast.

"You seem distracted today, Fiona."

"I'm fine." She spread butter over a biscuit and passed it to him.

"You haven't been yourself for days now." Malcolm nodded toward the pot of honey and, with a shrug, Fiona added the sticky sweet syrup to the biscuit.

"Well, I can't imagine who else I'd be," Fiona said with a forced laugh. When it wasn't returned, she concentrated on fixing her own biscuit.

"Is something troubling you, lass?"

"No." Fiona took a sip of tea, realizing she'd answered too quickly to be convincing. "I'm just restless, I suppose."

"You haven't been able to ride, have you?"

"No." Fiona seized on that excuse. "You know how I enjoy getting away to ride my horse. I did think I'd take a walk this morning, if you don't need me."

"Go on with you." Malcolm motioned toward the door.

"I was going to wait till later," Fiona protested. "Till your rest."

"Nonsense. I'll be fine. And morning's the best time of the day."

Fiona was forced to agree a short time later, as she trudged toward the gaol. She just wished her overactive mind would let her enjoy the beautiful summer morning.

Sergeant Keane was on duty, and he looked up, his eyes questioning in his dirty face when she laid the napkin-wrapped package on his desk. "What's this?"

"Biscuits. Fresh," Fiona added with a smile.

He took a deep breath, and Fiona could tell the moment he caught the delicious fragrance of the bread. His face split in a nearly toothless grin, and he tore open the napkin.

His manners really were deplorable, Fiona thought, as he wolfed down the food. The straining buttons on his grimy waistcoat testified to his fondness for food. He didn't look up until he'd finished every crumb, and Fiona silently applauded herself for finding the perfect way to please him.

However, when he finally glanced up at her, his

311

small eyes narrowed in suspicion, Fiona decided he might be shrewder than he looked.

"What you bringing me food for?"

"Well, I . . ." His question was so direct, so sharp, Fiona was momentarily speechless. She'd hoped they'd just chat for a while and then she could ask him if there were any new prisoners.

"Speak up, girl."

"I thought you might like them. And you did, didn't you?"

"They was good."

Fiona sighed. "I knew you'd think so." The sergeant's expression changed quickly from suspicion to something Fiona decided was supposed to be pleasant. She was so relieved that she barely noticed when he stood, scraping the chair over the wooden floor.

"So I was right all along."

"Right?" Fiona stopped formulating a question about prisoners and stepped back when she noted his approach.

"I knew you had a thing for me. I just knew it. Coming by here every day like you done."

"I came to visit my grandfather." Fiona tried to keep the fear from her voice, but she'd backed up as far as she could, and a furtive glance told her she'd cornered herself. The sergeant's lumbering form stood between her and the door.

"No one comes to see an old man that much."

"I did. Listen, Sergeant, I think I'd better leave." Fiona started forward, stopped abruptly when he grabbed her arm.

"Never took you for the shy type. Not with hair like this."

Fiona jerked her head to the side when he tried to

312

tangle his sausage-like fingers in her braid.

"Ain't no cause to get skittish. It ain't like we can do nothing here." He pressed his body against her. "Though you've got me wanting to bad."

It took a great effort not to gag. Fiona fought the waves of nausea, and tried to ignore the odor of filthy flesh. "I want to leave now." She tried to sound confident, even commanding, but knew she failed. An evil gleam came into his pale eyes.

"You can feel how much I'm wanting, can't you?" He ground his hips forward, and Fiona hated the whimper that escaped her. "Can't you?"

"Yes . . . yes," Fiona answered when he grabbed her jaw, twisting her face around to look at him. That she could actually feel nothing but mounds of fat was small consolation as he jerked her toward the door leading to the cells. "What are you doing?"

"I'm getting us what we both want."

"No!" Fiona grabbed for the doorjamb, but he pulled her inside, slamming her against the wall. Lights exploded behind her eyes as her head hit the logs. But it cleared instantaneously when his beefy hand closed over her breast. Tears sprang to her eyes, but she ignored them as her shoe connected with the sergeant's shin.

"Ouch! Hell, what you doing, woman?"

The instant he released her to grab for his leg, Fiona sprang for the door. "Oh, no, you don't." Fiona heard his growled words a heartbeat before he rammed into her from behind, wedging her against the wooden panel. "Think you can get away from me, do you?" His breath was hot, foul-smelling, on the back of her neck. "I'll show you what happens to girls who flirt with old Sergeant Keane."

313

"He'll kill you if you hurt me!" Fiona wasn't sure where that came from. In desperation she'd blurted out the first thing that came to mind. But the sergeant loosened his painful grip on her arm.

"Who you talking about, girl?"

"Colonel Kincaid!" He dropped her arm completely now.

"What's he to you?"

Fiona turned, unimpeded by his monstrous body. He seemed to be slinking away. "Certainly you know my grandfather was taken to his house."

"As his prisoner."

Fiona laughed, hoping he wouldn't notice the quiver in her voice. "As a favor to me. You see, Colonel Kincaid and I are . . . are . . ." Damn, how was she to describe it?

"You're his woman?"

"Aye!" Fiona let out a sigh of relief. That described it perfectly—at least for the sergeant's benefit. "I'm his woman. And he doesn't want anything happening to me. He gets very angry—murderous. Why, I've known him to break men's arms and legs before he finally gave in to their pleas to end the suffering." Fiona paused. Possibly she was carrying this tale too far. But the sergeant seemed to be buying it. His skin had turned a pasty white.

"You ain't going to tell him about this, are you?"

Fiona stepped away from the wall, brushing bits of wood from her skirt, and said nothing.

"I didn't know you was his."

Fiona shrugged. "I suppose there's no need for him to know." She pointed her finger at him. "Just as long as you keep your distance in the future."

"I swear."

314

"Good." After glancing around to assure herself that all the cells were empty, Fiona forced herself to leave the gaol slowly. She made it to the live oak ten rods from the door before her knees gave out and her body started trembling. Hidden by the low-slung branches dripping with Spanish moss, Fiona leaned against the wide trunk.

The sergeant's smell still lingered about her, freshening the memory of his attack. "You got away. You got away," Fiona repeated to herself, as her breathing steadied. "You lied and . . ."

Fiona stopped, her hand pressing against her mouth when she realized the obvious—the reason the lie had come to her so easily in the gaol. It wasn't a lie.

She was Ezekiel Kincaid's woman. What else would you call someone who lived in his house . . . lay with him?

No wonder the sergeant had been so quick to believe her. Fiona pushed away from the tree, stepping out into the sunlight. Did everyone else in town think the same thing? Telling herself she didn't care what the good Patriot citizens of Wilmington thought of her, Fiona hurried back to the colonel's house. Surely Duncan would show up soon. And if he didn't . . . "I'll take Grandfather to Armadale myself," Fiona mumbled.

By ten o'clock that night, Fiona's resolve to stay awake was faltering. She tried to concentrate on the words that snailed across the page propped up on her knee, but they continued to blur. If I'd only slept the last two nights, she thought, glancing at the bedside candle. The flame danced, mesmerizing Fiona as she let her eyelids droop. Perhaps she'd rest for a minute—just a minute.

The dream came to her again.

Zeke. Always Zeke. And usually blood.

In more rational moments, when she admitted that he haunted her dreams, Fiona realized she worried about him. Why else would she keep coming across him in her nightmares, and find him bleeding? By daylight, she could rationalize and accept. But that didn't help her when the darkness shrouded the line between fantasy and fact, and dreams seemed reality.

It seemed so real. The warmth of his body, the stale, metallic smell of blood. She touched his face, felt the rough stubble of beard, smiled when he opened his eyes, so blue in the darkness of his skin. She could tell he was weak when he lifted his hand, but his fingers drifting along her cheek still made her sigh.

Then his hand tightened, no longer gentle, covering her mouth, making her gasp. He knew. She could tell by the expression in his eyes, he knew she would betray him. She tried to explain. My grandfather needs to go home. *I* need to go home! I can't stand being thought of as your mistress, your woman. But the words wouldn't come out. Only "Zeke" escaped her lips.

"Damnit, Fiona, why are you calling out that Whig bastard's name in your sleep?"

Fiona snapped awake, abruptly leaving behind the image of Zeke, the blood . . . everything but the hand clasped roughly over her mouth. The bedside candle had burned down, now sputtering in the molten wax, but Fiona could see well enough to make out her cousin, looming over her. "Duncan," she whispered when his hand loosened.

"Of course it's me. Who else were you expecting, Fiona?"

316

"No one." Fiona tried to stifle her embarrassment. Had she really called out Zeke's name? "I've waited every night. You said you'd be back to get us before this."

"I got tied up with other business."

"What business?"

"Nothing that concerns you. Now get up."

"Are we leaving now?" Fiona swung her legs over the side of the bed, found the wooden step with her toe, and climbed down.

"Aye. I'll go for the laird while you dress. Make it quick."

"Maybe I should go with you." Fiona regretted her decision to keep her grandfather in the dark about their leaving. She should have given him time to adjust to the idea.

"You heard what I said. Stay here and get dressed. And be quiet about it. I don't want the whole house down on us."

"The servants sleep in the attic."

"You think I don't know that?"

Fiona's eyes widened at his tone. Apparently he *had* been spying on them. He'd reached for the doorknob before she remembered Jacob, the groom. Unlike the other servants, he slept in the stable to be near the horses. If they were going to take a wagon from the carriage house for Grandfather, Jacob might hear them.

When Fiona touched Duncan's arm and began to explain this to him, he shrugged her off impatiently. "I've already taken care of him."

"What did you do?"

"Damnit, Fiona, keep your voice down."

"Tell me what you did to Jacob. If you hurt him,

Duncan, I'll—"

"You'll what?" Duncan's hands bit into her shoulders, and his face lowered to mere inches from hers. "You seem to forget we're at war here, Fiona. How can you not remember all the clansmen that lay on the ground near Moore's Creek, slaughtered?"

They lived in her memory—always. But that didn't mean she wanted more killing. "He was just an old man, Duncan. An old man who loved horses." Fiona knew her sob had made him angry, for his fingers tightened.

"There's no reason to speak of him as if he's dead. I only tied and gagged him. Something I'm beginning to think I should do with you."

"You didn't kill him?" Fiona felt a rush of relief.

"Get dressed, Fiona," was all Duncan said as he slipped out the door.

It had been a long, hard ride north, after an equally long, hard stay at Fort Sullivan, a sweltering stronghold of palmetto logs near Charleston. Zeke had bivouacked his men outside of Wilmington this afternoon, planning to camp with them there and then ride into town in the morning. But he'd changed his mind.

Fiona had nothing to do with it, he told himself for the hundredth time, as he rode down a deserted street toward his house. The fact that she slept in one of his beds, warm and cuddly, with her wild red hair fanning over the pillow, was *not* the reason he'd ridden the five extra miles when he was dog-tired.

He wanted to find out what his new orders were. That was the reason. This way he could report first thing tomorrow morning. Colonel Moultrie had emphasized haste when he'd met with Zeke after the Patriots had repelled Clinton and Parker's invasion of Charleston.

"You and your men are needed back in North Carolina," the commander of the Second Regiment had said the day after they'd watched Admiral Parker's masts fade into nothingness on the sea's horizon. "Word just arrived this morning."

The message from the Provincial Congress had contained no other information, and Zeke had done his share of wondering what the problem might be, as he'd marched his men out of the fort to the cheers of the Charlestonians. The march north along the coastline had brought no enlightenment. As far as Zeke could ascertain, the British had abandoned attempts to conquer any of the colonies south of the Mason-Dixon line.

But it wasn't the British that occupied his thoughts as he rode into the crushed-shell drive at the back of his house. He couldn't think of anything but one slight, flame-haired Scottish Tory.

Though his horse was as tired as he, the stallion seemed to recognize he was home, tossing his head in welcome. Zeke understood his reaction, but knew it would take more than a clean bed and a good meal to satisfy him. Not that he planned to pressure Fiona. One thing Zeke had decided during their separation was that the last night they'd spent together had been special, and not necessarily something that would continue. Not the way things stood between them. But he also knew he couldn't stop thinking of her, of that night, and he wanted to keep her in his life.

How he was going to accomplish that eluded him.

He couldn't keep her grandfather prisoner forever, even if—Zeke dismounted, and shook his head when he noticed the sliver of light beneath the stable door. Leading his horse, Zeke reached for the iron latch. He hoped Jacob wasn't up at this late hour doctoring a sick animal—the freedman was getting too old to keep these hours. But the other alternative—that his head groom had fallen asleep without extinguishing the lantern—was just as bad. Whichever the case, he'd have to have a talk with Jacob.

But when Zeke creaked open the door and looked down the black hole of a pistol's muzzle, all thoughts of questioning the groom fled his mind.

Chapter Nineteen

"Zeke!"

At the sound of his name, Zeke shifted his attention from the pistol pointed at his chest. He would have known the voice anywhere, even if he hadn't ridden nearly two hundred miles with her haunting his mind. Fiona stood next to a stall, her hands lifted, frozen in the process of quieting one of his chestnut geldings. She didn't seem to be, as he'd briefly hoped, forced to be in the stable. However, she *did* appear shocked to see him, her violet eyes wide in disbelief.

"Going someplace, Fiona? It's a bit late for a ride."

"I'm—"

"Shut your damn whig mouth. Where she's going is none of your concern."

Zeke's eyes flashed back to Duncan, and he had a nearly uncontrollable urge to lunge at him and finish the trouncing he'd started months ago in Everly. Luckily reason, or perhaps the way Duncan shifted the pistol as though he'd dearly love an excuse to use it, prevailed. In this instance, Zeke agreed, discretion was the better part of valor. His mind fled to the pistols in his saddle bags, and he consoled himself by thinking what he'd do when he did get his hands on the Tory bastard. . . .

"I'm taking my grandfather home." Fiona stepped forward, her skirts swishing across the straw floor. Zeke deserved an explanation, she told herself. But she wasn't quite able to look him in the eyes when he turned to her.

Guilt. She recognized the emotion, even knew it was laced with something else she didn't care to name. But she had to remember her priorities. She just had to, Fiona decided as she gnawed on her lower lip. And they weren't Ezekiel Kincaid. But why, oh why, did he have to come back now?

Strange, Zeke thought, in all the times he'd imagined her — and sweltering in that South Carolina fort waiting for the English to attack had given him plenty of time for imagining — she'd always been waiting for him. Sometimes she'd been soft and sensual, sometimes tempestuous, her flaming hair tangled. But she'd always been waiting. He should have known better.

She hadn't liked it when he'd stared at her in that accusing way, but now that he turned his attention back to Duncan, Fiona liked it even less. She'd known he'd feel betrayed. What she hadn't expected was how much that would bother her. "He's gotten worse." Maybe if she could make him understand.

"You think a long journey over rough roads will improve his condition?" He spoke without even looking at her, as if he tired of pointing out the most obvious facts to her.

"Being at Armadale. That's what will heal him." Fiona could hear the desperation in her own voice, but didn't care. "I have to take him home."

"I can't let you do that, Fiona."

His words were deceptively low, his eyes when they

322

met hers, calm and sure. And suddenly she wasn't sure—of anything. The gelding behind her stamped his foot, the musty smell of crushed straw filling the air around her. What she might have done, had the choice been hers, she'd never know, for Duncan's angry voice vibrated through the stable.

"You don't have anything to say about it, you arrogant bastard! Fiona. Fiona!"

She jerked toward him the second time he yelled her name, nodding when he told her to take the horses out and hitch them to the wagon. Grabbing the reins, Fiona started toward the door. She needed to do something, to keep busy, so busy that she couldn't think. If she could just get away from Zeke, everything would be clear to her again. But he wouldn't allow it to be that easy.

"Adding horse stealing to your list of accomplishments?"

Fiona stopped, turning toward him. His eyes were cold, unforgiving.

"Go on, Fiona. The laird's probably wondering what's keeping you," Duncan ordered.

Duncan was right. She had no choice. Still she hesitated, twisting the leather reins around her fingers. "What . . . what are you going to do?" Her words were for Duncan, though she couldn't seem to break the hold of the colonel's stare.

"I'm just going to keep an eye on your friend, here."

Fiona didn't like the expression on her cousin's face when she turned toward him. It reminded her of the day in Everly. The heat of the evening didn't stop the chill that ran down her spine. "I don't want him hurt."

"Damnit, Fiona, this is war. When are you going to realize that?"

"Duncan! You heard what I said."

323

"Your concern for my welfare is touching, though perhaps a little belated." She appeared sincere enough, yet Zeke couldn't help wondering what she thought would happen with Duncan holding a gun on him.

"Shut up." Duncan's eyes narrowed and he leveled the pistol, the fingers of his hand twitching from the effort of not firing. "Get out there and hitch up the horses, Fiona."

"I won't. Not until you promise me!" Fiona would have lunged toward him if her hands weren't tangled in the reins.

"Hell, Fiona, I might as well hand the gun over to him, then. Is that what you want? Do you want to see me hanging from a gallows?"

"Of course not." This was the second time her cousin had referred to hangings, and it made Fiona's uneasiness build. As far as she knew, there'd been no punishments of that sort.

"Well, you make me promise not to hurt him and that's exactly what will happen," Duncan argued.

"He has a point there, Fiona."

"Oh, shut up!" Fiona turned on Zeke, glaring at him, more annoyed with the slightly cynical turn of his mouth than she could say. Didn't he know how eager Duncan was to retaliate for the beating he had taken? She glanced back at Duncan. "You're not to shoot unless he tries something."

"Such as?"

Fiona ignored the colonel's question. He obviously had no idea of the gravity of the situation. But she did, so when the idea hit her she could barely suppress her excitement. "We'll tie him up. You said you tied Jacob." Fiona assumed the old black man was in the tack room. "He can't do any harm that way. Duncan?" Her cousin didn't seem to embrace the plan with much enthusiasm. He simply shifted from foot to foot, staring at the colonel.

"All right. There's some rope hanging over there on the wall. You" — He motioned toward Zeke — "back up and clasp your hands behind you, up around that post."

The post was high, rising from the top of the stall to the ceiling of the stable, and Zeke had to raise his arms over his head to reach around it. It looked terribly uncomfortable, and Fiona considered pointing that out to Duncan, but decided against it. He didn't seem in a very charitable mood, and she imagined she'd dragged all the concessions from him she could. So she pushed and shoved at a wooden crate, finally positioning it behind the post. Without comment she gathered up her skirts and climbed on the box. Now she could reach the colonel's hands.

His hands were large, long-fingered, and strong. His skin when she touched it was warm, triggering memories Fiona didn't want to recall just now. To smother the vivid pictures her mind seemed intent upon projecting, Fiona wrapped the rope around his wrists with quick, jerky motions. "Hush," she chastised softly when he growled, complaining of her rough treatment. But her hands gentled. After glancing warily toward Duncan, she explained the obvious to the colonel. " 'Tis better than a ball in your gut," she whispered into the thick waves of his hair.

"And whom do I have to thank for such a charming choice?" Zeke didn't look back, but knew by the sudden yank she gave the rope that she heard his softly spoken retort. "Bitch." The word was little more than a hiss of air expelled through gritted teeth.

Fiona stiffened, but resisted the urge to twist the rope harder. And wasn't it just like him to blame her, when all she was trying to do was save his worthless life? If she didn't think Duncan would jump at the chance to carry out his threat, she would suggest a more creative way of tying the colonel — like hanging him by his toes from the rafter. As it was, she leaned forward and muttered, " 'Tis your own fault for coming home when you did." Her argument sounded ridiculous, even to her own ears, and Fiona was certain he'd point that out to her. But he didn't bother.

"The error is mine, to be sure," he said so quietly that Fiona's hair brushed against his ear as she bent forward to hear him. "I should never have trusted you."

Fiona blinked, refusing to give in to tears. His words hurt, but then they were meant to, Fiona reminded herself as she pulled away from him. Suddenly his smell, his warmth, so familiar even after a month of absence, made a mockery of the situation. Did he think she wanted to do this? She had no choice, but he refused to understand, or even try.

When she felt certain her voice wouldn't betray the emotion she felt, Fiona said in a tone loud enough for Duncan to hear, "That should keep him." She wanted to jump from the box, to get away from Zeke as quickly as possible, but she couldn't stop herself from loosening the knot just a little when she noticed the red welts already beginning to rub open on his wrists. "Stop fidgeting. You'll thank me for this later."

"I shall endeavor to remember that."

"Are you finished yet, Fiona? We need to be going."

"Almost." Fiona glanced over Zeke's shoulder toward where Duncan stood holding the pistol still aimed at Zeke's chest. He appeared restless, and Fiona knew the sooner she got him away from here, the better. But she couldn't resist one more chance to explain to Zeke.

326

"This is for the best. It would never work . . . my staying here. It's better that I leave . . . that my grandfather and I both leave." His snort didn't sound as if he were convinced. Or maybe it was just that Fiona wasn't too certain herself at this moment.

"And I suppose I should be grateful for you trussing me up like a Christmas goose?"

"I told you. It's better than—"

"I know, a ball in the gut. I just wonder what makes you so sure I won't get both?"

He'd twisted his head around, and Fiona found herself snared by his blue gaze. His breath was warm against her cheek, and she didn't have to try to keep her voice down when she answered. She could only manage a whisper. "Duncan would never. . . ." Her voice trailed off as his dark brow arched skeptically.

Jumping off the crate, she gathered up her skirts and hurried toward Duncan. "He's tied. You can put the pistol away now."

"I'm thinking I should watch over him while you hitch up the wagon. We wouldn't want him calling out for help before we can get away."

"He won't." Fiona glanced toward Zeke, wishing he'd endeavor to appear a little meeker. He stared at Duncan, his blue eyes narrowed as if daring him to do his worst. She would have kicked him if she'd been closer. As it was, Fiona grabbed Duncan's arm, the one that held the pistol, and gave it a yank. "Duncan. We have to get the laird home. He's waiting in the wagon, probably wondering what has become of us."

"Maybe you should go tell him. Hitch up the horses."

"I can't do it alone," Fiona lied, hoping Duncan wouldn't remember that she'd been raised around horses, tacked and hitched them to wagons since she was a child. "Come with me."

"Damnit, Fiona." Duncan turned to look at her, and it was all she could do not to back away from him. The hate, the desire to kill the colonel burned bright like a fever in his pale eyes.

Fiona tried to swallow, and found her mouth suddenly dry. Duncan's gaze slid away from hers, back to Zeke, and Fiona's followed. He made such a perfect target—*she'd* made him such a perfect target. By tying his hands high above his head she'd stretched his white shirt taut across his chest. It shone wide and bright as a beacon in the flickering light from the lantern. A vision of red blossoming across the pristine white flashed before her, and Fiona shook her head to clear it.

"We have to go now!" Her voice sounded frantic, but she couldn't help it. "Duncan." Fiona pulled on his arm again.

He gave no indication that he'd even heard her, only continued his stare-down with the colonel. A cock crowed in the distance, its sound a reminder of the new day about to dawn, the need for haste, but still Duncan didn't move. "We have to hurry, Duncan." Fiona felt as if she were talking to a child. "Zeke's tied. He can't do us any harm. But if we don't leave, leave now, we'll have more to worry about than one Whig Colonel."

"You go ahead. I'll be right out."

"No! No, Duncan. I'm not going to let you hurt him!"

He swung on her so quickly, Fiona stumbled on her skirts as she jerked back. "What in the hell is he to you, Fiona?"

"Nothing! He's nothing, Duncan. But we have to go. Grandfather . . ." Fiona latched onto the only

328

thing she could to remind Duncan of his duty. And it must have worked, she thought as a breath she'd been holding escaped her. His movements were slow, reluctant, but Duncan did lower the pistol, stuffing it into the waistband of his breeches.

Now that he'd decided to move, Duncan acted as if he'd invented speed. Grabbing the horse's reins, he nudged Fiona, propelling her out into the night air. He paused briefly to search the colonel's saddlebags, his teeth baring a slit in his red beard when he found the pair of pistols. Duncan tossed them into the wagonbed before backing the horses into place in front of the wagon.

The low-hanging moon offered some light, but Fiona wished they'd brought the lantern outside, when she began fumbling with the reins. But she didn't dare go back into the stable.

She'd tried not to glance toward Zeke before she was hustled outside, but hadn't been able to resist one last look at him. She should have tried harder. His expression had torn at her heart. He'd been angry; that was evident by the clench of his jaw. He had a right to be, she decided, but that wasn't what held her attention. It was his eyes. They were narrowed, the sweep of dark lashes all but concealing the brilliant blue. And they were sad. Sad and disappointed. In her.

He's nothing. Her words came back to haunt her, as if carried by the misty breeze drifting off the river. She'd said them to convince Duncan, but she feared they'd convinced more than just Duncan.

The gelding stomped, barely missing Fiona's boot, and she jerked her thoughts away from Zeke. She had to concentrate on what she was about. There was no time to worry about what Zeke might think. Moving back to check on her grandfather where they'd laid him on blankets in the wagonbed, Fiona decided she definitely was *not* going to go back into the stable and try to explain that she'd only been trying to help him. He would simply have to figure it out for—

The pistol report rang though the still air. Fiona's body jerked around, the blanket she'd been about to place over her sleeping grandfather slipping from her fingers.

Duncan. Fiona searched through the grainy darkness for her cousin. He'd been right here, helping, right beside her. But now she couldn't find him. He was—"Duncan?"

Fear flashed through her, stiffening her limp limbs. She dashed headlong toward the stable. Heart pumping madly, and winded as if she'd run a mile instead of the few rods from behind the carriage house, Fiona grabbed for the latch. At the same moment, Duncan exploded from the stable. The impact sent her sprawling into the dirt. She sat up, swiping hair from her face, gasping in mouthfuls of river-scented air. She was too breathless to ask the question that burned in her mind. But she realized there was no need. The expression of raw triumph on Duncan's face, the smoking pistol in his hand, were answer enough.

Jumping to her feet, kicking aside the tangle of skirts, Fiona hurled herself toward the pale yellow light drifting through the opening. Rough hands clutched at her shoulders, jerking her around.

"What do you think you're about, Fiona?"

Sucking in moist air, wondering why she couldn't seem to catch her breath, Fiona wriggled and twisted, trying to free herself from the fingers that bit through her cotton sleeves. "Let go of me."

"I will." Duncan shook her again, this time so hard she felt a dizzying vertigo sweep over her. "I'll let you

330

go when you've come to your senses. Now stop your female hysterics."

"Hysterics!" The word came out in a high shrill that at best could have been termed hysterical. "What did you do? Oh, God, Duncan, what did you do?"

"I shot him."

The blood drained from Fiona's face, even though she knew his answer before he spoke it.

"I had to shoot him, Fiona. He'd worked his hands loose." In that instant, his man's face, hard-planed and bearded, became once again a boy's. *I had to shoot him, Fiona. He came at me.* She'd helped Duncan bury the prize fighting cock, never telling her grandfather what had happened, though she hadn't believed her cousin's story for a moment. Shaking her head to dispel the memory, Fiona shoved at Duncan. This wasn't a stupid chicken, this was Zeke. "Get out of my way." Tears streamed down her cheeks. "I have to help him."

"Stop it, Fiona. We don't have time for this." Duncan swept his eyes around nervously. Dawn was already tingeing the sky with pale ribbons of light in the east. "We have to get out of here."

"I'm not leav—"

CRACK!

The slap was sudden and unexpected, and had such force that Fiona's head snapped back. A red welt blossomed across her cheek, and sheer pain blurred her vision as Duncan pulled her roughly into his arms.

"I'm sorry, Fiona. I didn't mean to . . . Oh, God, please forgive me. But we have to get out of here. If they find us . . ."

His body trembled and she could smell his fear. But she had no sympathy for him. Pushing herself away, her voice as calm as she could make it, Fiona said, "I'm not leaving. Zeke needs my help."

His hands dropped to his side, and with relief, Fiona realized he wasn't going to physically stop her from entering the stable. She moved with an air of desperation before his words rang through the silent early morning air. "You can't help him, Fiona. No one can. He's dead."

Her control, shaky even before hearing this, broke. Without thought, Fiona hurled herself at Duncan, her nails scoring down his face, the red welts disappearing into his beard. "You killed him. You killed him?" The first came out a sob, the last a questioning shriek.

"Damnit, Fiona!"

This time the blow didn't shock her as the first one had. She barely noticed the pain. All her strength seemed to have ebbed away.

"Would you listen to me? He would have gotten loose. He'd have come after us. Do you understand me? Do you?"

Duncan shook her, and she nodded. It seemed the easiest thing to do.

"Now we need to get out of here. Maybe you have no concern for my neck, but your own is in jeopardy now." Duncan paused. "And Grandfather's."

His words, or maybe the crazed expression on his face, filtered through to Fiona. "What are you talking about?"

"When they find him dead." Duncan jerked his head toward the stable. "Who do you think they will blame?"

"But Grandfather hasn't the strength. They'll know that."

"To lift a pistol, Fiona?" His smile was heartless. "Mere weeks ago they thought he had the strength to lead an insurrection. Besides, even if they lay the deed at your feet, they'll think he put you up to it."

He was right; she knew he was right. That's what she needed to concentrate on, Fiona told herself as she climbed into the wagon beside her grandfather. It was too late to worry about anything—anyone—else. Duncan motioned for her to sit on the seat with him, but she ignored him. She would ignore everything.

Her grandfather woke briefly when the wagon started rolling. But after she assured him that all was well and that they were going home, he drifted back to sleep. He was so weak, seemed to grow more so every day. She only hoped getting him home to Armadale would help. If not, she knew he'd at least prefer to die there.

Duncan kept up a running conversation—with her?—as they left the sleeping town behind them. Fiona wanted to tell him to be quiet, that she didn't care about his reasons, or anything else about him, but it seemed too much trouble. All her energy was consumed by blocking the thoughts of Zeke from her mind. Zeke covered with blood. Zeke dying. Zeke dead. The expression in his eyes when she'd walked out of the stable. Accusing. Betrayed.

Fiona shut her own eyes, but it didn't stop the vision, nor the tears that burned down her cut cheek.

"They won't know I had any part in this," Duncan was saying from his perch on the wagon seat. "I can take you someplace safe."

"We're going to Armadale."

Duncan jerked around, the motion causing the horses to pull to the right. "Well, you *can* speak." He made no comment when Fiona looked away, just straightened the horses and continued with his monologue. "It's too risky to go to Armadale now. They might not have your friend to tell them where we're going, but they'll figure it out."

"Is that why you shot him, so he couldn't say where we were going? Or was it so he couldn't tell anyone you were involved?"

"I shot him because he'd worked the rope loose."

Duncan glanced back over his shoulder, but Fiona refused to meet his eyes. Instead she stared out at the trees, silhouetted like giant creatures against the pearl-gray sky as they slipped slowly by.

"I was only trying to protect you and the laird." Duncan kept up his rambling and Fiona clasped her hands, weaving her fingers to keep from covering her ears with them. She didn't want to hear that Zeke's death was her fault, didn't want to think of the letter she'd sent to Duncan. It *was* her fault. It was. It was!

"You're angry now, Fiona. But someday you'll thank me for this. By the time they find your fine colonel he'll be dead and you'll not have to worry about him again. Why, I imagine—"

"What did you say?" Fiona scurried to her knees, scraping her leg across something hard in the corner of the wagon. She clung to the back of the seat, not backing away when Duncan twisted to stare at her.

"I said you'd be thanking—"

"After that." Fiona wondered if her voice sounded as strange to Duncan as it did to herself. It was so calm, deadly calm. "You said when they found Zeke he'd be dead. You told me he already was."

"Hell, Fiona."

"Is he dead, Duncan?" Her hands left the seat to clutch at the muslin of his hunting shirt.

"He could be. He probably is. Hell, what difference does it make? If he isn't now, he will be soon."

"Stop the wagon!"

"Fiona . . ."

"I said to stop the wagon!" Fiona shifted, knocking

her leg again, and remembering what the offending object was.

"You don't know what you're saying. This is exactly why I told you 'twas already accomplished. You're not acting rationally at all." Duncan had wriggled out of her frantic hold, but his body jerked, his spine straightening when he felt the press of steel against his back.

"Stop the wagon."

"Put that thing down, Fiona. For Christ's sake, it's loaded."

"You think I don't know that? Now, stop . . . this . . . wagon. Or, Duncan, I swear to God, I'll shoot." Fiona grabbed hold of the side as Duncan jerked on the reins, but she kept Zeke's pistol trained on Duncan.

"There, are you satisfied now? We're losing valuable time while you play at your little games. Now hand over the gun. Fiona! Where in the hell are you going?"

"Back." Fiona scrambled from the wagonbed and hurried around to the side, beside the horses. "Get down, and unhitch one of these horses."

"Fiona."

"Do it, damn you."

"They'll blame you." Duncan climbed down and unbuckled the trace, keeping his eyes on the pistol pointed at him. "When they find him, they'll think you shot him."

"I don't care."

"Have you lost your mind?" Duncan's question was asked in a mild enough manner, but she noticed beads of sweat breaking out across his brow.

"Perhaps I have. You know what a hysterical female I am. Now start this wagon, and don't turn back till you've reached Armadale. Katrine will take care of

335

Grandfather until I get there."

"Fiona." Duncan angled his hand down toward the pistol, but Fiona pulled back.

"Don't make the mistake of thinking I won't shoot you, Duncan."

"For him? For God's sake, Fiona, you'd shoot me because of a Patriot, an enemy?"

She didn't answer, couldn't answer. Instead, Fiona pulled herself astride the horse and galloped back toward town.

Everything looked the same when Fiona rode onto the crushed-shell drive behind Zeke's house. She slid from the horse, and sucked in her breath as she reached for the latch, almost afraid to open it.

The stable was dark, and hazy. It took her eyes a moment to adjust after the brightness of the new day. And then she saw him.

He was slumped against the stall, the rope around his hands keeping him from crumbling completely into the straw. She'd expected blood, had envisioned it often enough, but didn't know there would be so much. The whole side of his shirt was covered, drenched in varying shades of red and rust.

Fiona hurried toward him. Now that she was here, she wasn't sure what to do. Her hand flew to his neck, for the pulse point she'd seen so often throbbing against his tanned skin. Tears burned her eyes as she felt the flutter—not strong, to be sure—but definitely there.

He wasn't dead. She recited a hasty prayer of thanksgiving, hoping it was sufficient for now, as she worked at the stubborn rope at Zeke's wrist. Where she'd ever learned to tie such a wicked knot she couldn't remember. Her fingers fumbled, seeming to twist the hemp tighter as she strained to free him.

His moan startled her, made her work faster. When she finally felt the knot slip, and knew his body would drop, Fiona leaped from the crate to catch him. But he was too heavy to hold, and all she could do was soften his landing with her own body. For a breathless moment as she struggled to gulp air and roll him off her, Fiona feared she was trapped under him. But finally she pulled herself free.

Leaning over him, Fiona alternately plucked at his sodden shirt and searched his face, hoping for some sign he was conscious. His lashes lay like raven's wings across his taut, ashen skin, fluttering faintly when her fingers probed the jagged hole in his shoulder.

She had to stop the bleeding—helping to minister to her grandfather had taught her that much. Her petticoat was relatively clean, but even if it weren't, Fiona had no other choice but to use it. Pressing it against the wound, she closed her eyes, trying to shut out the low agonizing sound of his moan, the smell of his blood, as completely as she cut off the sight of his suffering.

It was foolish, she knew, and weak, but she couldn't bear to see what she'd done—what she'd caused to happen. His warmth seeped through her, the clammy fever of his flesh, the moist, sticky heat oozing through the linen. Her fingers bunched the cloth and pressed, willing the flow to stop.

And then she sensed a change. He'd quieted, and Fiona tore her eyes open, surprised when her gaze met his. The blue was glazed, slightly unfocused, but she could tell by the troubled expression that furrowed his brow that he saw her.

Fiona swallowed, trying to think of something—anything—to say, but her mind went blank. Finally she blurted out the only thing she could say with any certainty. "You're not dead."

"That's good," he said, his voice rusty and low. "I don't like to think angels can have bruised cheeks." His arm came up, the back of his knuckles just grazing the tender skin along her jaw before it dropped and he lost consciousness.

Chapter Twenty

It wasn't that he was so comfortable asleep, it was simply that the warning voices in his groggy mind predicted he'd feel worse awake. Despite the advice, his eyelids lifted, grating across eyes dry as dust. He should have listened to those voices.

The brightest flame he'd ever seen flickered near his head, sending bolts of light searing into his brain. Zeke squinted, shifted his head slightly, and tried to see past the candle. Shadows claimed the area beyond.

Licking his lips, suddenly aware of a raging thirst, Zeke tried to sit. The effort caused a poker-hot shaft of pain to radiate from his shoulder, spreading to the tips of his fingers. Sprawling back on the bed—his bed, he noted—drenched in sweat, Zeke let the memories engulf him.

"Damn!" He'd been shot by that Tory bastard, Duncan MacClure, after the she-devil Fiona had trussed him up for the kill. Fiona, of the flame-red hair and sweet, beguiling eyes—and the treachery. If he ever got his hands on her he'd—

"You're awake."

The words were softly spoken, but in his weakened

339

state, they startled him. Twisting his head around did nothing to ease his discomfort. Nor did it help that he jerked away from the cool hand placed on his forehead.

"What in the hell are you doing here?"

"Your fever seems to have broken. How are you feeling?"

"Like I took a ball in my gut. Now, are you going to answer my question?"

"It wasn't the gut. It was your shoulder," Fiona explained logically.

"Lucky me."

"Actually you were very fortunate that Duncan didn't aim farther right . . . or lower. The pistol probably throws a bit to the left."

He didn't need proof that Duncan had tried to kill him; just the memory of his face, distorted with hate, moments before he pulled the trigger, was enough. "You still haven't mentioned why you're here."

"I've been here." Fiona straightened Zeke's pillow, despite his attempts to stop her. His feeble effort was proof of the amount of blood he'd lost.

"Since I was shot?"

"Not exactly that long." Fiona pulled the Chippendale chair across the carpet and sat down with a sigh. "But I did come back."

"Are you expecting my gratitude?" Zeke tried to maintain the sarcasm in his voice, but he spotted the pitcher beside the candle. "Is there any water in that?"

"I don't want your thanks." Fiona poured some of the cool liquid into a glass. "Can you lift your head?" Pressing the goblet to his lips, she wiped with the back of her hand at the droplets that rolled down into his dark whiskers. He drank thirstily, complaining

340

when she pulled the water away. "I don't think you should drink too much at one time. Rest a minute."

Zeke was disgusted with how easily his body accepted her advice. She pulled the sheet over his chest and sat back in the chair, folding her hands and watching him. Zeke found her eyes on him rather unnerving, and something else. Familiar. He blinked, suddenly recalling other times when he'd awakened, not clear-headed as now, but disoriented by fever, to find her sitting just as she was now. He'd thought he was dreaming. Now he wasn't sure. "Have you been taking care of me?"

"Aye."

Zeke squirmed a little under the sheet, feeling vulnerable in his weakness. "Since when?"

"Since I untied you. You thought I was an angel."

"I was obviously delirious."

Fiona smiled. She couldn't help herself, his retort had been so heartfelt. "I'm thinking you probably were."

The corners of Zeke's mouth lifted slightly and he raised his good arm, drawing his hand over his chin to hide the fact that he'd nearly grinned at her—the woman responsible for getting him shot. His eyes widened when he felt the bristly growth of beard.

"You'll be needing a shave," Fiona said, "now that you're feeling better."

"How long ago was I shot?"

"Almost a sennight."

"I've been lying in this bed seven days?" Zeke tried to rise again, grimacing at the pain.

"Six and a half. 'Tis night." Fiona stood, pushing him back on the mattress with practiced ease. "You need to rest. This is the first time you've been free of fever, and it isn't wise to overdo it."

He settled back, feeling his eyelids grow incredibly heavy. "I still have questions. You never answered . . . my question."

"There'll be plenty of time tomorrow."

"Yes, tomorrow." Zeke's voice trailed off as his eyes closed. Fiona thought he'd gone to sleep, till she felt his hand nudge hers where it lay on the bed. "Will you be here tomorrow?"

Fiona hesitated. Would she stay? She felt his gaze upon her and lifted her eyes to meet his. His shone very blue and trusting in the candlelight—though she was certain he'd dispute her description. He didn't trust her, she was positive of that. The very fact that he needed to ask proved it, as much as her reluctance to answer.

How much did she owe him? She'd given him back his life. Did that repay nearly taking it? His fingers, warm and alive, covered hers, and she nodded. "Aye. We'll talk more tomorrow."

She wasn't sure why she'd agreed to stay. This was the perfect time for her to leave. He'd be all right—she knew that now. And that was to be her signal to leave, to go home to Armadale.

But then she'd changed her mind before. At first she'd only planned to stop the bleeding and let someone know of his condition. But she found she couldn't leave. Not without knowing. Not even when the local militia captain came to investigate Zeke's shooting.

The officer, a short, wiry man with sunken eyes, had seemed embarrassed to question her, especially when she'd refused to leave Zeke's side. He'd asked if she'd shot him, seemed satisfied with her succinct no. But Fiona knew it wasn't over.

"There'll be time enough to find out what happened once the colonel's better," the captain had said before excusing himself.

And now Zeke was better. All the more reason to avoid the folly of staying around. By this time tomorrow night she could be huddled in a cell in the gaol. Fiona shivered despite the warmth of the evening.

She had every reason in the world to leave, and none that she could think of to stay. Zeke's fingers tightened, and Fiona glanced down to the coverlet. Their hands lay there, hers and Zeke's, fingers entwined. He'd clasped her hand when she said she'd stay. Fiona didn't think he realized what he'd done. She assumed he'd been more asleep than awake when it happened. But she couldn't seem to pull away. Even now, with her arm stiff from stretching it toward the bed, she clung to him.

Yet another reason for you to leave, Fiona chided herself as she slipped her fingers free.

Bright sunshine spilled through the open drapes the next time Zeke woke. He turned his head, noticed the guttered candle, the fact that the room was empty, and bellowed. An indentured servant named Maggie—no Meg, he remembered after she looked as him askance—answered his summons. "Where in the hell is everybody?"

The woman stared at him with her small brown eyes as if he might bound from the bed and pounce on her, but she bobbed a curtsey, and began an explanation. "Mrs. Steel has gone out. She seemed much relieved that you're feeling better."

"And how did she come by that news?"

"I told her."

Zeke stopped studying the plump maid and

glanced toward the doorway, toward the woman who'd spoken. The one he'd been afraid had left. Fiona looked as bright as sunshine itself, though he couldn't imagine she'd gotten much sleep. It must be the hair, he thought absently, as he simply stared at her. Those red curls surrounded her with heat and light.

Entering the room, Fiona set the pewter tray on the chest at the foot of the bed. "Has he been giving you a hard time, Meg?"

"No, miss, only wondering about the household."

"Yes, I heard his *wondering* from belowstairs."

"I imagine he's feeling a bit out of sorts today," Meg said, her round face looking sympathetic under her ruffled cap.

"You're probably right." Fiona spread the drapes even further and shoved on the window till it opened.

"Will Colonel Kincaid be needing me for anything now, miss?"

"No, I don't think so. I'll just—"

"Now wait a damn minute." Zeke had been lying in bed watching the two woman discuss him as if he weren't there, and was getting tired of it. He didn't know exactly what he wanted them to do, but he didn't like being ignored. On second thought, he did know what he wanted . . . needed, but certainly wasn't going to ask for it—no matter how intimately Fiona had nursed him.

Fiona fussed with the drapes, straightening an imaginary wrinkle to keep Zeke from seeing her smile. He looked like a big, burly bear—the rumpled, deep-brown hair and heavy whiskers covering his jaw did much to enhance the image—awakened from hibernation. His temperament matched the look. But she guessed he had cause. At least she thought she understood his present complaint. "Meg, would you send Jacob up here, please," she asked the servant, who nodded and scurried away, obviously glad to be released from this duty.

When the black man knocked on the door, Fiona bade him enter, then slipped into the hall. Pacing the length of the corridor, still wondering why she hadn't left at first light, Fiona waited for Jacob. When he emerged, a nearly toothless grin on his wrinkled face, Fiona patted his arm and asked about the knot on his head.

"Almost gone, Miss Fiona. Don't trouble me none at all."

"You're sure?" Finding the groom in the tack room, tied, but with a nasty cut across the back of his head, had given her one more reason to be angry with Duncan.

"Yes, ma'am. I'm in much better shape than the colonel." He grinned again. "He sure don't like needing help. Don't like being in that bed, neither."

"Well, he's just going to have to not like it a little longer."

After politely knocking, but not waiting for a response, Fiona went back into the bedroom. "Feeling better?"

Zeke's only response was a steely-eyed glare. He hated the infirmity that confined him to bed, too lacking in strength to take care of his personal needs without help. Hated the fact that he was in bed and not out with his men where he belonged. Even hated the smile Fiona gave him, the smile that seemed a bit unsure. Well, it should be unsure, Zeke thought, as he noticed her bottom lip quiver. It should be a hell of a lot unsure.

Last night he'd gotten sentimental, caught up with

345

being alive and finding her there beside him, but today would be different. No hand-holding. Zeke grimaced when he remembered that. Might as well grasp hold of a snake as the hand of the woman responsible for nearly killing him.

Clearing his throat, Zeke crossed his uninjured arm over his chest. "I'm ready for some answers. Wait a minute; what are you doing?"

"Making you more comfortable." Fiona stuffed pillows behind his head, pulling him up further into a sitting position. He resisted her efforts, knocking at her hands until the sheet slid below his waist. Then he shifted his efforts toward keeping covered. Turning her head, Fiona tried to stifle a laugh. It wasn't as if she hadn't seen him before.

"Damnit, Fiona, I am comfortable; now—"

"But I can't shave you unless you're sitting."

"Shave me?" She spoke as if it were the most natural thing in the world, but Zeke had serious reservations. And a lot of them centered around a razor at his throat, wielded by a woman who'd at one time wanted to see him dead.

"Aye. I would think you'd feel better with those whiskers gone."

"I don't doubt you're right. But that doesn't mean I'm going to let you get near me with a razor." Now that she'd managed to hoist him up against the bolstering pillows, she went to the foot of the bed. Picking up the tray, she brought it to the bedside table, pushed aside the candlestick with her forearm, and put it down. Lined up on the pewter tray, nestled in a linen towel, were a bowl of water, soap, and his razor. His well-honed razor.

"And just why not?" Fiona turned on him, hands on hips. She'd just spent the last week saving his life,

346

and now he acted as if she weren't to be trusted. Well, if that's what he thought, let him say it.

Why, indeed? He had no intention of letting this slip of a woman know he feared her. His glance strayed to the razor, shining wickedly in the sunlight, then looked away as other thoughts assailed him. A candlestick crashing down on his head, her small hands jerking on a rope. His throat tightened, and he tried to swallow.

He wasn't terrified of dying, not really, though he conceded he'd just as soon it not be today. And if he did meet his maker at a young age, he'd prefer his death to have some meaning. Being killed in battle, fighting for the things you believed in, was one thing; having your throat slit by a vengeful woman was another. "You don't know how to shave a man." That he'd come up with an excuse made him smile.

"Nonsense. I shave my grandfather."

"Oh." Zeke sighed, leaning back, resigned to his fate, as she began brushing lather over his jaw. "Hell, Fiona!" He jerked up, getting soap in his mouth in the process. "Your grandfather has a beard."

Fiona laughed. She couldn't help it. He looked so ridiculous with bristly dark whiskers thrusting though the creamy soap bubbles and his eyes, wide and shockingly blue, staring at her warily. "I'm not going to hurt you." She supposed she should give him some assurance, considering their past relationship. "You needn't fear me."

"I'm not —" His muscles tightened as the blade scraped across his cheek. His voice sounded unnaturally high as he finished his thought. "Scared."

"Good." Twisting her head to one side, Fiona contemplated the best way to tackle his upper lip. "Do this." She stretched out her own lip, giggling when he mimicked her. She bent forward, blade in hand, only to feel his strong dark fingers close over her wrist. Her eyes, still full of mischief, met his.

"Let's stop laughing before we take another swipe at my face. I'd appreciate a steady hand."

After that he lay back against the pillow and shut his eyes, trying to relax. He did no more than suck in his breath when she slid the blade up his neck, skimming over his Adam's apple. But she didn't cut him, and Zeke found he began to enjoy her efforts.

She bent over him, and though his eyes were closed and he couldn't see her, he could feel the warmth from her body. And smell the faint, haunting scent of heather that drifted about her like a gossamer cloak. Strange, her fragrance all but blocked out the sharp scent of soap. Or maybe it simply made that stronger smell seem sensual.

When she stopped, wiping the last traces of soap away with the towel, Zeke opened his eyes. She stood back, hands on hips, examining him critically. Some curls had escaped her ribbon and fluttered about her temple as she turned her head first to one side, then the other. "That's better," she said finally, her voice carrying to him on a soft Scottish burr. "Now you look more human."

"Tell me the truth, Fiona." She raised her delicate burnished brow. "Have you ever shaved anyone before?"

Shrugging, Fiona hesitated only a moment before admitting the truth. "Actually, you're the first."

"I thought so."

His remark seemed to hurt her feelings. She came closer, a defiant gleam in her eyes. "Why? I did a good job. All your whiskers are gone." Her hand reached out, touched his cheek. "And there's nary a nick or scratch."

Zeke's hand covered hers, sliding it across to his lips. She stiffened when his mouth opened, the tip of his tongue wetting her fingers. She tasted of soap and Fiona, and he tugged gently. Her breath caught as she tried to pull away. At first he didn't let her, then reason sank in. What in the hell was he doing? Zeke released her hand, but not her eyes, as he stared at her. "We need to talk, Fiona."

"I know." She started to sit in the chair beside the bed, then stood suddenly. "After you've eaten. I'm certain you're hungry. Who wouldn't be after your ordeal? And I know for a fact that there are biscuits and ham, and eggs. I can tell the cook to fix them any way you wish, and—"

"Sit." The terse command sliced through her babbling. Her mouth clamped shut as she obeyed. "I'll eat later."

"But—"

"Later, Fiona." He watched her fold her hands, and nearly laughed at her rare submissive pose. This wasn't the Fiona he knew. But he decided he could get used to this one—occasionally. "Now would you like to explain things to me?"

"What would you like to know?" Her lashes lifted, giving him access to those violet eyes. Zeke steeled himself to be hard. The pain in his shoulder as he shifted helped.

"To begin with, what are you doing here?"

"Do you mean, why did I come back? Because I left, you know, with Duncan."

"I didn't know. I don't recall much of anything after your cousin shot me."

Fiona winced at his tone, but decided to continue. She might as well get this over with. "Well, I did. He told me you were dead. But later I found out you weren't. So I came back."

"Just like that?"

"Aye." Fiona didn't think he wanted to hear about her pulling a gun on Duncan, or riding bareback through the streets of Wilmington.

"Is your grandfather here, too?"

"No."

"Damnit, Fiona. He was my prisoner and my responsibility."

"Well, he shouldn't have been. And he's not anymore." Rising, Fiona paced to the foot of the bed. "He's back at Armadale, where he belongs."

"Where you belong?" The question was out of him before he could stop it, and he could have kicked himself when she turned, her eyes soft and luminous in the early morning sunshine. She didn't answer, didn't have to, and Zeke felt his body stiffen as if preparing for the inevitable. She was going to leave. And there didn't seem to be anything he could do about it.

"I think I will have some breakfast now." Though hunger gnawed at him, it wasn't the only reason he wished to eat. He simply didn't know what else to say — wasn't sure he wanted his last question answered. Yet when he sat propped against the pillows, a biscuit in his hand, he couldn't help asking, "How did Duncan know to come here?"

She dreaded that question more than any other. The answer was damning if she told the truth. And suddenly she knew she owed him that. "I sent him a message."

"Asking him to come?"

"Aye." The word was spoken softly, barely loud enough to be heard above the knocking on the door, but he heard her.

"What?" He barked toward the door, the unwanted interruption, but Fiona knew the unleashed anger was for her.

Mrs. Steel opened the door. "There's a gentleman to see you, sir."

"I'm not in the mood to receive callers."

"It's Captain Webster, and he says it's important that he speak with you."

Zeke sensed rather than saw Fiona stiffen. So she was familiar with the local militia captain. Well, he supposed there was no use putting this off. "Send him up, please."

"I'll leave you alone with your visitor." Fiona rose, gathering up the tray and heading for the door as she spoke.

"Stay."

Zeke's command stopped her. Shutting her eyes, Fiona took a deep breath. It was ridiculous for her to think she could simply walk out of this room and leave. She'd waited too late . . . too late. Slowly she placed the tray on the bureau, and walked toward the window. Ignoring Zeke, she watched a mockingbird sitting in the magnolia tree.

When the captain arrived, ushered into the room by Mrs. Steel, he nodded to Fiona before focusing his attention on Zeke. Mrs. Steel left, but just as she was closing the door, Fiona noticed the woman's satisfied expression. Had she brought Captain Webster here? It suddenly seemed less of a coincidence that the militia officer would reappear the same day Zeke was able to talk to him.

The captain moved a chair closer to the bed and sat down. "You're looking much better, Colonel Kincaid."

Zeke's brow arched. "You were here before?"

"Certainly. The day you were shot. I spoke with Mistress MacClure and your stablehand."

"Oh." Zeke glanced toward Fiona. "And what did they tell you?"

"Not much, I'm afraid. Neither seemed to know what happened. It appears your stableboy . . . Jacob, is it? Yes, well, it seems Jacob was struck from behind."

"Cowardly act." Zeke saw Fiona's fingers tighten on the sill.

"Certainly," the captain agreed. "I'm hoping you can tell me who the guilty party, or parties, are."

It sounded so simple. So simple. A word from him. An accusation. And justice would prevail. He shifted under the sheet, then opened his mouth. "I would love to assist you, Captain. But the truth is, I've no idea who shot me."

Fiona jerked her head around, sending red curls flying, and simply stared at him. Zeke wondered if the captain noticed her reaction. He didn't wish to go to the trouble of lying only to have her damn herself.

"You didn't see anyone?"

"Careless of me, I know." Zeke grinned sheepishly. "But whoever it was, must have been hiding in the stable."

Rubbing his hand over his large nose, Captain Webster nodded. "You weren't the only one, you know."

"Oh?"

"There were several other incidents in town last week . . . shootings. Luckily no one was killed. One of the victims was Francis Morgan. I believe you know him."

"Yes. He's a representative to the Congress."

Captain Webster leaned back in his chair. "Someone shot him as he walked in his garden. One of his servants caught a glimpse of the man. Said he had a red beard."

Zeke's fists clenched beneath the sheet. That Tory bastard had been busy. He watched Fiona move toward the bed. From her wide-eyed expression, he'd bet she'd known nothing of this till now.

"By the way"—the captain stood—"didn't you have a Scottish prisoner staying with you? Mistress MacClure's grandfather?"

"I did."

"May I ask what has become of him?"

"I had him moved." Zeke stared at the captain, trying to remind him without words who was the superior officer. But he couldn't blame the man for his questions.

"Hmmmm." Captain Webster rubbed his nose again. "But Mistress MacClure remained here?"

"Yes. With me."

"Oh." The captain's beady eyes raked Fiona. "I see."

"I imagine you do. Sweetheart"—Zeke shifted toward Fiona—"would you please show Captain Webster to the door? I'm very tired."

Sweetheart! He'd done it again—portrayed her as his lover! Rage boiled through Fiona and she knotted her fingers in the delicate silk overshirt. How dare he? She opened her mouth to tell him just exactly what she thought of his tactics, but slammed it shut. Without a word she moved toward the door. Opening it, she gave the captain her sweetest smile as he said his farewells. It wasn't until he'd gone, and she'd shut the door, that she turned on Zeke.

"I can't believe you did that!"

"What?" Zeke's brow arched. "Saved your neck?" He wasn't certain at this moment why he had done it, either, but he found the possible motives unsettling.

That left her momentarily speechless, but she recovered quickly. "You didn't have to tell him . . . to make him think . . . He probably imagines us in your bed this very moment." Fiona stopped, her cheeks coloring as her own imagination soared.

"I'm willing." Zeke flexed his shoulder, winced. "I think."

"Well, I most certainly am not."

Her haughty tone and the self-righteous set of her jaw did nothing to endear her in his mind. She acted as if there had been no long night of lovemaking. As if he'd implied there was more to their relationship simply to get a rise out of her. "And just what explanation was I supposed to give for your presence here? You weren't exactly supporting my story."

"I was too shocked!" Fiona's hands flew to her hips.

"Keep your voice down, or it will all be for naught anyway."

"Why did you do it?" Fiona's expression softened. "Why did you lie?"

Zeke shrugged to cover his own doubts. "I suppose in a roundabout way you did save my life."

"That doesn't explain your failure to expose Duncan."

How could he have exposed one red-haired Mac-Clure without implicating the other? And deep in his heart, Zeke knew he could never do that. But to admit that would make him more vulnerable than he cared to be, almost as helpless as he'd been right before Duncan had squeezed the pistol trigger. Zeke's eyes narrowed at the memory. "I won't delegate your cousin's punishment to a subordinate. When the time comes, I intend to handle it myself."

"I see." Fiona swallowed, turning away from the unmasked anger in Zeke's eyes. Not that he didn't deserve to be furious. She'd just thought . . . foolishly allowed herself to think . . . he'd protected her for another reason. Fiona shoved that notion from her mind. She had no time for such sentimentality, even if it were anything more than a figment of her imagination. "And is that why you failed to tell them about my grandfather, too? Do you plan to take care of that matter on your own?"

He didn't answer, but then she hadn't expected him to. She knew enough about Ezekiel Kincaid to guess what he was thinking. He wouldn't allow a prisoner of his to escape without doing something about it, any more than he'd allow himself to be shot without retaliating.

If this morning had done nothing else, it proved her need to be gone from this place. She was suspected by the local militia—for though the captain had been briefly fooled, she didn't think it would last. And she needed to get to her grandfather. Armadale wasn't safe for him. Duncan was right. It was the first place Zeke would go to look for him.

And Duncan? What could she think about Duncan? He was family, clan. He'd been like a brother to her. He had come to Wilmington at her request. But the war had changed him. Had he shot that man? Fiona looked down at Zeke, at the stark white bandage on his shoulder, and shuddered.

Picking up the tray, Fiona backed toward the door. "I'll leave you now. You look as if you could use some rest."

He nodded, not meeting her eyes, and Fiona was

glad. If he'd looked at her at that moment, or questioned her, he might have chipped away at her resolve. But he didn't, seemingly too deep in his own thoughts to worry about hers. Slipping through the door, closing it softly behind her, Fiona leaned against the whitewashed wall.

She shut her eyes and sighed. Her mind was made up. Tonight she'd leave for Armadale.

Chapter Twenty-one

"Thank God." Fiona rested her forehead against the windowpane, then glanced up to check the night sky once more. Not that she didn't trust the way the moon spattered its silvery light through the oak leaves; it was simply that she couldn't believe she was seeing it. The moon, the stars, even the clear, velvety black canopy of sky had been awash in dreary clouds and rain for five days.

Five days that had seemed like a hundred. Five days that had kept her stuck in Zeke's house. Five days that had nearly driven her crazy.

The rain had been monotonously steady, graying the sky and turning the roads to soppy red quagmires of mud. And it had started the morning she'd decided to leave.

But now it was over. This day had dawned clear and bright, with a healthy breeze off the river to dry up the puddles. And now the night lay ahead, equally clear, and thanks to the round ball of a moon, almost equally bright. A perfect night for traveling.

Fiona smiled, crossing her arms over her night rail, and glanced toward the riding clothes spread out on the counterpane. Beside them was a bundle contain-

357

ing a few undergarments and some food she'd smuggled from the kitchen. She wasn't taking any of the dresses bought with Zeke's money. There was no room in her saddlebags. That reason proved true enough. But Fiona knew she'd leave the gowns even if a coach were supplied to transport her belongings.

Little chance of that, Fiona thought, smiling despite the melancholy that suddenly descended on her like a shroud. Zeke was angry with her—she hadn't really needed Meg's delivered messages to tell her that—but even this fury was nothing to how he'd react when he found her gone.

As soon as the household slept she was leaving. No more delays, she promised herself, padding toward the mantel to see the clock face more clearly.

Half past eleven. Fiona tried to lift her spirits with the promise that her wait was almost over. She had a long, tiring ride ahead—and small doubts assailed her about fording the rain-swollen streams—but soon, God willing, she'd be home at Armadale.

Home. Her temple rested on the arm she'd draped over the mantel. It seemed so long since she'd been there, yet she could imagine quite easily riding up the oak-lined drive. She could almost see Lucy, her dark, work-worn hands bracketing ample hips, her turbanned head shaking. " 'Bout time you got back where you belong, Miss Fiona. Ain't I just been worrying myself to death? And look at you. Just like always, no hat on your head, and the sun burning like blazes. Why you don't freckle up like Duncan is a wonder to me."

Her homecoming would be tainted by the need to warn grandfather. Running a hand down over her face, catching a finger between her teeth, Fiona wondered if he'd leave at all. Would he stubbornly ignore

358

her warnings about Zeke?

If only she could get Colonel Kincaid to change his mind about pursuing the laird. Fiona sighed, pushing away from the hearth. That would be pretty hard to do without speaking to him. And since the day she'd decided to leave, she'd refused to do that.

At first it had seemed easy enough. She would be leaving, so why bother to stop in his room. But as the rain-dreary days wore on, it became obvious she was avoiding him. And then the summonses had begun. She ignored the first because it was a foul-tempered demand, and then as they kept coming she refused out of fear. Not that he'd hurt her, but that he'd somehow guess her plans, and force her to stay.

There was no chance of that now. He was asleep, she was confident of that. Today had been his first excursion out of his room, and he couldn't help but be tired. With all his stomping around and pounding, he was probably dead to the world by now.

The idea came to her, and she immediately wished it hadn't. But as much as she folded and refolded the skirt of her night rail, it wouldn't leave her mind. "What harm could it do?" Fiona mumbled to herself, then started toward the door before she could answer her own question.

Pools of light from the brass sconces and silvery splashes of moonlight spilling in the arched window lit the hallway. She hadn't thought to bring a candle, and luckily she didn't need one. Besides, she knew the way to Zeke's room.

The door opened silently, and just as quietly she slipped into his room. His curtains were open, letting the moonlight and cooling night breeze through the open window. Just one peek, she promised herself, as she crept toward the tall and imposing bed. It seemed ghostlike with the breeze catching its gossamer covering of mosquito netting.

Silly woman, she chided herself, aware of the quickened beating of her heart. It was only nerves caused by sneaking around in someone's room at night. But when she reached for the filmy netting, Fiona knew it was more. She really had missed seeing him, talking to him. She sighed, reluctant to admit that the rest of her life might be spent feeling the same way.

"Ach!"

The hand that whipped out, clamping around her wrist, nearly toppled Fiona onto the bed. She fought for footing, twisting her hand to no avail, and began a heartfelt tirade.

"In English, Fiona. I can't understand your gibberish."

"Gibberish! Gaelic is not gibberish."

"It is when you're throwing words at me at lightning speed. I can't follow it. And I'm sure you don't want me to miss a single thought."

"You lackwit, cretin, bastard . . ."

"Ah, that's better." Amusement laced his voice. "Those sentiments I understand."

He was laughing at her! Fiona took a deep breath, brushing tangled curls from her eyes with her free hand, and strove to appear calm. "Will you kindly let me go?"

"I don't think so."

Oh, she'd been so foolish — again. "And why," Fiona began calmly enough, but when she saw the flash of white teeth as he grinned, her anger exploded. She wriggled, the last word coming out as a frenzied demand. "Not!"

Zeke chose not to answer. He had hold of her, and that was all that mattered for now. "Is this why you've refused to see me in the day? You've been sneaking into my room at night?"

Oh, he'd like that, wouldn't he? Thinking she'd stood by his bed, mooning over him. "Most certainly not. This is the first night I've come."

"Really?" He sounded skeptical. "So why did you come tonight? You *did* come tonight, didn't you?" he added with just enough sincerity to make Fiona grit her teeth.

"Of course I did." Fiona yanked on her arm, felt his fingers tighten, and let it go limp.

"So why tonight?" he asked again, his tone more serious.

Did he know her plans? Fiona tried to make out his expression in the moonlight, but could only discern the curve of his jaw, a dark sparkle of eyes. She gnawed on her bottom lip. His grip loosened, but she knew better than to contest his ability to hold her, especially when he tugged her closer to the bed.

"If you've no other explanation, you must have come because you missed me." Again, Fiona caught the flash of white teeth as he grinned.

"I can assure you, *that* was not the reason."

"Then why are you here, Fiona?"

Oh, when his voice was smooth and low like that, like warm honey flowing over her senses, Fiona was almost tempted to stop resisting his persistent pull. But then she'd go sprawling across him. On the bed. And she couldn't have that.

Giving a futile tug on her ensnared wrist, Fiona shrugged. "I simply came to check on your progress."

"I'm healing quite nicely." Zeke glanced toward his shoulder, where a white bandage stood out in stark relief against his moon-gilded skin. "Hardly any pain."

Fiona doubted that. She'd seen the ragged hole in

361

his flesh, but if it meant getting away from him faster, she'd agree. "You seem to have gotten your strength back, at least." This remark, coupled with another tug on her wrist, brought a chuckle from deep in his chest. His bare chest, Fiona noted before training her eyes resolutely on his face.

"What have you been doing?"

"Doing?" Fiona thought she detected a caustic edge to his softly spoken question.

"I figured you must be excessively busy since you haven't had time to visit me." There was no mistaking the sharpness in these words. "Have you been making soap?"

"Don't be ridiculous."

"Mucking the stables?"

"No."

"Planning Washington's strategy for winning the war?"

"No, damn you. Would you let go of my arm?" Fiona twisted again, but couldn't break the velvet manacle of his strong fingers.

"No." Now it was he giving the negative response. "Not until you tell me why you've refused to see me."

"I thought you needed your rest," she lied.

"Is that what you thought when I pounded on your door today?"

"I . . ." How foolish she'd been to come.

"Is that what you thought, Fiona? Is that why you wouldn't let me in?"

"I thought it was for the best." Her voice cracked. Resolutely she pulled herself together. "If we didn't see each other."

"Didn't see . . . Then why in the hell are you here now?"

"I wouldn't be if you'd . . . just . . . let . . . go." Her

362

struggles were useless.

"I want an answer, Fiona."

"I don't have one."

"Well, at least that's honest."

"I'm always honest." Fiona bit her lip. She couldn't see it, but she was sure his brow arched at that declaration. The next moment she compounded her mistake by answering his snort of disbelief with a reminder of his own lie.

"Are you referring to the lies I told to save your sweet butt?"

Oh, he could be so crude. Fiona twisted, but found herself yanked forward till she had to support herself with her free hand to keep from falling over him. Her hair spilled over his skin like fire.

"Is that the one you're referring to, Fiona?"

"Aye." She could feel the heat from his bared chest.

"Well, since you're so displeased with it, I think you should know, I told it again."

"The captain returned?" She hadn't known that.

"Hell, no! This time the head of the Committee of Safety and two members of the Provincial Congress called."

"I thought they'd just come to wish you well." She thought she noticed a widening of his eyes at her admission that she knew his visitors, but she wasn't sure.

"Wish me well." He chuckled, or grunted, Fiona wasn't certain which. "Actually, they were concerned about my health. They wanted to know when I could take up my duties again. It seems the war hasn't ground to a halt just because your cousin shot me."

"Does this mean you won't be going after Duncan?"

This time he did laugh. "Oh, you needn't worry, Fiona. That redheaded Tory is going to get what he deserves."

"What about my grandfather?" Fiona's arm was beginning to quiver from holding up her weight.

"What about him?"

She couldn't bring herself to ask what Zeke planned to do about him. He'd been only too glad to tell her about Duncan. "Did the . . . did your visitors ask about him?"

"No." He slid over, allowing her room to rest her hip on the mattress. "The members of the committee either forgot or were too embarrassed to ask me outright."

So Grandfather was safe for the moment. But she still had to get him away from Armadale. Zeke would not allow his prisoner to escape without doing something about it.

"What are you thinking about?"

He started to lift his wounded arm, stopped, dropped his hand to her hip. It seemed to burn through the thin linen of her night rail, leaving her weak, unable to resist his pull.

"Nothing," she whispered, truthfully, for when he moved his hand in those slow, caressing circles, she forgot her own thoughts.

"I missed your visits."

His honesty forced her to act in kind. "I missed coming."

"Then why?"

His breath fanned her cheek as her arm gave up the battle and her upper body sprawled across his chest. "I don't know. . . ."

His lips were warm and gentle at first, then, with an abruptness that startled her, turned hot, demanding. Fiona tried to catch her breath as he tore his mouth away, burning a path down her neck. She should get up. He no longer clasped her wrist. His hands were too busy skimming over her back, down her hip.

He bit her earlobe, tangling his fingers in her hair before crushing her mouth down on his in a deep kiss filled with carnal delights. His tongue plunged and Fiona wriggled her feet off the floor, twisting till she lay full on top him.

"God, Fiona," his words rasped against her open lips. "If you hadn't come in here tonight." He left the rest unsaid as her tongue skimmed over his teeth. He sucked it into his mouth, moaning as Fiona spread her legs to accommodate his hardness. "I swear," he gasped between butterfly kisses placed along her jaw. "I was lying here deciding the best way to break down your door."

Fiona smiled, bracing her hands on the pillow beside his head, keeping just out of reach of his lips as he arched upward. "That would have made a lot of noise."

"I didn't care." He turned his head, wetting the wrist he'd held captive with the tip of his tongue, and Fiona dropped down to trace the bold swirl of his ear.

This was lunacy. In some deep recess of her mind, Fiona knew that. But she didn't care. Just this one last night to remember all the other nights of her life. All those empty, empty nights.

Fiona trailed her lips along his cheek, loving the whiskers that roughened her path, the male feel of him. He arched his head, exposing his neck, and she explored the tendons and muscles, the Adam's apple that moved as he swallowed.

And all the time she used her lips and tongue to work her magic, while he seemed to be lying complacently still for her, his hands were inching up the fabric of her night rail. The breeze touched her thighs, cooling the fevered flesh, then her buttocks.

"Oh." Her moan was muffled by the curve of his jaw

as he forced his hand between their bodies and his finger found her.

His touch was magic. She wanted to share the beauty with him, but all she could do was writhe and twist. Her hands sought purchase, grabbing hold, digging deep. Even through her passion-drugged haze she felt his body stiffen, heard the moan he couldn't contain.

She tore her hand away from the linen bandage, tears stinging her eyes for what she'd done. "Zeke! God, Zeke, are you all right?" She feared he'd passed out, because he didn't answer right away. "Oh, I'm so stupid."

"It's okay. I'm okay." His voice didn't sound very convincing. To add credibility to his words Zeke moved the hand that lay nestled in her tight curls.

"Oh, no, you don't." Fiona clenched her legs together only managing to force his finger deeper. "We can't do this."

"The hell we can't." She was so wet and tight.

"Zeke . . ." Against her will, Fiona felt her muscles relax. "Your shoulder," she managed, before the waves started rippling though her. Faster and faster they came. Fiona gasped for breath, vaguely aware that he'd jerked the sheet from between them. She heard his breathless command to mount him, might have wondered at some other time what he meant, but not now. Not now. Her body responded as if schooled in the art of love.

She slid up his body, stopping just as the tip of him slipped between her legs. He filled her deep and full, and it was all Fiona could do not to cry out. He did, and she froze, breaking the natural rhythm that seemed to flow by instinct. "Did I hurt you?"

"Oh . . . God . . . no. . . ." He grabbed her hips,

pulling her down at the same instant he arched up. "Don't stop . . . please."

She couldn't if she tried. Her body moved without thought from her. He yanked the night rail over her head, then found her nipples with his hands. They strained toward him as surely as the rest of her body. And then he stiffened, but she knew this time it had naught to do with pain, for her own body answered, shattering her senses as he exploded inside her.

She collapsed onto his chest, keeping just enough touch with reality to avoid his bandaged shoulder. His heart thumped beneath her ear, and she smiled, thinking it the most wonderful sound. Strong . . . steady. It helped draw her back bit by bit until she could notice things like the unconscious caress of his fingers as he opened and closed his hand, the musky smell of passion. His arm tightened around her, tucking her closer to him, and Fiona sighed. She felt so safe, so secure, so at home.

The thought made her jerk. She tried to rise, but his fingers tangled in her hair, lowering her cheek to his chest. "Stay," he murmured, his voice husky with sleep, and Fiona knew she had no choice—for now.

But thinking of Zeke as home was wrong, so very wrong. Armadale was home. Was all those things—security, a safe haven, love. While Zeke was . . . Zeke.

She tasted salt, thought it the sheen of sweat on his skin, then realized it was her own tears. They rolled silently down her cheeks, pooling in the hollow below his collarbone. Oh, why must she cry now? Fiona tried to roll to the side, hoping she could leave the room without his noticing, but his arm tightened around her. "Stay," he mumbled, again.

"Aye." He said nothing of the dampness on his skin, and Fiona hoped he was too near sleep to notice. She made a show of settling in, wiping her hand across his chest, wondering if she could stem the tide of her tears. He snuggled against her, his breath fluttering across her hair.

"Stay with me," he whispered, before sleep overtook him.

She could not judge the time, but she'd recited Flowers of Edinburgh to herself four times — not counting the verses she couldn't remember. That certainly had been enough time for him to be sound asleep. Feeling the steady rhythm of his breathing, the soft snoring, made her hopeful. Carefully she squirmed from beneath his encircling arm. The rope springs creaked, but Zeke made no movement as his hand fell onto the coverlet.

It took her a moment to find her night rail, tangled in the dust ruffle beside the bed. She yanked it over her head, impatiently grabbing her hair from beneath the collar. And all the time she kept her face turned away from the bed. Fiona didn't want to look at him, couldn't look at him, feared if she did she might not do what needed to be done.

She'd arranged her clothes so she could dress quickly, but hadn't expected to move so fast. Fiona doubted anyone ever pulled on a shift and skirt, laced up a corset, and plunged their feet into boots with as much speed. She kept her mind focused on her task, afraid to let it wander at all.

She'd think later, when she was safe at Armadale, and her grandfather was safely away. Then she'd allow herself time to ponder her feelings for Zeke.

Carrying a candle seemed too risky, so Fiona crept through the dark hallway, tiptoeing her way down the stairs. She hit the crushed-shell drive at a run, gathering her skirts in a tight bundle with her free hand.

Saying a silent prayer that she didn't have to worry about waking Jacob—he'd started sleeping in the attic after Duncan had hit him—Fiona pushed open the stable door. And froze.

"Going someplace, Fiona?"

Opening and closing her mouth seemed all that she could do. Finally Fiona blurted out the inconsistency in what she was seeing. "But, you're asleep."

"Obviously not." Zeke pushed away from the stall where he'd been leaning and started toward her, his facade of calm cracking wider as he stepped out of the lantern light into the shadows.

Running seemed the logical thing to do, but Fiona didn't think she'd get very far. Besides, just because his dark brows nearly formed a shelf above his eyes and his mouth stretched taut didn't mean she couldn't stand up to him. Fiona straightened her shoulders. "I'm going home . . . to Armadale."

"No, you're not."

Fiona sucked in air. "I most certainly am! You can't keep me here." She tossed her head; the hair she hadn't taken time to brush flew over her shoulder. "I'm not a prisoner."

Zeke stopped within a foot of her, and pointed out the obvious. "You were instrumental in helping the person who was my prisoner escape."

"Yes, but—"

"Consider yourself a replacement."

"A re—That's absurd."

The fact that he only shrugged fueled Fiona's anger. Her fingers opened, then closed, the forgotten parcel of food dropping to the straw with a soft plop. She kicked it aside as she began pacing. "I cannot stay here."

"I fail to understand—"

369

"Because of what just happened." She didn't stop her movements, but did look over her shoulder in time to see his questioning expression. "In your bed," she clarified.

"Ah." He bent forward, scooped up a piece of straw and studied it a moment before speaking. His voice was low, and despite her resolve to keep her distance, Fiona moved closer. "I wasn't aware you found *that* distasteful."

Fiona sighed, an exaggerated expulsion of air. He could be such a dimwit sometimes. "I don't find *that* distasteful. But don't you see what that makes me?" Fiona jammed her balled fists against her waist and answered her own question. "I'm your kept woman!"

"And that bothers you?"

She wanted to grab the front of the shirt he'd thrown on but not bothered to fasten, and shake him till his teeth rattled. "Of course that bothers me!"

"That problem seems easy enough to solve."

"Let me go," she cried, and stopped, her eyes widening in disbelief. "What did you say?" She was sure she hadn't heard him correctly.

He'd said it once, though for the life of him, he couldn't imagine why, but he had no choice but to repeat it. "Marry me." Never mind that he'd shocked himself by his proposal; she didn't have to look at him as if he'd suggested she peel off her skin with a dull knife. "Does being a wife bother you also?"

"No . . ." Fiona swallowed and tried again. "No, of course not."

"Well, then?" Why was he digging his own grave deeper?

"Well . . ." She gave a nervous laugh. He appeared self-assured except for the piece of straw he was crumbling to dust. He obviously wasn't thinking clearly.

Admittedly, she hadn't been either, at first, but now she'd set him straight. "We never get along."

"I wouldn't say that's true." The heated stare that accompanied his words made Fiona want to throw water on her cheeks to cool them.

"Oh," she gasped on a ragged breath. "You mean *that*."

"Well, *that* is important." He cocked his head to the side, a shadow of a smile playing across his mouth.

"But *that* isn't the only thing."

"Granted."

"And when we're not doing . . . *that*, even when we are doing . . . *that*, our loyalties are on opposite sides."

He seemed to consider this a moment, picking up more straw to replenish the piece he'd crumbled. His eyes snagged hers. "Do you hate me because of my beliefs?"

"Of course not." How could she hate him when she was half afraid her feelings were just the opposite?

"Have you taken some vow to kill every Patriot you encounter?"

"Don't be silly."

His broad shoulders under the white linen shirt lifted in a shrug. "I can accept your views on the war."

Fiona stared. He'd taken the main difference between them and reduced it to . . . to mere acceptance. What was she to say to that? It couldn't be that simple. "We fight," she blurted out. "Argue all the time. I have an awful temper. Everyone says so. You'd tire of it very quickly."

He *was* tiring quickly. But not of her temper. He'd been an idiot to suggest marriage in the first place, but since he had, she should be thrilled. Instead she gave him nothing but reasons why it wouldn't work — made him almost seem as if he were begging her.

Well, he needed to set things straight. "For God's sake, Fiona," he said, interrupting yet another deterrent to their union. "I wasn't proposing a love match."

"You weren't?"

Why did she have to look at him like that? It must be the lack of light, but he could have sworn tears clouded her violet eyes. Zeke's jaw tightened. What did he care? Tears, shed silently after they'd made love, were what had alerted him that she was leaving in the first place. He forced his voice to be harsh. "Hardly."

"Oh." Fiona gnawed her lower lip. "I never thought that's what you meant."

"Good."

"Aye. Good."

What in the hell did her agreement mean? Zeke studied Fiona a moment, wishing he could yank her back into the pool of light to better read her expression. He didn't think she was capitulating this easily, though why it was so important for her to do so, he couldn't imagine. He paused a moment before mentioning the one thing he knew would make her stay. "If we were married . . . well, I think the Congress would be more inclined to grant your grandfather a parole."

"You mean you wouldn't go after him . . . try to bring him back?"

Zeke tried to conceal his annoyance that it took this piece of news to excite her. After all, he'd known it would. "Yes, Fiona, that's what I mean."

"What about Duncan?" The moment she said that, Fiona knew she'd gone too far. She didn't even need to see Zeke's arched brow. "Well . . . I guess he'll have to fend for himself. He did shoot you."

"Exactly. Unfortunately, there doesn't seem to be anything I can do about it now. The Provincial Congress is anxious for me to clear up a problem in the western counties." He didn't think she'd care to know it involved capturing a band of Tories who were harassing Patriot families. If she accepted his proposal, Fiona would be removed from the problem, safe here in Wilmington.

Zeke let the straw filter between his fingers, brushing his hands together in a gesture he refused to accept as nervous. "Well, what do you say?"

Fiona swallowed. What choice did she have? If she married him her grandfather could stay at Armadale, the place he loved. But, oh, she didn't like doing this—not for the reasons he gave. Not when he spoke so derisively of love, and . . . She feared she was madly in love with him. But there was naught she could do but nod, and force an unsure "aye" from her tight throat.

It shouldn't have caused a shiver of joy to rush through him—after all, her acceptance had hardly been enthusiastic—but he couldn't help it. Any more than he could stop himself from taking her in his arms. Her face, when she lifted it toward him, was somber, her eyes a deep, searching violet. But her mouth was warm and familiar, molding to his easily as he deepened the kiss.

Chapter Twenty-two

"Do you want me to be fetching the constable, Missus Kincaid?"

Fiona blinked, not realizing for a moment that Jacob was addressing her. He had just explained what Mrs. Davis, the cook had told him, and now he was waiting for direction.

Married.

This is what being married to Ezekiel Kincaid had gotten her. Worries about runaway indentured servants. "Well, I . . ." A movement to the side caught Fiona's eye, and she glanced around to see Mrs. Steel descending the stairs. This was something else being married to Zeke had given her—his housekeeper. A woman who seemed more than willing to notice any mistake Fiona made.

And she made her share.

She didn't know how to run a household—it was as simple as that. Elspeth and Katrine had handled that at Armadale, and Fiona had thought that just fine. But now she was paying the price for her carefree ways.

Jacob shuffled his feet on the carpet, and Fiona knew a decision had to be made. In the absence of her husband, Fiona had to make it.

For there was one thing being married hadn't gotten her—Zeke. He had left the morning after their wedding and hadn't returned for over a fortnight.

"Did you say Peggy's been spotted at a tavern down by the waterfront?"

"Yes'm." Jacob fiddled with his sweat-stained felt hat. "Someone stopped by this morning to say they'd seen her down there"—he hesitated—"with some man."

Fiona bit her lip. She should be glad that someone had spotted her, because Fiona hadn't missed her. Thinking back, Fiona tried to remember the last time she'd noticed the sullen Peggy. She couldn't. Another mistake—not keeping track of Zeke's indentured servants.

Fiona reached through the folds of her skirt into her pocket. Her fingers tightened around the household keys. "Don't bother with the constable, Jacob. I'll handle Peggy myself."

"Are you quite certain you know what you're doing?" Mrs. Steel asked. To her credit she waited until Jacob was out of earshot.

"Aye." Fiona raised her chin, only to dislodge a strand of red hair. "Someone needs to fetch Peggy back, and I think it should be me."

"As you wish," was all the older woman said as she glided by Fiona, her starched skirts whispering across the carpet.

"As you wish," Fiona mimicked a quarter of an hour later, as she jammed a straw bonnet on her head. "As you wish." She yanked the ribbon into a knot under her chin, tying it in a crude facsimile of a bow. "Nothing is as I wish."

375

The sultry, hot day enveloped her like an itchy wool blanket as Fiona ventured out the front door. Wilmington was oppressively hot. Their thick-walled house kept out most of the heat, but whenever Fiona went out, she longed for the pine forests of home.

Sighing, Fiona pushed through the gate at the bottom of the walk. She'd sent a message to Armadale telling them of her marriage. She'd tried to explain why she'd done it — at least the reasons that involved Grandfather — but as yet there was no reply. They'd received her post. She knew that, because Elspeth sent a letter congratulating her, and telling her that Grandfather had made it safely to Armadale. And seemed to be doing better. At least she could take some consolation in that.

The letter hadn't mentioned Duncan, and Fiona had been just as glad. She didn't want to know where he was. She didn't want to think about what would happen when Zeke finished his mission and went after her cousin.

Touching a lace-edged handkerchief to her damp brow, Fiona decided that wasn't her concern. Right now her main worry was a runaway servant with dirty blond hair.

It was still her worry an hour hence, when she emerged from the tavern. She'd spoken with Peggy's "friend," a private in the local militia, but had seen no sign of Peggy. Nor had anyone seemed inclined to help her look for the girl. She'd accused the private of stealing her property, but he'd only grinned, showing teeth badly in need of extraction, and claimed not to know what she was talking about.

Well, Fiona decided as she made her way back to the house, maybe it *was* time to call in the constable.

Fiona shrugged, closing the iron gate in front of Zeke's house. It squeaked, and she made a mental note to have someone grease it, a decision that flew from her mind as the front door burst open.

"Zeke!" Fiona found her voice squeaking as badly as the gate. Running to him — her first impulse — was out of the question, for he covered the space between them before she could even start. But it wasn't a hug of welcome that greeted her.

"Where have you been?"

Fiona's violet eyes flew open at his demanding tone, and Zeke wished he could call back the words. If he hadn't been so damn worried . . .

"How dare you speak to me like that!" A nervous glance around the yard revealed the only witnesses to his outburst were the glossy-leafed magnolias. Still, he had no right to demand —

"I asked you a question, Fiona. And I expect you to tell me —"

"Well, you may bellow all you like, but that doesn't mean I'll answer, nor will I stand here and — Let go of me, you . . . you brute." Fiona's attempt to glide by him, head held high, was thwarted when his hand clamped around her arm.

"I want an answer," Zeke said, wondering how in the world the reunion he'd looked forward to for two weeks had regressed to this.

The eyes he'd dreamed of nightly were staring at him, not with the love he longed for, or even the passion he'd settle for, but with a fierce scowl. And the worst of it was, he knew he deserved her anger. She glared at him, her chin forward, her mouth set in a stubborn line as if daring him to pry the information from her.

Zeke wondered if they would stand there all day, waging a silent battle.

"Come on." Zeke's hand slid down her arm, clasping around Fiona's hand as he pulled her toward the door.

"Where?" Fiona dug in her heels. "I don't want to be going anywhere with you."

"Listen, Fiona. I'm . . . hell, I'm sorry I yelled at you. But I'd like some answers." Zeke ignored her "hmph". "And I think we need a more private place to hold this discussion."

As far as Fiona was concerned, there would be no discussion, but she would like a more private place to tell him that. So she made no protest as he led her into the house and down the cool hallway. Fiona thought at first that he'd take her to the library, but realized as they started up the stairs that their destination was the bedroom they'd shared on their wedding night. "Zeke, I don't think we should . . ." But it was too late. He pulled her inside the room, shutting the door, and the world, out.

Fiona found herself backed against the paneled portal, held there by Zeke's body. But she wasn't going to think about that, or the night they'd spent in this room. Anger would be her bulwark. But when he leaned closer, his finger catching beneath her chin, raising it, she felt her bastion begin to crumble. From the expression in his blue eyes, she expected words of love or, at very least, heartfelt apologies. What she got was a repeat of his original question. In a nicer tone, to be sure. But a repeat, all the same.

Well, why not answer him? Maybe then he'd move away from her before she broke down and begged him to kiss her. "I went to the Crazy Gull Tavern, and—"

"Hell, then she was right."

"Who?"

"Who, what?"

Fiona sighed in exasperation. "Who was right?"

"Mrs. Steel. Never mind." Zeke combed his finger back through his hair. "What were you doing there? Have you any idea what kind of place that is?" He tried to keep his voice calm, he really did. But he noticed Fiona's chin jut forward.

"I do now. And I went to get Peggy," Fiona explained through clenched teeth.

"Who in the hell is Peggy?"

"One of your indentured servants. She has nearly five years left and I thought—"

Zeke silenced her by raising his hand. A faint memory of frizzled blond hair and a sour disposition came to his mind. "Wait a minute. What is Peggy doing at the Crazy Gull Tavern?"

"She ran away," Fiona said in frustration. "Didn't Mrs. Steel tell you this?"

"No. No, she didn't mention anything about a servant."

"Well, what did you think I was doing there, for heaven's sake?"

"I don't know. I guess I didn't think at all." He braced his hand against the door, leaning his forehead on his upper arm. "Hell, when I got here, the first thing she said was that you were gone, and I thought . . ."

"You thought what?" Fiona twisted her head, but could barely see his face. Beneath his whisker-shadowed jaw and sun-darkened neck, the pulse that beat

379

steadily there seemed uncharacteristically vulnerable. "Zeke?"

"I thought you'd left me," he blurted out. "When I started to rage about, she mentioned the tavern. . . . And I guess I never did take time to think."

"Zeke." Fiona felt warm all over, and this time the weather wasn't to blame.

"What?"

He didn't sound too pleased with his admission, but Fiona was. She lifted her hand, touching the masculine curve of his chin, letting her fingers move up to his cheek. He tilted his head, and she smiled into his eyes. "I'm here."

The light kiss he skimmed across her lips made Fiona's knees weak, but it wasn't nearly enough for her. And by the way his breath caught when she pressed closer to him, Fiona knew it wasn't enough for him, either. Standing on tiptoes, she wound her arms around his neck, deepening the kiss.

"I . . . need to wash up." Zeke pressed his lips to her eyes, her cheeks, her nose.

"Later."

"Fiona, honey." Zeke swallowed as her hands trailed down his shirt, caught in his waistband. "I've ridden for two days."

"Mmmm."

"God, when you do that I can't—" Zeke tried to grasp reason. "I'm sweaty."

"So am I."

"And dirty." The words hissed through his clenched teeth.

Fiona fumbled with the last button. "I . . . don't . . . care."

Any other protest he might have made died on a

moan as Fiona's fingers curled around him. He yanked at her skirts, wading through the layers of silk and linen as she continued to caress him. He touched skin, soft and sweet. Her smooth hip. His hand splayed, tangling in the tight thatch of hair.

"Oh, Zeke." Fiona's legs opened and her head fell back against the door. His mouth burned a path down her neck to the edge of her gown's lace bodice. Frustrated with the material, he moved lower, biting at the nipples that strained against the silk. Fiona writhed. The coil of heat flamed hotter, and she clutched at him as her knees gave way.

But she didn't fall. Instead she felt herself lifted. Then filled. The coil wound tighter as he urged her legs up around his hips. She couldn't catch her breath, though she gasped in air. She couldn't get close enough to him, though their bodies were joined. Fiona clutched at Zeke's shoulders, digging her nails into his damp shirt, the corded muscles beneath. And all the time, he surged into her, the rhythm increasing until it matched the pounding of her heart.

Then suddenly there was no sound, just the movement of her body as it flowed around his, pulsing, squeezing, convulsing. He grabbed her hips, pressed deeper, became one with the motion.

She'd been floating through a sensual haze. Fiona realized that as the mist began to fade. She stood on the floor again, the door and Zeke's body the only things keeping her upright. Raspy breathing sounded in her ear, and Fiona opened her eyes, but still couldn't tell if it was Zeke or her. His forehead rested against hers in a touch as intimate as making love.

Fiona smiled, lifting her hands from where they

hung limply by her side, to touch him, his chest cowered with a sweat-slicked shirt, his jaw. "Will you be wanting your bath now?"

His lashes lifted, deep brown unveiling the blue of a summer sky. And he grinned. A grin that revealed dimples beneath the dust and whiskers on his face. "I haven't the strength to summon it."

"Oh, really?" Fiona fanned her fingers through his hair. "You hardly seemed lacking in strength a moment ago."

His deep chuckle vibrated through his body, hers. "That was then, my bonny wife. Now I doubt I could walk a mile."

Fiona pressed his face between her hands, moving it out to arm's length. He'd spoken lightly, as if in jest, but there had been truth in his words. Tilting her head, Fiona studied his face, seeing what she'd failed to notice before. New lines, lines of fatigue, bracketed his eyes, and the smudges beneath them were not dirt. "When did you last sleep?"

"Oh, Fiona." Zeke tried to turn his head, but she held firm. "I get my rest."

"Aye, and you just told me you'd been riding for two days."

"You're sounding like a wife."

"I am a wife, if you'll recall. Now wait here." Fiona slipped out the door, returning in a few minutes. Zeke stood as she'd left him. "You'd best fasten your breeches," she said, as someone knocked on the door. "That will be Meg with the water."

"Damnit, Fiona," Zeke mumbled, hurrying to do what she said, because Fiona wasted no time answering the door. Zeke watched as the copper tub was filled and Meg left the room for the last time. And

382

he waited.

"Well, are you going to be taking your clothes off? The water won't stay hot forever, not even in this weather," Fiona said, brushing a damp curl off her forehead.

"You're staying?" He felt like a fool when he saw her expression of surprise, but he'd expected her to leave.

"And who'll be washing your back if I don't?"

Zeke stared at her a moment, couldn't come up with an answer, so went to the hearth. Catching his heel in the bootjack, he leaned against the mantel and pulled off the boot.

"Is your wound bothering you?"

"No." The response was as automatic as the flexing of his shoulder, and the grimace that deepened the lines around his mouth.

Fiona watched him pull off his shirt, noting the way he favored his arm, and her lips thinned. He shouldn't have gone off so quickly after he'd been shot. But when she studied the pink puckered scar it appeared to be healing satisfactorily.

Warm water lapped to the edge of the copper tub as Zeke lowered himself in. He rested his forehead on knees bent so that his long legs could fit in the tub. Even in this position it felt good to bathe in something other than a meandering stream—and even that, not often.

Closing his eyes, Zeke allowed his other senses to bask in the feeling of peace. The warm water enveloped him. He could hear Fiona moving around the room, closing a drawer here, opening a jar there. He smiled when she touched him, her hands soft but firm. They slipped across his back, slick with soap,

383

and he gave a small moan of pleasure. He didn't re-call ever being taken care of like this, except after he'd been shot, and then he'd been too uncomfortable to really enjoy it.

But now . . . The swirl of water around his shins and thighs was hypnotic, as was the gentle touch of her hands, and the misty scent of flowers — Zeke jerked around, splashing a wave of water onto the floor. "What in the hell are you putting on me?"

"Soap." Fiona dropped a towel onto the puddle on the floor, and reached her bubble-covered hands to-ward him.

Catching one wrist, Zeke brought her hand to his nose. "This smells like a damn garden. *I* smell like a damn garden."

Fighting to suppress a smile, Fiona tilted her head. "I thought you liked this smell. You told me so on our wedding night."

"On you, Fiona! I meant on . . ." Zeke stopped when he noticed the devilish twinkle of her violet eyes.

"I know that," Fiona laughed. "But I don't have any other soap in the room."

"Look in my knapsack." Zeke motioned toward the corner by the wardrobe, sprinkling more water on the floor with his arm.

"All right." Fiona dried her hands before doing as he asked. "But I don't see what difference it will be making. You're just going to bed anyway."

Zeke's head shot up. Her newfound boldness sur-prised him, but he couldn't say he didn't like it. He watched her bend over his leather knapsack, and smiled. "Nothing would please me more than to spend the next few days in bed with you, but I do

384

have other duties."

"With me!" Fiona stood, swiping hair from her eyes. She could feel heat pouring into her cheeks. "I didn't mean *that*."

"You didn't?" Zeke wondered if she could hear the disappointment in his voice.

"Of course not. You're tired. Anyone can see that. You need to get some rest."

"Now, Fiona." Zeke flinched as she took up scrubbing his back with the lye soap. "I don't have time to take to my bed. There's the Provincial Congress to see."

"They can wait."

"Fio . . . n . . . a."

"Just a short rest?" She bent forward, brushing her lips over his ear, and before Zeke knew it, he'd agreed. But only to a short rest. It was early yet. He'd lie down for a moment—long enough to satisfy Fiona—then he'd confer with some of the colony's leaders about obtaining supplies for his men.

The next time he opened his eyes the lone candle in the room sent long shadows dancing on the white-washed walls. "Fiona?" Zeke rose on his elbows and spotted her sitting in a wingback chair by the hearth.

"Aye?" Fiona bit off a thread before dropping her sewing into a basket and moving toward the bed.

"What time is it?"

"Well past ten. There's no need to be getting up." She put the candle down and touched the leg he swung over the side. "Most everyone's abed."

"Hell, Fiona. You said you'd wake me."

"I most certainly did not." Her hands bunched in the waist of her white linen night rail. "*You* said you wouldn't sleep long." She smiled. "But obviously you

385

did."

"And I guess you think I needed it?"

Fiona only shrugged, and climbed onto the bed. "You're no use to the Patriots if you wear yourself out."

Zeke moved over, giving her room to lie down beside him. "Are you telling me you care about the Patriot cause?" There was just a hint of teasing in his tone.

"Hardly. But I do care about you," she said, and then bit her lip. Why had she ever admitted that? "I mean . . . we are married, like it or not," she added, as his arm slipped around her.

"Yes," Zeke agreed. "Like it or not." He nestled her head on his shoulder, noting she'd climbed into bed on the side of his good arm, and smiled up at the tester. He lay there, content to simply hold her, feel her warmth till the flame sputtered down into the melted tallow. "Fiona?"

"Hmm?"

"I can't go back to sleep."

Shifting, Fiona tried to make out his profile in the dim light. She hadn't been able to sleep, either. "Perhaps if you recite songs to yourself. That always helps me."

"Won't that disturb you?"

"And you're so worried about me you started talking, not knowing if you'd wake me."

"Did I?"

"No," Fiona admitted softly.

"Good," Zeke sighed, lying still except for the motion of his fingers on his wife's arm. The caressing circles widened. "What songs would you suggest I recite?"

386

"Ones from my childhood usually work for me," Fiona responded, snuggling closer.

"I don't believe I know any."

"Certainly you can remember something your mother sang to you, a lullaby, perhaps."

"No." Zeke felt her move at his side. "I don't recall her ever doing that," he said in a tone that brooked no further inquiry. "Do you know any?"

"Aye." Fiona hesitated. "But I haven't a very pleasing voice."

"Perhaps you should let your audience decide . . . Please."

She sang, haltingly at first, and then as the tune seeped into her soul, with more feeling. It was a haunting melody, and though Zeke couldn't follow the Gaelic, he guessed the lyrics to be sad. She was right about her voice. It wasn't pleasing if clear sopranos were what you sought. But it was true, and sensually low, and he felt caught up in a misty illusion that lingered after the last note echoed through the room.

Zeke rolled to his side. His fingers played in the hair that spread out on the pillow beside him. "Very nice," he murmured, before dropping a kiss on her forehead.

"But it didn't put you to sleep?"

"No."

"Shall I sing another?"

"Not now," he whispered into her ear before gently biting the lobe.

"Then what would you have me do?"

Rolling on top of her, Zeke grinned. "I thought you'd never ask."

"Oh, you . . ." Fiona sucked air into her lungs, and

shifted under his weight. "You never meant to go back to sleep, did you?"

"Not really."

"And you made me sing that song."

"It was pretty," Zeke said, kissing the underside of her chin, though pretty wasn't the exact word he would have chosen. "I liked it," he added more honestly.

"You're . . ." Fiona's breath caught as his mouth closed over a linen-covered nipple. "You're taking advantage of my good nature."

Zeke's hand trailed down between their bodies and she arched into his palm. "Is that what I'm doing, Fiona?"

"No," she breathed, as he pulled the night rail over her head, and settled down in the cradle of her body. No, he was asking naught of her that she didn't want herself. The touch of him, the taste, the knowing him safe in her arms were what she wanted.

But later, as they lay entwined, satiated, drowsy in the afterglow of passion, Fiona found her mind wanting more. Questions Zeke seemed reluctant to answer whirled through her head till she could do nothing but ask.

"Why did she never sing to you?"

The sudden stiffening of his body belied his casually sleepy "I don't know."

"Perhaps she didn't know any songs."

"Maybe." Zeke buried his cheek in the pillow.

"Or perhaps she sings even worse than I."

"I doubt that, Fiona. Now will you go to sleep?"

Propping herself on one elbow, Fiona ignored his caustic remark about her singing ability. "What do you think was the reason?"

"How in the hell should I know?" Zeke sat up, all pretense of sleeping gone. Using the flint, he lit a new candle. "What do you want from me?"

"Tell me about you and your mother. I mentioned her once before and you acted . . . well, just the way you're acting now. Did she die?"

Zeke raked his fingers through already tousled hair. "What is this, morbid curiosity?"

"I just want to understand . . . help if I can."

"You did." Zeke's voice softened as he touched the tip of her nose. "You sang me a lullaby."

"Zeke!" She didn't want him to put her off, though by the expression on his face, that was exactly what he planned to do. That was why his next words were all the more shocking.

"She's not dead. She left us . . . my father and me."

"When?"

"I was about seven, I believe."

"Why?"

Zeke jammed his pillow against the headboard and leaned back. "She had her reasons, I suppose." His mind shot back to the treehouse. The breeze drifting through the magnolia leaves. His parents' voices. "She thought she married beneath herself. My father was a merchant. My father was in business, and Mother — her entire family — didn't consider that appropriate."

"So she left?"

"Yes." Zeke studied the candle flame. "She never did think of Wilmington or us as home. She always talked of Fountainhead. It's a rice plantation below Charleston," he added, anticipating her question, trying to keep the bitterness out of his voice.

389

"And you never heard from her?"

"Not until . . ."

"Until when?" Fiona braided her fingers with his.

"I received a letter about two months ago. She wants me to visit her at Fountainhead."

"Are you going to do it?"

Zeke's laugh was bitter. "No, Fiona. I've no intention of going to Fountainhead." Zeke blew out the candle, watching the wick glow and then die. "Do you suppose we could get some sleep now?" he asked, flattening out his pillow.

Fiona had no choice but to do the same, though her mind still reeled with questions. Sleep did not come easily as she thought about a boy abandoned by his mother, a boy who'd never known a lullaby.

"I don't know why you can't stay one more day."

"I told you, Fiona. The only reason I was able to come at all was to talk to Congress about more supplies." He snorted, stuffing a change of breeches into his knapsack. "I should say any supplies at all. We're low on powder and ball . . . shoes."

"Well, maybe if everyone simply went home . . ." He stood, looking at her quizzically, and Fiona went on. "The British are nowhere near here, and the Loyalist army certainly can't be a threat. All of its leaders except Grandfather are in jail."

"Apparently not all of them."

Fiona glanced up from the shirt she was mending. "What are you talking about?"

Zeke picked up the pistol he'd just finished cleaning. He hadn't planned on discussing this with Fiona, didn't want to pull the war into their marriage any more than necessary. But it was too late now. She put down the shirt and moved toward him.

"What did you mean by that, Zeke?"

"Someone is leading raids on Patriot militia . . . families."

"And you think it's—"

"I don't know who it is, Fiona. I don't even know if there are any Scotsmen involved. I just know I haven't been able to catch them, and they're killing innocent men and women."

"Duncan wouldn't . . ." Fiona stopped, realizing how incriminating her remark was. But she'd thought of him immediately.

"For God's sake, Fiona." Zeke grabbed her shoulders. "I didn't say anything about him."

"But you think it."

"No." Zeke turned away, hoping he was being honest. "I can't believe it's your cousin. Whoever is doing this is little more than an animal. The last raid we came upon there were three dead men and two women in the farmhouse. Two children had survived only because someone stood them on a table in the fireplace." Zeke ran a hand through his hair. "The place was riddled with holes."

"It's not Duncan," Fiona said, her voice trailing off.

"I have to go." Zeke reached for the shirt she'd sewn. "Is this finished?"

"Aye." Fiona folded it, stuffing it in the knapsack he'd draped over his shoulder. "Do you know when you'll be back?"

Shaking his head, Zeke started toward the door. Fiona watched him go, a knot tightening in her throat.

"Zeke," she called out as he reached for the door

391

latch. Before he could turn completely she'd propelled herself into his arms. "Please be careful," she mumbled into his shirtfront, then lifted her face for the kiss she hoped he'd give her.

His lips were warm and she wound her arms around his lean waist, clutching handfuls of linen. He held her tightly, deepened the kiss, then pulled away and yanked open the door. And Fiona felt foolish tears stream down her cheeks.

Chapter Twenty-three

The letter gave her no choice.

Fiona folded the gown and stuffed it into a saddle-bag. Scanning the room she'd shared with Zeke, Fiona decided she'd packed all she needed for her journey.

Her eyes snagged on the folded parchment, and even though she'd read it enough times to commit the message to memory, she picked it up. The words blurred as tears filled her eyes, and impatiently Fiona swiped at her face. Crying wouldn't solve anything. What was needed was action.

She noted again the date written at the top of the page in Katrine's flowing script. September eighteenth, seventeen seventy-six. Nearly a month ago. It had taken Fiona that long to find out her grandfather was dying. "Damn war," she mumbled, folding the post and jamming it into her pocket. "Nothing is the same anymore."

Buttoning the jacket of her riding habit, Fiona descended the stairs. She stopped in the library to write a note to Zeke. He wouldn't like her going off by herself, she knew that. But what else could she do? Besides, she'd most likely be back before he returned.

And if she wasn't? Cringing at the thought, Fiona stuck the note under the inkwell. At least he'd know she was coming back to Wilmington — to him.

Less than a week later Fiona approached Armadale.

Remembering Katrine's letter, Fiona just hoped she was in time to see her grandfather once more before . . . Fiona forced her mount into a gallop as they neared the end of the oak-lined drive. Her breathing quickened as they turned the final bend and Armadale came into view. The house sprawled in front of her, gleaming white in the late-afternoon sun, beautiful and peaceful as she remembered.

But it wasn't the tranquility that had her sliding from the saddle even before the horse stopped completely. "Grandfather?" Fiona gathered her skirts and ran up the porch stairs toward the man sitting in the rocking chair.

Malcolm's head nodded to the side, then he opened his eyes, a smile of welcome creasing his grizzled red beard. "Fiona? Mary Fiona, 'tis really you?"

"Aye." Fiona fell to her knees in front of him, her hair spilling over his plaid-covered lap.

"You've come home, lass."

Fiona didn't respond to that, only reached up to touch his cheek. "You look wonderful. Your color." She sat back on her heels. "And you've gained weight. Katrine must be doing a fine job of taking care of you."

"It's being at Armadale."

"I'm glad. Oh, Grandfather, I'm so happy you've recovered. I was really worried. And I came as soon as I heard, but the message took so long getting to me." Fiona stopped, sniffled, smiled through the tears streaming down her face. "I was so afraid I'd be too late. But here I am, and I find you're better. It's surely a miracle."

Malcolm chuckled, and though it wasn't the hearty laugh she remembered from her childhood, it still warmed her heart. But his next words made her tilt her head and stare at him.

"I don't know if I'd be calling it a miracle, lass. My health has done nothing but improve since I returned to Armadale."

The war, or, more to the point, the Scots' attempt to march to the British fleet, had taken its toll on the after-dinner gathering in the parlor. Where, in the past, most of the chairs were occupied by family members, now the nearly empty room seemed to echo with only memories. Uncle Angus was gone, a prisoner of the Patriots in Philadelphia. His wife had taken to her room, and though she'd offered Fiona a warm greeting earlier in the day, hadn't joined the family for dinner.

Duncan was missing. Neither her grandfather nor Katrine mentioned him, so Fiona didn't, either. Information about her cousin could wait.

At the moment Fiona had more pressing questions on her mind, but she wanted to ask them of Katrine in private. She'd looked for the opportunity all afternoon, to no avail. Now, as Fiona followed Katrine down the hallway after bidding their grandfather good night, she planned to get some answers.

"I'll see you in the morning, Fiona. It's wonderful

to have you home." Katrine reached for the brass knob on her bedroom door, pausing when she realized Fiona was already pushing the door open. "I'm really very tired," she added, following Fiona into the room.

"And you think I'm not?" Fiona set the candle on the bureau before facing Katrine. "I'm the one who rode here from Wilmington."

"You always enjoyed riding," Katrine offered lamely.

"Aye. But not at breakneck speed. And not thinking the entire time I might be too late to see Grandfather alive."

"Did you think that?"

"You know very well I did." Fiona had a nearly uncontrollable desire to shake her cousin until her perfect blond curls bobbed. "You told me as much in your letter."

"About that letter . . ." Katrine smoothed a wrinkle in her skirt, seemed momentarily preoccupied, then shook her head. "I may have been a bit hasty."

"Hasty?"

"Yes." Crossing to the chair by the window, Katrine sat, folding her hands and looking up at Fiona. "Perhaps I shouldn't have written it."

"Perhaps you shouldn't . . ." Fiona flopped down on the chair opposite Katrine's. "I don't understand. Why did you tell me Grandfather was dying?"

"Well, he isn't in the best of health." Katrine clutched the chair arms.

"Katrine, Grandfather told me he'd improved steadily since coming to Armadale. Now, why did you lie to me?"

"It wasn't a lie, exactly."

"Not a lie. . . . Katrine, do you know how much I worried?"

"I didn't mean for you to do that."

"What did you think I'd do?"

"I don't know. Duncan . . ." Katrine clamped her hand over her mouth.

"Duncan?" Fiona sat forward. "What does he have to do with this?"

Katrine's eyes were large and rapidly filling with tears as she stared at Fiona. "He'll be angry if he knows I told."

"What does he have to do with it?" Fiona demanded, having little sympathy at the moment for either cousin.

"He told me to write it." Katrine jumped to her feet, then sank back into the chair. "He said it was the only sure way to get you home, to get you away from that Rebel. He said you really wanted to come home, but were afraid to leave him. He said you'd be glad I did it. You are glad, aren't you, Fiona?"

Ignoring her question, Fiona asked, "Where is Duncan?"

"Oh, I can't tell you that." Rising, Katrine paced to the fireplace, where a cozy fire helped take the chill off the air. "He made me promise not to tell anyone. The only reason I know is in case something happens to Grandfather."

"Katrine." Fiona rose and went to her cousin. Her hands were cold when Fiona took them in her own. "I need to talk to Duncan." She watched as Katrine began to shake her head. "Katrine!"

"He won't like it if I tell you."

"And I won't like it if you don't."

"But . . ."

397

"You don't really think he meant *me* when he told you not to tell anyone? I'm part of the clan." Whether he had meant her or not before, he certainly would now, if he knew what Fiona was thinking, but that information was best kept from Katrine.

"I don't know. . . ."

"And did he say not to be telling *me?*"

"No. . . ."

"Well, then?"

Making herself get on a horse again the next morning, knowing she had a full day's ride ahead of her, wasn't easy. Her muscles screamed out for just one more day's rest, but Fiona wouldn't listen. She'd gotten the information she needed from Katrine, and she refused to delay any longer. Duncan and she had things to discuss.

The directions were easy enough to follow, even though she wasn't familiar with the farm where Katrine had said Duncan was staying. Fiona had almost asked her cousin about the raids on Patriot families, and if she thought Duncan were responsible, but she hadn't. She doubted Katrine knew. Besides, it was better if Fiona found out for herself. They would discuss that after Fiona told him what she thought about shooting an unarmed man — possibly men. And sending letters to her full of lies.

"As if I needed that excuse to come to Armadale. I could have come back any number of times if I'd really wanted to," Fiona mumbled, then jerked back on the reins. The startled horse pranced to the side, and Fiona leaned forward, absently patting her mount's neck. Thinking about what she'd just said.

It was true. She could have come back to Armadale. Oh, Zeke had stopped her once, but there were other times, especially since her wedding, when it would have been easy to leave, to come home. If she'd wanted to.

But she hadn't. Hadn't even thought about why until this moment. A breeze fluttered the end of her ribbon across her mouth, and Fiona absently brushed it away. Why hadn't she left Wilmington? The answer was so clear, so obvious, Fiona thought herself a fool for not having realized it before.

She loved Zeke.

Differences they had—aplenty. But that did nothing to change her feelings for him. It didn't even change things that he didn't love her. "He shall," Fiona vowed, as she urged her horse forward. "When this horrible war's over, he shall."

By dusk, Fiona squirmed on her sore bottom. She'd followed the creek farther than she thought necessary from Katrine's directions, and still no farm. If anything, the area seemed more remote. Sighing, wondering how frightening it would be to spend the night here, by herself, Fiona glanced around at the ever-lengthening shadows. Going back would do no good. She'd traveled too far and, besides, her horse needed rest as badly as she. But to continue forward, down the narrow path that led into the darkening woods, seemed more than she could do.

Gnawing on her bottom lip, Fiona dismounted. She was close to convincing herself that spending the night here was her best choice, when a rustling in the bushes behind her jerked her around. "Just a rabbit," Fiona squeaked, her hand reaching up to cover her pounding heart. "Nothing to worry a—"

The hand that covered her mouth smelled of sweat and dirt, and it successfully cut off her words — and proved them false. Fiona's attempt to escape her assailant's bruising hands ceased when three men emerged from behind the straggly holly trees. Two were no more than boys, though their expressions were anything but innocent. Nor were the pistols jammed in their waistbands. The third man, tall and gangly, with spectacles perched on the end of his prominent nose, held up his hand as he approached.

"No need to go scaring the lass," he said in a voice that reminded Fiona of her childhood days at Armadale. But though he spoke with a soft Scottish burr, she knew she'd never seen him before.

"Scare her, hell!" This voice, rougher, and coming from the man whose hand still covered her mouth, lacked the accent. "The bitch bit me."

"We'll have none of that talk." These words, spoken to her captor, sounded like an order, and Fiona felt the fingers around her arm tighten. "Now, lass, if Private Smoot lets you loose, have I your word you'll behave?"

With Private Smoot's filthy hand clamping her jaw, the smell nearly making her gag, Fiona decided it best to agree. She nodded as adamantly as the private's constraining hand allowed.

"Good girl. Now take your hand away, Private Smoot."

"But, Captain . . ." The private obviously thought to protest, but when the captain lifted his chin, he decided against it. He pulled away from Fiona so quickly she stumbled forward and would have fallen, except for the steadying hand of the captain.

"Who *are* you?" Fiona asked, jerking her arm from

400

his grasp. They called each other by military ranks, but they didn't look like soldiers. Even Zeke's militia, most of whom lacked uniforms, managed to exude a military air. But these men were dirty, with matted hair and torn clothes.

"I'm thinking the more important question is what a young lady such as yourself is doing out here alone."

"Who says I'm alone?"

This desperate ploy made the captain chuckle, but when he stopped, his light brows drew together. "We really haven't time to play games, lass. What are you doing here?"

No ready lie came to Fiona's mind. Besides, the Scottish burr made her wonder if the truth might not be best. "I'm looking for Duncan MacClure."

"I told you we should have—"

"Quiet." The one-word order silenced the man behind her. Then the captain's hazel eyes were again on her. "Why do you wish to see General MacClure?"

General MacClure? When Duncan had marched off with the clan to meet the British, he'd been a mere lieutenant. Fiona considered his rise through the ranks phenomenal, unless he'd appointed himself to his present lofty position. But she let none of her thoughts show as she answered. "I'm his cousin, Fiona MacClure. I've word from home."

"Home?"

"Armadale," Fiona said, noticing the captain inclining his head toward the private.

"I've no reason to doubt you, lass. You certainly favor the general, but we have to take precautions. I hope you understand."

Before she could begin to understand what he

401

meant, a prickly piece of cloth covered her eyes. " 'Tis necessary if you wish to be taken to the general, lass," Fiona heard the captain say when she raised her hands, attempting to pull the blindfold aside.

Deciding it but another of the growing list of grievances she had against Duncan, Fiona allowed herself to be hoisted onto her horse. She did bat at the hand that clamped over her knee, positioning it over the pommel, but that gained her no more than a throaty chuckle from the private.

The ride was short. Though Fiona tried to determine their destination by direction, the blindfold disoriented her. The length of time she clung precariously to the saddle was all she could remotely estimate.

But Fiona didn't need her vision to tell her she'd arrived at some sort of camp. It hadn't been that long ago that she'd been with the Scottish army. The pungent tang of burning wood, the comforting smell of roasting meat brought back vivid memories of last winter.

And she could hear men. She couldn't tell how many, but by the murmur of voices when her horse stopped, it was more than a handful.

Suddenly she was yanked off her mare. Deciding she'd had enough of this foolishness, Fiona tugged at the blindfold. No one stopped her as she pulled it over her head.

Darkness had nearly fallen now, but the light from a half dozen campfires lit the area. Fiona blinked, and turned to stare at the men. Young, old, alike only in their straggly appearance, they gaped back at her.

"Come on now, lass." The captain took hold of her arm and guided her toward one of the tents. There weren't many — apparently most of the men slept outdoors.

The air inside the tent was smoky, but Fiona found Duncan immediately. He sat behind a makeshift table studying a book.

"Sorry to interrupt you, General, but there's —"

"What is it, Captain? My God, Fiona!" Duncan jumped up when he glanced up and saw her. "What are you doing here?"

"I should think that rather obvious. I was brought here — blindfolded — by your" — Fiona hesitated — "men. It seems to me the more important question is what are you doing here?"

"Captain?" Ignoring Fiona's question, Duncan looked toward the captain.

"We found her not far from here. Down by the creek."

Brushing aside the captain's restraining hand, Fiona stepped forward, but Duncan's attention continued on the tall man by her side.

"Was there anyone with her?"

"No. We followed her a while. She's alone."

"Of course I'm alone, Duncan. Who'd you expect me to bring?"

With a flick of his hand, Duncan dismissed the captain, then fixed his pale blue stare on her. "I repeat, Fiona. What are you doing here?"

"I was under the impression you wished to see me," Fiona began. "After all, you did your best to get me to Armadale." She thought this disclosure might shock him, but Duncan only sat down, and turned the page in the book he'd been reading. "A casualty of war, Fiona."

Reaching out, Fiona grabbed the book, tossing it to the packed-earth floor. "Aren't you even going to tell me your deception was for my own good?"

Duncan shrugged. "I wanted you back at Armadale where you belong."

"Well, what if I told you I don't belong there anymore? What if I said I belonged with my husband?" Fiona was keeping her voice calm with difficulty.

"Then I'd say you're a damn fool."

"Who's the fool, Duncan? What are you doing here . . . with these people?"

" 'These people,' as you call them, are part of my Loyalist army. *We* haven't given up. Nor shall we ever. We're fighting the Patriots, and—"

"Women and children, Duncan."

His laugh sent shivers down her spine. "I see you've been listening to that Rebel bastard you married."

"Is he wrong, Duncan? Can you be looking at me and tell me what he said was false?" Fiona grabbed for his arm, but he shook her away.

"This is war, damnit. It's time you realized that. War. They're all the enemy."

Fiona took a step back, her arms crossed over her waist. "Who's the enemy?" she whispered, repeating the question in a louder tone when he didn't answer. "Who, Duncan?"

"Anyone who believes in this idiocy. Have you heard what they've done? This declaration of independence?" Duncan's voice held nothing but scorn.

"I've heard, but it doesn't mean—"

"You're one of them now, aren't you? He's made you foresake your people . . . your clan."

"Don't be ridiculous." Fiona backed up against the canvas as he stood. "I just don't think there's any need to hurt innocent people. That's not helping England, nor is it anything for the *clan* to be proud of."

"And I suppose whoring for that Whig colonel is?"

Fiona sucked in her breath, letting it out slowly as she stared at her cousin. He'd changed. He'd become a stranger to her—worse, a stranger she disliked, even feared. She'd known it before, when he shot Zeke, but she had still hoped for the return of the boy she'd grown up with. Now she knew that person was gone, if he ever had existed.

Ignoring the prickle of apprehension dancing over her skin, Fiona began, "I came to talk to you, to try to make you understand that you can't do whatever you want in the name of war, but I see it's no use." She reached for the tent flap. "I'll sleep outside tonight, and at first light I'm going back to Armadale, and then on to Wilmington."

"Oh, I don't think so, Fiona." Duncan kicked over his chair in his haste to reach her. When he did, his hand clamped over her upper arm. "You're not going anyplace."

"Let go of me, Duncan." Fiona tried not to panic.

"Do you really think I'd let you leave here and tell your husband where we are?"

"I don't know where we are. Blindfold me tomorrow; I don't care. I just want to leave." She resisted the urge to twist out of his grasp even though his fingers dug into her arm.

"You know too much, Fiona. Besides, I think you should be our guest for a while. Maybe then we wouldn't have to worry so much about the militia. That damn husband of yours dogs our every step,

405

but so far I've outsmarted him. And if I hav
you . . ."

"He won't care. Having me won't keep him from
catching you, Duncan. And when he does—" Fiona
gasped when his fingers tightened. "And when h
does, he'll make you sorry you ever crossed him."

He flung her to the ground before Fiona could us
her hands to soften the fall. She landed hard on he
hip, closing her eyes as the pain shot through her
But Fiona refused to show Duncan how much he'
hurt her. Rising on one elbow, swiping at the hai
covering her face, Fiona stared up at him. "You'll b
sorry, Duncan."

But the only one who was sorry now was she
Fiona lay on a narrow cot in Duncan's tent feeling a
a complete loss as to what to do. She'd sneak out o
camp in the darkness, except that her hands were
tied to a slat on the cot and, try as she might, she
couldn't loosen the knot. So she lay there, listening to
Duncan snore and thinking what a fool she'd been to
come here. But even berating herself grew tiresome
and near dawn she fell asleep.

She must have slept, because the first gunsho
jerked her awake. Trying to sit up reminded her tha
her hands were tied above her head. "Duncan!" Fiona
twisted around, but saw only his profile in the pal
morning light as he rushed from the tent. By now
the gunfire was steady—and close. She could hear
men yelling—curses of surprise, shouted warnings.

Squeezing her eyes shut, Fiona prayed—every
prayer she'd ever heard and some she made up on
the spot. She didn't know who was shooting, or why
but it was closing in on her. And she couldn't move

Her eyes flew open when a ball ripped through the

nt fabric, striking the lantern above her head with a
netallic clang. Fiona pulled on the ropes, wriggling
er hands until her wrists burned.

Muskets exploded, horses' hooves pounded, and
en screamed in agony, but they all seemed to fade
to the distance. All drowned out by the sound of
er own whimpering, and the loud drumming of her
eart.

And then Duncan came tearing back into the tent.
iona screamed when the knife flashed toward her,
nd it wasn't until Duncan yanked her to her feet
hat she realized he'd cut her ropes, not her. But she
ad scant time to be thankful. With another down-
vard slice, he cut a hole in the back of the tent and
ushed her through.

Fiona's toe caught on the canvas and she went
prawling onto the dirt. But again she felt herself
anked up. "Oh, no, you don't, you bitch. You're
oming with me," Duncan hissed near her ear as he
lragged her through the weeds toward a stand of
ine trees.

The shooting had stopped. Fiona realized that the
nstant before she heard someone yell. "Stop right
here, MacClure!"

Fiona didn't have time to rejoice in the sound of
hat voice before Duncan dragged her around, using
er body as a shield between himself and Zeke. He
rabbed his pistol from his waistband and jammed it
nto her ribs.

Her husband hadn't seen her when he yelled.
iona could tell that from the shocked expression on
is face—the expression that quickly turned to rage.
lis eyes left her to focus on Duncan. "Let her go,
MacClure."

"It's General MacClure, and I don't think so. You're not going to shoot as long as I have your little wife."

"Don't bet on it, MacClure." Zeke raised his pistol and aimed.

Duncan believed him. Fiona could feel her cousin's trembling, sense his fear as he stared into Zeke's steely blue eyes. He thought Zeke would shoot him around or through her. Fiona was glad Zeke was so convincing, but it wasn't really true. Zeke wouldn't take a chance on hurting her. Would he? Fiona searched his face for a sign, any sign of a bluff, but saw none.

Apparently Duncan didn't see any either, for with one shove, he sent Fiona flying toward Zeke.

Catching her was more reflex than anything else, but Zeke set her aside quickly. "Simpson, Pierce!" he yelled as he started off toward the woods where Duncan MacClure had disappeared. "Get some more men. Fan out and help me find him."

Men rushed by her, following Zeke into the thicket. Fiona stood for a moment trying to decide what to do, then slowly started back toward the tent. That was where Zeke found her several hours later.

She was sitting on the cot, her chin resting on her knees. She looked up when he threw back the flap.

"We haven't found him."

His tone made her wary about jumping up and running into his arms, so she sat there, wondering what she'd been wondering for the last few hours. "Would you have shot me?"

The silence grew heavy as he stared at her, his gaze never wavering. Finally, when Fiona thought she would surely scream from the tension building in her he moved. Out of the tent. Fiona could hear him call someone, and she supposed it was the same man who entered the tent with him moments later.

"Sergeant Williams," Zeke said, his voice void of emotion. "You're familiar with Armadale, I believe."

"Yes, sir. I know where it is."

"Good. Would you please escort this lady there?" Without waiting for an answer, he turned on his heel and left the tent.

Chapter Twenty-four

Rushing to a window when she heard horses behind the house was a habit that Fiona seemed unable to break. A habit that had led to nothing but disappointment for the fortnight since she'd returned to Zeke's house in Wilmington. He hadn't come home. Fiona reminded herself of this, slowing her steps as she laid aside the petticoat she mended and brushed back the curtain.

The yard was empty. With a heavy sigh, Fiona leaned her forehead against the smooth, cool pane. Moisture marbled the glass as she wondered again why she'd come back.

Zeke had sent her to Armadale. That was obviously where he wanted her—away from him. Out of his life. So why hadn't she stayed there? "Because you're stubborn and impetuous, and headstrong, and all those other things he said you were," she said, adding past the lump that formed in her throat, "And you love him."

Fiona sighed again. "And now you've started talking to your—" Blinking, she rubbed at the glass with the heel of her hand, then sucked in her breath as she saw the stable door open and a man walk into the yard.

Zeke was home.

As she watched, unable to tear herself away from the window, he strode toward the house through the maze of neatly trimmed boxwood. It wasn't until he disappeared from view beneath the magnolia that Fiona moved.

Pushing away from the window, she glanced down and groaned. Her chintz gown was hardly her best, but there was no time to change. When she'd first come back to Wilmington she'd dressed with care every day, thinking *that* would be the day she'd see him. But as the days ran into weeks . . . At least the deep violet color was becoming.

Fiona hurried to the bedroom door, let go of the latch and ran back to the mirror. "Oh, no." The hair she'd braided and loosely wrapped around her head this morning was coming undone. Jabbing at the wooden pins, Fiona tried to secure the braid, while slicking back the tendrils that curled around her face. "It's no use," she moaned, giving her pale cheeks a pinch before rushing from the room.

She was descending the stairs, four steps from the bottom, when he came through the front door. He stopped, stared at her, and the expression on his face told Fiona how shocked he was to see her here. Her hand clutched the banister as she waited for him to say something . . . anything.

But he didn't. With a resounding slam, he shut the front door. His boot heels echoed the bang as he headed down the hall.

Furious, Fiona rushed down the stairs and rounded the newel, her skirts swaying about her legs. By the time she reached the library the thick-paneled door was shut. Without hesitating, she opened the door, entering the book-lined room.

Seemingly oblivious to her presence—though Fiona knew better—Zeke stood, his back to her, calmly pouring whiskey from a glass decanter. In frustration, Fiona kicked the door, slamming it shut in a parody of his earlier action. She'd hoped it would make her feel better, but as she stood, staring at his back, her breasts rising and falling with each breath, she realized it didn't.

"What are you doing here, Fiona?" Zeke tossed his drink back, relishing the burning heat as it slid smooth as silk down his throat. If he could just concentrate on that feeling, maybe he could forget the pain around his heart. He'd thought it no more than a dull ache, had hoped it would eventually disappear, and then he'd walked into the house and seen his red-haired wife.

Fiona stepped forward, hesitated. His broad-shouldered back had never seemed so wide, so distant. "I live here." She wanted her voice to be strong, matter-of-fact, but it came out little more than a whisper.

But he heard her. He glanced over his shoulder, and Fiona forced herself not to cringe at the expression in his narrowed eyes. "Oh, really?" His tone held a derisive quality that cut nearly as deep as his piercing stare. "I was under the impression Armadale was your home."

"It was." Fiona swallowed past the lump in her throat. She'd rushed in here angry that he'd ignored her. But now it wasn't anger that forced her to continue. "I suppose to some extent it always will be, but—"

"Then I suggest you return there. I'll provide you with an escort." Zeke poured himself another drink, watching unconcerned as amber liquid sloshed onto the silver tray.

Fiona's chin jutted forward. "Is that what you want—for me to go back?"

Zeke's harsh bark of laughter answered her question. "Since when have my wishes had any bearing on your actions?" The second shot of Scotch wasn't nearly as satisfying as the first.

"I had a reason for being at Duncan's camp. I—"

"Though I'm certain this is an entertaining tale, I'm not in the mood to hear it."

"Oh, you're not in the mood, are you?" Rushing forward, grabbing fistfuls of his coat sleeve, and jerking him around gave her a certain satisfaction. "Well, maybe I'm in the mood to be telling you. You—"

His strong fingers gripping into her shoulders cut off her words. "Don't push me, Fiona." He enunciated each word carefully, fighting to keep control of his emotions. "In a battle of brawn, you'd come in a poor second."

"Especially if you had a pistol pointed at me."

"You little idiot!" The shake he gave her before dropping his hands had Fiona's braid sliding down the side of her head.

"Idiot, am I?" Fiona slapped at the arm reaching for the glass decanter. "And I suppose I imagined the gun you aimed at me, the look in your eye?" When his hand continued toward the whiskey, Fiona didn't think, she acted. Picking it up by its narrow neck, she hurled it toward the fireplace. "Answer me, damnit." Oh, how she hated the sob in her voice. But he didn't seem to notice as he grabbed her shoulders again, backing her up till their leather soles crunched glass shards and her back felt the edge of wooden shelves.

"You want to know if you imagined my expression?" He shook her again when she didn't answer, dislodging more hair. "Is that what you want to know?"

413

"Aye."

"If I looked angry, you didn't imagine it. If looked furious, you didn't imagine it. If I looked as if I could throttle you, you didn't imagine it!" His hands tightened on her shoulders. "When I saw you there with him, when I knew you'd left me, I . . ."

"But I didn't—"

"When I knew you'd left me to go back there," he continued as if she hadn't spoken. "I don't think I ever felt so . . ." Hurt, miserable, heartbroken, betrayed. All the emotions he'd tried to block out since that moment Duncan had turned and Zeke had seen Fiona, flooded over him. It was like the time he'd realized his mother wasn't coming back, only worse . . . much worse.

Dropping his hands, Zeke strode to the window, tearing back the curtains and leaning his arm on the sash. "But I wouldn't have shot you. I can't believe you'd even think I could do such a thing."

Fiona slumped back against the leatherbound books, staring at his dark form silhouetted by the bright sunshine streaming in the window. "But, you said—"

"Hell, Fiona." Zeke turned back to look at her. "What did you expect me to say? 'Well, Duncan, since you have Fiona with you, by all means escape, run off with her. And while you're at it, kill me while I stand here and drop my gun.'"

"You could have told me this . . . earlier."

"You shouldn't have had to ask. You're my wife, for God's sake. I'd sooner turn a pistol on myself than shoot you." Zeke balled his fists as he turned back toward the window. He was sounding like a lovesick boy. Well, he'd told her what she'd come to find out; maybe now she'd leave him in peace. The hand that touched his sleeve didn't do much for his peace of mind. He hadn't heard her move toward him.

"You're my husband, and you believed the worst of me."

"You forget, Fiona. I saw you there."

"But you never asked why."

"Explanations didn't seem necessary at the time."

Oh, he could be so infuriatingly arrogant—almost as if he used it as a wall around his emotions. Fiona squared her shoulders and moved closer. She knew now that he hadn't intended to shoot her, though she'd felt it in her heart from the beginning. Now he was going to hear the truth about her trip to Armadale. "I received a letter from Katrine saying Grandfather was dying. And I . . . What is it?"

"If this is the thrust of your explanation, I think you should know I visited your grandfather not a month ago, and he appeared far from death."

"He didn't mention you'd been to Armadale."

"I don't think he was overjoyed to see me."

Fiona couldn't help smiling, though her expression quickly sobered when she glanced up at Zeke. "Aye, well, anyway, I didn't say he *was* near death; I said that's what the letter stated. I rushed to Armadale, of course."

"Of course."

"I left you a note," Fiona explained, ignoring his arched brow. "It's on your desk." When he made no move to get it, Fiona continued. They both knew she could have written it anytime since she'd returned. "When I got to Armadale, I discovered my grandfather much improved, *and* I found out he never had been close to dying—not since he'd arrived at Armadale, anyway. Katrine had lied to me."

"Why would she do that?" Lord save him from the

415

fool he was. He wanted to believe her.

"Duncan had made her do it . . . or at least suggested it. Katrine had this idea that returning to Armadale was what I really wanted."

"And wasn't it?"

"Would you believe me if I said no?"

Shrugging, Zeke pretended a nonchalance he didn't feel.

With a sigh, Fiona continued. "I was so angry with Duncan for . . . well, for everything—shooting you, and lying to me. So I made Katrine tell me where he was and went there."

"Hell, Fiona, don't you know how dangerous that was?" Zeke grabbed her upper arms and had to force himself not to draw her nearer.

"I didn't at first. But when I got there and saw all those men— Then I knew he was the one you were after, the one attacking the Patriot families. But he wouldn't let me go. He thought I'd tell you where he was." Fiona touched his shirtfront. "I know you won't credit this, but he's changed. Duncan was never like this before." Her hand dropped away. "Well, then you came, and I could hear fighting but I didn't know who it was. And Duncan came back into the tent and grabbed me, and then . . . You know the rest."

"Yes, I know the rest." Zeke moved past her, slumping into the chair behind his desk.

"Well?" Fiona demanded, following him.

"Well, what?"

Hands on hips, Fiona looked at him as if he were daft. "Do you believe me?"

"Yes. How can I help it? Not even you could make up a story like that."

"Oh, thank heavens." Fiona sank down in front of him, her skirts whooshing softly. "I was afraid you

416

wouldn't, and then I didn't know what I'd do." She rested her cheek on his knees.

Zeke's fingers itched to touch her hair, but he pulled his hand back. "I can't take you myself, but I'll have someone escort you back to Armadale."

Fiona's head shot up. "I thought you believed me."

"I do. It's just—"

"Then why are you sending me away?"

"Fiona, I . . ."

Jumping to her feet, Fiona grabbed the letter off his desk, thrusting it toward his face. "Read it. I was going to come back. I didn't leave you." When he made no move to take it, she balled it up and threw it at him. It bounced off his shoulder. "You think I want to leave you like she did."

"Damnit, Fiona, this has nothing to do with anybody else." And damn himself for telling her about his mother.

"Doesn't it? Then why are you trying to send me away?"

Zeke blew air out through his teeth. Why in the hell was she making this so hard? "You don't belong here."

"I'm your wife."

"A position you didn't want and I forced upon you."

"Forced? I agreed to this marriage and you know it."

"After I pointed out the advantages for your grandfather." Zeke started to rise, but she shoved with the palms of her hands, pushing him back down. "Stop it. I'm not proud of what I did, so—"

"Why did you do it, then?"

"It's not import—"

Fiona moved between his legs. "Why?"

"Because I love you, that's why." She was standing over him like some avenging angel—or she-devil—her hair curling wildly about her face. "Though Lord

417

knows why I do. You are the most stubborn, hot-tempered, impetuous — umph!"

Fiona flopped onto his lap and threw her arms around his neck. "This doesn't change anything," he said, just before her lips crushed down on his.

"I love you, too." Fiona kissed the corner of his mouth, the curve of his jaw. "And I'll never leave you." Leaning forward, Fiona meant to kiss him again, but his hands framing her face stopped her.

"But I'm going to be leaving you." Zeke splayed his fingers through her hair. The braid lost its last few pins and fell down over her shoulder.

"I don't understand."

Soothing the worry lines from her forehead with his thumb, Zeke explained. "I offered my services to the Continentals. The war isn't going to be won here in North Carolina. At least not now. They need more men in the North."

"You're going there?"

Nodding, Zeke lowered his thumb, sliding it across her lower lip. "I tried to make you believe our differences could be worked out, but —"

"I don't care about the war."

"I didn't catch Duncan, but, by God, I spent the last few months trying. And if I had . . . if you hadn't been standing in front of him, I'd have brought him in or died trying."

"I don't care about Duncan," she said, but saw the doubt in the depths of his blue eyes. "I don't. You, Zeke. I care about you. Just y —"

His kiss was quick and impulsive, and Fiona molded against him, trying to show with actions what she feared he doubted. "I do love you, Zeke," she murmured against his lips.

"But I have to leave with the army."

418

"I'll wait for you." His hand cupped her breast, and Fiona moaned, clutching his shoulders.

"It could be years. I don't know how long—"

"I'll wait." His arms tightened around her, and Fiona wove her fingers though the thick curls at his nape. "I'll never leave you." She wanted him to believe her, to trust her, but as he lowered her across his arm she couldn't be sure of any emotion but passion. It shone in his eyes as he watched her face. It sang through the hand that followed the curves of her body, setting her aflame with desire.

Fiona stood before the cheval mirror clad only in her shift. The fire roaring in the hearth couldn't completely drive away the January chill, and goose bumps shivered across her arms. But Fiona didn't notice as she turned, studying her profile.

"Hmmm." She moved closer, her bare toes curling as they hit the icy floor, and flattened the linen across her stomach. Still not satisfied, she jutted her hips forward. "Aha," she laughed, smoothing her hand across the slight bulge. "That would be more like it."

Finally giving in to the cold, Fiona sidled closer to the fire. She pulled on her wool stockings, tying the garters below her knees, and stepped into her quilted petticoat—her best quilted petticoat. She expected Zeke home today, and even though he'd been away less than a sennight, she couldn't wait to see him.

He hadn't left with the army. More to the point, his regiment hadn't left Wilmington. The rumors that they would be sent to New York to bolster General Washington's army had proved false. The North Carolina Council of Safety had declared the soldiers should remain in the Wilmington area to regain their health.

Initially, Zeke had balked at the order, but after examining his men he agreed with the Council. So he'd spent the winter training the troops. . . . "And staying with me," Fiona finished, pulling her gown over her head. This trip to Halifax was the longest he'd been away all winter. And it had been the week Fiona had started feeling queasy in the mornings. She was fairly certain she was pregnant.

Humming a Scottish lullaby, Fiona ran the brush through her hair, grinning at herself in the mirror when the curls sprang back in place. The sound of the bedroom door opening surprised her—she hadn't expected Zeke till later in the day. But, hoping he'd missed her as much as she'd missed him, Fiona turned, a welcoming smile lighting up her face.

It froze. The blood in her veins froze.

"What are *you* doing here?" Fiona's tone was brittle.

"Now is that any way to greet your dear cousin?"

"I want you out of this house. Now!" Fiona started toward the still-open door. "Jacob!" She tried to keep her panic under control. "Mrs. Steel!"

"They can't hear you, Fiona. As a matter of fact I've taken precautions to ensure our privacy."

"What did you do to the servants?" Fiona turned on Duncan.

"Nothing they won't recover from."

"I'm going to help them."

"Oh, no, you're not." Grabbing Fiona's arm as she moved past him, Duncan pushed her back into the room, kicking the door shut with his boot. "Your husband and I have some unfinished business."

Catching hold of the bedpost to keep from falling, Fiona flung her unbound hair from her face. "He's not here. He's with Washington's troops in New York."

Duncan's laugh sounded evil as he leaned against

he door. "He left six days ago for Halifax and he'll be back later this morning."

Fiona sucked in her breath. "He's in New York, I tell you." But even as she spoke, Fiona knew the words did nothing to convince him.

"Your Colonel Kincaid and I traveled together, Fiona. Oh, he didn't know it. You see, I stayed behind him, out of sight. But I was there. Watching and waiting."

"I don't believe you." Fiona dug her fingers into the mahogany post. "If you followed him, why are you here?"

"I could have shot him, Fiona. Any number of times. Never doubt that. But I thought it would be more fitting to carry out the deed here . . . with you to witness it."

Duncan didn't say what deed, but Fiona had no doubt he meant to kill Zeke. Later, as she sat in the wingback chair near the fireplace, she tried to think rationally. She had to find a way to save her husband. But as she stared across at Duncan sitting in the other chair, nothing came to mind.

She'd tried reasoning with him, when he first made her sit, but that accomplished nothing. If anything, he'd become even more irrational, finally screaming at her to shut up. So she had, and now she sat studying him, studying the pistol lying in his lap.

It was the only thing about him that seemed in good shape. Duncan looked so different, so dirty and disheveled, with his matted hair down around his shoulders and his beard scraggly and unkempt, that Fiona wondered how she'd recognized him. But though his clothes were tattered and mud-stained, the brass on the pistol's handle shone bright with the look of recent care.

Fiona wondered if it were the same gun he'd used to shoot Zeke before, then forced her mind off that thought, knowing it could do nothing to help her now.

"He's taking his time getting here." Duncan glanced at the bracket clock on the mantel. "The way he lit out this morning before dawn, I figured he'd be here by now."

"Perhaps he's not coming."

Duncan chortled, wiping away spittle with the back of his hand. "You still trying that, Fiona? He had to stop at the camp outside of town. He'll be along directly."

She hoped Duncan was wrong. Maybe Zeke had decided to stay with his men. Maybe he had fallen off his horse and broken his leg. Maybe—

Fiona jerked when she heard the front door slam. Before she could hide her reaction, Duncan had her by the arm, yanking her forward. They were out of the room and to the top of the first landing before Zeke had climbed halfway up the stairway.

When Zeke saw them he froze, one foot on a higher riser than the other, his hand clutching the banister. Duncan had a pistol pointed, not at him, but at Fiona. Afraid to breathe least he cause Duncan to pull the trigger, Zeke turned his gaze from Duncan to Fiona. Her eyes appeared frightened, and she bit her lower lip to keep it from trembling.

"We've been waiting for you, Fiona and I." Duncan shuffled from one foot to the other, relaxing his hold on Fiona's arm. "We've been waiting for this moment."

Fiona felt rather than saw the pistol shift from her side to point down the stairs. Before Duncan let go of her arm, his hand quivered, and she knew what he was going to do. There was no more time to think, to plan what she might do. Duncan aimed at Zeke, and

Fiona shoved. With all her might she shoved, pushing Duncan off balance and down the stairs, losing her own footing as well. Screaming when the pistol report rang in her ear.

Fiona felt herself falling and grabbed for the banister, wrenching her arm as she landed against something hard, warm, and wonderfully familiar.

"Fiona . . . Fiona, honey!" Zeke knelt on the step after catapulting himself up the stairs to catch his wife. His hands were shaking as he pried her fingers loose from the wooden railing. He slid around, sitting on the landing, pulling her onto his lap.

Duncan lay at the bottom of the stairs, one leg folded under his body and his head twisted at a grotesque angle.

Zeke glanced down at Fiona. Her eyes were gaping open as she stared mesmerized at the figure below. Zeke heard her breath catch on a sob, and pressed her head against his shoulder. "Fiona, honey, don't." He scooped her up in arms that trembled, and carried her to their bedroom. Placing her in the chair, he knelt in front of her. "Honey, look at me." Her hands were like ice—cold and motionless, small in his.

She didn't want to see it. But the vision wouldn't leave her, even with her eyes closed. She saw Duncan lying there, twisted and— "Zeke!" The reality of what he'd done came rushing up to meet her . . . and the reason.

"I'm right here, Fiona"

Touching his face, trailing her hands down his neck and shoulders, Fiona studied him. "Are you hurt? Did he shoot you? I heard the pistol fire."

"No. No, I'm fine."

She couldn't stop reassuring herself. Her fingers played over his chest, pushing aside the wool jacket to

smooth across his linen shirt. "I was so afraid. He wa
going to kill you, and I didn't know what to do. An
then I pushed him, but I thought it was too late when
I heard the shot, and I thought he'd shot you anyway
and . . ." Fiona took a breath as she ran out of words
"You're sure you're all right?"

Zeke nodded, looking up at her stricken face. "M
heart's thundering. Feel it?" He flattened her hand
with his palm, a hint of a smile playing on his lip
when her eyes widened. "God, Fiona, I thought you
were going sailing down those steps."

"You caught me." Fiona touched his hair, still feel
ing the cold of the winter morning as he laid his head
in her lap, hugging her knees. His love seemed to sur
round her like a soft, cozy quilt, and Fiona drew in a
shaky breath, realizing he really was safe beside her
She traced the contour of his ear, smiling as he snug
gled closer.

"Zeke, I . . . My heavens, I almost forgot. How
could I? The servants . . . Jacob, Mrs. Steel, the
others. I don't know where they are, but Duncan did
something to them." She jumped to her feet when he
did, but he gently pushed her back down.

"You stay here. I'll find them." Zeke paused at the
door. "You going to be all right?" Her answer reas
sured him; he still wished he didn't have to leave her
but there were things that needed to done. Twenty
minutes later, when he returned to the bedroom to
find her standing by the window, he'd taken care of
most of them.

"They're fine. A little shaken, but no one is hurt."

"What had he done with them?"

"Tied and gagged them and put them in the pantry
He didn't hurt them," Zeke repeated. He didn't tell her
how he and Jacob had dragged Duncan's body out to

the tack room. "You better now?" Coming up behind her, Zeke wrapped his arms around her middle, burying his face in her hair.

"I guess I'm a little shaken, too." Fiona's laugh was nervous.

"You have a right to be." Zeke's arms tightened. "You saved my life, Fiona."

Smiling, Fiona turned in his arms. "I'm glad."

"So am I, but—"

"But what? Fiona leaned back in his arms, searching his face.

"Don't ever take a chance like that again. God, Fiona, when I saw you falling . . ." Zeke took a steadying breath. "My life wouldn't mean anything without you."

"I'm here." Fiona touched his jaw. "I said I'd never leave you. *We* will never leave you."

"That's good, because—" Zeke paused, looking down into violet eyes alight with happiness. *"We?"*

"Aye. 'Tis we, now." Fiona smiled, watching as understanding hit him and a dimple-deepening grin spread across his face.

Epilogue

November, 1781

As a pine-scented morning breeze drifted through her open window at Armadale, Fiona snuggled closer to the hard warmth behind her. It felt foreign, yet wonderfully familiar, and she smiled as a hand tightened over her breast. A lazy thumb circled her nipple, then slid across the aroused tip.

"I thought last night tired you out," teased a low, seductive voice.

Fiona smiled saucily up at Zeke as he turned her onto her back. "You were the one who'd ridden all day and half the night."

"And pleasured his wife the rest of it," Zeke reminded with an answering grin, as he settled comfortably into the cradle of her body.

"Not quite all." Fiona touched his whiskered jaw, letting her fingers drift down the strong pillar of his neck. "As I recall, you slept some."

"Ah, so the lovely Missus Kincaid has complaints." Zeke nosed aside a tangle of red hair and nipped at a creamy white shoulder, sending Fiona into a fit of giggles. "Because if you do, I think I can take

426

care of the problem."

"No, I was only jok—" Fiona's breath caught on a sigh as he entered her. At first, when he didn't move, only rested on his elbows, his face buried in her curls, Fiona didn't think anything of it. But as the seconds passed, she turned her head, brushing her lips across his ear. "Are you all right?"

She *had* only been joking with him. Their lovemaking had been wild and wonderful last night. They'd come together almost frantically at first, scarcely making it through the bedroom door before tearing off each other's clothing. Then again on the big tester bed, and again, they'd tried to make up for all the lost time. He had every right to be tired.

But it wasn't fatigue that brightened his blue eyes when he lifted his head, staring down at her. "I'm fine. It's just. . . ." Zeke paused, not knowing exactly how to explain. "It's just you feel so damn good. I've dreamed of this. I've lain awake, sometimes in a tent, more often under the stars, and fantasized about waking up beside you, about this." He let his hand skim down their bodies to where they were joined.

Tears welled in Fiona's eyes. "I know. I've missed you so." His lips when they touched hers were soft and sweet, innocent. The perfect foil for the intimacy of their bodies. He brushed her mouth, sharing his breath, the silky warmth of his tongue as it wet her lower lip, while he swelled, filling her completely.

"Zeke." His movements were unhurried at first — long, slow withdrawals, deep consuming thrusts — and Fiona thought she would die from the beauty of it. She clung to his powerful arms, arching to meet him, opening her mouth when his kiss became hard and demanding. Drowning in him.

When she could stand it no more, when the pres-

427

sure built up inside her, Fiona clutched the sweat-slick muscles. "Please, oh, please." The last word was little more than a moan as she bowed up, and her world exploded around her.

Her eyes drifted open to see her husband looking down at her, a totally male grin deepening his dimples. "I've dreamed of this, too," he whispered, his breath coming in ragged gasps. "Of seeing you consumed by passion . . . by me." His fingers touched her mouth. "Beautiful."

Her tongue touched his callused skin. "Let me see." He was right. It was beautiful. He plunged deep, his head thrown back, and let the fire rage out of control. Again and again he drove into her. The tendons stood out in bold relief on his bronzed neck, and the skin across his cheekbones stretched taut. And Fiona watched the man she loved become one with her.

Flopping on his back, Zeke pulled Fiona across him. Her breasts flattened on his chest and he reached up and tweaked her nose. *"Now* I'm tired."

"And you have every right to be," Fiona assured him with an exaggerated sigh. "Why don't you stay here in bed, and—"

"Can't do that." Zeke shook his head.

"Why ever not?" When he'd gotten to Armadale late last night, Zeke had told her he thought the war was all but over. General Cornwallis had surrendered his army to combined American and French forces at Yorktown in Virginia.. Zeke had been there after stalking the British general through much of South and North Carolina. Unless the British launched another offensive, something Zeke said he seriously doubted, he planned to stay home with his family. Now he talked as if he needed to be up and about. "Well," Fiona prodded, when he just lay there grinning at her.

"I want to see our babies."

Fiona smoothed dark brown hair behind his ear. "You saw them last night."

"Peeking at them asleep in their beds doesn't count."

"It doesn't?" Fiona smiled down at him, loving him more than she could say.

"Nay." Zeke's finger followed the length of her spine. "I want to hold them and see them up, running about."

Laughing, Fiona shook her head. "You may well rue the day you said that." When she noted his confused expression, Fiona continued. "The 'babies,' as you call them, are full of mischief—especially the twins. They bedevil the cats, and—What are you laughing about?"

"Just thinking it's probably their red hair."

" 'Tis not!" Fiona rested her elbows on Zeke's chest, her own red hair forming a curtain around them. Though it was true their two-year-old twin daughters' heads were covered with red ringlets, she didn't think that the reason for their limitless activity. "Nathan acted the same way when he was their age."

"Did I ever thank you for naming him after my father?" Zeke grinned, thinking of the son born when he'd been in South Carolina.

"Aye, when you came home and saw him for the first time." Tugging at a clump of chest hair, Fiona added. "I'm thinking that was when you gave me the twins."

Zeke's grin widened. "I wonder what I gave you this time."

Fiona batted at the hand that trailed down her hip, but her eyes were twinkling when she called him an arrogant man.

For a moment they lay there, both thinking of the handful of times they'd been together over the past four years. Zeke touched his wife's cheek. "I'm sorry I wasn't there with you. My own children don't know me . . . I don't know them. And it was hard for you. I know it. When I sent word for you to get out of Wilmington and go to Armadale, it was all I could do not to desert and come for you myself. The war was heading straight for you, and I couldn't do a damn thing but. . . ."

Fiona's fingers on his lips stopped his words. "We managed fine. The servants and I packed the children in a wagon, and here we are." Her eyes found Zeke's. "You're the one who had all the hardships. I was so afraid for you."

"The fighting times were few—except at Yorktown. But there I made sure I kept my head low," he teased, not wanting her to know how awful the war had really been. At Camden. At King's Mountain. Zeke shook his head to dispel the visions of death. "Mostly we just marched . . . then marched some more."

Sensing he didn't want to mar his homecoming with talk of war, Fiona refrained from questioning him. But when he remained quiet, a pensive expression furrowing his brow, she snuggled closer. "What is it?"

Zeke took a deep breath. "I went to Fountainhead while I was in South Carolina. We were close by and, well, I'd gotten that letter, and . . ."

"Did you see your mother?"

"Yes." Zeke tangled his hand in Fiona's hair and pulled her head down to his chest. "You know, I didn't recognize her. All these years I never imagined her changing. But she has. Older. . . ." Zeke's voice trailed off.

"Was she glad to see you?" Fiona could feel his

430

shrug.

"She wanted me to stay and help her with Fountainhead. When I refused. . . . I think she's just looking for an heir to the place, and I'm a convenient choice."

"Zeke, I'm sure it's more than that." Her arms tightened around him.

"No. Her brother's only son died a few years back—right before she wrote me. Now she's all alone." He paused. "I offered to bring her to Wilmington, to live with us. But she refused to leave her *home*."

Fiona couldn't help feeling pity for the woman who'd abandoned her son. She would never know all that she'd missed. "You know the children and I will go back to Wilmington anytime you say."

Zeke stared up at the sincerity and love in his wife's violet eyes and felt his somber mood evaporate like a whisper of mist. "I know."

"We only came back here because you said to. But my home, Zeke, is wherever you are."

His kiss was warm and sweet, full of the love he felt for her—and cut short by a commotion in the hall. It was followed by pounding on the door. Fiona jumped from the bed and began searching through the clothes strewn on the floor.

"What are you doing?" Propped on his elbow, Zeke watched her, a smile of appreciation on his lips.

"Trying to find my . . ." Fiona tossed garments onto a chair. "Here it is." She jerked the shift over her head, then scooped up his breeches and tossed them toward the bed. "Pull those on," she whispered. Turning toward the door, her voice lifted. "Just a minute, darlings."

Glancing back at Zeke, who was hurriedly stepping into his uniform pants, she explained, "It's the children. They wake me up every morning. It's a game we

431

play. Grandfather keeps them occupied for a while, but—" The rapping came again, more urgent this time. "Ready?" Fiona smiled at Zeke's apprehensive expression as he nodded, combing his fingers back through his hair. "They'll love you, as I do," she said, then opened the door with a flourish.